On Point

A Basketball Novel

Roger Johnson

ISBN 978-1-7364368-0-6 (pbk)
ISBN 978-1-7364368-1-3 (ebook)

website: Roger_Johnson.com
email: rogerj47@gmail.com

For my family: Cheryl, Mike, Luke, and Jennifer

--

Roger Johnson

...and to Leadville, Colorado, where my
love of basketball began so long ago.

ACKNOWLEDGMENTS

For the nearly two decades that I have been writing novels, several people have read and supported my "hobby" enthusiastically. First and foremost are my wife Cheryl and my sons Michael and Lucas. It was Luke who encouraged me to write a sports novel after I had completed a half-dozen recent historical fiction books. His critiques of my works have always provided keen insights for improvement.

Some of my readers have read one or two of my books, a few all ten. Regardless, I am grateful. For *On Point*, I would especially like to thank my brother Jay Johnson and good friends Kal Fallon, Wally Towne, Wendy Constantine, Jonna Christensen, and Betsy Kalmeyer for their comments.

Joe DesGeorges formatted the manuscript, provided professional talent to help design the cover, and showed tremendous patience with my lack of technical skills.

Finally, my boys teams over three decades furnished many of the specifics of games described in these pages. My one JV girls squad showed me the joy of coaching with tenderness. Every one of these teams became a part of my extended family, and every player one of my kids.

Roger

Books in the Cheetah Series

On Point

Gifts

Coach Izzy

On Point

Roger Johnson

IngramSpark

2021

On Point

"Great point guards don't play on the outside thirds, Molly.
Attack the paint!"

Coach Morgan Summitt.

Approximately 400,000 girls participate in high school
basketball every season in the United States alone, and
hundreds of thousands more around the world.
Basketball truly is a global game.

CHAPTER 1

Opportunity often conceals itself as failure

After chasing down a loose ball just outside the three point line, Molly stood motionless, slightly arched at the waist, her head up, her knees bent. Surveying. *Move the defense.* She dribbled to her right pushing her teammate to the corner. Molly sensed the opening before it became visible, before the opponent realized its weakness and could close the gap. Switching the dribble from her right hand to her left, she dipped her right shoulder hard into the seam, exploding past two perimeter defenders and into the lane. Now, she had options. She had given herself and her team a chance. A retired coach in the stands tensed. *Complete the play, young lady!*

Morgan Summitt focused all his attention on #14, Molly Rascon. He watched her eyes: wide, alert, and searching, much like a feral African cat stalking her prey. The Oro Hills sophomore point guard, a five-foot-three-inch package of passion and tenacity, moved with purpose, as if seeing the plays before they occurred, finding space where none existed. Blessed with quickness and agility, Molly controlled the opponent, and now, Morgan sensed, she would determine the outcome of the game. Academy Prep also sensed this turn, felt the momentum shifting, and altered its defense to keep the basketball out of her hands, to limit her touches.

Earlier in the day, while shopping downtown, Morgan noticed Molly and three of her junior varsity teammates at the dollar store, giggling while trying on winter caps, posing in the mirror. They left without buying anything and crossed Main Street to the thrift shop. Happy fifteen-year-olds on their lunch break before afternoon classes. He decided then not to miss their last game of the season. Now, he sat uncomfortably on the wooden bleachers, his back propped against the brick half-wall separating the lower seats from the upper stands, his legs extended across the next row. Four dozen other spectators, mostly the families of players, sat in groups of three or four on one side of the gym watching the junior varsity game, over half of them supporting the visiting Academy Prep Antelopes. Outside, on this third Friday in February 1995, a winter storm swirled. A bank of lights flickered over the west basket, making the gym seem colder. Across the court from the spectators sat the Oro Hills coach wearing jeans and a sweatshirt and two substitutes clad in faded uniforms, a stark contrast to the colorful A-Prep bench where seven subs, two managers, and two coaches cheered louder than the home fans. In the far corner of the gym, the A-Prep varsity team, ten girls in their powder blue warmups, stretched and bounced in preparation for their game, the final contest of the regular season. They had already been crowned league champions, undefeated in the conference for the second straight year. The playoffs awaited. For Oro Hills' varsity, its season would end after this contest, without a win in nineteen games. Only the top eight teams in the conference advanced to the district tournament, and Oro Hills finished ninth out of nine.

With four minutes remaining in the game, Molly Rascon split the double-team and scored a layup over a tall defender, giving Oro Hills a one-point lead. She reacted back to steal the inbounds pass and scored again, this time with her left hand. Rather than running back into the zone with her teammates, Molly harassed the A-Prep guard, almost causing another turnover. After her coach yelled out at her to "Get back!" into the two-three zone, she joined her friends and waited for the opponent to attack. Academy Prep passed the ball into their center, who was fouled by a heavy Oro Hills girl in a too-tight uniform. The buzzer sounded sending in the two girls from the Oro Hills bench, one of them for Molly, the same pattern her coach used in the previous three quarters. Morgan's jaw tightened and his eyes narrowed, accompanied by a subtle shake of his head. He noticed Molly's glare as she trotted by her coach to take a seat on the bench. The free throw bounced off the rim, but the visitors rebounded and scored. Seconds later, Academy Prep scored again to retake the lead. Molly remained on the bench for the last three minutes, watching Academy Prep score the final eight points. Morgan watched #14 as she and her teammates walked the line to congratulate their opponent.

She tapped each girl's hand and then scurried off to the locker room, the only Oro Hills player to leave the court right away.

The P.E. locker room sat under the bleachers. Molly shoved the door open with such force that it slammed against the wall and bounced back at her. She strode to the end of the locker room as if avoiding a nagging mother at a family reunion and then walked back and sat in the same spot on the locker room bench that she had occupied before the game to listen to Coach Thulen's instructions. Her eyes were fixed as if by a flash, looking inward more than out. In a few moments, she regained control of her breathing and her eyes. She looked up to the chalkboard and reread her coach's words. Two lines. "Have fun" and "Uniform check-in on Tuesday after school." Molly stood and stepped to the board. She erased the first line with the palm of her hand and wrote "That's it?", then pivoted and hurled the chalk across the locker room where it shattered against the far wall. She burst into tears, went to her locker to grab her clothes, and left the empty locker room still wearing her uniform.

In the bleachers Morgan looked at his program to check the heights of the visiting team.

"Excuse me."

Morgan turned to an old man standing next to him.

"You wouldn't happen to be Morgan Summitt, would you?"

Morgan stood and removed his cap, scattering his thinning, unruly head of hair. "Yes, I am. And you are?"

"Oh, you probably don't remember me, but I'm Jake Considine. I played on that good '48 team with you, or at least I sat on the bench and watched. I was two classes behind you."

"Jake," said Morgan, "I'm sorry. I didn't recognize you. What's it been, forty-five years?"

"Forty-seven to be exact, but who's counting? Lot's changed here in our hometown, lots of brown kids. My granddaughters play for Academy, and I attend all their games. The youngest is #55, the tall girl who scored so many points." Jake smiled a grandpa's smile.

"She had a great game, Jake. Is she a sophomore?"

"Yes. She's the first sub off the varsity bench, and she gets extra quarters playing with the JVs. She and her older sister are a potent duo. We have high hopes for them; lots of camps this summer."

"Well," said Morgan, "that's how you get better. Basketball's a year-round sport these days."

"What are you doing back here in Oro Hills, Morgan? Last time I heard, you were coaching in the Denver area. Saw a picture of you in the newspaper at State."

"Retired up here about three years ago." Morgan motioned for Jake to sit with him.

"No thanks. I need to get back to the family. I just thought it was you and wanted to say hi. You're looking good, Morgan. Maybe I'll see you again next year."

Morgan returned his attention to the floor as the two varsity teams warmed up, one disciplined and one unfocused. The game displayed these traits, and Morgan left before halftime with Academy Prep leading 33-7, and both teams laughing. He waved back to his high school teammate before entering the commons area, where he passed Molly, sitting alone at a corner table.

"You played very well," he said.

She glanced up with swollen eyes, hurt eyes. "Thank you, sir, but it wasn't enough."

Morgan nodded. "You did your part, young lady. Hold your head up."

§

Morgan drove directly into his garage, the snow depth approaching a foot with more predicted. As always, when his wife Andrea heard the garage door opening, she met him with a hug and a kiss, a habit they had cultivated over forty-plus years of marriage.

"Cold nose. How were the games?" she asked.

"Frustrating . . . again."

She could usually ease her husband's tension, but not tonight. "Tell me about it." She led him into the living room, where they sat on a couch in front of a gas fireplace. Cousy, their cat, lounged on the carpet in front of the fire.

The concept of equal playing time for all players on a team bothered Morgan. It had always been a peeve of his. Equal time was not fair, he believed. Some kids worked harder than others to develop their skills and earned more time. Plus, a score was kept. Tonight, he told Andrea about

4

the JV point guard being removed from the game to give a sub a few extra minutes, but it cost her team an opportunity to win the game, which would have been their first and only victory of the season. "To take that away!"

"Same old with the varsity?" Andrea asked.

"Yeah. Mercifully. Their season needed to end, but the JV girls were getting close."

"You enjoy watching them, don't you?" Andrea had attended all of Morgan's games when he had coached but chose to read a good book these days and was now finishing one for next week's book club, the Mountain Matrons.

Morgan breathed out heavily. "Yeah. As I've told you before, . . ." he stopped and smiled at his wife. "Did I ever tell you how much I've appreciated your patience with me with this other love affair of mine, especially when I go off on a rant?"

"I know."

He paused and finally nodded. "Anyway, thank you. Yeah, the JV girls like each other and play with a bit of heart. I think they're all sophomores, maybe a freshman or two. Unlike the varsity, there are a few of the younger girls who seem to want to win. I just wish their coach didn't use that silly zone. He coaches like it's an intramural game. He could utilize their quickness more effectively. I think those girls could have won a half-dozen games if they would have been turned loose. And that little point guard is really something. Why she isn't on the varsity . . ." Morgan caught himself again. "How was your evening?" he asked.

"Just this low-grade headache. Worried about Kathy."

"You should have told me; I didn't have to go to the game."

"Cousy is good company. You needed to attend the last game."

Andrea repositioned herself with her head in Morgan's lap, so he could massage her temples. She soon fell asleep, and he gently rested one hand on her shoulder and the other on her scalp. Over the next several minutes, Morgan replayed the JV game. He smiled at the sight of the referee sprawled out on the court, after Molly had knocked him over rushing for a loose ball, his partner trying to decide what to call. Morgan shook his head slightly remembering the JV coach yelling at his girls not to take chances or come out of their zone and having Molly and her sidekick ignoring his instructions. Morgan understood why Molly wasn't starting on the varsity; she wasn't a part of the senior-junior clique that had long ago accepted losing. She couldn't laugh during or at the end of lopsided losses, or any loss. He wondered what those JV girls would do now that the season ended. He guessed it wouldn't involve any more basketball. His experience had been with high school boys on the court, but he taught talented girls in advanced placement classes. He knew what they were capable of when given the opportunity. *Opportunity*, he thought. *Just like tonight's contest; a private, prep academy versus a poor, rural school.*

CHAPTER 2

You're always practicing habits, either good ones or bad ones.

S pring in Oro Hills ushered in mud season, a frustratingly long two months for the town's residents, a time when lower elevations along the Front Range experienced the re-birth. In the Colorado mountains, winter lingered, snow continued to fall, and the frozen ground delayed overturning the soil, or as Andrea said, "the soul." While Morgan made his annual pilgrimage to the State Basketball Tournament in Denver on the second weekend of March, Andrea laid plastic sheeting on a ten-by-twelve-foot area of their backyard to hasten the thaw, to prepare her garden. Across the street, a new family moved into the small, two-bedroom rental. When things quiet down, thought Andrea, I'll walk over and introduce myself. Maybe after my book club leaves in the late afternoon.

The Mountain Matrons book club invited Andrea to join almost as soon as she had arrived in Oro Hills. She and Morgan retired in May of '92 from teaching jobs in Lakewood, a west Denver suburb. They told people who asked that moving to the mountains was their reward for thirty-five years in the classroom. Andrea worried Morgan had retired too soon, worried he still had his passion for the classroom and the gym, worried he would have regrets. His joke about becoming a hermit and a ward of the state, living off his pension, concerned her. And there was his guilt over his daughter.

It was Queenie Roberts who invited Andrea to join the Mountain Matrons. They had shared a table in the local coffee shop one morning, each lady reading and sipping coffee. "Sweetheart," said Queenie, "I haven't noticed you around town, and I notice everyone. Are you new?" Thus, a friendship between a mostly private retired teacher and an idiosyncratic lawyer was hatched. Forever thirty-nine, Queenie was also forever curious and loud. Her significant other was Mercedes Spinelli, a leathery, fifty-ish woman from a Pueblo Italian family, who now owned a cattle and horse ranch south of Oro Hills.

This month's meeting of the Matrons was at Andrea's. The March meeting had been scheduled for Anita Pagel's motel lobby, but in this tourist off-season, Anita and her husband decided to close the motel for three weeks and go south for some sunshine. The other four members of the club were Mitzi Risso, a high school English teacher, Lorna McCaffrey, the manager of Coffee, Tea, or Me, Octavia Wick, owner of the Get Drilled bar on Main Street, and B.J. Pacheco, editor of the *Oro Hills Tribune*. This month's book was unusual in that it wasn't a novel, but a history of Oro Hills, written by an aunt of Mitzi's.

Lots of food remained from the potluck, and Andrea made a request. "Would you mind if I kept the leftovers and delivered them to my new neighbors across the street? Moving is always hard. We'll keep working on the wine while we discuss the book."

"No offense, Mitzi, but your aunt's book is pretty dry. Next month needs to get back to sex and romance," said Mercedes. "Still, it is interesting to know some of this stuff."

"Oro Hills is a hard town," said Mitzi. "My aunt's family were all miners. I remember the men as seeming older than they were. Died young."

"My father opened our bar while Oro Hills was booming after the war, but between the periodic closings and the union strikes, we knew tough times. But, dang, the good times were sure glorious," said Octavia. "I'm a few years younger than your husband, Andrea, but I'll bet he has some stories."

Andrea sipped her wine and leaned forward in her wingback chair. "His father worked the mine until he was drafted into the Army for World War II. He went to the Pacific and never came back. Morgan keeps most of that locked up. He grew up poor. He joined the Army when the Korean War began, and he seldom talks about that either. He tells me about the good parts of this town."

"The chapter on Oro Hills being a union town was interesting, I thought," said Queenie. "You guys know I get riled up about the decline of unions, because I think they improved working conditions and pay for the workers of this country."

"Moving on," kidded Mercedes. "It's amazing how often the book mentions the schools, especially from the end of World War I in 1918 on. Made it seem as though the high school was the center of all culture in Oro Hills."

"It was," said Octavia. "For me, for my brothers, even for my parents, there was a great pride in being a Miner. We still have a school banner up over the bar, and I donate to a few of the fundraisers for both the elementary and high school. It's frustrating now, because the old families don't seem to care as much. Their children and grandchildren have moved on, so there's not much ownership. Many of the new families live out in the trailer courts and aren't as connected. Schools once held towns together, a common purpose and obligation. Now, with the proliferation of those small charters, it's so fragmented." She paused. "And several families send their kids to nearby towns."

"Well," said Queenie, "it's about that time." She reached into a large shopping bag by her side and pulled out six paperback copies of the next book. "Some of us might have a little in common with the three women in this novel. They're a bit odd at times." Queenie smiled broadly as she moved her eyes around the room.

"Any sex?" asked Octavia.

"Read the book, sweetheart."

§

The high school basketball tournaments over for another year, Morgan returned to Oro Hills after the 5A championship game, arriving home at midnight. Andrea awoke to the sound of the garage door and met her husband in the kitchen. Her look told him of her concern.

Morgan smiled and kissed her gently on the lips. "They're predicting heavy snow; thought I'd beat the storm. How was your book club?"

"Fun, as usual. Queenie went on a small rant about unions, and Octavia suggested we get a 501 status and become a service provider, but that didn't go anywhere. We just want to read books, sample new wine, and giggle once a month." Andrea told Morgan of the new neighbors, a young mother with two kids, a teenage daughter and a son in elementary school. There was no sign of a husband.

"By the way," said Morgan, "my old coaching buddies all said hi. Cherry Creek won the 5A and Pueblo South the 4A."

"You miss it, don't you?" said Andrea.

"I'm good. Nice to be home. I visited with Kathy for a while before I went to the games."

§

The predicted storm dumped only four inches of light powder, but the temperature hovered in the low twenties with a stiff breeze. Spring? Morgan sat at the breakfast nook with his coffee and newspaper. The nook absorbed the morning sun and looked out across the neighborhood.

Across the street, the garage door opened, and a bundled-up girl emerged with a snow shovel. Morgan watched as she cleaned the sidewalk and then the sloping, one-car driveway, pushing the snow into the street. When she finished, she put the shovel away, removed her gloves and parka, and grabbed a rubber basketball.

"Do you recognize her now?" asked Andrea.

"Molly Rascon. Did you know?"

"When I took the book club's leftovers over last night, I met her."

Morgan didn't respond; his attention already had turned. He ate and watched as Molly shot at the rectangular, wooden backboard with a frayed net mounted over the garage door. Ten powers from the right, ten from the left with the left hand. Ten Mikans. Jump shots from the forty-five, all banked. Ten free throws. Repeat.

"She's determined, isn't she?" asked Andrea.

Andrea placed her left hand on Morgan's shoulder and smiled to herself. "What are you waiting for?" Morgan nodded slightly but said nothing. "It's not like you don't have time, you know," she said. "Grab your jacket; it's freezing."

The sun raised the temperature into the upper twenties. Morgan crossed the street toward Molly. "Need someone to rebound?" he asked.

"Sure," answered Molly. "I guess." She looked at her rubber ball, took one dribble to her left, and swished a twelve-footer.

Morgan retrieved the ball on one bounce and passed it back to Molly, a crisp, two-handed chest pass that hit her right in the hands. She bounced the ball again and shot, and a routine began to develop. From ten to twelve feet, Molly was accurate; further out she labored. They worked in silence with only an occasional "nice" uttered by Morgan when she swished a shot. Even her misses stayed close to the rim, a soft touch. After each pass, the old man rubbed his hands together to generate a little heat, but the girl seemed not to notice the cold. Only her visible breaths revealed how cold it was.

After a dozen minutes, Molly asked, "You want to shoot a few?"

"Nope. You won't get better with me shooting, and my glory days are in the past."

"You played?"

"A little. High school and small college." Morgan stepped forward and extended his hand. "I'm Coach Summitt and I belong to the lady across the street who you evidently met yesterday."

"Molly Rascon."

"I hope I didn't bother you coming over," he said.

"No, you worked me pretty hard." Molly smiled. "Where did you coach?"

"In the Denver area. High school boys. Retired now. You're very good; I watched you play a few times this season."

"You watched us play? You came to our games? Nobody comes to JV games." Molly smiled broadly. "Thank you for the compliment, but I'm not that good."

Morgan waited for a moment. "Don't underestimate your talent. You've got some game. Would you like a few pointers?" He raised his hands to his mouth and blew into them.

"I can't afford anything."

Morgan let out a soft laugh. "Anything I do will be free. My wife might pay you for getting me out of the house occasionally."

Molly stared at the old man, sizing him up. He had the frame of a basketball player, long and lanky, and a kind face, maybe because of how he nodded his head frequently, which seemed like a gesture of gentleness. "Okay, give me something to practice."

"All right, Molly, a couple of things. Don't take a dribble each time you shoot. Use your left foot as your pivot foot and rise up to shoot. If you're practicing by yourself, spin the ball back to yourself. Second, your drive-way slopes away from the basket, especially from about here." Morgan pointed to a crack in the decaying cement. "Your three-point shot ends up making your target about eight inches higher. You're developing a bad habit with that shot just to get it up there."

"Not much I can do about that."

"Actually, there is, Molly. Don't practice your threes here. Work only on your close-in shots, in front of this crack."

"My high school coaches don't want me shooting threes anyway. Nothing over fifteen feet."

"Ah, the magical fifteen-foot range." Morgan shook his head. "Well, today's point guards need to be able to shoot the three from the top of the key, so you'll just have to get so good at that shot, they'll beg you to shoot it."

"How can I do that if I don't practice it?" asked Molly.

"Let me work on that." Morgan smiled and indicated to Molly to begin shooting again. As she did, he talked. "Stay in balance. Good. Way to use your legs. Basketball is played with bent knees. Show me target hands." Morgan began to sweat under his jacket as he moved to rebound, but he was no longer chilled. He rebounded a made shot and walked over to Molly. "Your right-hand action is exceptional. Don't allow your left hand to get in its way. It's only useful as a balance hand. Otherwise, it's the devil." Morgan demonstrated. "See how it lays against the side of the ball with your thumb pointing back into your left eye? Now, as you move to shoot, don't allow your left arm to fully extend."

"I'm so used to using it. It just seems natural to me. How do I break that habit?"

"Try this. Before you go to bed each night, tape a flat paper plate on your left hand. Lay on your back and shoot the ball straight up above your head. Only three or four feet. Try to get the ball to return to your right hand without moving it. The plate should keep you from thumbing the ball." Morgan took the ball and laid down on the driveway to demonstrate.

Molly looked concerned. "Will you be able to get up without my help?"

Morgan stood and laughed. "And don't shoot any shots over twelve feet for the next week. Nothing past this crack in the driveway. Those long shots are when your technique begins to break down. We'll get back to the threes right after that."

Molly's mother emerged from the garage holding a cup of coffee and a cigarette in gloved hands. "I thought I heard another voice." She was a short, plump woman who looked more like Molly's older sister than mother. "Aren't you cold?"

"Mom, this is Mr. Summitt. He lives over there." She pointed to his house.

"I met your wife. Such a charming lady! She brought dinner over while we were moving in." She smiled and shook Morgan's hand.

"My wife's a little friendlier than me. I tend to hold up in the house and hibernate during the winter. Nice to meet you, Mrs. Rascon."

"Anderson. Miss Anderson. Molly's father and I never officially tied the knot. We tried, but we were too young. He's a no-account somewhere in Pueblo working on another family now."

"Mom, do you have to tell everyone. Let it go!" Molly's voice showed both irritation and frustration.

"Your daughter has a bit of fire in her belly for this game. Anyone out on a morning like this deserves my respect. She also has an impressive shot. My wife kicked me out of the house and told me to come rebound for her."

"Well, that was nice." Miss Anderson turned to Molly. "Remember, you have to babysit your brother this afternoon while I work, and you need to clean you and your brother's room today. Wash the sheet between your beds. Don't forget." She turned to Morgan. "Don't let her infringe on your privacy, Mr. Summitt." She shook Morgan's hand again and went inside.

"Where does your mother work?"

"She has two jobs. She manages the laundromat and cleans houses. We got this house because a friend of hers wanted someone in it for the rest of the winter. I don't know how long we'll be able to stay, but it's nicer than the trailer. Mom didn't finish high school. She blames me sometimes." Molly frowned and took the ball from Morgan's hands. "You don't have to do this, you know."

Morgan nodded. "Yep, I know." He caught Molly's eyes and held them. "This series, no dribbling. Shoot, come down in balance, and move. Catch and shoot. Remember, show me target hands."

§

Later that day, Morgan drove to a local realty office to check on rental rates. He learned about the disparity between houses and trailers and about the number of Oro Hills residents who worked out of town where wages were higher, but who remained in town because of affordable housing compared to surrounding towns.

Morgan didn't see Molly on Monday, a six-inch snowstorm the probable explanation, but she knocked on his door on Tuesday afternoon just as Morgan and Andrea were sitting down for dinner. Andrea answered the door, since she was still standing, and invited Molly in.

"I hope I'm not interrupting, but I wanted you to check on whether I was still thumbing the ball," said Molly. Seeing that dinner was already on the table, she apologized and then said, "You guys sure eat early."

Morgan rose and laughed as she made her last observation. "Old people do that. What time do you have dinner at your house?" he asked.

"It depends on when mom gets home, usually around seven or eight."

Andrea glanced at her husband and then turned to Molly. "Is your brother at home?"

"No, he usually stays with a friend until my mom picks him up," answered Molly.

"Well," said Andrea, "I over-cooked tonight, so you put the ball down by the door, take off your jacket, and sit down. Morgan can look at your shot after dinner." Her tone indicated that Molly could not refuse. She removed her jacket, slipped off her wet boots, and sat across from Morgan.

"How was school today?" asked Morgan.

"Okay, I guess."

Morgan looked over to Andrea. "Are you a good student? Do you have a favorite class or teacher?"

"I'm maybe a little better than average, I guess. What did you teach, Coach?"

"History, mostly American history. Some government. Mrs. Summitt was an English teacher." They chatted about school for the rest of the meal, both Molly's and the Summitt's.

Morgan wiped his mouth and set his napkin on the table. "I ordered a backboard yesterday. It should be here by Friday, and weather permitting, I'll have it up by the time school is out, so you can start working on your three-point shot. In case you hadn't noticed, my driveway is level all the way out to the gutter. That's about twenty-five feet. It's not wide enough on the sides, but it will do fine for working on your technique. After dessert, we can go over your basketball questions."

"I just wanted you to see how I'm doing with the lay-on-the-floor drill you showed me on Sunday. Since I couldn't shoot outside, I spent a couple of hours working on it last night, and I want to make sure I was doing it right and not practicing it wrong."

"Yeah, I can look at your form. By the way, you didn't neglect your homework, did you?"

§

Molly and Morgan worked on her shot for about an hour on both Wednesday and Thursday afternoons. At a comfortable distance, Molly had stopped thumbing her shot and her accuracy was improving. When she returned from school on Friday, Morgan's new hoop was in place over his garage, and lines had been drawn at the free throw and three-point distances. He wouldn't allow her to shoot from the three-point line at the beginning, making her go through her progression first. After about ten minutes, he relented.

"Okay, Molly, let's see if this makes a difference. Get your left foot down and step into the shot. Get your momentum moving forward. Use your legs."

Molly stepped behind the line and displayed target hands for Morgan's pass. Her first shot hit the front of the rim, bounced up and in. Her left arm stayed bent and her thumb remained back. She made an emphatic fist pump with her right hand.

"I'd say your floor practice has done you some good. That looked smooth and easy. Now, I won't say anything unless your left hand starts flying out; make or miss, keep your technique true." He passed her the ball and a routine began anew. *This girl*, he thought, *has some serious talent and dedication.*

§

On Sunday evening Molly knocked on Morgan's door again. They had already completed their workout and darkness had descended. Inside, she looked a little uncomfortable. "Mr. Summitt, there's something I want to ask you. You can say no if you want. The winter sports award ceremony is Tuesday and my mom has to work, and I was wondering if you would . . ." Her voice trailed off, but Morgan waited as she kept her head down. Finally, she looked up. "I would like to take you as my guest." She looked to Andrea. "And you can come too."

"I'd like that very much, Molly. We'd be honored," said Morgan.

"I don't even know if they give junior varsity players anything, but we're still supposed to be there. Anyway, I'm bringing my brother too."

Mrs. Summitt placed small cakes on the kitchen counter and poured Molly a glass of milk. Morgan slid into the nook bench with a glass of tea. "When did you start playing basketball, Molly," he asked.

"In fifth grade. My teacher set up a lunch league and I got to play with the boys. They needed another player and I was big enough and athletic, so I got to play. The rims were lower, and I could make shots. Making baskets in a real game is such a rush, plus dribbling came easy for me. I just fell in love with it. Besides, it was cheap, my trailer court had a hoop, and I could get off by myself and shoot. My mom thinks I waste too much time just shooting a basketball. She wants me to get a job, maybe as a server or house cleaner."

"How long did you live in the trailer court, Molly?" asked Mrs. Summitt.

"All my life. This is the first house I've ever lived in."

Morgan nodded. "Being good at anything can give a person confidence, can show us how to succeed in something else."

CHAPTER 3

I vividly remember every game that season, but I most treasure my time on the driveway with my basketball and best friends.

Morgan remembered his end-of-season banquets. Heavy on senior recognition, but every player at all three levels received a hand-written note. Held in the school commons area with decorated tables and a potluck dinner, Morgan would stand in front of a full house of players and families and recall the highs and lows of the season, but always celebratory. The banquet marked the end of one season, but more importantly, the start of the next. *Always be moving forward*, thought Morgan, *always forward. The next season.* To be a head coach, basketball had to course through one's veins.

The Oro Hills awards ceremony was held in the gym. Lowell Exeter, the high school principal, said a few words to begin the evening. Exeter stood a half a head taller than any of his coaches. In his late fifties, he still had a flowing mane of hair. In all ways, Exeter was a big man: big hands, big head, booming voice. And yet, to both Morgan and Andrea, he seemed bored and satisfied, like a man leaning toward retirement. His words were generic, words that could have been given to any number of schools on such a night. Tonight, awards would be given to boys and girls basketball players and the wrestling squad. None of the teams had experienced much success. No wrestlers had advanced past districts, the boys' basketball team was beaten in the first round of districts, and the girls did not win a game. A losing culture.

The girls' JV squad was called forward first. Coach Thulen commented on their spirit and desire, that they had tried hard in every game, that his team simply did not possess the talent or size that the other schools did. He mentioned nothing about their basketball skills, nor did he speak about any specific games. No girl received individual attention. While he spoke, one of Molly's teammates kept poking her in the side, causing both girls to giggle. He concluded by saying that many of the girls would be on the varsity next year and provide strong support to the returning varsity players. Then, he passed out form certificates of participation. Molly returned to the bleachers and handed her certificate to Morgan without expression, who handed it to Andrea.

The girls' varsity followed. Coach Abby, as the girls called her, tried to massage the winless season, saying there were wins left on the court, possibly because of injuries, eligibility issues, and inexperience. She praised the five graduating seniors for their leadership and perseverance and wished them well in the years to come, saying she would miss them. Coach Abby then spoke about the three returning juniors, Stephanie, Elena, and Sophia, and what a strong nucleus they would be for the next season. Morgan remembered how difficult it was to find public words for losing teams that would ring true and satisfy parents, yet at the same time encourage the underclassmen to work hard for the coming season. He considered Coach Abby's attempt admirable.

After the girls received their awards, the boys' teams received theirs, and then the wrestling squad theirs. Morgan noted that the eight boys standing with the wrestling coach were not enough to fill every weight class. Morgan wondered why participation for these sports seemed so low; there certainly could not have been cuts made. That would have been self-defeating. Did more students begin the programs and then quit or simply drift off?

The event closed with a few words from the activities director, a man in his early thirties, who also wore a tie. He complimented the young athletes on their achievements and commitments, and his words seemed sincere. He added that it was not too late to try out for track or soccer, and Oro Hills needed as many of its students to be multiple-sport athletes as possible. He closed with a comment on the value of extra-curricular athletics to the all-around education of the student, that if such an endeavor was deemed valuable by Ivy League universities, that same value should apply to small schools in the Colorado mountains. He then closed the ceremony with a note of thanks to the parents in attendance.

"Molly, would you introduce me to the athletic director please," asked

Morgan. He helped Andrea navigate the wooden bleachers and was then led to the podium where the activities director stood."

"Hi, Molly. Where's your mother?" asked the A.D.

"Mr. Vincent, this is Mr. and Mrs. Summitt, my neighbors. Mom couldn't make it, so I asked them if they would come with me."

Morgan extended his hand. "Morgan, and this is my wife Andrea. Molly's mother had to work, so we're filling in. I wanted to say that I appreciated your remarks about the value of sports in the over-all framework of a student's education. Both my wife and I are former educators."

"Thank you, Mr. Summitt, I appreciate that. Call me Kane. It's a nickname my wrestlers gave me back when I coached. How are you adjusting to the long winters?"

Morgan laughed. "Andrea and I just turn up the heat and stay inside. There's a rumor going around that spring will show up eventually. Andrea's just reading through the winter. It was nice to meet you, Mr. Vincent. There are a few other parents who would like your attention. If the trenches get you down too much, call me and I'll take you out for beers and let you vent." Both Andrea and Morgan shook the A.D.'s hand as they left.

"He seems like a sincere man," said Andrea.

§

Molly turned sixteen on March 24. It was a Friday and her mother threw a party, complete with beer and a birthday banner strung across the garage eave. Around seven-thirty Molly brought two pieces of cake to Andrea and Morgan and lingered just inside their door to make small talk. She warned them the party could get out of control because of the alcohol and older guests but assured them she had tried to get her mother not to serve any, but to no avail.

"My mom is trying to re-live her own missed celebrations, because she had me so early. She's already half-torn," said Molly.

Morgan had never heard the phrase "half-torn," but he understood its meaning. "Do you need us to watch Alex?"

"No, he's sleeping over with a friend tonight."

"If you don't mind my asking, how old was your mother when she became pregnant with you?" asked Andrea.

"Fifteen. Delivered when she was my age. She's only thirty-two now. No, she never finished high school," said Molly in what seemed to Morgan as an apology. "I don't drink, so I'll see you tomorrow morning. Enjoy the cake." She smiled and ran across the street.

§

When Molly came over in the morning, Morgan asked her in before they began her shooting routine. A large, wrapped box sat on the kitchen table in front of Andrea. "We didn't know it was your birthday. Morgan bought this last week when we went to Denver." It was a basketball, a composite, indoor/outdoor ball to replace her worn rubber ball. Morgan took a black magic marker from a coffee cup on the kitchen counter. Carefully, he wrote MOLLY RASCON on the ball. "It's your ball now, Molly. Take care of it."

§

In the afternoon, Andrea woke Morgan from his nap on the chair to a new development. Molly and three other girls were playing two-on-two in the driveway. All three were in sweats and seemed physically interchangeable. Four girls, each with dark hair about the same length held in place by a scrunchie, and all physically fit, although Molly was the most muscular of the group. Morgan sat at the breakfast table and watched with a smile. When Molly saw him, she motioned for him to come out.

"This is Izzy, short for Isabella. This is her cousin Elena; she's a junior, and this is Stevie."

Morgan shook each girl's hand. "I recognize each of you from last season's games. I enjoyed watching you all play."

As it turned out, both Izzy and Elena had some basketball skills, especially Izzy. Stevie, however, struggled to make a layup, but she was the quickest of four quick girls, and it was difficult for the others to effectively play when Stevie guarded them. Morgan recalled the zone defense these girls sat in during the season and shook his head. Andrea watched from the nook. After a while, she invited them in for hot chocolate and cookies. It was still late winter in Oro Hills, and the temperature remained in the low forties.

"You guys go back outside and play. I've got to go watch March

Madness on TV, sort of my duty, you know, to make sure those college teams are playing the game the right way," said Morgan. "By the way, Molly, you'll be on your own this week. The missus and I will be staying with our son in Denver and visiting our daughter too. We should be back next weekend. Feel free to use the driveway." Morgan waved them away with the back of his hand.

"Sweet girls," said Andrea.

"Next year's team, I imagine," said Morgan.

CHAPTER 4

Never foul the jump shooter! Contest, but don't foul! That's the shot we want them to take.

The Mountain Matrons Book Club held their April meeting in the conference room of Anita Pagel's motel. Spring peeked into Oro Hills, or at least winked, and Saturday's temperature hit forty-seven degrees under sunny skies. Anita was close friends with Lorna and Octavia, and all three were concerned about the continued recession in Oro Hills affecting their small businesses.

"Is Oro Hills' problem race or poverty?" asked Octavia. "In my bar I don't even notice."

Queenie sat and shook her head. "They're intertwined, sweetheart, but I think it's more poverty-based. Rich Latinos seem to fit, unlike us Blacks. Poverty just complicates everything. Oro Hills was at the top of the mountain, so to speak, before the economy went south. Now, our businesses, our schools, even our reputation suck."

"Little harsh there, aren't you, Queenie?" said Mercedes.

"I mean *suck* in the sense that everything is an uphill struggle when you're poor." There was general agreement with Queenie's last statement and the club went silent for a moment. Queenie stood, said, "Well, hell, I didn't mean to put a damper on things. Guess we'll just have to look into Octavia's suggestion from last month."

§

As the weather improved, Molly's time on Morgan's driveway extended. He dug out an instructional tape on ball-handling and they watched it together. Her dribbling skills were already advanced, but she spent hours with the new drills. "Forget the spin dribble," advised

Morgan. "Develop that ankle-breaking crossover, low and hard." Morgan bought a second basketball for those drills requiring two balls. He sat in a patio chair and made her look him in the eyes while she dribbled. "Tell me how many fingers I'm holding up. Pull the dribble back, go between your legs, behind your back, but always keep your head up."

§

When Cindy joined the four other girls on Morgan's driveway, Andrea kidded them that they now had a real team of five. Elena finally spoke, saying they might need a center someday, someone over five-foot-six.

"Do you guys know any tall girls who play basketball?" asked Morgan. "What about the girl who played center on the JVs last season?"

"The big one or the skinny one?" asked Izzy.

Morgan said he was referring to the heftier girl.

"Oh," said Molly, "Alondra's going to love your description. Mr. Summitt, *hefty* is not a compliment." Morgan started to correct himself before he realized Molly was teasing. "Alondra doesn't have time. I'm sure she'd like to come and be normal, but that's not going to happen."

Morgan's expression asked why. The girls looked at one another. Izzy finally answered. "She's on a tight leash. Her mom puts her in charge of the whole family, and there are ten kids in her trailer. She's the oldest."

"Ten in one trailer? I hope it's a double-wide."

"It's not," said Molly. "One of those old ones just outside of town. In the summer, they put up a tent in the yard for the boys to sleep in, but winter is hard."

While the girls shot baskets, Morgan couldn't stop thinking about ten children in an old trailer, and about a sixteen-year-old girl already saddled with the responsibility of taking care of nine siblings. He knew Molly sometimes substituted for her mother at the laundromat, doing the tasks of an adult, but Alondra's life seemed like such a burden.

Shortly, Izzy, Cindy, Stevie, and Elena left, leaving Molly to catch-and-shoot with Morgan. "Coach, I thought of a couple of others." This was the first time Molly called him Coach.

"A couple of other whats?"

"Tall girls. Penny Mathews is tall, but really skinny. She played with us early in the year but got ineligible. She's not very good though." Morgan remembered her, and Molly was correct. Mostly, Morgan recalled how weak Penny was. "And there's a new girl. Bianca. I don't know her last name, and I don't know if she ever played basketball. She moved in after Christmas."

"How tall?"

"I don't know, but a lot taller than any of us."

"Do you know anything else about her?" asked Morgan.

"Well, she's pretty and she stays mostly to herself, almost like she's uncomfortable about being in Oro Hills."

"Be brave, Molly. Talk to her and invite her to come shoot baskets with you."

§

Winter returned on the ides of April, and the weekend basketball gatherings on Morgan's driveway had to be postponed. While their mother worked at the laundromat on Saturday, Molly and Alex ate lunch with the Summitts. It was becoming another of the routines in Morgan's and Andrea's lives, one they enjoyed. On this afternoon, Morgan showed Molly a game film from one of his State teams, a team that advanced to the finals before coming up a few points short.

"We rode the back of our point guard this year. All my really successful teams had a great point guard. This one actually had two terrific point guards. I wish one of them would have played for me during those lean years. Without a point guard, I was kind of lost as a coach. Watch what he does here, Molly. He fakes an attack on the double-team, pulls his dribble back, and then attacks the outside shoulder of the inside defender. By doing that, he takes away the third defender, the sideline. Now, he's turned this possession into an advantage situation." Molly nodded. Morgan returned to the game tape of the quarterfinal game. "In this game, we were struggling with their half court press; long-armed kids. At halftime my point guard suggested we set our center right behind their middle defender just to keep him occupied, and then he would handle the other defenders by himself. Not a single turnover in the second half. We came back from a double-digit deficit to win easily."

"You let your point guard give suggestions during the game?" said Molly. "I can't imagine that."

24

"Get so good this summer that you make it happen for your team next year." Morgan turned off the tape. "What do your coaches have going on over the summer?"

"Nothing."

"No open gyms or camps or games?"

"Nope. Nothing. We didn't have anything last year either, but at least we have this this year. The other girls are having fun coming over here. Coach Abby said she might take a year off. I don't think she wants to, but there's something about working on her next degree. Coach Thulen would just step in if she goes, but he works all day, and in the summer, he helps with the football team," said Molly.

Alex returned to the kitchen and tugged on Molly's sleeve. "Mom's home. We'd better go check in."

Morgan smiled at Alex and turned back to Molly. "Be proud of your mom. She works hard and has done a good job with her two kids." Molly rolled her eyes, but Morgan caught her. "Don't let me ever see you do that again. We all have our faults, but your mother works and comes home. It's a difficult situation out there these days, but she's trying. Okay." It was a stern look, but not an angry glare.

"You're right." Molly stood and headed for the door where Andrea hugged her around the shoulders.

"Give your mom a hug just like this one. You don't have to make it a big deal, just hug her and ask her how her day went. She'll appreciate it," said Andrea.

Morgan watched Molly and Alex kick through the snow across the street. "It is tough out there these days. We were fortunate to have taught during the glory years."

CHAPTER 5

Anticipate! See the next play before it happens.

On April 19, 1995, a deranged man blew up a federal building in Oklahoma City, killing over one hundred and sixty men, women, and children. Another five hundred were injured. Two days later, the mad man was arrested. Morgan and Andrea watched the continuing television coverage and sipped their coffees in the breakfast nook on Saturday morning.

"What kind of a man can do such a thing?" asked Andrea. "Where do you get that kind of hate?" They sat stunned and silent as pictures of the bombed building flashed across the screen. They had no words.

Around ten o'clock, as she had done since Morgan put up his hoop, Molly crossed the street and began shooting. Morgan could almost hear Molly coaching herself. He got up and turned the television off. "No sense in this," he said to Andrea. "I'm going outside and try to put this out of my mind for a while. Do you have something to read?"

"It wouldn't stick. Maybe I'll drive downtown and visit Lorna, have my coffee there." Andrea stared at her husband and began to tear up. "All those children." He drew her into his arms and held her tightly without saying a word. Her head fit in the crook of his neck and his arms went across her shoulders at just the right angle. Even on a day such as this, his body comforted hers. "Thank you. I'll be all right."

"I know you will. You just have this big heart that always takes in the suffering." He pulled his head back to see her face, and then kissed her on the forehead.

"Go on out there and be with Molly. Put this out of your head for a while. I'll bring you back a cinnamon roll." Andrea sniffled. She leaned back and patted his chest with her hands, a nervous gesture and tried to reassure him. "I'm okay. I am. Go."

On Point

§

"Morning, Coach." Molly passed Morgan the ball. "I raised my three-point number again."

"How many now?"

"Just one more. Five. Izzy tied me yesterday, but I got her. She tried to mess me up by giving me bad passes and standing next to me, but it didn't work."

"She's good for you, challenges you, you know. She'll be good for the team next season. I'll enjoy watching the two of you play together. She's really improved."

"So has Elena. Not as much as Izzy, but she's getting good too. It's been fun."

"Are they coming over?"

"Yeah, probably before eleven. I just wanted to get my routine in before they get here. Stevie has a track meet in Colorado Springs, but maybe Cindy will show up, so we can play two-on-two."

"Stevie gives you a difficult time when she guards you," said Morgan.

"She's just so quick. If I fake her out, she catches me before I can get to the basket, and I thought I was fast. She can't make a layup or a jump shot, but she's a great defensive player." Molly gave Morgan target hands and the routine began. Shoot and move. "Why do you think Stevie has such a hard time shooting layups, Coach?"

"I can't figure it out either. I've tried several different things, but whenever she jumps off one foot, it seems like the rest of her body becomes disconnected. Way back when, I started as a junior high coach, and teaching layups was the first thing I taught. When I held little kid camps, same thing, and I don't remember it being so difficult. Everyone struggles with their weak hand and the coordination of that, but a simple layup is teachable." Morgan shook his head.

"I'm starting to look forward to next season," said Molly. She caught Morgan's pass, jab-stepped, and then took two left-hand dribbles into an eight-foot jumper. "I wasn't sure I would after last season, but when the other girls started coming over, I realized that with the returning players on varsity, we might actually win a few games." She received the pass, jabbed again, but this time stepped back and swished a shot at the foul line. "What's that like, Coach?"

"What's what like?"

"Winning?" Losing for Molly was the way of things—for all the girls on the Oro Hills team. She didn't fear it, because she lived it. She played basketball for fun, to be with her friends, but she hated losing, and something told her it didn't have to be.

Morgan held the ball and his body stopped. He chewed his bottom lip and shook his head slightly. "Well, immediately, it's exhilarating. It makes you feel good about yourself and what you've put in to achieve it. Success is a building block. Maybe you've heard the saying, 'Success builds success.' It's true, just as lots of losing is a hard habit to break." He wasn't satisfied with his answer. "Molly, winning makes it easier to remember, makes you want to remember, and when you win, you learn that losing is no fun."

"I know losing is no fun. That's why we never thought about it in practice last year. Coach Abby concentrated on making our practices fun."

Morgan thought about what practices must have been like for Molly. *Phony fun*. It had to have hurt. "What else was fun for you last year?"

"Bus rides, I guess. Getting out of town. I liked the drills where I could compete and when the coaches let the JV scrimmage the varsity. We beat them a couple of times, and I loved that."

"Remember those moments next year when you're on the varsity, and never, ever let the JVs beat you."

§

At school on Monday, Molly spoke with two girls who played on the JV team with her about coming over to Morgan's to shoot occasionally, but they didn't seem interested. Molly also learned that the boys coach had started open gyms twice a week and was setting up a short list of games for the summer. She ate lunch with Izzy and Elena, more like giggled her way through lunch, as Elena revealed her crush on a senior boy. Molly noticed Bianca sitting with Rosa Leon. Rosa and Molly were friends in junior high, but Rosa had moved away to New Mexico for a year-and-a-half before returning at the semester. They were still friendly, but Rosa wasn't in any of Molly's classes, like she had missed an entire year of school and was taking freshmen classes. Rosa was a pretty girl, not beautiful like Bianca, but small town attractive. There seemed to be nothing small town about Bianca. Remembering Morgan's words about being brave, Molly excused herself from Izzy and Elena and crossed the commons to meet Bianca. Molly spoke with Rosa first, asking her to join the shooting group, and then turned to Bianca.

"Hi. I'm Molly." She extended her hand to Bianca and was somewhat startled when the new girl stood and shook Molly's hand with a firm grip.

"Rosa said you guys used to hang around a little bit."

Molly acknowledged they did before telling Bianca she would also be welcome to come to Mr. Summitt's driveway to shoot baskets and get to know the other girls. She learned that Bianca was a sophomore also; for some reason, she had it in her mind that Bianca was a junior. Maybe it was her physical maturity. When she turned to rejoin Elena and Izzy, she thought about being brave. This wasn't the test, and she understood that Mr. Summitt was telling her something different than giving her a lesson on bravery.

§

Winter returned with a vengeance on Thursday. School was cancelled and Morgan spent the day plowing snow from his sidewalks and driveway and from the sidewalks throughout the neighborhood. Around two in the afternoon, Andrea answered a knock at their door and invited in a snow-covered figure before finding out any information about why she was there.

"Is Coach Summitt here?" she asked.

"Morgan, honey, someone's here to see you," Andrea called out. "He's downstairs and probably didn't hear me; he's a little deaf. Take off your coat and have a seat while I get him." Andrea left the girl while she went to the top of the stairs. "Morgan, can you come up here? You have a visitor." She returned to the living room to find the girl had only unzipped her coat and removed her stocking cap.

"I don't want to get snow all over your carpet, ma'am."

"It's only water. Here, let me take that."

Morgan appeared and introduced himself. "Miserable out there."

"I hope you don't mind, but since there's no school, I thought I'd come over. I'm staying just a few blocks away." She held out her hand. "I'm Bianca Steele. Molly said you give basketball lessons." Bianca stopped, waiting for a response.

Morgan smiled. "Well, I sort of do. Suggestions mostly." He paused trying to figure out what Bianca was looking for. "First, slip off those boots and let's have some hot chocolate. Two blocks in this weather is a long way, especially with the wind. I know. I've been out in it a few times already." He held her hand while she slipped off her boots.

"Thank you."

Andrea was already heating milk when her husband and guest came into the kitchen. "Have a seat, my dear," said Andrea. "It won't be but a moment."

Bianca smiled. "Thank you. I didn't mean for you to do all of this. After Molly invited me to come, at first, I didn't think much of it, just thought she was being nice, but the more I thought about it, it sounded fun. I like basketball. I used to play back home a little, but I just came here. During the season. Mostly, I just know Rosa."

"Where's home?" asked Morgan.

"Espanola, New Mexico. That's where I met Rosa when she moved down a year ago. It's a tough town. Lots of drugs. That's why I'm here, to get me away from all of that."

"There's drugs most everywhere these days," said Morgan.

"Not like Espanola. Meth, cocaine, even heroin. It was everywhere in the high school, and you couldn't go to a party without being offered something. Scary. I'm living with Rosa's aunt. Rosa was so scared down there that she dropped out of school. Now she's behind, but at least she's trying to catch up. I help her every night. We started talking about Molly's offer, because I said I was going out for the team next year, but I don't want to just play. I'd kind of like to be good at it."

Morgan was surprised at how quickly Bianca opened up. Being invited in and given hot chocolate probably eased her apprehensions. Andrea's nature. "I know Molly and the girls would welcome you to their group. You know they weren't very good last year."

"A little. Me and Rosa went to a game, but I don't remember talking about how good they were. Rosa may want to come out too, but her grades are pretty bad."

"The team will do better than last season next year, that's for sure. Tell me, Bianca, what do you do best on the court?" asked Morgan.

On Point

"Rebound, I guess. My shooting's not too good."

When Bianca finished her hot chocolate, she thanked the Summitts and rose to leave. Morgan offered to drive her home and she accepted. They talked briefly on the short ride back to Rosa's house, and she promised to come back when the snow melted.

"I keep the driveway cleared, so it will be dry by the weekend if the snow stops. It was nice to meet you. I can help you with parts of your game. Rebounders need to make two kinds of shots: putbacks and free throws. You seem pretty athletic. Those will come fast."

At Rosa's house Bianca turned to Morgan. "That was really nice of your wife to ask me in." She paused. Then, "I mean that." She stepped out and closed the door before Morgan could respond. He waited until she was inside the house before driving away.

At home Andrea wanted to talk about Bianca. "What did you make of her?"

"My first impression is that she's lonely and scared. Well, that, and she's almost six feet tall. She seemed much more mature than Molly and the others, but you know how first impressions are," said Morgan.

Andrea was still sipping her hot chocolate. "I didn't get that she was scared, but maybe scarred. I wouldn't know about what that might be, but to leave her family to live with a friend that she might have known for only a year says something. What do you know about that town in New Mexico?"

"I never heard of it before, but she sure painted a grim picture, didn't she? I can't even imagine the home lives of some of these kids. That they make it to adulthood at all is often a victory," said Morgan. "The girls talk about their families and I hear snippets. Seems like the only kids from normal families are Elena and Izzy and maybe Stevie; all the others are missing dads or are being raised by aunts or grandparents. Molly has daytime responsibility for her brother, and Alondra, the invisible Alondra we only hear about, cares for nine or ten siblings."

"Seems like you're offering a safe, comfortable environment for them." Andrea smiled.

"I think they're giving me a meaningful retirement hobby."

§

Finally, a mid-fifties day in the middle of May under a cloudless sky with no wind. Molly and Bianca wore shorts and tee-shirts as they worked on their skills. Molly worked on her ball-handling routine while Morgan taught Bianca the techniques of a basic power layup. He had Bianca hold the ball over her head with arms extended and bounce on two feet. "Feel that bounce, Bianca. Now, as you do it, imagine you're strong and determined." After a minute of bouncing, he had her toss the ball up to the backboard, jump off two feet to grab it, and then jump up quickly to shoot the ball against the backboard. "Remember the bounce, Bianca. Keep your arms extended for this drill and just use your wrist to shoot it. Keep your shoulders square with the backboard. That's good, real good." It was a simple drill using only her right hand from the right side. "Be fluid but think power. Secure the ball and bounce back up. Head up, eyes up. See the spot on the backboard where you want the ball to make first contact. Higher. Never up, never in. Good, very good." He pointed to Molly. "Watch how she practices; I've never seen a player so committed to improvement. Learn from her."

Morgan stepped back and allowed the two girls to practice with no supervision. He noticed something and said, "Take a break, Molly. I need to work on Bianca's footwork for a minute." Morgan took the ball from Bianca. "Often as not, the rebound won't just fall off the rim, and you'll find yourself farther than three feet from the hoop and in an awkward position. That's when your footwork comes into play." He showed her how to gather herself into a strong position, to take one power dribble to move back into the three-foot area near the rim, and to power up again. "It's not easy, but if you work at it, it will become second nature."

"One more thing, Bianca, and you need to remember this too, Molly. Almost every drill involves passing, and while the emphasis may be on shooting or rebounding or something else, there's always a pass. So, remember this. Every drill is a passing drill. After your part of the drill, Bianca, you throw a pass back to Molly. Make it a good one. In the back of your mind, I want you to hear me saying to you, *Every drill's a passing drill.*"

§

If the Mountain Matrons were anything, they were loose. No

drunks, but silly occasionally. Queenie and Mercedes were a couple; A tall black woman and a tightly wound Italian who met in Pueblo when they attended a union meeting protesting working conditions for steel workers. "I heard about this protest meeting, and since my hometown of Birmingham was a steel manufacturing city like Pueblo and had a bit of a reputation for protests, I thought it was my duty to attend. This little bit of a woman stood up and electrified the crowd. Fell in love with her that night." The other Matrons laughed.

Octavia broke in. "Changing the subject, Queenie, darling, we talked about being more proactive in our community a couple of months ago. After our discussion about Oro Hills, it seems like most of us would like to help, but just don't know where to start. Mitzi and I talked about it and thought maybe we could begin with the schools. Early education seems to be the hot topic these days, so maybe that would be a place to start. All of our schools seem to be struggling for a few extra dollars."

"As long as I don't have to sit with kindergarteners and have them touch me, I'm in," said Mercedes. "Can I just donate money?"

"Money's always good," said Mitzi. "Commitment to the cause."

§

When Andrea returned home, she found Morgan cooking a quick batch of spaghetti for himself. She sat with him and related the club's news while he ate. B.J. was angry with the high school principal because of his indifference to the school's low scores. He blamed it on the make-up of the student body and the changing demographics of Oro Hills. He had the gall to say to her face he was okay with it, that the town shouldn't expect more.

Morgan shook his head in a concerned way. "And if Anita was relating the club's discussions for the day, what would she tell her husband you said?"

"Probably about this team of girls you've adopted who show up most every day on our driveway. Mitzi says she doesn't know them because they're underclassmen, but she does recognize their names. She asked me to ask you why you aren't working with the juniors."

"Tell Mitzi I'm not out recruiting; just whoever shows up. I did have a fun day with Molly and Bianca today though. And Rosa."

CHAPTER 6

Don't ever let them get comfortable out there.
Their comfort is our enemy.

W
ith three weeks left in the school year, spring in the mountains arrived. The Oklahoma bombing remained at the forefront of the news along with the O.J. Trial. Coach Abby called her team together after school on May 18 to tell them she was going back to college for one year, a sabbatical, but she would return for the 1996-1997 season. They would be in good hands with Coach Thulen. Morgan heard about it later that Wednesday from Molly who was frustrated the girls wouldn't have a summer program.

"Coach Thulen said he'd open up the gym a couple of nights each week, but he couldn't take us anywhere because he's working his second job in the summer. The guys team is playing in a Memorial Day tournament in Pueblo and going to team camp in Grand Junction. It isn't fair." Molly wasn't looking for a response from Morgan; she was just venting. She began her ball routine in her own world. Shortly afterward, Stevie arrived, the first Morgan had seen of her in two weeks.

"How did you do at State?" ask Morgan.

Stevie beamed. "Two fifth places. I got to run in the finals in both."

Elena, Izzy, Bianca, Rosa, and Cindy also came over and practiced for an hour. Bianca took Stevie across the street to Molly's driveway to demonstrate how to shoot power layups. The girls played their first three-on-three game, which Morgan thought was painful, as if they had never been taught this basketball staple. Elena guarded Bianca, and that was a total mismatch. Elena, at five-five, was six inches shorter and thirty-plus pounds lighter. Morgan liked the battle between Molly and Stevie, at least when Stevie was guarding Molly. Still, Molly's skills were improving at such a rapid rate, she could frequently get around Stevie. Mostly, whoever had the ball shot it, and then there was a scramble for the rebound. No one set a screen or blocked out. Worst of all, but not unexpectedly, there were more turnovers than shots. *Passing*, thought Morgan, *continues to be basketball's least taught skill.*

Dinner times differed for each girl, and they drifted off beginning around five-thirty, but daylight savings time allowed Molly to keep shooting until her mother and brother returned just after seven. Andrea had made a sandwich for Molly an hour earlier, knowing her mom would be too tired to fix a proper supper. Molly sat in Morgan's patio chair while he shot set shots and hooks.

"You know, Molly, there are other things in life than basketball," he said as he moved to retrieve a missed shot. He faced her as he rolled the ball in his hands. "And there are young boys more fun than an old man."

"This from a retired coach who spends as much time on his driveway as I do? I'll bet you were a basketball geek in high school too."

Morgan turned to shoot a short hook shot that banked in. "Yeah, I guess I was, but not to your extent. When coaches around the state warn their players that there is a player somewhere who is outworking them, these coaches are referring to you." Morgan smiled.

"I'd leave you alone if there was somewhere else to play, but then you'd get lonely and sit in your kitchen missing me and growing older." Molly was teasing her coach. "Are you encouraging me to get a boyfriend, Coach?"

Morgan laughed aloud. "No, not really."

"High school boys are mostly jerks, and they only want one thing, and you know what that is. Ask Alondra. Promise you won't tell, Coach?"

"Promise. What?"

Morgan stopped shooting to give Molly his full attention. She finished the sandwich, lifted the chair back onto the small front porch, and stepped over to Morgan to take the ball. "One of those kids she has to take care of is her own. Had it in junior high. We all know. She just wanted to get married; talked about it all the time. In ninth grade. She got her baby, but her boyfriend was probably twenty, and he took off when she got pregnant." Molly turned away and shot a baby left-handed hook. She retrieved her own shot and turned back to Morgan. "I don't know where I'm going or what I want to be, but I sure know I don't want to get pregnant and left behind. I don't want my mom's life." Molly's eyes teared up as she looked into Morgan's. He stepped to her and pulled her into his body for a grandfatherly hug.

Gently, Morgan said, "I don't think there's any reason to believe you will."

Molly sniffled. "Maybe I could join the military after high school."

Morgan could tell Molly had said that in jest. "Or go to college."

Molly pulled away and wiped her nose against her sleeve. "I need to get through high school first."

Morgan stepped to the far side of the basket, motioning with his head for Molly to shoot. "Yeah, that's probably a good first step to getting out of Oro Hills."

They shot until Molly's mother drove into the driveway. "Remember, Coach. Don't say anything about Alondra."

Morgan nodded. "What you tell me stays between the two of us. Always."

Molly smiled and started to walk away. She turned and said, "You can share things with Mrs. Summitt if you want."

§

While Andrea sat on the couch reading her book club selection for the month, Morgan sat in the recliner with a yellow legal pad. He listed the names of the girls who had come to the driveway to shoot, a total of nine at one time or another. He made a calendar beginning on this Thursday, May 18, and taking it through the middle of July. A little over eight weeks.

"Can I interrupt you for a minute?" he asked his wife. "Do we have any plans for the next couple of months?"

§

Early Friday morning, Morgan was on the phone with Kane Vincent. "Can I buy you that beer this afternoon? After four? That would be great. How about Get Drilled? See you then."

Morgan chose the Get Drilled Bar because he knew Octavia Wick from Andrea's book club. Kane Vincent arrived just before four-thirty, flopping into the booth seat across from Morgan. "It may not look like it, but I won again. Survived another week," he said with a smile.

Morgan said he learned the girls coach was taking a year off and her assistant worked two jobs, leaving the girls without any program for the summer. He wondered if there would be any problems if he ran an open gym a couple of nights each week, and if he could set up a few games for them if he could find any schools that were willing.

"No legal problems that I see," said Kane. "The problems I do see are that our gym has been scheduled pretty tightly by the boys, girls volleyball, and cheers on most nights for the rest of the year." The high school principal Lowell Exeter entered the bar and seemed to know everyone, reminding Morgan of Norm from the TV show *Cheers*. Exeter noticed Kane and stopped to say a few words. Kane introduced him to Morgan before the principal took a seat at the end of the bar where he could see and be seen. As they talked, other patrons stopped by the table to say hi to Kane, and he introduced each one to Morgan.

"How many girls do you think might be interested in playing in the summer?" asked Kane. "I know Abby struggled to get participation. The best player is more interested in volleyball; she plays club in the spring and summer."

"Maybe eight or nine. More if word gets out. I'd just work with those girls who wanted to be there. I think it would be helpful for Coach Thulen next season. Losing by fifty isn't a good thing."

Kane lifted his next beer and said, "The battle's getting a little fuzzy." He swallowed and said, "We might be able to get you into the old gym."

Morgan smiled. "I played in that gym when I lived here. Fond memories."

"You're an alumnus?"

§

Back home, Andrea had dinner waiting. "Well, what did you find out?"

Morgan related his conversation, said he had spoken with Octavia, who said hi, and told about the activity in her bar. He told Andrea he had Kane Vincent's permission, but space could be a problem. He would meet Kane at the Elm Street Gym early in the week to check on its condition, to see if it was usable. "The girls can't use the school's equipment or uniforms over the summer; no money in the budget in case any of it was lost. I think I'll go over to the outlet mall to see if they have any cheap jerseys; that's all they would need. Before I say anything to Molly and the others, I need to make some calls to other schools to see if they have any openings in their leagues or would want to just scrimmage."

"How many games are you looking for?" asked Andrea.

"Whatever I can get. I didn't realize how easy it was with the boys in Lakewood. I always had plenty of kids wanting to play. Fifty games a summer. Two leagues, an underclassmen league on Saturday mornings, team camp, weights, open gym. I didn't know I was coaching in heaven."

§

His old copy of the Colorado Association for Co-Curricular Activities directory allowed Morgan to call several girls coaches on Saturday. Varsity leagues were full, but he was able to secure a spot in a JV league playing on Tuesday and Thursday nights beginning the first week in June. Two games each evening for four weeks against higher classification teams, a prescription for sixteen ass-whoopings, but Molly would get her games, and that was a positive. Now, Morgan needed to make sure he had seven or eight girls each night, and that involved considerable planning and coercion. Nearly every girl had a summer job and family responsibilities. If the Elm Street Gym wasn't available, his driveway would have to do.

§

Molly generally worked at the laundromat on Saturday nights, subbing for her mother. Date night. Molly didn't mind because she had no interest in hanging with the drinking crew. At ten-fifteen, the last of the women finished, and Molly closed. When she pulled into her driveway, she noticed Morgan sitting in the kitchen.

She called first. "Hey, Coach. I saw you were still awake, and I just got home from working, and I can't sleep yet, so I was wondering if I could come over while I eat my dinner?" Morgan had seen Molly drive up. He met her at the door so that she didn't have to knock.

"Mrs. Summitt is already in bed, but she won't hear us," said Morgan. "What do you have there?" he asked pointing at her plastic bowl.

"Beans over cornbread. Do you have any milk? I forgot to bring it."

"Do you want to re-heat it in the microware?" Morgan went to the refrigerator for the milk and then sat with Molly, who indicated her dinner was warm enough. After the small talk, Morgan asked, "If you could, how many games would you like to play this summer?"

"You know, Coach, if we could just play seven or eight, that would be great. Just something to show us our improvement and to be able to compete. Izzy and Elena came over to the laundromat tonight, and we talked about it. I love shooting baskets and working on my game, and they do too, but we would like to play some games."

"How would sixteen do?" Morgan asked. "I was on the phone all day trying to set something up. I called lots of schools our size trying to get into a league or at least some weekend tournaments, but everything is full. I got a tip that the Jeffco League might have an opening in their JV league, so I called about it." He paused. "We're in." Molly stopped eating and stared at Morgan. He could see she had a thousand questions to ask. He began to lay out the details for her. "Even though it's a junior varsity league, it's 4A and 5A JV teams. Some will be as good as Academy Prep and Benson. Every team will be bigger than us with more players. And they will have their regular coaches."

Molly interrupted. "Will you be coaching us?"

"For this league, yes. We'll play every Tuesday and Thursday beginning June 6. Two games each night. We'll have to drive about forty-five minutes each way. We'll need to leave here around four-thirty, and we won't get home until after ten. Four weeks. All of June."

"Sixteen games?"

"Yeah. I signed us up. Now, we need to get at least eight girls to go every time. I promised we would never forfeit. Molly, I must tell you, you might not win a game, because the teams you'll be playing have all the advantages. We've never even had a practice." He looked at Molly and realized the only thing she had heard was "sixteen games." Morgan moved his head from side to side to get her to come back to the obstacles they would face. "Molly, the very first thing we have to do is get a commitment from seven or eight of the girls to show up. Most of you work and it's a huge time commitment, I know. Jeez, I don't know how your mother will react, much less the parents of the other girls, parents whom I've never even met."

Molly reached across the table for Morgan's legal pad and began to list names. First on her list was herself. "One. No matter what." Izzy and Elena came next. "Their parents will let them play." Then, Cindy and Stevie. "I know both their moms; I'll make sure. That's five. We need Bianca. We've got to have her, and if she can come, then probably Rosa can too. Seven." Morgan had already counted this group. It was eight and nine and hopefully ten that he worried about.

"What about Penny?"

They talked until eleven and then Molly said she probably needed to go home. Morgan worried about her, but she said this happened occasionally and she was fine. He watched her cross the street and waited until he saw a light come on. A moment later, her porch light blinked on and off. He sat down at the kitchen table and read the list of players who might be available. A thin list, but doable. His thoughts turned to strategies. This bunch had one point guard and one center; the others were interchangeable. Besides Molly, only Elena, Izzy, and Cindy could handle the ball a little, but they would struggle against the competition. Molly needed to stay on the floor. Rosa and Penny did not have the skills for this level, but they would still need to play. Sofia, if she played, and Elena, the two seniors, at least had the physical size to compete as did Bianca, plus they would defend. Morgan smiled a warning to himself: *Don't make Molly and Bianca play the entire game.*

He had a good idea about what he would teach, both offensively and defensively. No set plays and no zone defenses. Motion offense, probably four around one. Every girl a guard except Bianca and Penny— and Alondra if she ever played. Molly would be the trigger for it all. Defensively, the big school girls would have to deal with man-to-man pressure. Morgan laughed softly. *Girl-to-girl. Player-to-player.* He would turn Stevie loose.

Morgan wasn't tired. On his legal pad, he listed several items the girls would need for summer play. At least two new indoor basketballs for warmup drills; he didn't want them to seem rube-ish to the suburban girls. Some kind of uniform. At least jerseys. Morgan didn't want them to be self-conscious about the trimmings.

A car pulled into Molly's driveway at midnight and her mother emerged with a man. They walked to the door, but after a kiss he left, and she went in alone. That mattered to Morgan on this night.

§

Molly was shooting by ten. She told Morgan she had called Izzy to tell her the news, and she was sure they would always have six to play. "We can do it. None of us are fat."

Morgan noticed Bianca walking up the street, dribbling Molly's old rubber ball. She waved from a few houses away and Molly jogged down to meet her. Morgan knew what Molly said to Bianca by the way she grabbed her arm and by Bianca's reaction. Their excitement made Morgan smile again.

"Is it true . . . what Molly said? We're going to play in a league?" asked Bianca.

"It is if we can get enough of you to commit to this. It's a big-time commitment," said Morgan.

"Can Rosa play?" asked Bianca.

"We're counting on her."

"Can I use your phone and call her?"

Both girls went inside with Morgan and made calls to the others, making plans to meet in the driveway at one.

Bianca and Molly were joined by Izzy, Rosa, Elena, Stevie, Cindy, and Penny—all arriving before one. Every girl said she was in and that their parents would let them go. Morgan worried the adults might have concerns as they learned more. When the pizza arrived, the girls sat around the dining room table and giggled. *Enthusiasm*, thought Morgan, *is a wonderful and contagious feeling.*

Morgan stood behind Elena to get the girls' attention. "There is more to this than just playing games. We'll need to practice a few times in order to have some understanding of how we'll play the game. I need to tell you all a few things before we begin. First, I've never coached girls before, only guys, so I'm going to treat you just as basketball players and not think about sex." Bianca laughed first and then the other girls giggled. "Gender. Whenever we practice, there will be some conditioning, some running." As he spoke, he watched the girls' reactions. Every one of them kept her eyes on his. "As we move into a practice environment, my behavior may be a bit different from what you see here on the driveway. I'm too old to

41

yell anymore, but I may get more pointed in my advice. I don't know, but just understand I could be a little different. I've been out of this for three years." He looked at each girl. "Any questions yet?"

Rosa raised her hand just over her forehead. "I want to come, but do I always have to play?"

Morgan nodded. "Rosa, the purpose of this is to get better. Each of you is starting with a certain set of skills and abilities. I want you to improve upon them by playing. No, if there are times when you don't want to be in the game, just tell me. But I want you to get in there, to compete, to battle." Morgan looked at each girl again. "I want each of you to support one another's growth. Summer ball is a time to have fun, to get better, and to come together as a team. Some of you are better than others, and that means some will play more minutes, but each of you can help. One of my goals is to teach you not to be afraid."

§

On Monday Morgan drove twenty-five minutes to the outlet mall. At the Nike store, Morgan found enough mesh jerseys in almost the right shade of gold, but he realized that mesh works for boys, but maybe not for girls. It was then Morgan realized he had no idea about the sizes for the girls. He thanked the clerk, telling her he would be back.

He returned home to find Andrea asleep on the couch. He sat down with his legal pad and tried to sketch out a budget, but again he was unsure as to the costs of the various items. With his boys' teams, he budgeted accurately. He decided he would call Morey to get some idea of what could be expected. The junior varsity league fee was $400, a reasonable amount, but coming out of his pocket. *Money well spent*, he thought. *An investment in education*, he kidded himself.

Seven girls came by after school to practice, still giddy with excitement. "Teach us a play, Coach," said Molly.

"No plays this summer. We're going to run what's called motion offense, and even that will be simplified. It's all about passing and cutting. Every one of you will learn how to do it, but I might put Bianca on the post during games sometimes. When she's playing the post, she'll mostly be a screener and rebounder, but, Bianca, I want you to learn some guard skills just to improve your overall basketball ability. Molly, what did I say about every drill?"

"Every drill is a passing drill," she answered.

"Good. Now, for the first drill," . . . and for the next hour, Morgan taught his summer team the details of motion, patiently but purposefully.

§

Morgan reviewed his list while drinking his morning coffee with Andrea. He asked her about sizing and whether the girls' bust sizes mattered. She laughed at how he phrased his question, but said it might if it was extreme, and to her knowledge none of the girls had a problem with that. She said he might consider getting two or three extra jerseys and make one of them XL.

"How many girls said they could play?" asked Andrea.

"Eight, maybe nine. Better than I thought, but we'll see if they can always make it. A few said they might only be able to come sometimes. Still, better than when I made the commitment to play. I was worried about not having enough some days. We'll see."

"You didn't ask me about my lunch with the Matrons."

"If I remember correctly, you slept through most of the evening," said Morgan.

Andrea smiled back at her husband. "Yes, I did. Anyway, we talked about you and your girls. My friends think what you're doing is remarkable and want to help. So," and Andrea paused her sentence. "Do you want more coffee? I'm going to warm mine up." She stood to retrieve the coffee pot and refilled both of their cups. "As I was saying, they want to help. I copied your list before I went to meet them and showed it to them. For now, they pledged to buy the items the girls need immediately." Andrea scrunched her nose and waited for Morgan's reaction.

He started nodding his head before he spoke. Then, "Do they know how much this might cost? One basketball goes for seventy dollars. Screened jerseys will at least double the cost. We're talking around five hundred now."

Andrea nodded her head in return. "Yeah, we know. I kind of made a call to Morey to get a better idea. He says hi, by the way. He's always been a nice guy. He wants you to call him today, so he can get the jerseys to you as soon as possible. The club is also covering the cost of the league. All of it. Seems like you've discovered some sugar mamas. Be nice to Mercedes and Queenie. They've got more money than I knew about."

Morgan could only say, "Wow, this is really nice of the club. Tell them thanks. I need to do something for them."

"We talked. All of us are public school brats, as Octavia said. No prep schools or private academies. Some were poor growing up, or at least not rich. For each of us, someone along the way gave us a boost." She touched Morgan's arm. "I'm not done. If any of the girls don't have the proper shoes or need something else, they want to continue to help, so check on that. Shoes will just automatically appear. They won't be the most expensive basketball shoes, but Morey said he had some good, inexpensive shoes he could give you a deal on."

"If that happened, the girls would think I was buying them, and that can't be. I'll need to tell them about your club," said Morgan.

"How about if you just tell them they have some supporters in the community who want to help?" said Andrea.

"Maybe I could tell them that we went over to Blackhawk and won big on the gambling tables."

CHAPTER 7

Pass away from the defense.

After breakfast Morgan drove to the south side of town to meet the activities director at the Elm Street Gym. True to his nature, Morgan was early, but the sun shining on the south facing wall of the old building made waiting pleasant. The gym was once an old warehouse, converted sometime in the 1920s into a gym. A faded wooden plaque affixed to the wall near the double-doors commemorated the boys consolation championship in mid-fifties. Most of the players' names were unreadable, but the date, a basketball, and the word *Champions* could be made out. Oro Hills last state championship in any sport. Kane Vincent arrived late and apologized. He unlocked the door from a ring of keys befitting an assistant principal whose boss delegated nearly every responsibility to him. It had been forty-six years since Morgan last set foot in this building, the year after his high school graduation, the year he joined the Army and escaped Oro Hills and the mine. One year underground had been enough.

"You once played here?" asked Kane.

Morgan stood just inside the doors and surveyed the gym. Memories flooded back. "A long time ago. Who uses it now?"

"The recreation department holds exercise classes here occasionally. I think that's all, but it keeps the gym functional. The bathrooms work and the lights come on."

The two men made a pass around the court's perimeter. The floor was warped in two spots, but not severely. Morgan shook his head at the myriad of lines painted on the court, lines for basketball, of course, but also for volleyball, cross-court basketball, and a half-dozen other games physical education teachers deemed important. "The elementary school

45

used to use it before they revamped their gym," said Kane.

The backboards on the main court were glass rectangles, probably fifty-years old, and cloudy. Regulation, but the rims were worn silver, the nets frayed, and there were no basket pads. Four fan-shaped metal backboards remained in place on the sides. Only one of these had a net. Seating hadn't changed: the balcony, which made this gym such a pit, such an advantage for the home team, extended out to the boundary lines. Back in the day, Oro Hills fans would fill the gym before the "B" team game, denying seating, and thus entry, for the visitors.

"I understand you were quite a star," said Kane.

"No. I was the biggest kid at six-one. Played center all three years. My sophomore year began the year the war ended, and I graduated in '48. I liked to mix it up, and the game was rougher back then. Lots of fights."

"Did you take part?"

Morgan grinned. "Oh, yeah. I was no choir boy. My senior year, I even got suspended for the last game of the season because of a fight the previous weekend. We lost and didn't get to go to the State Tournament. Back then, only the league champion got to go. Not like today where three teams from each league advance to the round of twenty-four."

"Do you like this way better?" asked Kane.

"I do. A team can improve through the season and make noise in the district playoffs. Might not make it to the final eight, the real State Tournament, but can be rewarded and recognized for its improvement."

"Well," said Kane, "will this work?"

Morgan nodded. "Do we need to fill out any paperwork?"

"No. I'm the paperwork." He smiled and removed the key from his ring. "It's all yours."

§

Morgan didn't have to make phone calls to organize practice; the girls made sure everyone knew. The first practice took place Tuesday evening at 7:30, a school night. After his meeting with Kane Vincent, Morgan had driven to Lakewood to MoJo Sports to pick up some items and talk to Morey. "Let me know about shoes as soon as possible." Morey helped load the equipment into Morgan's truck. "You got a nice benefactor, Coach," said Morey.

Promptly at 7:30 Molly got her wish, she and her friends started *Summer Ball*: dribble layups from the right side, then, zigzag. The girls had not done this drill, so Morgan explained what he expected from both the dribbler and the defender. "Go slow and get your footwork correct." Only Molly could dribble with her head up, and Morgan noted how much work would be needed on this skill. "Cindy, you're going to be called upon to do this next year, so work hard." After that, the girls partnered for passing drills. "Slide with your hands up. Give your teammate a target. Two-handed chest pass; throw it hard. Make her learn to catch a hard pass. Good!"

Already, the division between what might be considered a first team and a second team was beginning to emerge. Certainly, Molly, Bianca, and Izzy were the offensive leaders. Stevie and Elena were next. Cindy and Penny were trying and good enough to work into the drills without messing them up. Rosa was trying. Morgan encouraged her. "Way to go Rosa. That's much better!" After the passing drill, Morgan called for a water break and sat them down.

"Really good, so far. I'm proud of you! Because we don't have a lot of time to prepare for our first game, I won't condition you with line drills, but we will do plenty of full-court stuff. I want to emphasize the fundamentals, so you'll be ready for the regular season and whatever Coach Thulen wants to run. We'll do two more things tonight, a rebounding drill and then a full-court fast break drill. This drill is what I call the *run to rebound* drill. You'll work in groups of four." Morgan demonstrated the details and walked the girls through it, smiling all the while. It was far from perfect, but the effort was. *I should have coached girls earlier*, he thought to himself. It had been a fun and productive practice.

§

No Wednesday practice, church night, so Molly shot in Morgan's driveway. Morgan was tired; he hadn't run a practice in over three years, so he sat in the patio chair while she practiced.

"How did you think it went, Coach?" she asked.

"Pretty good, but at some point, we may need to actually play against a live defense." He laughed. "You know, don't you, you're going to have to carry the load?"

Molly held the ball and looked at him. "What all does that mean? I mean, I know I'm the best player, but what are you asking me to do?"

Morgan sat up straighter. "It means that you can't get hurt, you can't get in foul trouble, and you always want to have the ball. It means you have to play through fatigue, both mental and physical, and always take responsibility when things aren't going our way. I won't kid you; I don't know what to expect this summer playing against the Jeffco League. They'll be good and your teammates will be outmatched, with the possible exception of Bianca. The two of you can compete."

Molly dribbled the ball side to side without moving. "I'm looking forward to it."

"When I need to take you out is when we'll really struggle," said Morgan.

"Why would you have to take me out?"

§

On Thursday Morgan put the girls through a rebounding drill. "We aren't dancing here. Before you go for the ball, put your body on your man. Girl. Woman. Lady." The girls started laughing. Morgan smiled broadly. "How about if when I say *man*, I don't correct myself?"

"Why don't you just say *player*, Coach?" teased Molly.

Sofia was in attendance, but Rosa stayed home to do homework. Morgan liked Sofia; she was stronger than most of the others and liked contact. As a senior to be, she wasn't in Molly's clique, but she was good friends with Elena. After a two-on-one drill, Morgan showed the girls how to play four-on-four half court with a shell drill.

"We're going to challenge the other teams to throw the ball cross-court, so we will really over-play one side of the court." He realized the girls didn't grasp what he was saying, so he sat them down and pulled out his clipboard. He drew lines dividing the court into thirds. "We want to push the ball to one of the outside thirds, and then we'll all play that third and the middle. At all times, we will put extreme pressure on the dribbler. With your quickness, we can make it very difficult on them to execute their offense." At each pause he stressed the need for pressure on the ball.

"Good job again tonight. I hope you're having some fun and feel good about our progress. I've reserved the high school gym for Saturday."

On Point

§

Molly had several of her teammates over on Friday night for a sleepover, but she turned it into a review session on Thursday's practice. "Coach is saying we all crowd the one side of the court when we play defense and not hug our girl. On offense we do just the opposite and try and stay wide, to create space." She would put down her pencil, stand, and demonstrate what Coach meant by "Jump to the ball." She emphasized that Coach had slight adjustments for "the bigs" and for Stevie. The questions the girls had that Molly couldn't answer, she would write them down to be posed to Morgan on her own. Years later, each of Molly's teammates would remember these nights with fondness.

§

On Saturday ten girls showed up. Alondra was one of them. Five-feet-seven and *hefty*, she made Morgan wonder if one of the jerseys he had recently ordered would fit her. Every girl came up to Alondra when she entered the gym, an obvious sign of how well she was liked. Her skills mirrored those of Cindy's or Penny's, not as good as Sofia's, but certainly better than Rosa's. With Alondra, Morgan could demonstrate five-on-five situations for the first time. It was also the first time Bianca was pushed around physically, the first time Morgan could get a gauge on her toughness.

§

At 12:30 Mrs. Summitt and three of the Mountain Matrons arrived with pizza. Andrea introduced them to the girls as Mrs. Risso, Ms. Roberts, and Mrs. Pagel. "You all recognize Mrs. Risso." The Matrons determined three of the girls—Rosa, Bianca, and Alondra—needed real basketball shoes.

After lunch Morgan walked the girls through situational sets: free throw alignment, two basic out-of-bounds plays, and quick press-break. "If we're pressed, get the ball to Molly. Bianca, fill a spot in the middle of the court, our two and three players are to run wide and deep, and whoever throws the ball in is to stay behind and slightly to the side of Molly." Morgan walked them through the press break, explaining how it fit into the overall scenario or how the team was going to play this summer. "Everything will be fast. We're going to be out of control early and confused, but you'll learn. You'll get it. The teams you play against will be bigger, but none of them will be as quick. And our bigger girls give us a nice mix." Morgan wasn't as convinced about his last statement, but he sold it to his girls. "Our pressure defense will have to carry us early on. Stevie, you'll be the trigger."

§

The ten days between the first organized practice and the first summer league game went fast for Morgan, but slow for the girls. They had finals and their anticipation for a real game dragged the hours out. School ended on Friday at noon, the final day being a "waste of time," according to Molly. Practice was held on Saturday in the school gym with no Sofia, but with Alondra and Rosa. Rosa did not wear her practice clothes and was crying. When Morgan asked her why, she told him she was ineligible, that she was going to have three Ds for the semester.

"You passed all your classes. Why would you be ineligible?" he asked.

"If you get one D, you're ineligible," answered Cindy. "That's our contract."

Morgan was confused. "What contract?"

Izzy tried to explain. "Our eligibility rules. That's the contract. It's a one-D policy. One D makes you ineligible."

Still, Morgan was puzzled. "You're saying that if you get just one D, not an F, but a D, you're ineligible?"

Izzy and the others nodded. "Last season, lots of the team missed games because they received a D. I didn't, and Elena didn't, but I think everyone else missed at least one game." Izzy looked to her teammates and they all agreed.

Morgan scrunched his face as he thought about this. Finally, "First of all, there is no eligibility during the summer, so, Rosa, you can play. How many classes do you guys take each semester?"

"Six or seven, depending on your schedule," answered Izzy.

"So," Morgan analyzed as he spoke, "even if you're passing five or six, if you get a single D, you're ineligible?"

"That's what I just said," answered Izzy.

Morgan rubbed both hands over his face. "That's not a state policy, unless the Association changed something in the last three years. I know schools can make it harder, but a single D . . ., that's crazy." He paused again. "Rosa, you can play this summer; I know that. I'm going to look into this one-D policy, because it makes no sense to me."

"I didn't bring my shoes," said Rosa.

Morgan smiled. "Then take off those," he said pointing to her flats, "and shoot in your bright socks." He hugged Rosa and put the team to running full-court layup drills.

Just after noon Morgan called the girls together at center court. He told them he wanted to meet on Monday in his driveway to finalize plans for their ride to Denver. They were to come with bags packed so he could check on their readiness.

"Coach," said Molly, "we've all been to away games before."

§

Molly, Bianca, and Rosa came by on Sunday afternoon to shoot on Morgan's driveway. He wasn't at home, and Mrs. Summitt told them he often drove to Denver on Sundays to visit their daughter, but he would see them on Monday afternoon.

§

"Let's go inside," said Morgan to the nine girls who were shooting in his driveway on Monday at three. Inside, he gave them game schedules with the list of the other teams in the Jeffco Summer League. He said their first game on Tuesday would start at six. Games were played in two eighteen-minute halves with a running clock, except for the last two minutes of the second half if the score was within ten points. "It's summer, so fouls and violations won't be called as rigidly, so be ready for that." He advised them to bring a banana for between games, their second game was at eight, and to bring a snack for the ride home. "Because we'll be getting home late, I don't think we'll stop for anything."

He answered a few questions before lifting a box from the side of his chair. He passed out the new jerseys, "Make sure the number you want fits you. Most of you will be wearing smalls. Bianca and Alondra, check to see if the larges fit you. Penny, you might want to wear a medium still." As the girls tried on their jerseys, their excitement was obvious. "I was

51

going to wait until tomorrow just before the game to give them to you, but I decided we needed to check for sizes." He reminded them the book club ladies were responsible for the new apparel. "If you see them on the street or downtown, be sure to thank them." Finally, he said the ladies who brought pizza to the gym a couple of weeks earlier noticed three of the girls didn't have decent basketball shoes. "These are the least expensive, but they'll serve you well for the summer."

CHAPTER 8

Get up into the passing lane! Make them beat you back door!

Eight girls squeezed into Andrea's mini-van for the forty-five-minute ride down the mountain to Denver's most western suburb, Golden, for their first summer league game ever. Penny sat shotgun, while the four smallest—Stevie, Cindy, Molly, and Izzy—shared the far back bench, leaving Rosa, Elena, and Bianca in the middle seat, which was designed to hold two adults. None of the girls complained and no one felt uncomfortable. The combined weight of the four girls in the back totaled about four hundred pounds, about what two of Morgan's boys players weighed. Driving a second car, or in this case Morgan's truck, was not necessary. Morgan attached a luggage rack on top for the equipment, freeing the entire interior for the girls.

During the trip, Morgan stayed mostly silent as the girls talked and laughed among themselves. Stevie communicated as she played, in quick starts with busy hands. She and Molly drove the conversation, but the others were actively involved. Penny said nothing but swiveled in her seat to listen to the others and laughed frequently. Listening and observing what he could through the rearview mirror, Morgan began to learn more about his summer team. As he had surmised during the winter season, these kids liked one another, and the new additions—Bianca and Rosa—fit in comfortably.

From the back as the van entered Golden, Molly yelled, "Hey, Coach, I'm a junior now. We all are."

It wasn't accurate, and Elena quickly corrected her. "I'm a senior, so you all need to treat me with the requisite respect." Izzy oohed and asked Elena where she learned the word requisite. Elena then asked Morgan if the two sophomores, Cindy and Penny, should carry the balls and other equipment.

"We'll share that duty. We aren't going to make these artificial layers that sometimes develop on teams. They can hurt our growth and divide a team. I want all of you to pull for each other and not make anyone feel uncomfortable. You're teammates now." He paused and looked at them through the rearview mirror before adding, "Family."

"Does that make you our dad?" asked Molly jokingly.

"I'm way too old for that. I'm old enough to be your grandfather."

"Or in my case," continued Molly, "my great-grandfather."

"Hey, hey, hey," admonished Morgan. "I'm not that old. Just your old fart grampa."

Bianca raised both hands as a sign for silence and the van's attention. "Our O.F.G."

Being a head coach in Jefferson County for twenty-plus years and teaching for thirty-five, Morgan knew every gym in the district. He knew where to park, which doors to enter, where the locker rooms were located, and many of the girls coaches' names. He knew the schools' colors and mascots. Tonight, his Miners were playing the Farmers and Rams. For him, this was a homecoming and he was entirely comfortable in the surroundings. "Here we are," he said as he parked the van. "Start enjoying this."

The gym was warm. June 6 and no air-conditioning. Morgan's girls had all worn their jerseys in the van along with their basketball shoes. Morgan would later require them to wear "street shoes" in the van. But this was the first game and they had much to learn about how to play, how to dress, how to act, and what to think about this game of basketball at a higher level than they had ever experienced. Wide-eyed, they watched Ralston Valley's junior varsity dismantle Green Mountain.

"They're so big!"

"They're better than Academy Prep's varsity."

Morgan listened and smiled. *Yep*, he thought to himself, *both true statements, and this is why you play summer league.* He also knew he had two girls who wouldn't be intimidated long. Nervous at first, but ready to go. And one girl who probably never gave a second thought to who she was playing and would be a whirling dervish on the court. Arriving early for this first time was beneficial. He gathered the girls at one corner of the gym and began coaching them.

On Point

"Big, aren't they? And that Ralston Valley bunch is really good. When I signed us up for this league, I was told they were the team to beat. I guess they're playing girls who will be on their varsity next winter. That gets me to my first point. Coaches have different goals in the summer. We don't have the same issues, and so they will approach these games differently. I'm pretty sure Ralston Valley has a chance to win the state tournament next year, so their coach wants to teach his younger girls how to win now. We're in a different boat here. Goals are extremely important to growing. Tonight's goal for me is to get your feet wet. I will not let any of you drown tonight, but some of you will be in over your heads for a few minutes. Rosa, you will play for a few minutes. Penny and Cindy, a few more minutes. All of you are going to be overwhelmed at times. That's good!" Morgan paused and gave them an encouraging look. "We'll start with Molly, Stevie, Izzy, Elena, and Bianca. Man-to-man defense. Rebound and run. If any of you gets stuck with the ball, look for Molly. Molly will come get it. She'll take care of you." Morgan looked at Molly and nodded. Eight girls with different thoughts nodded back. "Okay, let's go."

Morgan had given them a warmup drill, so they wouldn't simply stand around and shoot haphazardly before the game. Layups and free throws, then outside shooting. When the buzzer sounded, he found himself nervous, but excited. The girls gathered around him. "I'm looking forward to this. You'll make some mistakes, but you're going to do lots of good things too. This is where we start." Oro Hills stacked hands.

Molly said, "One, two, three, Miners!"

The Wheat Ridge team was taller at every position. They won the jump ball and passed to their guard in the back court. Morgan called out to Stevie who immediately moved up to guard her. Oro Hills matched up as Morgan had instructed them to do, and before the Wheat Ridge guard had made one pass, Stevie stole the ball from her. Stevie "found Molly," who dribbled up the court and passed ahead to Izzy. She looked to shoot, but was guarded, so she returned the ball to Molly. #14 beat her girl off the dribble and attacked the basket. Her short jump shot swished, and Oro Hills led 2-0.

The speed of the game was what surprised the girls the most. Wheat Ridge won 37-23, clearly the better team, the deeper team, the more practiced team, but Oro Hills competed. Molly finished with eleven points, Bianca had six, Izzy three, Stevie two, and Elena one. Nobody off the bench scored or even took a shot. As the girls shook hands with their opponents, Morgan talked briefly with the Wheat Ridge coach, who spoke highly of Molly and Stevie. "They're a tough duo. Going to cause other guards some headaches."

Morgan took his team outside on the lawn to debrief and cool down. "I'm proud of your efforts. That was a very good start." He walked around and gave each girl a high-five. "How's your butt, Penny?" She had been run over by the Wheat Ridge center late in the game, a collision that brought tears to her eyes.

"I'm fine. I'm just so clumsy."

"Put some ice on it," kidded Bianca. Penny smiled and the team laughed. *A good sign*, thought Morgan.

He kneeled on the grass with his team. "We did some good things, lots of good things. Now, as the summer progresses, we want to do those things more often. Each of you did some good things."

Rosa giggled. "What did I do good, Coach?"

"Don't minimize this, Rosa, but when I sent you in the first time, you didn't hesitate. You went directly to the scorer's table and ran onto the court. You overcame your initial fear. When you dropped the first pass, you didn't say, 'I'm sorry,' you said, 'My fault,' to Molly."

Molly interrupted. "It was my fault, Rosa. It was too low."

Morgan continued. "There is a world of difference in how we say things. 'My fault' is a basketball term, and that's positive. Good first step."

"Coach, you didn't ask us if we had fun," said Elena.

"Nope. I know you did. It was obvious to anyone who was watching."

§

Oro Hills ran out of gas in the second game. Bianca, who played nearly every minute of each game, finally hit her wall with ten minutes left. Molly and Stevie tried to fight through their fatigue, but neither could execute her specialty, and Green Mountain surged in the second half to win 32-21. Just as it had in the first game, the Miners hit only one three point shot. One for eleven in the first game and one for twelve in the second.

"Now I know why Coach Thulen didn't want us shooting threes last year," said Molly.

Morgan shook his head. "Well, he's not coaching you this summer. I am, and I want you to continue shooting them. A great old coach once told me that a missed shot was nothing more than a high pass. If you're open, chuck it up. I think Bianca scored two baskets on put-backs from missed threes and her other points off rebounds. We practice them, you were open, and we had rebounders. That's the definition of a good shot. Don't second guess. If you're open, I want you to keep shooting threes."

In contrast to the ride down, the van ride back to Oro Hills was quiet. Most of the girls slept, but not Bianca, who made Penny sit in the middle seat, so Bianca could talk with Coach Summitt. "Thank you for this, Coach. It means a lot to us. We'll do better next time."

Morgan turned his head slightly to respond. "Bianca, you guys performed beyond my expectations. Really. I'll bet I had more fun than any of you."

"I need to get in better shape. Back in New Mexico, I never got tired."

"You never stopped trying, and my guess is in New Mexico you didn't play two games in one night against big schools like this. We have three players right now who can compete against those big schools: you, Molly, and Stevie. Stevie is a one-dimensional player, defense, but she was very effective. Izzy and Elena will get there. With Sofia and the other senior who's playing volleyball this summer, you have the makings of a good team. You and Molly did so many good things, and we haven't had many practices. I hope you don't get discouraged."

"Back in Espanola, there was so much trash talking even on our own team. Tonight, the girls on the other teams were so nice to us. Maybe that one girl in the last game wasn't, but she wasn't terrible. She was mostly frustrated because she couldn't move me too much."

"No," said Morgan. "You held your ground and more. You're a tough kid, Bianca."

"That's one thing I learned in Espanola, to be tough. If you aren't, you get run over." She went quiet for a few minutes. Then, "I hope I don't have to go back."

§

Just after ten Morgan dropped each girl off at her house before arriving home. Each one thanked Coach Summitt before leaving. Molly remained as Morgan pulled the van into his garage.

"How'd we do, Coach?"

"Much better than I expected from everyone but you, Molly. Your play didn't surprise me at all. In both games, you were the best guard out there."

Molly smiled. "Yeah, but we lost them both."

"Hey kid, we're going to lose most of the games we play this summer. Those schools are made up of players who've been coming up through their systems, their feeder schools. They're bigger, stronger, and there's more of them. But, Molly, we're not going to lose all of them. I promise you that. Don't let your teammates get discouraged. Keep learning."

"How do we overcome our littleness?" asked Molly.

Morgan hugged her around her shoulders before sending her across the street. "By getting into great shape and out-quicking them."

§

Unlike the initial trip to Golden on Tuesday, Thursday's van ride was mostly basketball talk. Morgan had thrown the girls into the water, they hadn't drowned, and now they were eager to get wet again. League games were played at two sites, Golden and Alameda, but Oro Hills was always scheduled at Golden to ease travel requirements. Tonight, the Miners were to battle Tigers and Pirates. For Oro Hills the same eight girls made up the roster—still no Sofia or Alondra or any recruit—but they would be enough. First game jitters and procedures were over, so the focus was the game itself.

"Even though our three point shots didn't fall," said Morgan, "I want you to keep shooting them when you're open. Molly, you passed up several good shots at the top of the key because you were looking to get your teammates shots." While directing his advice to Molly in particular, the team's best outside shooter, he wanted the other girls to hear that she was being unselfish in her game. Morgan told the team to "get after it" on defense, to be aggressive, even if mistakes were made. "For this summer, our purpose is simply to disrupt any plan or system the opponent might have. Create chaos. Stevie, you did a great job in both games on Tuesday.

Keep that up. The rest of you, as Stevie makes the other team's point guard put her head down, step into the passing lanes. Remember what those are?" he asked. They had gone over that several times, both at the Elm Street Gym and on Morgan's driveway. "Take away the first pass, the easy pass. Create turnovers. Don't be timid out there on defense. Bianca will cover the basket; trust her back there." There was so much to teach, but Morgan wanted first to instill an aggressiveness in their defensive soul, and he knew he had three toughies to build around: Stevie, Molly, and Bianca.

The Lakewood Tigers lacked the size of Tuesday's opponents, but were more skilled offensively. Stevie was less effective in disrupting their point guard which led to several easy Tiger baskets, and their one-three-one zone defense confused Molly and her teammates. The Tigers made dribble penetration difficult, and their defensive transition took away most fastbreak opportunities. Oro Hills lost 36-17.

Playing against a less disciplined team in the second game, Molly's game flourished. Oro Hills led most of the way, but Stevie fouled out in the second half along with Izzy, allowing Alameda to win 33-30. Molly set up Elena for a three point attempt from the left side on the game's last play, only to see it rim out. Bianca rebounded the ball and passed it back to Molly just as the buzzer sounded, leaving no time for a follow shot.

Bianca sat in front again on the ride home, but instead of sleeping, the girls were excited about how close they had come to winning a game. Elena apologized over and over for missing the shot, but the girls supported her. Morgan knew Molly had again passed up a three at the top of the key to get Elena that shot, and he knew she would internalize her choice. The van quieted down for the final few miles, allowing Bianca to talk with Morgan.

"Different games, huh?" she said.

"Yep. You didn't get to touch the ball much in the first one, did you?"

"Hardly at all. What do we do in that situation?"

"For summer league, there's not much we can do. Teams need to have a method of attacking a zone, and that involves daily practices. I wouldn't worry about it; it's kind of a summertime gimmick which gives a team a false sense of success."

"The second game was so much fun. I could have shot the ball at the end, but I knew we needed three points and not two, so I didn't."

Morgan smiled. "You were thinking about time and score, and that shows awareness. Let me throw out a thought. What do you think Alameda would have done had you tried to shoot that last shot? Do you think one of their girls might have tried to block your shot?"

Bianca went silent while she thought about Morgan's query, then, "If I maybe would have given her a little fake, she might have fouled me, huh?" Bianca made a little sound. "Maybe a three point play?"

"We'll never know, but maybe. We'll work on your shot-fake after a rebound. It can be very effective in getting shot-blockers off their feet and fouling." He paused. "Bianca, last time you said something about moving back to Espanola. Is there a chance you might have to?"

Bianca bit the inside of her lip. "There's always a chance. My mom's still down there and Rosa's is too. We live with her aunt, and she's a little older. Now that summer is here, Rosa and I are both working to help pay for our living there, but it's hard. I just don't want to go back, and it would kill Rosa."

§

For the opening day of the Oro Hills Little League baseball season each summer, the town held a parade on Main Street, a central business street, down to Mahan Field. Morgan made it a point to watch the parade; it was so small-town hokey, but that's why he liked it so much, because it was small-town hokey. He stood with Andrea and Molly waiting for the Dodgers to pass by, waiting for Alex in his pressed blue jersey to pass. Morgan asked Molly if she had heard anything about Rosa and Bianca returning to New Mexico.

"Coach, all of us are one . . ." Molly paused. "We're one bad thing away from moving. All of us, except maybe Izzy and Elena, could go. We all live in rented houses or trailers. There's a reason for that." Molly kept her eyes on the parade as she spoke. "This is my third time around for Oro Hills. I like it, but I know I could be back in Pueblo or off to some small town where a relative lives who's willing to put us up for a while. We're all poor, but Rosa and Bianca and Alondra are really poor."

§

60

Later in the day, as Molly shot baskets on the driveway, Morgan helped Andrea erect her makeshift greenhouse over the small garden in the backyard. Morgan was a capable fix-it man, and Andrea always had a project for him. He labored away in his own world on this Saturday, but Andrea generally knew his thoughts. Today, it was the tenuous condition of his girls, about the lack of security in their lives, about Molly's earlier comments. They had seen Lakewood change its demographics over three decades, and he was certainly aware of how Oro Hills was no longer the town of his youth. The mountains remained constant, the local rivers and reservoir hadn't changed, but the town bore scant resemblance to its former self. The natives had grown old and tired, frustrated with its evolution. The town had browned, as the old timers referred to the influx of Hispanics. The schools suffered the most, as the tax base declined and family support for school projects and activities lessened. Why put much effort or allegiance into the school if you might up and move within a year or two? Why fight the locals, who remembered a different world than the one existing in Oro Hills in 1995?

"Growing up," said Andrea, "I lived in one house until I was in the seventh grade. Then we moved a few blocks away where I stayed through graduation." She held a piece of plastic sheeting while Morgan attached it to a plastic pole. "Care to talk about what's rolling around in your head."

"Every one of those girls works in the summer." Morgan stopped there to redo the connection. "They have to be tired when we play our games, but not one of them complains."

"It's a different type of tired."

"Yes and no."

Andrea smiled. "Do you want to talk about this, or am I going to have to pry it out of you over several days?"

"Penny was sick last week, which means there's a good chance she'll pass it on to the others, but that's beside the point. Penny was sick, but still showed up to play. They all work; they all have lives that give no certainty to tomorrow. This is all new to me," said Morgan.

Andrea aped her husband. "Yes and no."

He understood, leaned into her, and kissed her on the cheek. "I thought I was just going to help Molly with her shot."

§

As a teenager in the late-Forties, Morgan loved his high school gym, the Elm Street Gym. He played every game in front of a full house, a crowd of obnoxious miners and their equally ornery wives. World War II was over, and it was time to optimistically move forward. As an angry player, he knew the town had his back. Returning to the gym with Kane Vincent a month earlier brought back these emotions. The irregular basketball floor size, the metal poles along the sidelines that supported the balcony, the scoreboard with the moving hand. Visiting teams called it "The Barn," but it would be considered unsafe now, especially the balcony seats. Now, he saw his girls developing an affinity for it, but for a different reason. Except for their own voices and the echoes, it was a quiet place, a place of their own. They seldom called what they did "practice," instead, they went to "basketball." They weren't practicing, they were playing. "Mom, I'm going to play basketball."

For the opening minutes of basketball, Morgan wanted them to jog with a ball, always with a ball. The girls didn't arrive at the same time but came in twos and threes when they were able. Maybe they finished work late or couldn't get a ride until a teammate or teammate's mother picked them up or they had to babysit a sibling. They came when they came. In pairs they would zigzag the length of the court twice, once as a ball handler and once as the defender. Almost all the drills were with a partner. Full-court layups, right and left. The power series. Paired shooting. "Game shots at game speed," Morgan would say. The team played an inordinate amount of three-on-three with lots of passing and cutting, some screen-and-roll, some pick-and-pop. Molly set a tone early, but Izzy, Elena, and Bianca bought in immediately. Stevie was ADD., but she was all in regardless. Cindy and Rosa became Molly's students, but without the athleticism. Morgan believed Cindy could be an effective junior varsity point guard next season. Skinny Penny learned from Bianca. Not once was Morgan able to have a five-on-five drill, so he ran lots of five-on-oh to teach spacing and transition. The one part of basketball where Morgan demanded physical play was rebounding drills. "Put a body on your girl. You can do better! You need five stops in a row before we turn it around." Routines and repetition.

"We did rebound drills last year, but never like this. And it wasn't every practice, just sometimes. The varsity did it more," said Izzy.

"Who do we play tomorrow?" asked Stevie.

"It's on your schedule," answered Molly. "Ralston Valley first and then Golden."

"We're going to get killed in the first one," said Elena.

Morgan blew his whistle to get their attention. "Circle," he called out. The girls came to half court and sat in the jump circle, the signal basketball was over for the night. "We'll meet at my house at the same time. Yep, two tough ones, but keep in mind that playing difficult games in the summer will improve your chances to win next season. Anybody have any conflicts tomorrow?" There were none, so they stood and Molly stacked their hands.

"One, two, three, Miners," they shouted in unison.

§

Arriving in Golden for their game against Ralston Valley, Morgan learned Ralston Valley would not be playing tonight, that they were attending a team camp at a local college with their varsity and freshmen level teams. Ralston Valley's other opponent was already playing the five o'clock game, but wanted to play a second game, so they would be Oro Hills' opponent at six o'clock. Stanley Lake would be playing two games in a row, but they had twelve girls on their bench. Morgan wasn't displeased that his team would not get to play Ralston Valley; they had lost the first four contests last week and didn't need to get blasted to begin this second week of summer league. He told the girls of the situation, and they, too, seemed relieved. Good competition was one thing, but Ralston Valley was not equitable competition at this moment.

As it turned out, playing back-to-back games affected Stanley Lake, especially with their best players. Oro Hills' pressure defense caused multiple turnovers leading to easy layups for Molly, Stevie, and Izzy. While Stevie missed most of hers, Molly and Izzy were there to rebound and score. Stanley Lake resorted to a two-three zone because of fatigue, allowing Oro Hills the space to shoot threes. Izzy and Elena each made one, and Molly hit three. Bianca scored on a couple of missed shots, and Morgan's girls won their first game of the summer.

Sitting on the lawn after the game, Morgan congratulated and complimented them. "How does that feel?" he asked.

After the giggling and cheering subsided, Molly said, "We were lucky they were tired from the first game."

Morgan smiled as he sat down with them. "They were worn out a bit, I'll admit, but not twelve points tired. You beat them fair and square; luck had nothing to do with the outcome. It seldom does. Maybe if a team hits a full-court heave at the end of a game to win, that's luck, but mostly luck doesn't determine who wins or loses. You guys just took it to them." He paused. "And how about those threes. Five of them!" Morgan noted each girl's contribution, a rebound or a defensive play, that each one had made a completed pass. "Rosa, Penny, Cindy. Nice going." Cindy and Penny had each taken a shot, and even though they missed, these were positive steps to Morgan. "Now, in our second game, I want you to remember one thing. When you were up pressing hard and Stanley Lake got past you, did they score easily?"

It was a rhetorical question, but Morgan waited. Finally, Molly asked, "Did they ever score that way?"

Morgan shook his head. "They made one basket, that's all. Our big stud was back there protecting the rim." Bianca beamed. "You little girls do your job, and Bianca and Penny will do theirs. Never confuse your roles. Take care of your assignment and trust your teammates."

§

Oro Hills second game, this one against the host school, Golden, was close, but a loss. Still, the van ride home was loud. Oro Hills had finally won a game, and Molly could examine what winning felt like. In the front seat, Bianca said to Coach Summitt, "So I'm a *big stud*, huh?"

§

On Thursday Oro Hills won their second game of the summer, this time against Jefferson, the only other lower division school in the league. After losing their first four games, Oro Hills had split the next four, bringing their record to two and six.

"That's twice as many as we've ever won," said Stevie.

"No, that's an infinite number of wins than ever before since we never won a game," responded Izzy. Stevie looked confused about the math, but

Elena supported her cousin's assertion.

To Molly, an infinite number seemed correct.

§

On Friday Molly, Stevie, Izzy, Elena, Bianca, and Rosa sat in Morgan's kitchen eating cookies and drinking sodas, waiting for Coach to return from the men's golf league. He had tried to beg out, saying he would be unable to play on Tuesdays because of basketball, but the golf men rearranged the schedule. When he drove into the driveway around four-thirty, five basketballs were laying on the lawn. As usual, Andrea greeted him in the mud room with a kiss.

"The girls are waiting for you," she said.

"Hey, Coach, we have a question," said Molly, now the unquestioned leader of the squad. "We want to know about team camp. What's all involved?"

Morgan sat down at the head of the table. "Well, your boys are going, so you know what it is. There are camps all over, some have already been held. The boys are going next week, I think. I always took my teams because I thought they were beneficial. Some years, I had as many as forty kids go; other times as few as eighteen or twenty."

"Do players stay in motels?"

"No, no. These camps are always held at colleges or universities, and you stay in the dorms and eat in their cafeterias. It's all self-contained. You arrive and check in, play your first game, eat, and play again. The next day, you get up and have breakfast, play, eat lunch, play in the afternoon, eat dinner, and play again in the evening. That's the routine; it's all basketball. Some camps give you seven or eight games, and some give you ten or eleven depending on how many days you stay. I think the boys are staying two-and-a-half days and playing eight games. I'm not sure."

Molly had spoken with the boys. "Can we go to one?"

Morgan tilted his head in a negative fashion. "I suppose we could, but it might be too late to get into one. They usually want teams to sign up in the spring, but the main obstacle is cost. They all charge about $200 per player. A couple of you might be able to raise the money, but most of you wouldn't be able to. Also, with only eight girls, assuming you all could clear your work schedules and get your parents' permission, all those games would wear you out." His girls' faces indicated he was correct about the cost and getting time off. "Hey, what we're doing now is preparing you for next season. You're going to be so much better."

Elena judged the mood at the table and jumped up. "Okay, then, let's go outside and work on our routines. In case you all have forgotten, I made two threes last week, and I intend to make even more next week. Thanks, Mrs. Summitt." Elena led the girls outside, all except Molly, who lingered behind.

"It would have been fun, you know," she said before heading out the door.

§

Morgan took Andrea on a date on Friday night: dinner and a movie. As they laid in bed later that night, she asked her husband about team camp.

"Two hundred dollars, huh? Pretty steep. Still, I could talk to my book club girls if you'd like."

"They've already been more than generous, and I really do think it's too late. I keep wondering what their coaches were thinking with these girls. No summer practices or games. Don't they get it?"

Andrea turned onto her side to face her husband. "Low expectations. You know that. That's what you've been fighting all summer."

"I know. You get what you demand, and no one makes any demands here." He paused for a moment.

She touched his nose with her finger. "How about you check on some camps tomorrow, and I'll call the girls. It probably is too late, but you'll fret if you don't look into it."

§

Morgan called six Colorado colleges and the University of Wyoming about their camps. All except one were either day camps, already completed, or full. Adams State in Alamosa indicated they might be able to fit Oro Hills into the junior varsity schedule. A JV schedule again, thought Morgan. The cost per player would be $160. It was a three-day, two-night camp providing seven games to be held between July 6-8, but he would need to let them know by Tuesday, because the coaches would be making the camp schedule on Wednesday. Morgan was told that he would receive the standard kickback of $20 per player.

"I appreciate your desire to help me here, but I have a couple of questions still. Since you haven't made your schedule yet, is there any way possible my girls could play in the small school varsity league. They are currently playing in the Jeffco Summer League and holding their own. The small school JV pool wouldn't help us much. Also, if I didn't take the coach's pay, would you lower each girl's cost by $20?" The discussion between the Adams State assistant coach and Morgan went on for several minutes, but Morgan was successful in getting both requests. However, he could not commit to attending at the moment, but he said he would call back on Tuesday.

Andrea invited her book club women to lunch to consider another sponsorship, this time to the tune of $1120 or more. "My husband didn't want to pursue this, but since we have talked about it, I overruled his reluctance. However, I don't think you need to do this, especially since Morgan doesn't even know if enough girls can go."

The women discussed the issue over sandwiches and brownies, with most of them indicating they would be unable to contribute any more than they already had. Andrea apologized for asking but was forgiven with humor. Queenie had been surprisingly quiet through lunch, but finally she said, "Each one of y'all has been generous in supporting these girls, and I'm proud of our contributions. I also think that down the road, y'all will be giving more, but to promise over a hundred dollars each to fund this when Morgan doesn't even know if he can get enough girls to attend, isn't prudent. That being said, let me promise to fund this little endeavor. Andrea, you tell your husband that this club will provide what his girls need, if he can get the necessary number. What is it? Eight?" She paused, but then quickly added, "But this stays within the club. This is a *we* contribution. He's not to know who is giving how much."

§

"Six yesses and two maybes," said Morgan.

"Did you tell them it was all or none?" asked Andrea. She winced at her wording. "Is there a chance for eight?"

"I don't know. Fifty-fifty. I don't know if I should call Sofia to see if she would be interested in going. She's kind of faded away for the summer. I'm not even sure whether I should call Penny's or Elena's mother." When he stopped, Andrea stepped to him and gave him a hug.

They were interrupted by a knock at the door. Molly, Izzy, Bianca, and Rosa stood there with Cheshire-like grins. Once inside the house, Izzy explained how easy it was to convince Elena's mother to let her go. "She's so protective of Elena and her sisters, so I told her there would only be girls, and we would look out for her. Besides, she's worried about Elena's current boyfriend." Penny's mother had mistakenly believed the camp would last an entire month, and when she understood it was only three days, she immediately said yes.

"Have any of you spoken with Sofia to see why she's backed away?" asked Morgan.

Molly tightened her lips and looked to Izzy for what looked to Mrs. Summitt like permission to tell. "There's a rumor she's pregnant, and I think it's true. She works at the auto parts store, but she looks terrible, like she doesn't care or nothing. Sofia always used to put on her makeup before she went out. Even to work."

Izzy nodded in agreement. "She's got a serious boyfriend. They've been dating for over a year."

Morgan looked to his wife and then asked the girls if any of them had reached out to Sofia. Molly shook her head. "Sofia will never ask for help. She's the most together person I know. She'll make it work."

Sitting on the couch, Andrea leaned forward toward the girls. "Sometimes, it's those girls who most need support. What about her family?"

"Her mom's good; she'll be there," said Izzy.

Bianca knew where this conversation could go, so she changed the subject. "With eight girls, can we attend the camp? You said we just needed eight."

Morgan smiled and nodded his head in a way his wife interpreted as saying yes, but being surprised it was really happening. Andrea watched the girls as they squealed in excitement, and she worried for Sofia. Andrea also thought of Queenie and her generosity and wished she was here to see the girls at this moment. And in all the years Andrea had shared in the coaching experiences of her husband, she couldn't remember one such as this, when something that wasn't known became known. And possible.

§

Oro Hills won two more games in the second half of their summer league, finishing with a 4-12 record. In the second round, they finally matched up against Ralston Valley and were swamped, 51-18. Molly scored fourteen of the points and Bianca added the other four. Except for Molly, the girls were over-matched. It didn't help that Stevie did not attend this game due to a cold, but it would not have mattered, as Ralston Valley used a solid press-break strategy. Still, the other games were more competitive, and Morgan's girls had fun and improved. One scary moment occurred during the third week when Molly crashed into a large player from Golden and stayed down. The Miners were forced to finish the game without her, but it turned out not to be anything more than a bump. In that same game, Cindy got a black eye. On the final night, one of the opposing coaches approached Morgan about having Molly transfer to her school where she could "play at a level commensurate with her skills," that she wouldn't get much better playing against 2A teams. Morgan thanked her for the compliment, but politely said her offer was out of the question and out of line.

One of the primary purposes of summer play was team building, and the Oro Hills girls formed a bond in Andrea Summitt's van. As much as if they were given a seating chart in high school English class, they remained in the places they staked out on the first trip to Golden. The return trip always found Bianca sitting up front with Coach Summitt to discuss her basketball skills and topics unrelated to the court.

"If I learned I had to return to New Mexico and live with my mother, could I still go to team camp with the team?" she asked.

"Of course," answered Morgan. "Playing this summer is for improving your skills, not as a tryout for next season. This all began on my driveway as a way to get better. We have no official connection with the high school. I sincerely hope to watch you play here next season; I know you want that too, and your friends love you." He paused. "Is there someone I could talk with to help you?"

There was some shuffling in the van. Molly traded places with Penny so that she could talk with Morgan and Bianca. Molly pushed Bianca's shoulder. "You aren't going back. If you have to, you'll move in with me. And Rosa too. You aren't leaving." The other girls listened to Molly tell Bianca her future. Blended families existed throughout Oro Hills, throughout poor communities everywhere. "I asked Coach earlier this summer what it felt like to win. I like the feeling. A lot, and I know we wouldn't have won a game without you."

In the dark Bianca scrunched her face. "I helped, but you were the one."

"Yeah, we all helped, but we wouldn't have won a single game without you."

All the girls laughed, and Morgan knew that the team bonding had been successful.

CHAPTER 9

There is no time between offense and defense.
The transition must be instantaneous.

On Monday, July 3, part of the long Independence Day weekend, Kane Vincent sat at his desk at Oro Hills High School examining new guidelines for the "Pity League," as he often referred to the Discovery League. Two years earlier, when the Colorado Association for Co-Curricular Activities realigned the three-hundred-plus schools into the five classes based on updated enrollment figures, it created a 2A league designed for schools with less than stellar winning records, schools which tended to finish at the bottom of their conference year-after-year. The Association hoped to give these schools a taste of success by playing schools with similar socio-economic circumstances. Kane Vincent, silently fumed. *A league for losers.*

The schools were not geographically aligned, which made for long bus trips to contests resulting in extensive lost time from the classroom and an expensive endeavor. Unintended consequences. While the schools in the new conference did win more games—in the conference—they had no greater success in the post-season, in any sport. Compounding its misguided action, CACA included a new high school, Academy Prep, a private school with an enrollment at the top of the 2A cutoff. Evidently, the Association was led to believe A-Prep would grow beyond the 2A classification in two years and move up, leaving the Discovery League to the under-achievers as originally designed. The new guidelines stated this would *definitely* be A-Preps last two-year cycle in the league. Alone in his office, Kane Vincent slapped the guidelines down on his desk; he had read these two years earlier. "Two more years. Shit!" he said aloud.

§

71

Oro Hills' Independence Day parade leaned heavily on cars and politicians, and not enough on bands and floats. The high school's band marched in matching tee-shirts and jeans, just fourteen teenagers behind their band director. Stevie, Elena, and Izzy all played the flute. After the parade, they joined up with Alondra for lunch at Coffee, Tea, or Me before walking Main Street and socializing with their classmates. On the previous weekend, a kitchen fire had slightly damaged Alondra's trailer, forcing the family to relocate some of the children. Her six brothers were sent across town to live in a separate trailer park, leaving the four girls with Alondra's mother and aunt. And no usable kitchen.

§

The girls met at Morgan's house for burgers and hotdogs on Wednesday night. As instructed, they brought their bags or suitcases, so Morgan could check to see they had the essentials for playing, and so Andrea could insure they had the toiletries for two nights and three days away from home.

At the patio table, Morgan explained the camp as he remembered team camp "There will be two of you to a room, four to each suite. You can pick your roommate, but I want to know tonight before we leave, so we don't have to go over that when we check in. After check-in we will get settled into our rooms and then eat a little bit. Then, we'll play our first game. After each game, we'll meet to discuss our play. Then, and for the rest of camp, we'll eat in the cafeteria together. That should give you a sampling of college food. Some of you will have a lot more of that in the years to come."

"Me first," said Elena.

Morgan smiled. "Anyway, the routine becomes eat, play, eat, play, eat, play, shower. It's going to be hot in Alamosa, and I doubt if the gyms will be air-conditioned, so expect to sweat a lot. I'm bringing some Gatorade too, and Andrea is sending along a bunch of oranges. If Adams State is like the other team camps my teams attended, the cafeteria will have plenty of food, so you won't need to bring anything." Morgan paused to check for questions. The girls had none, so he continued. "I won't be staying in your dorm, so you'll be on your own. I expect you to be on your best behavior. Stevie, can I count on you?" The girls laughed and she nodded.

"Coach, how good are the teams we're going to play?" asked Molly.

"I'm not sure. We're in a small school varsity league. My guess is none of them will be as good as Ralston Valley was, but maybe as good as the other schools in our summer league were. I hope so. It's a varsity league though. There is also a large school division you can watch to see how good those schools are. This really is three days of basketball. I think you're going to enjoy it enormously." Morgan nodded his head.

"How long is the drive, Coach?" asked Izzy.

"Probably a little over four hours. We'll meet here at seven, okay?"

"I'm not sure Stevie can sit still that long," teased Izzy.

When Morgan sent the girls home around eight, he loaded their gear into the back of his truck. He wanted this one experience to go perfectly for these kids, who had been so excited, so committed, and so cute all spring and summer, who had added a measure of purpose to his life again.

§

Molly told Morgan she would stand with him while he checked the team in; the other girls could wait by the van. He told her he wouldn't know any of the other coaches, unlike the boys team camps, where for him, he knew the majority of the coaches and went out in the evenings to discuss their teams or past contests.

"Did you coach your boys differently than us?"

Morgan thought about that, and it showed on his face. It hadn't occurred to him that he did, but then again, he hadn't considered what he was doing with Molly and her friends as formal coaching; it was teaching and facilitating. He saw Molly shooting baskets and went over to rebound, and everything since was simply an extension of shooting baskets on the driveway. He hadn't planned on the other girls appearing. He hadn't thought of a summer league or team camp. Molly had asked, and he had contacts.

"Hello, Earth to Coach Summitt." Molly poked him in the arm.

"Hey, I'm old. Give me a minute to consider your question." He smiled. "Yeah, I did, but this hasn't been a job; more like a . . . a hobby, a very pleasant hobby, but not a job. You guys have made it easy."

"Did you demand more of your boys?"

Morgan's head bounced up and down slowly. "A good coach has to be demanding or he gets run over."

"Did you yell at your boys? You've never raised your voice at us."

"Oh, yes. And swore. I especially liked the term *ass* to get them moving, but there were others too. Over the years, though, I think I yelled less."

"Did you coach to win? Last year, we never played to win; it was never part of the equation. We just played. Coach always told us not to worry about the score, so we didn't."

"I watched you, Molly. You played to win. Every game. I honestly don't know how to coach—or why a person would coach or play—without that great desire to win the game. I knew there were certain opponents my teams couldn't beat in certain years, but even with them, at the beginning of the game, the score was nothing-to-nothing, and we were going to get the same number of possessions. Yes, I coached to win. It wasn't the only thing, but it was a major thing."

Molly stared at Morgan as he talked, almost unblinking. They came to the check-in table, but she could tell he was still considering the answers to her questions. For four months he had been this gentle man willing to give his time to her and her friends, but now she sensed another side to him. She wished she had played for him back when.

Morgan introduced himself to the college assistant coach behind the table. "Hi, I'm Morgan Summitt and this is my assistant, Molly Rascon. We're from Oro Hills." He handed her a check from Queenie Roberts for $1120.

"Your team will be staying on the third floor in two suites, four girls to a suite. You will be staying across the street in Girault, but there will be a dorm monitor for your girls."

Molly interrupted. "Our girls will be fine. No worries there."

The Adams State assistant smiled. She knew Molly was a player and not Morgan's assistant, but she grasped what the young girl was saying and appreciated her words. She directed Molly to another table to pick up the camp tee-shirts, room keys, and meal cards. "We've changed our mascot from the Indians to the Grizzles, so our shirts reflect that change." When Molly left, the woman smiled at Morgan, "Seems like a pistol. Point guard?"

"Yes, and she is."

On Point

§

For the girls from Oro Hills, the suites were like rooms at a Hilton Hotel. Four girls to a suite, each with her own bed and a bathroom in each room. Izzy, Elena, Penny, and Cindy staked out one suite, with Bianca, Rosa, Molly, and Stevie in the other. Morgan watched as the girls touched their beds, turned on the sink tap, checked out the bathroom, and looked out the windows on the third floor. Morgan thought of how Alondra might respond to such a living arrangement and wished he had reached out to her.

"I'll meet you in the lobby downstairs at one-fifteen, and we'll walk to the gym together. Molly will have one ball and Cindy will have the other; point guards should always be in charge of the balls. For now, unpack and eat." Morgan turned to leave.

"Coach," said Bianca. "Thank you."

§

Oro Hills' first opponent was Bayfield, from the southwest corner of Colorado. The game was competitive, close from the outset, but with two contrasting styles of play. Deliberate versus chaos. One-two-two zone versus player-to-player. Bayfield had a plan for attacking the full-court press, which proved successful in the first half, but Stevie was relentless pressuring the ball, and Molly and Izzy began to predict the passing lanes. In the second half, Bayfield's guards became anxious and rushed their passes. Additionally, both Elena and Izzy hit a three point shot, and Bianca's size and strength wore down Bayfield's center. Oro Hills won its first game by seven. Rosa made a free throw in the last minute, her first point of the summer. Since two games were being played at the same time and other teams were in attendance, the gym was crowded and noisy. Oro Hills had never played in such an environment.

After the end-of-game handshakes, Morgan led his girls outside to find shade and a quiet spot. "Well?" he asked.

The response was predictable. Such fun. One girl would respond, and the others would clap and agree. Cindy interrupted, "We forgot the balls." Morgan indicated she and Molly needed to go back to the gym and retrieve them. They returned in an instant with both basketballs, and Morgan began a brief summation of the game.

"We made four threes and Bianca scored two more baskets on those missed shots. I was pleased that we went to the line eight times, but you need to concentrate on those shots. We only made three. Penny, what does Bianca call you?"

Penny smiled. "Big Skinny."

I liked how busy you were, but you had a couple of balls knocked away after you rebounded them. Pushups?" He paused. "Seriously, you played your best game, and I'm proud of you."

Molly raised her hand. "Coach, we trailed at half. What happened to them in the second half."

Morgan walked behind Stevie. "Pressure. It wears teams down and as games stay close, pressure causes more mistakes. I want you all to appreciate what Stevie does for this team. She's our energizer bunny. No team we've played so far this summer has anyone like her, and the rest of you are figuring out that you can be more aggressive. It's called closing the passing lanes; it's what good defenses do. They close the passing lanes. Almost all of our steals today were because Stevie pressured the ball. While none of you have her quickness, you can all get up tighter. You're getting it." Morgan kept it brief. His girls heard enough for their first game. "Dinner begins at four-thirty. Our next game is at seven. This may be the only time in your life you've heard this, but feel free to go back to your rooms and lay on your beds. I'm going to go back inside and watch more games. Any of you can join me if you want, but you don't have to."

All eight girls followed Morgan into the gym.

§

Dorm food for rich kids carries a certain negative connotation. For the Oro Hills girls, it meant an entirely different thing. It meant variety, quantity, seconds, and soft-serve ice cream without limitations.

The evening game was against "Oklahoma," the only small school team from that state. They had made it to their Sweet Sixteen last year and returned three starters and several subs from a team that won seventeen games. They constantly threw passes over the top of the press and attacked Bianca with precision. Bianca fouled out and Penny was unable to offer much of a defense. Oklahoma won by a sizable margin despite Molly's first twenty-point game.

On Point

§

The Adams State coach spoke with Morgan before their morning game. "I've heard rumors about your point guard. What's her name?"

"Molly Rascon." He pointed her out in the layup line.

"Little bit of a thing, isn't she?"

"Plays big," joked Morgan. "Five-three or so."

"Senior?"

"No, just a junior. She's just learning the game. Plays every day. Really."

"I think I'll stay around and watch. I'd hate to have missed a prospect when she was right under my nose."

Oro Hills versus Springfield. From southeast Colorado, Springfield was known for excellence in athletics, especially baseball, but the school took pride in all its teams. Two of its girls sat on the chairs nursing sprains, two starters, as it turned out. Oro Hills' pressure exerted itself again, and without a full crew, Springfield wilted. Oro Hills won easily, and Morgan was able to give Cindy, Penny, and Rosa extended minutes. With Molly, Stevie, and Bianca on the bench, Springfield was able to close the score to nine by the end of the game, but those three had built the lead to over twenty early in the second half.

The Adams State coach had walked past Morgan at halftime, nodded her head, and said, "Impressive. I'll keep an eye on her."

§

Because Morgan took his girls on a campus tour, the girls did not get any time off their feet before their second game. They struggled in the first half against a New Mexico team, but got just enough from Bianca and Molly in the second half to win by two points. With the score tied and time running out, Molly dribbled into the lane as she had all game, but this time when the center stepped up to help, Molly gave Bianca a sweet bounce pass for a power layup just before the buzzer.

Outside on the lawn, Morgan talked about the importance of conditioning before reviewing the game. "On that last play, Molly, what would have happened if the defender wouldn't have stepped up then? What would you have done?"

"Time was running out. I would have taken a jump shot."

Morgan made his point. "All of you listen, especially you, Bianca, and you, Penny. We like layups better than anything, don't we? So do our opponents. Jump shots are less accurate, even when a good shooter like Molly is taking them, so if we have to give up one, make it the jump shot. So, here's the phrase to plant in your brain. 'Don't help up, help across.' Don't help up, help across.'" Morgan had them all repeat the phrase, and then he said, "Way to go. Winning a close one. Now, go lay down and take a nap before dinner. I'll see you back here at five-forty-five. Do you have the balls?"

Oro Hills' game had ended at two. Dinner didn't start until four-thirty, so Morgan walked back into the gym, found a folding chair, and looked for the game with a team most like his. A large Colorado Springs school, Sierra, was in a tight game with Durango. As he set his chair down to watch, his *assistant* unfolded a chair next to his, and they watched Sierra's player-to-player press wear down Durango.

§

Izzy made three threes in the evening game against Holt, a tiny school on Colorado's eastern plains near Yuma. Morgan wondered how close Holt was to Joe's, an eastern Colorado small town that won the Colorado high school basketball championship back in 1929 and went on to the finals in the national competition. The game reminded Morgan of the Jeffco Summer League where his spirited small school went up against taller and more talented larger schools, and while competing valiantly, still lost. Oro Hills won by ten but knew it had been in a battle against a courageous competitor.

His post-game message: "No matter the circumstances, you will always battle like Holt did tonight. Give the game its dignity. Show up and battle! I want you to remember this game and the name *Holt* as we move forward."

§

Most of the girls went to bed early and were eager for their games on Saturday. After the morning game, they would clean their suites and eat an early lunch. After the afternoon game, they would shower, pack, check out, and head for home. Mrs. Summitt would be there to drive the van, this time accompanied by B.J. Pacheco, editor of Oro Hills' newspaper, who wanted to watch the girls play.

At ten Oro Hills played a Catholic school from Denver, Bishop Machebeuf, a team that could have played in the large school division. Morgan knew Machebeuf was a 6-12 private school with an exemplary academic program and, in regard to its basketball teams, an effective feeder system, something Oro Hills did not have with its transient demographics. Only two of his girls had attended Oro Hills schools all their lives. Fatigue played its part as the girls went zero-for-twelve on three point attempts. Molly had sixteen points, Stevie added six, and Bianca scored nine, including five free throws. Nobody else was able to put the ball in the basket.

With the girls sitting on the lawn, Morgan kept his comments brief. "Izzy and Elena took the shots when they were open. Because we're into our third day, they didn't fall, but you did the right thing. Our legs are just too tired to get the ball to the basket properly. Rosa, why didn't you put that layup shot up on the last rebound? Remember, when you rebound under our basket, go right back up. Take the ball into your opponent's chest and get fouled. You can do that."

Rosa smiled. "I panicked a little. All I could remember was your phrase, 'Find Molly.'"

Morgan smiled. "Remind me to tell you a story about bad coaching advice sometime. You did good, Rosa. You're getting lots better."

§

A dorm advisor escorted Morgan to his players' suites before lunch so he could inspect the cleanup. He should have known they would be spotless. "Elena's a drill sergeant, Coach!" He sat with them at lunch, and they enjoyed their last soft-serve cones before heading over to play their final game. Bianca wanted to know if she and Rosa had to return their shoes to him when team camp ended. He hugged her and told them they weren't on loan but had been given to them. Molly commented that if Sofia were here, it would help a lot, and when Stephanie rejoined the team for the season, she would make a huge difference.

"You don't know her, Coach, but she was our second-best player last year. She's Bianca's height and really athletic."

"She's the one playing club volleyball with a traveling team, isn't she?" asked Morgan. "I remember watching her a little last season. She is athletic, that's for sure."

"Yeah. She's kinda like Coach Abby's pet. And Coach Thulen's too."

§

In the seventh and final game, Oro Hills played Alamosa High School, the local 3A school. Alamosa had been scheduled to play a New Mexico school, but that school had been hit with minor injuries and chose to forfeit and begin their long drive home early. Oro Hills' scheduled opponent had not won a game and asked to play a junior varsity team where it might have a chance. Before tip-off, Morgan told his team to be flattered that the camp directors thought highly enough of their play to schedule them against Alamosa. He also warned them to be ready for a tough game. "It's our last one of the summer so leave it all out there."

Ever the naïve novice, Rosa asked, "What are we supposed to leave out there?"

And they did. Alamosa, fresher because of numbers and able to sleep in their own beds each night, pulled ahead early, but Oro Hills stayed close. The Mean Moose press was ineffective against Molly's ball-handling skills, while Stevie's pressure disrupted Alamosa's plan. For the final two minutes, the clock was operated under normal game conditions. Worried about Molly's ability to blow past her, the Alamosa defender played off just enough for Molly to hit a three with thirty-seconds left, tying the score at 34. Stevie was called for a reaching foul a few seconds later, and the Alamosa girl hit one of two. Morgan called time out and set up two options. The first was simple: get the ball to Molly and let her make a basketball play. If Alamosa denied her the ball with two defenders, then Elena was to get the ball into Cindy. She was to throw it into Bianca for the shot. "Everybody run to rebound."

Alamosa's double-teamed Molly, one face-guarding her. Elena in-bounded to Cindy who couldn't get it to Bianca, so she passed to Izzy who made a convincing shot-fake before dribbling past her girl. Her jump shot rimmed off, but Molly had sprinted from the backcourt to rebound. She captured the ball and put in the follow, giving Oro Hills a winning record for the camp. The girls hugged and screamed until Morgan instructed them to line up and shake the Alamosa team's hands.

Morgan was exhausted. Andrea and B.J. congratulated the girls and passed out treats. The two women stood to the side as Morgan talked to his girls. "Well, I'll bet I had as good a time this summer as any of you. You guys were like cheetahs out there in the second half, just swarming all over the Mean Moose. Where did you find the energy?"

"Bianca told us she'd kick our fannies if we acted tired," said Izzy. "She scared me." Izzy said this jokingly, but her tone indicated some concern.

"She didn't use the word *fanny*, Coach," said Rosa. "She used your word."

"Remember that next season when you're up against Academy Prep. Look at them and see Alamosa and think *cheetahs*. I'll be watching from the stands." He looked at his wife. "Give a hand to Mrs. Summitt for all her support and to Ms. Pacheco for hers." The girls stood and clapped and then each one gave both women a hug. B.J. took a half-dozen photos of the team "all sweaty and raggedy and smiling."

"Okay, back to the dorm and shower."

"Coach, can I say something?" asked Bianca. Morgan nodded. "This was the most fun thing I ever did."

"You're welcome," said Morgan. He watched the girls run to the dorm for showers, but Bianca's comment stuck with him. *The most fun thing I ever did.*

CHAPTER 10

When you pass by each other, you touch. Maybe a hand pat or slap, but something. Always.

In its Tuesday edition, The *Oro Hills Tribune* ran a short story with a photo, titled "The Girls of Summer." When asked why the girls decided to get involved so heavily, Molly said, "We didn't win a game last year, and we don't want that to happen next season." The article provided a little history. Since the high school formed a girls program in compliance with the 1972 Title IX edict, not once had a team won more than four games in a season, and their total number for all the years was just twenty-six. The story quoted Morgan saying, "I'm the old guy who drives the van."

§

"Nice story," commented Lowell Exeter to Kane Vincent. "It's always good for our students to get a little publicity and recognition. Did I meet this Morgan Summitt guy?" His A.D. reminded Lowell that they met in the bar one afternoon in May. Exeter nodded. "By the way, have you gotten all the coaching contracts back from the non-teachers?" The principal wasn't expecting an answer; it was a subtle reminder. He turned and disappeared into his office leaving Kane Vincent to handle the details.

§

Two summers earlier Morgan crafted himself a wooden fly box large enough to hold sixty-four separate fly patterns. Eight rows across by eight rows deep. *If I can't catch a fish with one of these, no amount is going to make me a better fisherman,* he told himself. Since basketball ended, he could turn his attention to his two summertime hobbies with greater energy. Fishing and golf. On Tuesday he rejoined the golf league with regularity.

Matches were scheduled for either the early mornings or the late afternoons. He preferred the mornings, even though they were often cooler, but being behind, he played both times this day. He returned from the course to find Molly shooting on his driveway. She hadn't taken any time off.

"Hey, Coach," she said when he got out of his truck. "Did you see the paper?"

"I did. Nice little story and picture."

Molly flipped him the ball when he got to the driveway. Morgan lofted a short jumper that bounded off the rim. "Coach, is that story true about the number of wins all-time?"

"If Ms. Pacheco says it is, then I would believe it. She's pretty meticulous about her facts. Why?"

"Then my goal is to win at least five games next season. We'll be the winningest team in the history of Oro Hills." Molly smiled.

"Pretty low bar. Have you ever set goals?"

Molly thought about it for a moment. She pounded the basketball side-to-side a couple of times. "For basketball, you mean? I have dreams, so I need to improve my skills."

"Yeah, for basketball or for school."

She shook her head. "No."

"Come on inside and grab a drink. I think Andrea has some cookies or something available. Let's sit down and I'll show you how to make some realistic goals for improvement. By the way, did you get your grades for last semester?"

Molly sat with Mrs. Summitt until Morgan returned, dressed as usual in his jeans and a tee-shirt. "Okay, grades?"

"Not so good. Four Bs, a C, and a D," answered Molly.

Morgan nodded and pushed his tongue behind his lower lip. "Well, from just hanging around you these past five months, I would have thought you would do better. You're pretty sharp." Morgan understood some of her difficulties, but he didn't bring these up. "What kind of grades would you like to receive?"

"All As and Bs, I guess." Her answer showed a lack of confidence.

Andrea slid the yellow legal pad that was a permanent part of the kitchen nook over to Molly. "You'll have to forgive us, Molly, but we're life-long teachers. It's in our blood, and we haven't been able to find a cure." She smiled. "Okay, list your classes and the grade you received." As Molly started, Andrea patted her on the arm in a reassuring manner and waited.

When she finished, Molly looked up. Andrea turned the pad and noted the results. "A B might be a good grade and for now, let's assume that it is. Remember, you said you wanted to get all As and Bs. Let's focus on the C and D. Biology is the C and English is a D. Can you explain that?"

Morgan had never heard Molly excuse poor play on the basketball court all summer, but he sensed she didn't know how to explain her poor grades without looking outward. "Mr. Grayson doesn't review for the tests, and I don't take tests too well." She kept her head down. "English has a lot of reading." She didn't finish her thought, but Andrea suspected the conclusion.

Matter-of-factly, Andrea continued. "It seems to me the problem might be your reading skills are low. It shows up directly in English, but there's always a bunch of reading in science too. In an ideal world, an A represents a student's skill level and the amount of effort she puts forward. As a basketball player this summer, I would have awarded you an A+. Does that seem fair?"

Molly nodded.

Andrea continued. "Did you give the effort in English that you do for basketball?"

The answer was obvious, and Molly shook her head.

"I wouldn't expect you would, but my guess is because it's hard, you got frustrated frequently. Understandable, but we need to push past that." Andrea pointed to Molly's B in history. "History can have lots of reading, but you got a B. How do you explain that?"

"Mr. Knapp showed lots of films."

Andrea smiled. "Do you miss much school, Molly? Are you absent frequently?"

"No. Almost never, unless I have to take care of Alex when he's sick."

Andrea turned to Morgan. "What's the name of that basketball book you used to have your kids read?"

Morgan knew where his wife was heading. He stood. "I think I have a copy downstairs. I'll get it."

"I taught reading, Molly. It's the basis for every one of your core subjects. If you aren't a good reader, it makes every other subject hard. I'm guilty of this too, or at least I was guilty when I taught reading. We English teachers tend to assign books that we like, not what our students might find interesting."

Morgan returned. "*Stuff Good Players Should Know*," he said handing the book to his wife.

Andrea handed it to Molly. "I've never read this book, but my husband, the coach, passed it out to several of his players over the years, and every one of them read it cover-to-cover. He only gave it to players who loved basketball. Take it home tonight and take a look, but beginning tomorrow, part of your basketball time will be spent with me reading this book. Together. Aloud. We're going to improve your reading skills rapidly." She pursed her lips and held Molly's eyes. "Deal?"

§

Later that evening, after dinner, Morgan looked at Molly's grades. As he understood it, the one D would render her ineligible for the first semester. He had neglected to follow up on his promise to learn about Oro Hills' eligibility standards. He would call the athletic director in the morning.

§

"Did you get a chance to look over the book?" asked Andrea. Molly said she had and indicated it was really good. They sat down to quiche, and Molly's first reading session of the summer. Morgan waved as he left to meet Kane Vincent. Andrea handed Molly a spiral notebook and pencil. "Reading is an active process, Molly. I want you to be engaged to whatever it is you're reading, to form a partnership, so to speak. Most of your school reading assignments are to collect information for tests, a transfer from the book onto a piece of paper. Okay, our first reading goal is to learn what's in this first chapter. One chapter, that's all. As you read aloud to me, I'll ask you questions, and you'll begin to underline and make notes in the book."

"You want me to mark in Coach's book?"

§

Kane Vincent handed two pages of information across his desk to Morgan. "We've had this policy in place for three years. It holds our students accountable at a high level. The teachers drew it up after looking at several other schools' plans. We want them to work as hard, to give as good an effort in the classroom as they do in athletics. Our teachers felt we needed a club to motivate our students to take their studies more seriously."

Morgan perused the paper. "Were you a part of putting this together?"

"No. A committee of teachers, parents, students, and administrators worked for two years to write this. Then, it was presented to the school board for adoption. It was put into place the year I came here. It was my first year as an administrator." He paused. "I was put in charge of implementing the policy."

"Were you a teacher before you turned to the dark side?" Morgan grinned.

Kane understood the joke and chuckled. "Yeah, math/science teacher and wrestling coach."

"Math and science, huh? So, you understand the value of facts and evidence then."

Morgan turned back to the paper of statistics. "It appears that, correct me if I'm wrong, the number of participants in athletic teams decreased as the season went on. In every sport, it appears. As you probably know because of your experience as a coach, athletic participation increases the academic performances of the athletes. The state association pushes those statistics all the time to justify the amount of money schools spend on athletics, which, by the way, is still a small percentage of the budget. Is there any chance those kids who quit just gave up because of prolonged ineligibility?"

"I'm not sure there was any follow-up on that. Our teachers generally like it because the athletes behave better in class."

"From these statistics it would seem like only a small percentage of your student body participates in athletics," said Morgan. "Does one D at the semester make a student ineligible for the whole next semester?"

"No, Just for six weeks."

"Kane, I don't have all the facts, and my information comes from six girls, so blow me off if you have better information, but four of the girls said they missed some games because of this policy. Only one of them had an F. If I remember correctly from my coaching days, if an athlete was passing five subjects, he could participate. This policy you have is the most restrictive I've ever seen, and its purpose seems to be punitive rather than helpful to increase participation."

Kane Vincent nodded. He was listening. "Let me do some checking, and I'll get back to you."

§

Mercedes and Queenie hosted the Mountain Matrons on Saturday. B.J. and Mitzi were lavish in their descriptions of the girls team.

Mitzi said, "Those kids were so excited driving down to Alamosa last week, and it was mostly about basketball, not just getting out of Oro Hills. I don't recall girls ever talking about the sport or the game itself. I don't personally know any of these girls, except Elena, but over the years, I don't recall girls talking basketball in my class or around school. A whole new experience for me."

"Morgan would tell you it was basketball itself," said Andrea. "He'd become a philosopher and go on about the magical powers of the ball and the hoop, and in this case, a girl by herself on a driveway or in a gym. One-on-one against Michael Jordan. This summer, that girl would be Molly Rascon and the hours and hours she spent shooting or dribbling on her own."

"She's the little one who's so talented," said B.J.. Andrea nodded and B.J. went on. "She was like the focus of the game; everything was concentrated on her. Both teams. Kind of fascinating to observe. It's my job to notice things like that, so I was amazed by her eyes and body language; this from a woman who has never shot a basketball in her life. We only watched the last day, but it was such a treat."

"Morgan told me to tell all of you thanks for making it happen. He knows they wouldn't have gone to the team camp without your financial support," said Andrea.

§

On the driveway Bianca faced Morgan, who simulated a post defender on the low block. She placed her left foot between his feet, crouched, and did a reverse pivot with her butt against his thighs. As she performed this move, she raised both arms to shoulder level to create space. From the wing Molly spun a one-handed bounce pass to Bianca on the baseline side. Bianca hopped her body slightly forward to catch and secure the ball. Simultaneous with the catch, she turned her head to locate Morgan.

"Excellent! You're in a strong position now to make a post move, and you can use either foot as your pivot foot. Why did Molly throw you the ball on this side of your body?" asked Morgan.

"Because you were playing on my top shoulder," answered Bianca. She stood and passed the ball back to Molly.

"Remember," said Morgan, "go get the ball; don't wait for it. Otherwise, the defender can step around and steal it. That four-inch hop is all you need, but it's important." He looked at Bianca for confirmation. "Now, in this position you can reverse pivot to create space and make your move." He demonstrated. "When Molly isn't around to pass to you . . ."

Molly interrupted, "*If,* not *when.* I may just shoot and make her rebound."

Bianca laughed. "Sort of like team camp, then." She flinched when Molly fired the ball at her.

"Anyway," said Morgan, "*when* Molly isn't around, you can practice this by spinning the ball back to yourself. Hop forward, secure, locate, reverse pivot. Over and over and over again."

"It's his favorite word, Bianca. 'Again, again,'" said Molly with a smile.

"If you're on defense and find yourself on the high side, what do you do?" asked Morgan. He waited for Bianca's response.

Before Bianca could answer, Molly offered the phrase. "Never get beat high side."

"Oh, yeah," said Bianca, "I need to shuffle quickly and create a little cushion."

"Probably too late now," teased Molly. "That Academy Prep center has already used you. And her sister too, the one who played JV last year, and they're laughing at us again."

§

Kane Vincent couldn't believe it. Every sport in the previous year showed a decline in numbers from the beginning of the season to the end. He remembered his coaching days in Iowa. Wrestling was the state sport almost, and his school fielded three squads. Quitting was not acceptable; it was the eleventh commandment. *Thou shalt not quit*, and yet here in Oro Hills, it was commonplace. There seemed to be no stigma attached to quitting. Was this a direct result of the eligibility requirements, of the one-D policy? In his three years as activities director, no coach had come to him to request a modification of the policy. The boys basketball coach was the policy's biggest supporter, and he held his players to a very high standard, but his program began with twenty-three kids and ended with eleven. Did they quit because of how much he ran them or because of the one-D policy? Kane got up from his desk, went to his filing cabinet, and searched for any record of the process that went into formulating this eligibility policy.

§

Unbeknownst to her book club friends, Anita Pagel and her husband had offered their motel for sale since the beginning of the previous year. A serious offer was tendered around Easter, and after negotiations settled on an acceptable price, the deal was concluded in mid-July. The Mountain Matrons held a going away party for Anita at Andrea's house on the last Saturday in July.

Anita sniffled. "Motel ownership changes hands frequently. We love Oro Hills, but we just got worn out making ends meet every month. It wears on a person. It really wore on Trevor; he felt as though he was letting me down."

Queenie rearranged her large body on Andrea's couch. "A poor town wears people out. What you described, Anita, reminds me of my home town. Well, not much of a town, but a city." Queenie gave a loud sigh to remember. "Birmingham, Alabama. My mother worked in the textile industry. Worked hard, and every month she worried we wouldn't have enough to cover the rent or put food on the table. Only thing that saved us was the union."

Mercedes cut off her partner. "Stay on point, darling," she cautioned.

Queenie nodded. "Well, that and the church. But I see this in our little haven here. It's a good town with good people, but it's difficult for so many, including some of you in here. Poverty reaches in and grabs your soul. I admire y'all for being so positive and successful, especially you." Queenie looked to Octavia and Lorna, the two women who ran small businesses. "Y'all have my deep respect."

§

Saturday summer evening in a small town. Around eight, just as the sun had dropped behind the mountains, Bianca and Rosa knocked, waking Morgan from a nap and startling Andrea. She answered the door and invited them in, giving Morgan time to act as though he had been reading.

"What brings you two here? Don't you have some boys to chase?" asked Morgan.

Bianca's mother had overdosed and been taken to a Santa Fe hospital. Bianca cried and tried to talk, but mostly just wanted comfort, to be with an adult she trusted. For all her aloofness around the basketball team because of her size and maturity, on this night she was just a scared teenager living apart from her mother. Rosa did most of the talking.

"Is your aunt at home?" asked Andrea.

"No," answered Rosa.

"Can you get a hold of her?"

"She's the one who told us. She called from somewhere about three hours ago," said Rosa.

"What do you want to do about this, Bianca?" asked Morgan gently. "Do you want to go see her?"

"No, I don't want to see her. I've seen her too much like this. She'll just slobber out her love for me and that she wants me to come home. She'll be good for a week and then nothing will change. I can't help her." Bianca wiped her face with the flat of her hand, trying to get herself under control. "I'm not going back there. If they make me, I'll run away again."

Morgan glanced at Andrea. They heard the same word. *Again.* They waited.

It was Rosa who spoke next. "We won't go back. When we rode in the van and everyone made fun of Oro Hills, . . . you never heard us say anything negative. This is like heaven to us. Those girls don't know."

When Morgan sensed Bianca was calmer, he took the legal pad that always sat on the table and began to diagram basketball plays.

"How many of these do you know?" asked Rosa.

"Oh, one for every situation, I guess. Certain things just stick in people's mind, and these stick in mine. I coached basketball for over thirty years at one level or another, so there were plenty of styles to learn. Mostly, I did what we used this summer, with a bit more structure, but when I coached junior high, I ran lots of plays. As the players changed, with differing skills and physical abilities, I altered what I did."

"What did you do when you had bad players like me?" asked Rosa.

Morgan smiled up at her. "I kept teaching them. When they worked hard like you, it was easy and very enjoyable."

Bianca took the pen from Morgan's hand and reversed the pad. She put her left hand on the yellow pad with her fingers outstretched. Then, she traced the outline of her hand over the basketball plays, signed her initials, and slid the pad back to Morgan. "We should go now, Rosa."

Andrea hugged them both at the door. When they were gone, she hugged Morgan tightly and spoke into his shoulder. "I never knew the depths of this thing called poverty. I'm so naïve."

"Nor me. On our van trips, they referred to things, and I never comprehended. I'm just a basketball geek."

CHAPTER 11

Be physical when you step in front of her. Love contact.

Kane Vincent sat with Coach Thulen over coffee at his jobsite. The formalities needed to be completed with him taking over the head coaching duties for one year while Coach Abby was on leave. "What do you think about our one-D eligibility?" asked Kane.

"Never gave it much thought," replied Thulen. "It's how we operate."

Kane nodded to himself and went on. "Some of the girls played a lot of basketball this summer. That should help you next winter."

"I wouldn't expect much, given neither team won a game last season. Abby told me to just run what we did last season and hope Stephanie Miles has a good season."

"Did she play with the summer team?" asked Kane. "Seems like she told me she was playing club volleyball all summer."

"No, she didn't play any basketball, but she's still going to be my best player. At least the volleyball team should win a few matches."

"Coach," asked Kane, "what would you think about asking Morgan Summitt, the guy who ran the summer program, to be your assistant for the season? He was a head coach for most of his career."

"Pretty old, isn't he? I'm not sure he would understand our girls after all those years with city boys. Summer competition is pretty different from league play."

"He might be able to give you a different perspective," said Kane.

"Maybe, but I already promised a friend of mine he could be my JV coach. He played some high school ball."

Kane popped his forehead with the palm of his hand. "Dang it, Coach. I just remembered, I'm supposed to be at a meeting over at the junior high. Let's pick this up in a couple of days. Sorry."

On Point

§

Morgan Summitt stood in the middle of the river in his chest waders, slightly bent over at the waist, as if being four inches closer to the end of his pole would provide him with some advantage over any fish silly enough to take his fly. Kane Vincent watched the old fisherman from fifty yards upstream, noticing the meticulous way Morgan drew back his line from the water before returning it to the river. Morgan paused and stood motionless, like a statue, intent on something moving in the water near a huge boulder. Then, as gracefully as a ballet dancer, he strung the line on the river, placing his hook in a seam of water flowing into the deep pool. Kane crouched on his haunches and observed Morgan for another ten minutes before Morgan noticed him.

"Lost?"

"No," answered Kane as he walked up to Morgan. "You're right where your wife said you would be. What fly?"

"Adams 16. It's an imitation of a mayfly, a general searching pattern. I tend to search more than find."

"Got a minute? I've got a couple of cold ones in my truck," said Kane.

So did Morgan, as it turned out. They sat on the tailgate of Kane's truck as they talked.

"Did you research that eligibility policy? I'm kind of interested," said Morgan.

"I did, but it's not what I came out here to talk to you about." Kane took a drink of his beer and held it in his cheeks. "Catch any?"

"One little one."

"Wonder if you'd work with the girls basketball team a little longer?" Kane took another drink from his beer.

Morgan thought about it. "I thought Thulen was going to do it?"

Kane nodded. "That was the plan, but I'm kind of a jerk sometimes." Morgan sipped his beer and waited. Kane finished his first beer and popped the tab on his second. "Drinking beer along a river when I'm supposed to be working; that's my idea of a good time."

"Maybe you are working," said Morgan.

"I asked Thulen to come in and see me in June, but he was always busy. Kind of pissed me off, but a lot of what I'm supposed to be as an assistant principal slash activities director does. We don't always get to select the best candidate when we fill jobs here in Oro Hills. Low pay. Second lowest in the state. Funny thing: if you don't pay people well, they tend to stay away."

"Big surprise, huh?" Morgan opened his second beer.

"Exeter told me yesterday to get Thulen on contract and fill the two junior high positions before the end of the week. Told me we'd be fine for one year with these guys, so that's where I was this morning, having coffee with a guy who assumes he's going to get the job because he's available." Kane's voice remained even. The two men drank silently for a moment before Kane resumed. "I asked him if he would take you for his assistant for the year. He told me he'd already asked a friend of his to help. He didn't even have the job yet."

Morgan thought about what was to come. "I'm not sure I'd be interested in being his junior varsity coach anyway. He and I have a bit of a philosophical difference as to how the game is to be played, but as the head coach, he'd have the final say. And there's that thing about expectations."

"I understand," said Kane. "You don't happen to have any more beers, do you?"

"No, I'll plan better next time."

Kane turned his head to Morgan. "Well, then, how about you be the head coach next year, and we'll look around for an assistant for you. Won't be Thulen."

§

Kane Vincent met with the football coaches for their pre-season huddle on Monday, August 6, the head coach and his five assistants to review new guidelines from the Colorado Association for Co-Curricular Activities. Coach Ryan would meet with his boys on Wednesday, and the first official practice would be the following Monday. Two-a-days. High hopes for a winning season.

"As always, CACA's emphasis is on safety, so read over the guide's directives on when you can use pads and begin contact. Coach, we jumped the gun last season, so let's be careful this year." Kane covered the remainder of his agenda and then asked Thulen to stay for just a moment after the meeting. Thulen had been one of those volunteers until three years ago, when he assumed the role as special teams coach and gained a meager salary.

"We've got a football meeting now. I can come in after that," said Thulen.

"This won't take long, Coach." The other coaches left for the gym, and Thulen indicated he would be there in a moment. "Coach," said Kane, "I've noticed how busy you are with your job, and I know how much time football takes, so I've decided to hire Morgan Summitt as our girls basketball coach for one season. Football goes into November, and you wouldn't have time to run open gyms and adequately prepare for the early part of the season, so I'm freeing you up to give the football job its just due."

Thulen's eyes narrowed. "I got time for both. Besides, Coach Abby told me I would take her place."

"Well, Abby doesn't do the hiring and firing here, and frankly, I'm a little tired of letting the girls programs get the short stick. A head coach must be all in to his primary assignment, and you've always put football first. Even this summer." Kane didn't blink. "As an assistant coach, we were able to work around it."

"I was counting on that salary." Thulen said this as a demand, and Kane recognized the intent.

"There are lots of other jobs that pay more on an hourly basis; you know that. Head coaches don't do this for the money; never have." Kane paused. "When Abby returns next year, we'll review this decision."

As Thulen turned to go, he said, "I'm not going to be that guy's assistant then. You'll need to find someone else." He turned back and strutted to the gym.

Kane thought of several retorts but held his tongue. He nodded to himself like a man who had just completed a fine woodworking project.

§

Information leaks out quickly in small towns. Kane told Morgan there might be some disgruntled Thulen supporters or players, that Thulen would be quick to spin a story. Morgan met with Kane just before noon to sign his contract when they discussed the issue. Morgan decided to tell the girls before they heard it in the form of a rumor. Molly, Cindy, Izzy, Bianca, and Rosa were shooting baskets on his driveway when he returned from the high school, and he invited them in for snacks and sodas.

"Mrs. Summitt told us you played golf this morning. Did you finally win a match?" teased Molly. How Molly conversed with Morgan surprised the other girls; there was little formality to it and lots of subtle bantering.

"I did," said Morgan. "It was the second-best thing that happened to me this morning."

Bianca noticed a smile, an expression of giddiness, something a little different, as though he might have won something of value or received unexpected good news. It reminded her in a way of his expression on the last day of team camp when he told the team that he had enjoyed the summer more than they had. She removed her hands from her soda, put them in her lap, and sat up straight.

"What was the best thing?" asked Molly.

"Well," he paused and glanced at Andrea. "I signed a contract to be your coach this season. Just came back from meeting with Mr. Vincent."

Molly turned sideways and pumped her fist with the accompanying "Yes!"

Izzy offered her congratulations and shook Molly's shoulders. "This will really help Coach Thulen. He's going to like working with you."

Morgan realized the misunderstanding and held up his hand. "Ahh, no, not quite." Bianca knew, but waited. Beneath the table she tightened her thighs against her clasped hands. Morgan squeezed into the nook next to Molly and continued. "As the head coach. Mr. Vincent believes Coach Thulen has too much on his plate with the football team and his regular job to be the head coach this season. He wouldn't be able to give the basketball job all the time necessary at the beginning of the season to get you started on the right track, so Mr. Vincent asked me to take the position. I'm going to be the varsity coach."

A quiet moment of surprise ended with excitement. Molly turned and hugged her new coach and then turned to Izzy for another hug. Andrea noticed Bianca smile with pursed lips and begin rocking gently, her hands still locked in her lap. Bianca looked up to Mrs. Summitt with tears in her eyes, and then her face began quaking. Andrea smiled back and nodded. The other four girls were looking at Morgan or each other, but Bianca was tied to Mrs. Summitt. Andrea mouthed to her, "You're staying, no matter what."

After a few moments, Morgan continued. "Coach Thulen was

disappointed, but he had a conversation with Mr. Vincent and has now decided to step away from the program for this year and return when Coach Abby comes back."

"So, he's not going to be the JV coach either?" asked Cindy.

"No. When you see him, tell him you'll miss him, but understand his decision, and you'll be excited for the following season when he returns along with Coach Abby. This is a one-year deal for me. I'm sure he'll come watch all your games."

"Who's going to be the JV coach then?" asked Cindy.

"I don't know yet. Mr. Vincent is on the lookout for someone. We only briefly talked about that, but I said I'd kind of like a woman to help, someone with a fiery temper who can yell at you guys when you get lazy, since I haven't been able to. I'm too nice."

"I'll do it," said Molly. "I can yell at these guys."

"Do the other girls know?" asked Izzy.

"No. You're the first. I was hoping Stevie and Penny and Elena would have been here," said Morgan.

"Elena's working, but I'll call her," said Izzy. "I don't know where Penny is, and I think Stevie is in Denver shopping with her mom. For school clothes. She'll be surprised."

"When do we start?" asked Molly.

Morgan slid off the nook bench and stepped back to Andrea's side. "I start today and the driveway's available, but we can't do anything formal now. It's volleyball season and I'll let them get a good start before we begin open gyms. Some of you will be playing volleyball, I assume."

"Me," said Cindy.

"Me, too," said Izzy, "and Elena and Penny." Izzy looked across the table to Bianca. "You ought to go out, Bianca. We could use your height."

Bianca shook her head no but said nothing.

§

Morgan called Kane to see if he could get a look at the girls' equipment, to do an inventory of uniforms, balls, and any other items available to him. He also wanted to see what his budget looked like in case he needed to order anything immediately. Morgan met Kane at four in the gym, while he was searching through dozens of keys hoping one might fit the girls' storage units.

"It has to be one of these, you would think. When I got the job, the secretary handed me a ring of keys befitting the president of Yale Locks. Never used most of them." Kane led Morgan through the girls' locker room and down a tunnel to a set of enclosed wooden storage shelves. He took one look at the locks protecting the two large units and put his keys away. "Looks like Abby put her own locks on these. I won't have the key. Wait here a moment; I'll be right back." Without waiting for a response, Kane headed back up the tunnel.

Kane reappeared a few minutes later with a bolt cutter. "How many times do I have to tell coaches to give me a spare key." He snapped off both locks and left Morgan on his own to assess his equipment.

Varsity uniforms: eleven home whites, probably about five seasons old, and ten away browns, maybe a year or two older. It wasn't the age, but the styles that made them unattractive, especially the trunks. An assortment of warmups, no three of which seemed to match. A cracked vinyl ball bag with the name *Miners* stenciled on the side. The junior varsity uniforms had not been folded or sorted from the previous season and were piled on a bottom shelf. Had they even been washed after the last game? Morgan stashed these in the ball bag to take home for cleaning and counting. The second storage bin contained balls, an air-pump, clipboards, and an array of practice jerseys. One ball, labeled "game ball," was in a box, but the other nine were of varying quality, only two of which were as good as the ones Morgan purchased in May for summer league.

He sat down to assess his booty. It was clear to him that girls basketball in Oro Hills was a low priority with low expectations. The girls truly did play for fun and fun only. *What a waste of taxpayers' money, but more, what a waste of talent!* The summer proved his girls would be able to compete in the Discovery League, probably not at Academy Prep's or Benson's level, but certainly with the remaining six schools. Last season, there had been eight girls on the varsity team and eight on the JVs; sixteen girls in total. Morgan didn't know how many students attended Oro Hills High School, but he assumed it was around one-hundred and fifty. And only sixteen girls were out for basketball with no competing sports in the winter.

Morgan hooked the broken locks onto the storage bins, but then laughed. Who would want to steal any of this stuff? He stuffed the dirty JV uniforms into the ball bag and headed back to the office to speak with Kane. Morgan wanted clarification of his budget and to talk about an assistant coach. He could funnel his meager salary into the program, but that wouldn't be available until well into the season. He did have an idea about where he could get an infusion of cash, however, and he wasn't going to be reluctant to ask.

Upstairs, he knocked on Kane Vincent's jamb. Kane waived him in. "Well, what did you find?" asked the athletic director nodding at the ball bag.

Morgan briefly told him about the condition of the uniforms and that he would need a half-dozen new basketballs but turned the conversation to the assistant coach. "Is there someone in the building, a woman, who's a little feisty, who mingles well with the kids?"

The word *feisty* described Gloria Fawkes. Six-feet tall, bleached-blonde hair, single, thirty-ish, school nurse, strong and fit. "She went toe-to-toe with the hospital her first year, because they wanted thirty-five dollars for school physicals. It was her contention that these kids' families didn't have money for health care, that they didn't carry insurance, and the hospital and local doctors needed to set aside a Saturday morning before school began in August to do free physicals. Community service. Since she also works at the hospital during the summers, she had some clout. Actually, we're doing ours Saturday starting at nine at the hospital. Come on over and meet Gloria, see if she's interested," said Kane. When Morgan left, Kane laughed out loud. Yeah, *feisty*.

Bianca and Rosa did not know about the free physicals on Saturday. Not having participated in any activity in the spring, they had not been advised by a coach to sign up for one, and if a flyer was mailed to their home, they did not see it. Morgan asked the girls on his driveway which ones were getting the physical. All were, except Bianca and Rosa. Morgan told them he would pick them up and take them over to take advantage of program, that it would cover them for the entire year.

"Will I get a shot?" asked Rosa.

Morgan assured her she wouldn't.

§

With Coach Summitt standing by their side, Bianca Steele and Rosa Leon were told they could not get a physical without the proper paperwork, primarily a parental permission slip. None were available at the hospital, so the girls would need to schedule a physical on their own. Before they left, Morgan looked around for Gloria Fawkes and spotted her at the table where the male athletes were lined up, a queue of about twenty-five. It appeared to Morgan as though her task was to keep the boys behaving respectfully to the women seated at the table checking their papers. While he observed, Kane Vincent walked up behind him and tapped him on the shoulder.

"That's her. Has she grabbed anyone yet?" Kane asked.

As the two men shook hands, Morgan answered no and asked if Kane had approached the nurse about coaching. Kane said he hadn't but would introduce him to her and let him broach the subject.

"You're having too much fun with this, and I don't know why," said Morgan. "What's the catch?"

Kane just raised his eyebrows and said, "You requested someone feisty. Just trying to meet your needs."

With Bianca and Rosa in tow, Kane introduced Morgan to Gloria. "Morgan's going to be our new girls basketball coach, and he's on the lookout for an assistant."

"Nice to meet you, Coach." Gloria turned away immediately to quiet the boys line, which had bunched up to talk and roughhouse. "If you guys would ever hit the opponents as hard as you hit each other, you might win a few games. You come in here and behave disrespectfully to adults who are doing you a favor. Didn't your parents teach you anything? Get back into an orderly line and shut up." She grabbed the shirtsleeve of one boy, said his name, and challenged him to take charge of his teammates, before turning back to Morgan. "Sorry about that. Boys just need constant monitoring." She looked at Rosa and Bianca. "And who are these two young ladies?"

"I'm Bianca."

"Rosa."

"They came for physicals, but we don't have the proper paperwork," said Morgan. "The lady over there said we'd need to go back to the school to get it or reschedule."

"Oh, hell. It's a damn walk-through so the school can claim innocence for liability." She frowned at Kane. "You watch these boys. You girls come with me."

Kane moved closer to the line of boys, but they were behaving now. Morgan watched as Gloria Fawkes escorted Bianca and Rosa to the front of the girls line. She spoke briefly to the lady checking paperwork and then walked the girls past a curtain and into the examination rooms. Two minutes later, Gloria returned to Morgan.

"On Monday, go over to school and pick up that paperwork for them. Our poor girls don't even know how to ask for permission. They're so vulnerable, it's scary. Have someone who knows the girls sign it and return it. For all I care, you can sign for them. Doesn't appear either of their mothers are around." Gloria breathed out heavily. "Such baloney!" She took another deep breath to change the subject. "Now, what's this about needing an assistant? Not sure I can help you find one."

Morgan looked back to the curtain. "Thank you for that. Coach Abby is taking a sabbatical this year to work on her master's degree, so I'll be filling in for one year. I need an assistant." Morgan let that hang in the air for a moment.

Gloria nodded and grinned slightly. "You might want to know if I know anything about the game?"

"Do you?"

"Yeah, a little. Do you?"

Morgan smiled. "Some. I'd ask for a lot of your time starting after Labor Day. Don't know what you would be willing to commit to."

"I can't stand bullcrap; you might want to know that up front. I don't like to be outworked. Kind of a thing of mine. Have you ever been a head coach?"

"Twenty-two years."

"This here is going to take all day" said Gloria, "so how about I meet you somewhere this afternoon, and we'll see if we could work together. I'm not easy to be around for long periods of time."

Morgan opened his wallet and took out his card. "See you for dinner around five. I'd like for my wife to meet you."

§

That the uniforms were old was no reason not to take care of them. Morgan grew angry as he folded the newly washed junior varsity gear. Eleven faded jerseys with the screened numbers peeling off, originally purchased for the varsity eight years ago. Molly unfolded #14 and held it against her chest.

Morgan smiled. "Best number. Oscar's number. Cousy's number. My son's number." Time with Molly always relaxed him, and Morgan let go of the condition of the uniforms.

"Your son played for you?" asked Molly.

"Yeah. Pretty good shooter."

"He lives in Denver, doesn't he? I think you told me that once."

"Yep." He pushed aside the jerseys and began folding the trunks. Just nine pair.

"And you have a daughter down there too, don't you? She's the one you visit on Sundays? Do you have any other children?"

"No, just Brian and Kathy. No grandchildren." Morgan shook his head. "It's a good thing you girls are all small or else these trunks wouldn't have fit you. Old style."

Mrs. Summitt entered the laundry room to check on the progress. "Oh, that's not good," she said trying to flatten out a curled number. "What time are you expecting Gloria to show up?"

"Around five. What are you fixing?" asked Morgan. "What are you doing for dinner tonight Molly?"

"Can't tonight. Mom's having some family over, so I'm helping with that, but thanks."

"What do your kids do for a living?" asked Molly, directing the question to both Andrea and Morgan.

Morgan answered. "Brian sells insurance, kind of a workaholic, and Kathy's taking a cooking class just now." Morgan glanced at his wife.

Andrea nodded. "Before you head outside to shoot baskets, why don't we sit and have a snack and something to drink?" It wasn't a question, but a signal for movement out of the laundry room and into the kitchen. She put a small plate of cakes on the table and poured iced tea for all three.

"Molly, keep this between the three of us for now," said Morgan. "Our daughter is in prison, and when I go down on Sundays, it's to visit her. She got mixed up with drugs several years ago, and then compounded her mistakes by getting with the wrong group of people. Led to some stealing. She still has a few years to serve." He stopped there and let Molly process the information.

"Wow," she said softly. "I'm sorry. I didn't mean to pry. It's just like you seem to be the perfect parents."

"It's okay. We know you weren't. Kathy's doing much better and we're hopeful."

§

Gloria arrived slightly before five with an appetite and a bouquet of flowers for Mrs. Summitt. She had stopped in the driveway to talk with Molly, whom she knew slightly from school. Molly popped her head in the door after Gloria entered to tell Morgan she was leaving, and she made a funny face as if to ask, "What?"

Gloria related a bit of her past when they sat down. "I've never coached; don't think I have the patience. Little things set me off, like Lowell Exeter." Gloria cut her steak in tiny pieces and ate most of it before beginning her baked potato. She swallowed and leaned back. "Okay, I have some questions. I knew Abby and liked her; wasn't surprised she took a year off; she was so frustrated. Kane told me last spring he was going to hire Thulen. What happened to that and how did you get roped into this?"

Morgan related the *Saga of Molly*, about how her passion reawakened his coaching spirit and how it brought her friends into the mix. He told Gloria about the summer league and team camp, and then took the high road about Kane's decision not to hire Thulen for the job. "I think the main reason was the attitude of the girls. They're a special lot."

Gloria resumed eating. "Thulen's a likable guy, but he doesn't want to rock the boat. He has very little drive and no imagination. I watched them practice a few times. He just wants to be the girls' friend. They like him. I assume you know they didn't win a game last year and have never been good. Participation is real low."

"That would be one of my goals, to get more girls to go out." Morgan paused. "And keep them out. It would be nice to get twenty to twenty-five girls out."

"You are a dreamer. What else?" asked Gloria.

"Win some games. Molly wants to be the winningest team in Oro Hills history; that would mean winning a half-dozen. I think they can do better. I want to get this program on the right track, so when Abby returns, it'll be in better shape than when she left it."

Gloria remained uncommitted throughout dinner, posing questions during her second helping. Andrea cleared the plates and brought out cheesecake. Her questions became more specific. "Those two young ladies you brought in this morning, Bianca and Rosa, what's their story?" Morgan explained and Gloria went on. "Nice and polite. Really stuck together during the physicals. Not real comfortable in the situation. I called over to the district office to check on previous records. Rosa has a file, but Bianca doesn't. That young woman has secrets."

"If you take the job, I'll fill you in on some of the details," said Morgan.

"Whether I do or not, I'll need to create a file on her, but I'll tell you what. I'm in, but I won't just be the woman to check the locker room when you can't. I want full responsibilities. I want the JV team to have its time during practice. If I disagree with something you do, I'm going to tell you, but I'll do it behind closed doors. And I want a no-cut policy for the lower level team."

Andrea stayed silent through most of the dinner, but when Gloria extended her hand across the table to Morgan, she also shook Andrea's hand. Andrea smiled. "Do you read much?"

CHAPTER 12

Point guards can't foul out, can't get tired,
can't get hurt, can't come out.
Not this game, but every game, the whole season.

By Wednesday, the fifteenth of August 1995, the football team was practicing twice-a-day in pads. Stevie was running cross-country and still trying to persuade Bianca and Molly to join her. Elena, Izzy, Penny, and Cindy were practicing volleyball in the gym, along with fifteen other girls. With another substantial contribution from the Mountain Matrons, Morgan ordered two sets of uniforms, home whites and away golds. He began daily conversations with Kane about shooting shirts or sweatshirts for the girls.

"I don't know where you'll get the money, Kane, but administrators always have a secret stash somewhere," kidded Morgan.

"I may end up regretting hiring you. You always come into my office with an open palm. Can't you get your secret sugar daddy to buy those too?"

Morgan smiled. "It's all matching funds. If you or the district shuts off the spigot, my donors will too. Think of it this way, you're getting two for the price of one." Morgan knew Kane's funds were limited, but he also knew he had to be persistent to get anything from the District. If the book club bought everything, the school would allow it and transfer the girls' funds to other programs, setting a bad precedent. He hoped the Matrons would see a return on their investment in the number of wins both teams could attain. Zero-win seasons, regardless of how well dressed the girls were, were still zero wins. "I think my repairs to the ball rack will save you a few dollars there, and I won't bill you for labor."

"Mighty generous of you, Coach." Kane liked Morgan's approach. He hadn't demanded a single item, simply explaining how proud the town would be of its teams and what a morale boost new uniforms would be for the girls. What they were wearing was old and embarrassing. *Miner Pride.*

§

The first day of school for the 1995-1996 school year was Wednesday, August 22. Molly's reading lessons continued through the beginning of school, and she was a quick study. Molly, Bianca, and Rosa continued to practice basketball on the driveway, even as late-August weather brought temperatures into fall-like conditions at 8500 feet. After school volleyball practices and cross-country kept the other girls away. Gloria Fawkes decided she and Morgan needed to meet on a regular basis, and she was invited to join the Mountain Matrons too. Andrea joined her husband on Sunday when he drove to Denver to visit their daughter.

The football team played its first game on the first Saturday in September, but seven players stood in street clothes due to ineligibility, five with a single D. The volleyball team opened its season on Tuesday missing two varsity starters. Elena's first weekly report card included four As, one B, and one D, making her ineligible for this first contest. Morgan attended both games, and Andrea joined him at the volleyball match. They spoke briefly with Elena, who explained that she scored poorly on her only trig test but was getting some extra help. Later, Morgan spoke briefly with Kane Vincent.

"They played hard; would have been nice to have a full squad," said Morgan.

Kane agreed. "You know, Coach, I hadn't realized how accepting I've become of this situation, of our teams always playing short-handed. The post-game talk always has a caveat, always the excuse that if so-and-so would have played, we'd have been right there. It's true, but it gets old. Our rationale is the same; we hold our athletes to a higher standard." Kane turned away to speak to a couple of students, teacher-talk. Then, he returned to Morgan. "You've become a real pain in the butt for me. This eligibility plan, more money for the girls basketball team, I've got an upset football coach. What's next?"

Morgan understood that Kane wasn't angry with him but was re-examining his role as activities director. "That's why they pay you the big bucks." Morgan smiled. "Elena being ineligible really makes it stark, doesn't it?" Kane nodded and then spoke quickly to another pair of students. Molly and Stevie came over to say hi to Morgan and Andrea but left to be with their friends. "Need a beer, Kane? It's still early. Bring your wife; we'd like to meet her."

§

Labor Day was warm and sunny, and the eight girls who had attended team camp shot baskets on Coach Summitt's driveway. Alondra and her "sister" joined her classmates. Izzy won the first game of twenty-one, but Molly won both games of knock-out. She teamed with Penny to win four two-on-two games before losing to Stevie and Bianca. Molly demanded an immediate rematch, but Bianca told her she had to wait until her turn came up again. Bianca and Stevie beat Cindy and Elena handily, but were pushed into overtime by Izzy and Alondra before winning 9-7. Alondra knocked Bianca to the concrete on one screen allowing Izzy to score easily. Nobody seemed too concerned except Rosa, but Bianca stood up and scored the next three baskets for the win. *The championship* was on.

"This one's to eleven," said Molly. "You could get lucky to seven."

"Like the last time?" said Bianca in mock response.

Stevie slid past each screen that Penny tried to set, forcing Molly to develop shots off the dribble. When she did beat Stevie one-on-one, she had to shoot jump shots. Bianca simply did not cover Penny and played a one girl zone at the basket gathering every defensive rebound. Still, Stevie was ineffective against Molly's defense, forcing Bianca to move away from the basket just to get the ball. Penny could defend Bianca on the perimeter. Ultimately, Molly's tenacity prevailed.

"You would have fouled out if Coach was calling fouls," said Molly.

"Quit complaining, Molly. You won, didn't you?" responded Stevie.

Morgan watched from the nook with Andrea, who held Alondra's child. Morgan kept nodding his head and making notes on the table's yellow pad. *There's a team out there; a real team.*

§

Morgan reserved the high school gym for the girls beginning on Monday, September 11. Starting at seven, it would give a girl time to go home after practice to eat, and the open gym would end promptly at eight, allowing for some homework time. Mondays and Wednesdays for one hour of offensive skills and shooting. No games, just individual drills. Gloria volunteered to work with Bianca and Penny and any other tall girl, repetitive post moves and lots of free throws.

"My high school coach specialized in post play. I shot more free throws than any girl in my conference my junior and senior years. He was always screaming, 'Take the ball up strong into her chest!'"

"Were you better than Bianca?" asked Morgan.

Gloria nodded her head. "As a senior maybe, but she's a much better athlete. She's just sixteen and a junior, and it's obvious she's much more conscientious than I ever was. Big upside, and she'll do anything you ask of her."

"Rebound and power up. Be strong with the ball. If you rebound, you shoot. That's what I want you to work on with her. Repetition."

Gloria liked these discussions about basketball and the kids. "By the way, I still haven't been able to get all her records from New Mexico. Don't know if her old school is lazy or doesn't have them."

§

At the first open gym, Morgan found the volleyball team just finishing practice. He was sure he had checked the practice time, that practice was to end at 5:15. He sat with nine girls in the bleachers waiting for the volleyball team to leave the floor and take down their nets. Coach Holmes blew her whistle and gathered her girls for the post-practice summary at 7:10. When she finished, she approached Morgan.

"Coach," said the girls' coach, "I'd appreciate it if you kept your girls out of the gym until my practice is over. They're a distraction."

Morgan remembered a similar power ploy several years back when a new football coach at Lakewood demanded full gym usage when the fall weather turned cold. Morgan apologized. "I'm sorry, Coach. I was under the impression your practice would be over by five-fifteen. Did I misread the schedule?"

Coach Holmes looked over her shoulder to her student managers. "Just leave the nets up; I'll use them in gym class tomorrow." Then, she looked at Morgan. "I've never had to clear my practice time before. Abby never started practice in my season; she waited until we were done, and everything worked out fine."

Gloria started to say something, but Morgan cut her off. "I don't want to get off on the wrong foot here, so is there a time when I could use the gym without disrupting your practice?"

Coach Holmes made a contemptuous noise before saying, "November," and turned to walk away.

As she turned to go, Morgan said, "If I recall, you practiced out of season last spring and this summer and monopolized some girls who wanted to run track, but you discouraged them." Coach Holmes turned back to respond, but Morgan was quicker. "These are not your girls, and they're not mine. They're Oro Hills' girls and they deserve every opportunity to be successful." His tone was even, but firm. "I will bend over backward to help these girls become successful in whatever sport they're in, which means I'll cooperate with you if you're doing what's best for them. But I will not stand aside. Schedule your practice time whenever you like, but don't play games with me or these girls."

Gloria thought she saw Coach Holmes flinch, but if she did, she recovered. "I doubt if you understand our kids here, coming from the big city and everything." She turned and walked away.

Morgan stood and faced the nine girls waiting to shoot baskets. "You can take the floor now." He looked at Gloria. "For now, let me fight these little battles. She'll go to Kane and complain, but he'll make her write her schedule down, and we'll work around it."

"That was a pissy thing to do, like she was marking her territory. To say we don't understand these kids!" Gloria clenched her jaw.

"She's talked with Thulen. He said the same thing to me, same words. At some point this week, I suspect she'll come talk to you to get you on her side."

"Don't worry, I won't," said Gloria.

Morgan grinned. "I know. Let's go to work." As they stepped off the bleachers, Elena, Cindy, Izzy, and Penny asked if they could stay and shoot. "Probably not a good idea tonight. Go home and eat and get your homework done. You have a match tomorrow, so you'll need your rest. Maybe Wednesday if your practice is over by five."

§

Coach Holmes did not go to Kane Vincent. She skipped the chain of command and went directly to the principal, Lowell Exeter. In doing so, she lost Kane's support for any future endeavor and allied herself with a man who looked to avoid confrontations whenever possible. Lowell met with Morgan, telling him about Coach Holmes' long and distinguished service to Oro Hills, taking her side in the current dispute, asking him to avoid overlapping practices, and encouraging him to be a team player by knowing his place. "Your season will come soon enough. Let's let the volleyball team have their time."

"That's what I'm afraid of, that my season will come too soon, before the girls have an opportunity to be successful. Individuals get better in the off-season, in the summer and fall; teams get better during the season. Schools with successful athletic programs aren't selfish with their kids, especially small schools, the 1A and 2A schools. If you tell me I can't meet with the girls who are only trying to get better until my season starts, I won't. You're the boss, but I'd think this school would get damn tired of losing all the time, especially when it doesn't have to." Morgan kept his eyes focused on Exeter, who averted the new coach's glare.

"None of us like losing, but we have problems other schools don't have. It's very difficult," said the principal.

"Success is always more difficult for poor communities, but we don't have to accept it. The volleyball team plays Academy Prep tonight, and I can guarantee you that their basketball girls are holding open gyms at least twice a week. Some of their best players will play three sports and get private coaching on the side." Morgan knew he was stepping on the line. "Did Coach Holmes tell you what she's afraid of by denying me the use of the gym?"

Lowell Exeter sat in his chair behind a big desk that, despite his size, made him look small. "Can you guarantee a winning season by holding open gyms?"

"Nope. But I can tell you that those girls who attend open gyms will be better when the season rolls around."

Exeter hated arguing. He didn't like Morgan challenging him. "Well, work with Kane to find some common ground. Coach Holmes just wants what's best for her team."

Morgan held his tongue. Exeter would have to explain to Coach

Holmes how he had compromised, and it would sound to her as if he still had her back, but he didn't.

§

That night, Academy Prep demolished Oro Hills in straight sets, 25-3 and 25-2. The next afternoon, Coach Holmes ran her team hard, except for Stephanie Miles, who sat at the end of the gym icing her knees. Holmes denied permission for any of her players to attend open gym. Morgan and Gloria worked diligently at open gym with twelve kids, nine girls and three boys. Molly practiced crossovers against Stevie, who had come in after cross-country practice, working to get into the lane for twelve-foot jumpers. Then, Stevie worked against Molly, trying to make right-handed layups against pressure. One-foot takeoffs continued to be difficult for her, but jump-stops were getting better. At another basket Bianca worked power moves against Gloria, who knew how to defend the post. After an hour Morgan called the girls together. "The volleyball team plays at home on Friday. They had a tough loss last night and will need some support, so try to attend." As the girls dispersed, Morgan put his arm around Alondra's shoulder. "It was nice to see you again. Do you have a ride home?"

"Coach Gloria is giving me a ride. Thanks. I'll try to make it next week." Alondra joined some other girls putting on their coats and gathering their things.

"How'd she do?" asked Morgan.

Gloria had a big grin. "Well, she's rough in more ways than one, but she had fun, and the others enjoy her company. She has a quick wit. From what I could gather, her mom has a new stay-at-home boyfriend, so she's there to watch her sisters. She can get better."

Molly and Stevie emerged from the tunnel after putting the balls away. Morgan gave Molly and her brother Alex a ride home, along with Rosa and Bianca.

§

Gloria joined Morgan and Andrea on Saturday noon for the home football game. The aspen to the west were in full colors, and a gentle wind began to blow at halftime. The game was competitive against Edgewater, another team without a victory in the young season. Morgan had played high school football on this same field, but back in the Forties, there were no elaborate bleachers or scoreboard. He remembered larger, more vocal crowds. He also remembered rivalries. Post-game fights were common, especially after night basketball games when the darkness provided faux courage for teenagers. Buses often were the targets of eggs or rocks and needed to be guarded during the games.

On the field Oro Hills scored a touchdown to take the lead over Edgewater. As they stood to applaud, Gloria pointed to the student section where many of the basketball girls where gathered. "Who's missing?" she asked Morgan.

Morgan studied the clique only for a moment. "Molly, huh."

"She's probably on your driveway, relentlessly pursuing the perfect step-back cross-over." It was a statement both of admiration and concern.

The Miners missed the extra point, and the crowd settled back into their seats. "In this case," said Morgan, "she's working at the laundromat. Her mom's sick, but otherwise, that's where she'd be. I don't know if I ever worked with a player so dedicated, and that's saying a lot."

"Coach," Gloria called Morgan *Coach* most of the time, "I played sports with passion and a desire to win, but it was play, and I had the opportunity to compete beyond high school, but she works at the game. Sometimes when I watch her, when I watch the two of you together, it's a laboratory. Her devotion, her commitment to learning the finer points is amazing. The two of you are dissecting the game, studying not only her game, but the games of the other girls. I wish I'd have been with you this summer. It had to have been something."

Morgan nodded. "Yeah. Something." He kept nodding, much like a bobble-head doll. "At team camp the Adams State College coach watched her a couple of times and is interested in her development. One of the coaches from Jefferson County approached me to see if Molly would transfer to her school because she was too good for 2A." Before he finished his thought, Gloria jumped in.

"That's bullcrap!"

"I know, and I let her know." Morgan had started calling Gloria *Coach* too. "Coach, Molly sees basketball differently; she feels it."

"Sort of like you, I suspect," said Gloria.

Still nodding, "Yeah, but mine didn't happen when I was sixteen years old. I grew into it; Molly's owned it from before I met her."

"She trusts you completely, you know."

"I know."

Down on the field, Edgewater fumbled, and Oro Hills ran the game out, winning 18-13. Kane Vincent threw his arms up in the air with fists clenched and walked briskly onto the field to shake Coach Ryan's hand. Kane high-fived several of the players. Morgan liked that. "That's what an administrator should do," he said to Gloria. He nudged Andrea. "Pretty cool, huh."

§

Andrea returned a bit sleepy from her book club, the only time each month when she indulged in more than one drink a day. She pecked Morgan on the cheek, laid her hand on Alex's shoulder, and told Morgan about Queenie's plan to sue the State of Colorado over school funding. "The inequality of property taxes has long-term consequences," said Andrea, paraphrasing Queenie.

"Yes, it does," said Morgan. "Did you get enough to eat?'

"Yes, of course. B.J. was happy the football team won so she could write a positive story about high school sports. She said the consequences of unsuccessful teams goes beyond the school walls, that her circulation would increase if the teams won more games."

§

Coach Holmes took her volleyball seriously, even if Morgan disagreed with her policy on sharing the gym and her girls. She was also, according to Mitzi, a very good teacher. Forty-seven years old, a high-altitude runner, outspoken, a member of the local gun club, with penetrating eyes, the volleyball coach intimidated many of her students. Like so many of her colleagues at Oro Hills, her teams had never experienced a winning season, which, Morgan believed, colored her attitude toward him and intensified the spat over gym usage. Unfortunately, Coach Holmes expressed her dissatisfaction to Molly and Bianca in side comments during class. Holmes saw a setter and outside hitter in those two girls and believed Morgan had told them not to go out for volleyball, to spend their time practicing only basketball.

"Did you explain to her that you've never wanted to play volleyball?" asked Morgan to Molly.

"She doesn't listen. I played as a freshman but didn't like it. We didn't have open gym back then, so it didn't interfere with basketball, but I just didn't like it. I only played because my friends played. Coach Abby tried to get me to go out, but I just *didn't like it*, so I didn't play last year. She nagged then too. Now, she's blaming you."

"Do you want me to talk with her?" asked Morgan.

"No. She'll just take it out on me more. Her mind is made up. I'll deal with it."

"What about Bianca?"

"She just laughs. I don't think she's ever played volleyball, and she doesn't do anything without Rosa, and Rosa wouldn't make the team, so it's not going to happen."

§

Kane Vincent called Morgan a week later to tell him his basketballs had arrived and wanted him to come get them out of his office. To Morgan, it seemed like Kane wanted to talk with him, and this was a reason to get him in.

"Coffee?" asked Kane. Morgan waved him off, but Kane poured himself another cup from his office maker. "Thought we would get another one this Saturday. The kids just needed to hold onto the ball on that last drive."

"That fumble was the killer. They played with a lot of heart," said Morgan. "How good is Arroyo?"

"We won't get that one . . . for lots of reasons. They gave A-Prep a good go on Saturday; probably the next best team in the league. Too big up front for us, and we've got some injuries and eligibility problems." The junior varsity game against Slater had to be cancelled for lack of numbers; the squad was down to twenty-seven and many of the reserves were freshmen. "I call it the 'Elena Salazar Corollary.' A kid passes five or six classes with all As and Bs, but gets one D, and we declare him ineligible. You were right. Kids just fall away and quit. Coach Ryan's seeing it, and I think Coach Holmes has lost a couple of players."

"Probably can't change it in the middle of the year, can you?"

"I discussed it with Lowell, and he didn't think that would be fair." Kane said the word fair with some disdain. "He said we could begin looking at it to maybe tweak it for next year. Get a committee together and look at the data. You know what school committees are good for, don't you?" It was a rhetorical question.

The two men talked for a while longer, with Morgan catching up on the latest excuses for Oro Hills' teams' lack of success. "The Blame Culture" as Kane described it. "There's a faction in town that will tell you our kids don't deserve to win, that they just don't have it in them," said Kane. "Lowell buys into that theory and tells me winning is not a big deal to our students and their families. Remember," said Kane with a shake of his head, "our kids are different."

§

When the current semester began, Molly decided to come home from classes and devote an hour to her game while the temperature was at its warmest. She would then do her chores and fix dinner. Afterwards, she would work on her reading with Mrs. Summitt. Since the Summitts ate early, this schedule worked for both of them. As the days shortened and winter approached, especially in the mountains, Molly's anticipation for the season heightened. Bianca and Rosa joined her on several afternoons. Coach talked to her about "roles," and she began to understand. She would do her part, and every girl had a part. Coach always made a point of congratulating Rosa on her defense and told all the girls that teams were based on defense. On the driveway in the fall, she liked playing defense against both Molly and Bianca while they worked on their offensive skills. Often, it was Coach Summitt guarding Bianca and Rosa guarding Molly. "Make it difficult for Molly to throw that entry pass. Don't foul Molly when she shoots the jump shot; just contest. Block out. As Molly moves closer to the basket, get more physical." "Good" and "well done" from Coach were the warmest compliments she had ever received.

Returning from the last open gym in September, Morgan asked the girls about their hobbies outside of school and basketball. "So, what do you do on the weekends?" Morgan remembered from his high school years in Oro Hills. Lots of parking. "Any boyfriends these days, Bianca?"

he asked lightly.

"She's stopped going with her man boyfriend. He was such a loser," said Rosa.

"Did he have a job, Bianca?" asked Morgan. "Unemployed young men are the most dangerous. They've got nothing to offer except their charm."

Molly laughed. "In case you didn't get it, Bianca, that's another one of Coach's truisms." She turned to Morgan. "That's a good one, Coach. I'll write it down when I get home along with the others."

"You write them down?" asked Morgan.

"Oh, yeah. This one will go below 'Don't foul the jump shooter.' Both good advice."

Morgan wondered if any of the girls had received *the talk* between mother and daughter about the dangers of pre-marital sex. In Rosa's and Bianca's case, an aunt-to-niece or friend-to-friend talk. Through the back door, he thought. "Has anyone heard how Sofia's doing?"

Molly nodded. "She miscarried. She'd been going to school at the start but dropped out. Then, this week she showed up. She didn't say anything, but she's not pregnant anymore, and she's Catholic, so that one thing wasn't an option."

To Morgan, that Molly didn't use the term abortion was telling. "Are all of you Catholic?"

The girls looked back and forth. "Most of us. We are, and so are Izzy and Elena," said Molly. She checked off the names of the basketball girls. "Alondra is. Not Stevie or Penny. Cindy is."

Bianca asked, "Are you, Coach?"

"No. I was once, when I was a kid. My mom was Catholic." He paused. "Her parents were born in Mexico, as we said back then. Now, you're all Hispanic or Latin, but since my dad was white, I was always considered white. Never gave it much thought. Mostly we were just poor miner kids. I stopped going to church a long time ago. Mrs. Summitt goes most Sundays. She prays for my heathen soul." The girls laughed.

"I will too," said Rosa.

CHAPTER 13

We're none of us just anything.
We're mixed breeds. Mutts. But cuddly mutts.

Four weeks before the opening practice—Morgan refused to call it tryouts because he and Gloria were determined to keep every girl who showed up—Morgan and Andrea packed for a week-long vacation. Morgan reserved a motel for two nights in Durango, one of his wife's favorite Colorado towns, and then they would drive to Phoenix where they would spend four days. On the way home, they would stay for two days in Santa Fe, returning on Tuesday, October 24. Molly would take care of Cousy, feeding him twice daily and changing out his litterbox once. Gloria would run the three open gyms and begin collecting parental permission papers and physicals. She was anxious to be put in charge, since Morgan tended to micromanage the planning. Being the only adult in the gym would provide her with a bit of credibility heading into the season. Most of the girls attending open gym would end up on her junior varsity, as at least four and maybe more of the varsity were playing volleyball and unable to attend open gym. Izzy, Cindy, Elena, and Penny all wanted to attend, but Morgan would not allow it after Coach Holmes' edict about participating in only one sport at a time.

During the day on Thursday, Molly and Bianca stopped by Gloria's office "just to talk." They had enjoyed both open gyms and were encouraged about the number of freshmen attending. Neither girl thought any of them could help the varsity this season, but maybe as sophomores they could be valuable. Gloria told Bianca her old school was not being helpful in sending her records in a timely manner. Bianca shrugged her shoulders and shook her head but said nothing about it. When they left, Gloria placed another call to Espanola High School, hoping to get someone other than a student receptionist. A student answered again, but transferred Gloria to the secretary, who couldn't give out any information about students over the phone. She suggested Gloria send a letter on school stationary, and then it would be handled quickly. "We've done that. This student was enrolled last semester, but is just now going out for a sport." The secretary wondered aloud how a transfer student could enroll in any school without those medical records. When Gloria hung up, she wondered the same thing.

§

Oro Hills' volleyball team won again on Friday, meaning they would get the eighth seed in the district tournament, which meant their season would last until the first week in November. Unfortunately, their opponent would be Academy Prep. Kane Vincent called the three remaining schools on the football team's schedule to cancel junior varsity games because of dwindling numbers. Their last game would be November 4, the first Saturday of the month. The boys basketball coach had not held any open gyms, but informed Kane he would like to get a jump on the season by holding open gyms on each night after football ended. He said these wouldn't be mandatory, but hoped he could get most of the football kids to attend. He expected to be a league contender this season, even though his team probably could not crack the top three. Kane had heard the same expectations from the coach the year before, and they finished seventh and were eliminated in the first round of districts. Still, hope was good.

§

Molly practiced every afternoon on Morgan's driveway, even on Monday and Wednesday before the open gyms. To her, the season was just around the corner, and she didn't want to miss any opportunity to get better. Bianca and Rosa joined her on Tuesday and Thursday. At open gyms she, Bianca, and Rosa used one side of the floor to work on drills, while Coach Gloria spent her time with the younger girls. Molly decided the girls should call Gloria by her first name because her last name sounded too much like the bad word. They all had a good laugh at that. Alondra was unable to attend this week.

On Saturday Stevie won the Discovery League cross-country championship by eleven seconds over the second-place finisher. No other runner from Oro Hills, boy or girl, finished in the top twenty. She would compete for a state title the following Saturday in Denver, all five-feet-two and ninety-pounds of her. When she showed up at Morgan's driveway on Sunday with her trophy, Bianca asked Stevie if she needed a running partner for the rest of the week. "I'll keep up."

Morgan called Gloria on Sunday night from Santa Fe to see how things had gone for the week. He knew about Stevie's victory, and he was happy a few more girls were at the gym on Wednesday. "They're probably more comfortable with someone closer to their age than an old man."

"Coach, I called down to Bianca's old school, and they won't give out her medical information. Seems kind of weird; do you know anything about that?" asked Gloria.

"Nothing specific, but Kane also said he was having trouble getting it." Morgan made an old-man thinking noise. "Her old school is just up the road a bit. Maybe I'll drop off Andrea at the art galleries and drive up, see if I can speed the process a bit. I'll check in on Wednesday, if not at school, then at open gym. Don't say anything to Bianca about my visit to her old school. She doesn't seem to be too proud of it. Or Rosa."

§

After feeding Cousy on Sunday night, Molly sat at the nook in the Summitt's kitchen and did her homework. Comfortable. She poured herself a glass of milk and read her history assignment, making notes as she did. Homework was no longer difficult; tedious at times, boring sometimes, but not difficult. When she finished, she closed her text and wrote down the starting line-up for the first game in December. Saturday, December 2. She couldn't wait. Molly, Stevie, Izzy, Stephanie, and Bianca. Cindy, Elena, and Penny as substitutes. Coach told her he needed eight for the proper rotations. A sub at each position. All the ballhandling duties would fall on her, but she wanted that. "It's your ball, Molly," said Coach. *Yes, it is, Coach. Yes, it is.*

§

Morgan guessed Espanola High School had seven or eight times as many kids as Oro Hills, but he didn't know. It seemed about the size of Golden, but more hectic. The language of the hallway was Spanish as much as English. Morgan made his way to the office where a Latina woman smiled and asked what she could do for him. He identified himself and asked to see an assistant principal or the athletic director about a former student.

"Was one of our students rude to you?" she asked.

"No, no. Nothing like that. This girl goes to my school now and wants to play basketball, and I'm trying to get her records on file. She's a great kid."

"What school did you say you coached for?" asked the secretary.

§

When Morgan and Andrea returned home on Tuesday afternoon, the first thing he found was Molly's starting line-up on the kitchen table. He smiled. Cousy jumped up on the bench and onto his lap. Molly had fed her too much, and now he would have to limit her intake for a few weeks. *What a good kid Molly is*, he thought. Three weeks until the first real practice, the day after fifteen to twenty girls show up to play basketball, to have fun. But Molly? Molly's on a mission, and Morgan was going to help her achieve goals she didn't know she could achieve. *Five wins, Coach. The winningest team in Oro Hills history.* Double that, Molly. The first *winning team* in Oro Hills girls' basketball history. After twenty-two years, it was about time. Title IX made sports available to girls, given them an opportunity, but Oro Hills had not experienced the second part of the law, that it had made *winning* available to them too.

§

Morgan and Gloria sat with Kane Vincent in his office on Wednesday afternoon. Outside, it was snowing lightly, and the wind blew hard across the front sidewalks. Classes had just ended and several of the students were running to the buses or their cars without coats, having come to school when the sun was shining. Three teachers stood near the buses on duty. Gloria sipped a soda, Kane his coffee, and Morgan drank bottled water. Kane raised his cup in a mild toast. "To teachers."

"So," asked Morgan, "what do we do about Bianca?"

"I can get her a full physical, reconstruct her medical records. That's not a problem," said Gloria.

"Good. Keep it under the name she uses now. Steele." Kane shook his head. "Wonder why she chose that name?"

"Maybe she didn't choose it," said Morgan. "It was clear Espanola had a gag order. I was just hoping to walk in, talk with a counselor or administrator about her, go down to the gym to speak with a coach, and come home. Their A.D. slid the article across his desk, had me read it, and then took it back. Wouldn't comment. Just told me to take it for what it was worth. Honestly, I couldn't tell whether he cared or not, but the secretary did. As I was leaving, her eyes expressed the greatest concern, almost as if we were Bianca's guardians now. It was as if she was imploring me to act."

"Lowell doesn't know," said Kane. "Doesn't need to know. My guess is Rosa is aware and probably Rosa's aunt, but nobody else needs to. Gloria, you take care of her health records, and I'll proceed with her academics. I think we're good. Morgan, you've got the hardest job. You've got to take care of her spirit."

"I'm concerned, just wonder what's best for her, whether it's to play or to hide. My gut tells me she needs these other girls, Molly and the team," said Morgan.

Kane watched Morgan and Gloria walk to their cars on the same wind-blown sidewalk the students had traveled minutes earlier. Kane liked his choice for Morgan's assistant, a pick he made on a whim because Morgan asked for someone feisty. Gloria was proving to be a strong, trusted faculty member, even though she wasn't technically an educator. A season as a coach would alter that designation. Morgan was a no-brainer. Kane only wished he could retain the old fart for many years to come.

§

Because of the weather, open gym was sparsely attended. Molly, Alex, Rosa, and Bianca rode with Morgan back to school. Three freshmen girls also attended. Gloria played on the freshmen girls' side in a couple of four-on-four games. Despite his small size, Alex was much better than two of the freshmen girls, and Molly and Bianca were too good to lose. After each loss, Gloria feigned anger. Morgan watched Bianca with different eyes, saw a different side of her. He tried to remember more than a half-dozen times when she wasn't with Rosa, either on the driveway or during the summer. They had roomed together at camp, eaten together in the cafeteria, slept together once in his basement when the heat went out at their aunt's house. He checked on their schedules and found they attended different classes because Rosa was making up work from sitting out a semester. Bianca's grades were all As and Bs, Rosa had a couple of Cs, but neither of them had received any Ds this semester. Bianca looked older tonight and Morgan noticed she bit the inside of her lip ever so slightly. When Gloria gave instructions, Bianca gave her complete attention. Molly had a mission but was still a teenage girl; Bianca was completely focused, and in some ways worked as hard as Molly, but for another reason. He wondered when the last time either Bianca or Rosa had been warmly hugged, and then he remembered that he would give them side hugs occasionally, like he did the other girls. On the return trips from summer games, she rode up front with him.

Gloria stopped the four-on-four game to give instructions to her freshmen. "Watch how Bianca does it! I know she outweighs you by fifty pounds, but she'd bump me even if she were your size. She's not doing it because she doesn't like you; she's doing it because that's what Coach Summitt taught her to do. That's the way the game's played."

Molly looked up to Morgan and laughed. "Coach Gloria forgot to say '*Again*.'"

Morgan ended open gym a little early. The freshmen girls all had rides waiting, so Morgan told Gloria to come over to the house for a bite to eat. He would bring Alex and the girls along. He called Andrea, asking her to prepare some hot chocolate. She knew what he knew about Bianca and Rosa; there were no secrets between them. Bianca rode up front in the van where, tonight, she said it warmed up quicker.

Alex ran from Morgan's garage across the street to his house with no hat and only a light coat. Molly yelled at him to do his homework, which caused Gloria, who pulled onto the driveway behind Morgan, to question homework for an elementary student. Inside, the guests hung their coats on wall hooks in the laundry room. Andrea had a fire going, so the girls sat on the carpet with steaming cups of hot chocolate while Morgan eased into his stuffed chair and Gloria and Andrea sat on the couch.

"Do you need to call your aunt, Rosa?" asked Andrea. Rosa shook her head no.

"This is what my life has become," said Morgan. "A room full of females. If not you guys, then it's Andrea's book club, although you guys treat me with more respect than the older women do. I'm their favorite punching bag." Five pairs of eyes looked at him wondering what he was going to say next. He tilted his head slightly and looked at his cup. "I'd say I have it pretty good."

Molly placed her hot chocolate on an end table and laid back on the carpet. "This is nice. Our carpet is old, and we don't have a fireplace." She giggled. "And Alex would jump on me if I did this."

"We don't have a fireplace either," said Rosa.

"I don't have one where I rent," said Gloria. "It's just a tiny, smelly, two-room apartment." She looked at the girls on the floor. "I think I'll let the Summitts adopt me and live in luxury downstairs."

"It's big enough for all of us," said Bianca. "And really comfortable."

Molly sat up and swiveled on her butt to look at Morgan. "What do you think, Coach? Are we going to win some games this season?"

Morgan stretched his neck from side-to-side to intentionally delay his answer. "Maybe if I can find a point guard, we will. Someone who can handle the ball a little." He looked to Gloria. "Do you think one of those freshmen girls might be the answer, Coach?"

"Maybe little Jenny. And those other two who showed up tonight could play center and off-guard with a bit of toughness. Yeah, we might win a game or two with them."

Morgan sat forward in his chair. "I figure we sit back in a tight two-three zone and slow the game down. Yeah, that might work."

Molly shook her head and looked to Bianca. "Maybe we could get Coach Thulen to coach us again. He loved that zone. 'Get back, get back,' he'd say. That worked so well, last year." She threw her hands over her face in mock exasperation and fell back onto the carpet.

"He wasn't my coach last year, Molly. Remember? Rosa and I were just spectators." Bianca looked up to Morgan. "Are we going to play the season like we did this summer?"

Morgan understood the seriousness of her question, that the joking was over. He pursed his lips and nodded. "Faster, I hope. You showed me this summer that you were all willing to run, and we did it better than anyone we played. We weren't always successful, but we were starting to get it by team camp, and that was without organized practices. Every one of you got better." Morgan looked at Rosa as if to say, *you especially.* "We have a lot to overcome, most notably Oro Hills' culture of losing, but we started doing that this summer. We won eight games. Eight games! Our summer opponents would look at us as if they had a sure win, what with our recent history, but they sure didn't think that way after playing us. I'll bet not one of the teams in our league improved as much as you guys did, and none of them saw us play. They'll be in for a surprise. Up here, at altitude, they'll think they're dying. I won't kid you, we aren't the best team in the state by a long way, but we will compete. Teams will know who we are and not take us for granted in the second go-round of conference play. No team ever scouted Oro Hills in the past, but I'll bet they do this season." He let that sink in and kept his eyes moving between Molly and Bianca. Then, "I've got a point guard and a center who will own their position, and a bunch of others who are tough kids. We're going to do just fine."

"I hated that last year," said Molly. "Not just losing, but that other schools just took us for granted. They ignored us, like we were an automatic win. None of those girls talked with us after a game."

"They'll have to this season," said Morgan.

Gloria shuttered. "I don't know about you guys," she said to the three girls on the carpet, "but I've got goose bumps."

The phone in the kitchen rang. Andrea got up and answered and then called, "Molly, it's your brother."

"Probably wants me to come home," she said as she arose and went to the kitchen. It was a short call. She returned with a happy face. "We may not have school tomorrow. Alex said something about the heater being down." She looked to Morgan. "Is there any way to check?"

Gloria stood. "I can find out. Let me make a call."

Alex's information was correct. Sometime between when open gym ended and the second cup of hot chocolate, the high school boiler shut down, and Thursday's classes were cancelled. The night janitor thought it seemed a little cool, checked on it, and found the giant fan not functioning. A part needed to be replaced, but it would have to come from Denver, requiring a morning delivery.

"Guess I'd better heat up a little something to snack on," said Andrea.

The crew congregated in the kitchen while Mrs. Summitt searched the refrigerator for leftovers. At the nook table, Morgan took the legal pad, glanced at Molly's line-up, smiled, and then turned the page. "Coach Gloria and I have been meeting to talk about the season . . ." he paused. "You don't have a boyfriend waiting for you, do you, Coach?" he asked Gloria. She narrowed her eyebrows as if to say, *Don't go there*, and he proceeded. "Let me show you my thinking."

Andrea laughed as she placed a plate of mini-cakes on the table. "Morgan's in heaven. A captive audience to talk basketball. I'll be by the fire reading in case you need something."

Morgan drew a basketball court on the pad. "Eighty-four feet by fifty feet." He drew lines connecting the two foul lanes. "Now, I divide the court into thirds; a middle third and two outside thirds. On defense we defend the middle third and one outside third. We will direct the ball to one side and do our best not to allow it to be reversed. Always ball pressure." He looked up to the girls. "Always."

Around ten, Rosa called her aunt. At eleven, Gloria drove Rosa and Bianca home, and Molly walked across the street. Andrea had already gone to bed. Morgan poured himself a glass of milk and stood looking out the window across the street at Molly's house. *And I dare any team to effectively cover that little girl one-on-one.*

§

The snow continued to fall, seven inches and counting. The ski slopes cheered, hoping for an early base and an early opening. The Denver newspaper was late, so Morgan looked over last night's diagrams and drank his coffee. It was Andrea who saw two bundled up figures walking to the door. "Company," she said.

"You two are up early. Have you had breakfast?" asked Morgan letting them in.

"Cereal," said Bianca. Andrea set out to fix a little something and poured them each a glass of juice. As the they sat down, Bianca looked seriously at Morgan. "You know, don't you?"

Morgan sat down again with his coffee and nodded. "So does Mrs. Summitt, Coach Gloria, and Mr. Vincent. Nobody else, and it's our secret. Nobody else needs to know."

Tears welled up in Bianca's eyes. Rosa put her arm around Bianca's shoulders and watched her face. Bianca sniffled and swallowed hard. "I'm sorry."

"You have nothing to be sorry for." Andrea slid next to Bianca, putting her arm around Bianca too.

"I just snapped. I'd had enough." Tears streamed down her cheeks as she tried to continue.

"Hey," said Morgan gently. "I think you did what you had to to protect yourself and Rosa. That's not snapping; that's doing what's right." He put his hand on the table, palm up, and waited. Bianca lifted her hand from under the table and put it in Morgan's. He wrapped his fingers around hers. "For you and for Rosa, this is your safe house. Any time, night or day, whether I'm here or not, this is your safe place." All eyes were on Bianca. She kept crying, a sixteen-year-old victim of some of the worst types of child abuse, who had fought back and beaten the hell out of her abuser, her mother's boyfriend. Later, it would matter some, but this morning, whether Bianca could rebound or shoot a power layup mattered not at all.

CHAPTER 14

Low expectations are just like a drug, an evil, addictive poison.

Bianca wished aloud that she could watch Stevie compete at the State Championship meet, so rather than attend the home football game, Morgan and Gloria drove Bianca, Rosa, and Molly to Denver to cheer for Stevie. The last Saturday in October had dawned cold in Oro Hills, but cool and bright on the Front Range, excellent running conditions. As the Discovery League champion, Stevie received a favored position at the start and was the tiniest girl on the first line. She started out fast in the 5k run and stayed with the lead group for the entire race. With two hundred meters to the tape, it became a sprint between three courageous runners, and ended in a photo finish. Stevie finished second by less than two-tenths of a second and won the silver medal. After the medal ceremony, she received permission from her coach to ride with Morgan and the girls to Colorado Springs where the volleyball districts were being held.

Oro Hills, as the eighth seed, went up against Academy Prep, who had several players on the squad who also competed in basketball. The match was quick and lopsided. In the second game, Stephanie Miles sat out with an icepack on her left knee. Morgan watched as Academy Prep walked through the congratulatory line with Oro Hills. They showed little respect for Elena and Izzy and Cindy and Penny and their team-mates; no words of encouragement or taps on the shoulder, just the feeble high-five with stationary hands held at head level. They didn't give Oro Hills a second thought.

With this day over, the fall sports ended for Oro Hills' girls. One young Miner brought glory to the Gold and Brown, a second-place finish in cross-country, but the teams had struggled mightily. Morgan thought about this as he drove home. The work Molly and Bianca had put in all summer was now going to be displayed, put up for review. Morgan hoped he hadn't over-valued their ability, after all, he had never coached girls. He didn't know their stamina over the course of a season, and the style of play he envisioned would require tremendous conditioning. The helter-skelter pace with sixteen-year-old girls at high altitude. His crew had won one-third of their summer games against mostly junior varsity competition, albeit quality JVs, but how would it transfer when the opposition was being coached to handle specific situations? So much would depend on Molly; was he being unrealistic about her talents? And Bianca. A mature exterior masking a fragile core. Stevie would be a terrific on-ball defender; she had proven that, but her offensive skills were limited. Izzy was another key, and much would depend on whether her driveway shooting skills would transfer to the hardwood. She would be asked to shoot a half-dozen threes each game and make one or two, but they all had to look like they had a chance to go in. Morgan smiled. Izzy was no head case; she simply listened to his instructions and went out and did what was asked--and then smiled with excitement. The other girls were of junior varsity quality, but unless the transfer gods smiled on Oro Hills, Elena and Cindy and Penny and Rosa would have to do.

Morgan remembered Molly's starting five. *Stephanie Miles at forward.* He recalled a few instances from last season when he watched the varsity, before he became frustrated with their lack of toughness and focus. Stephanie was athletic; she could run and jump and defend, but she was part of the graduating seniors' clique and not tied in with this summer's core of girls. Still, having another five-eleven player on the court with Bianca, especially one with Stephanie's experience and potential, could yield tremendous benefits to the four juniors who would most likely be starting.

§

Monday's open gym was busy. All eight girls who played together in the summer attended along with a handful of other volleyball players. Alondra came with Elena. Stephanie Miles was a no-show, but that was expected, since her knee deserved a few weeks of rest. Molly organized a three-on-three game, but Izzy and Elena chose not to play; instead, they paired up to practice shooting, to shake off the rust. Unlike the open gyms Morgan ran in Lakewood with boys, this one was organized and efficient. There wasn't a full-court game with the winners holding the court all evening with a loaded team and a couple dozen boys standing along the wall waiting to get in. Morgan's young assistants often played in those pick-up games, and he imagined Gloria playing if a full-court game broke out, but it never did. Morgan watched Molly work with Stevie on her layups: "One-two-up. One-two-up. You can do this. Try it again."

§

The Oro Hills football team traveled beyond Denver for its final game, the longest road trip of the year. It was just as well, as the depleted roster numbered fewer than the twenty-two boys needed to field a complete offense and defense to practice against. Despite early season optimism, they had won only one game; injuries and eligibility had taken their toll. The boys' rest between seasons would be just one week, and the basketball coach told them he expected them to be at open gym on Monday, to get a little shooting in before tryouts. *No rest for the weary.*

Morgan had met the boys basketball coach three seasons earlier, when he and Andrea moved to Oro Hills. Morgan went to the games and found much to appreciate. The coach did the most important thing coaches need to do; he got his boys to play hard. Andrea attended with Morgan that first year, but found the games not so interesting without knowing the players or watching her husband standing in front of the bench. She did remark to Morgan that the young coach reminded her of him when he was young, always yelling and battling with the officials, kicking his heal against the bleachers, showing visible signs of frustration. She liked that Morgan matured and settled down over the years. He still stood most of the game, but he was calm. He hadn't received a technical over the last sixteen years of his career.

What did frustrate Morgan when he watched the boys games were the extraordinary number of turnovers committed by the team without the coach seeming to care. Wild passes especially. The turnover count numbered in the thirties and often hit forty. *Thirty possessions without a shot; can't win a game that way*, and they seldom did. The boys did storm the offensive glass though, and Morgan liked that. He had never approached the boys coach about helping or with suggestions during his three years in Oro Hills. He introduced himself that first year and stepped away.

To accommodate the boys and their short pre-season, Morgan moved his open gym up an hour allowing the boys to play as long as they wanted and not have to share the gym with his girls. The boys would also have access to the gym Monday through Thursday, and both the boys and girls would officially begin on Saturday; the girls in the morning and the boys in the afternoon. The boys coach said he might have to cut a few seniors to make room for some talented sophomores, youngsters, Morgan knew, who might be more skilled than those seniors, but who would not help the team win a single varsity game this season. At the 5A level, that philosophy might have some merit, but in small schools, kids who had been in the program were of value for the current year. They were a part of the fabric. Let the freshmen and sophomores have success on the JV team rather than learn the culture of losing. Quit building for the next season every season.

Morgan smiled at the number of times he had had this philosophical discussion with his colleagues at clinics and team camps. How many seniors do you keep; do you include the most talented sophomore on the varsity; if a junior isn't playing on the varsity, should you cut him? Now, thought Morgan, at Oro Hills in 1995, operating under a one-D policy and a previous losing season, seniors should be kept at all costs. Regardless of what the boys coach decided, Morgan would not be cutting any girls. If, by some strange occurrence, more girls tried out than the school had uniforms, he would get the Matrons to buy extras. He loved Queenie and Mercedes more and more. One of his primary goals for the season would be to not forfeit a single JV game. In all his previous years of coaching, this concept never entered his thinking.

Morgan returned home on Wednesday after open gym excited to begin this new chapter. He sat with Andrea on the couch. "This should prove interesting," he said.

Andrea placed a bookmark in her novel and set it on the end table. "Do you have everything you need?" Morgan nodded. "What about managers and stat girls? A film person?"

Morgan dropped his head on the back of the couch and let out a small laugh. "Let me guess. The book club?"

Andrea smiled. "We thought we might show up on Saturday morning to get the lay of the land. For away games we'll go in my van. I'll be the designated driver. We might not all make it every game, but we'll make sure it's all covered. I'll teach them what they need to know, but you may need to help me with that at the beginning. I'm a little out of practice." She paused. "Your entourage."

§

Since Molly, Bianca, and Rosa rode to the gym with Coach Summitt, they were there with Gloria at eight on Saturday. Practice was scheduled to begin at nine-thirty, but Morgan wanted everything to be ready. The floor swept, two ragged nets replaced, a sign-up table in place, the balls out. The first day of a first-class program. A first impression. The two coaches would sit at the tables and sign the girls in. Andrea would write each girl's name on athletic tape and affix it to her shirt front. Mitzi would check to ensure the girls were adequately dressed, and Mercedes and Queenie would weigh and measure each one and make her feel comfortable, especially the freshmen and sophomores. Morgan mused that he would be the only male in the gym surrounded by nearly thirty girls and women. Indeed, this would be a new experience.

Morgan and Gloria hoped to get eighteen girls to come out on Saturday. The weather cooperated and twenty-one girls were in the gym by nine-thirty: seven freshmen, six sophomores, six juniors, but just two seniors. The two seniors were Elena and Sofia, who brought her paperwork with her, including a note from her mother saying Sofia had been cleared by her doctor from her previous condition. Not surprising to Morgan, Stephanie Miles was a no-show, although it disappointed Molly, and Elena told Coach that Stephanie's knee was still bothering her, and she might come out later if it felt better.

When every girl was checked in, Coach Summitt gathered them all on the bleachers for introductions. "I want to thank all of you for being here this morning. This is not a tryout, but our first practice day. No one will be cut from the team regardless of your skill level. If you want to be a part of this program and commit to making every practice, you will be on one of the teams." Morgan surveyed the girls to check for understanding. They looked so young to him, younger than the boys of his past. He realized some of the girls were only fourteen and most did not have their driver's license. "Before I go on, I want to introduce the women here who helped this morning. You'll be seeing lots of them because they're going to keep statistics for our games. They have already worked behind the scenes to get this program rolling." He did not elaborate, but he made each lady stand when he said her name. When he announced Queenie, she stood and said, "Y'all are a mismatched group of darlins, so when Coach finishes talking, line up over here, so we can hand out practice jerseys to y'all."

Morgan hadn't noticed the large box behind the table. Now he glanced at his wife and shook his head. He turned back to the girls in the bleachers. "For those of you who haven't met Ms. Fawkes, she is your school's nurse and she will be the junior varsity coach and my right-hand man this season."

"Woman!" yelled Molly with a smile.

"Right. Woman." Morgan nodded to Molly. "Now, starting on the top row, I want each of you to stand and tell us your name. Speak clearly because I'm a bit hard-of-hearing." When this was done, Morgan said, "Line up to get a practice jersey and then get a partner and a ball. Just slip the jersey over whatever you're wearing." As the girls climbed out of the stands, Morgan went over to his wife to ask about the jerseys.

Andrea smiled. "I remember that you delayed handing out practice gear until after cuts, but you just said there would be no cuts, that this was the first practice day, so we ladies thought they needed to start out looking like a team. We had a little cash in our account, so we decided 'what the heck.'"

Morgan leaned in and kissed his wife on the cheek. "Thank you. Pass that on to the club." He turned, strode to the center of the court, checked to see that each girl had a ball, looked to Gloria, and started the first drill of the first practice. Simple ball-handling skills: around the back, around the head, between the legs, and then tossing the ball above the head and catching it. "Again." Balls were dropped, balls of varying quality, half new and half very worn, and Gloria moved mostly around the younger kids. Both coaches looked at the name tags trying to learn names and giving comments to each girl. Next, full-court dribbling. Morgan directed his seniors and juniors, plus Cindy and Penny, on one side of the court with the sophomores and freshmen on the other. Down and back. Right hand down, left hand back.

He blew his whistle. "When either Coach Gloria or I blow the whistle, it means stop what you're doing and hold the ball. Our next drill will be a passing drill. Pair up with a girl in the opposite line with one ball. Get one of the good ones for this drill. Get twelve feet apart and we'll pass to each other." Coach Gloria partnered with the twenty-first girl, a lanky freshman, and Morgan gave instructions. "The first passes will be two-handed chest passes. Throw it hard and try to hit your partner in the chest." Morgan called over Elena and the two of them passed the ball back and forth. "If you're receiving the pass, put your hands up like this." He held up both hands in front of his chest. "We call this 'target hands,' and it gives your partner a target. Remember, throw your passes hard."

At the water break, Gloria met with Morgan at center court. "Gawd, these young ones are raw," said Gloria. "You may need to give me Cindy and Penny just to get a shot."

Morgan laughed. "That would mask your teaching skills." He smiled at his rookie coach. "And it probably won't happen. If we're going to play like I hope to, I'll need a full ten. Having Alondra and Sofia out may just allow it to happen, but we'll see."

"Sofia looked good. I hope she's okay."

"You're the nurse; you should know. I've talked with her a little, and she seems happy to be here. She did say she's out of shape, but she didn't say it out of frustration. Keep an eye on her," said Morgan. "Okay, water break's over," he said with an elevated voice. "I want the seniors and juniors down here with me and the sophomores and freshmen with Coach Gloria. We'll work on layups and close-in shooting." Morgan intentionally sent Cindy and Penny with Gloria to be with their classmates and for the purpose of demonstration. Over the summer both girls improved their shooting skills, and working with Gloria, they could show leadership skills. Morgan wondered if the number of quarters a player could play had changed. *Was it per night or over the course of the season?*

Gloria was on her own to teach shooting techniques to the girls on her end of the court, while Morgan's group moved through more advanced drills. He turned and watched the younger girls at times. A few of Gloria's players showed some promise, but most were unskilled. None of them revealed abilities that might place them on the varsity, but all of them seemed to be having fun and enjoying their friends. Her JVs would not be able to play the same style as his varsity, wouldn't be able to shoot three point shots and rebound the long miss, but their defensive pressure would mimic the varsity, Gloria would be teaching basic skills all season. The second hour passed quickly, and Morgan called the girls to the bleachers for closing remarks,

"How many of you attended every practice last year?" asked Morgan. Only Molly raised her hand.

"We were allowed one free miss every other week," said Elena.

Morgan nodded. "At the beginning of today's practice, I said you couldn't miss practice. Coach Gloria reminded me that what I meant was you couldn't miss practice without a valid excuse. If you're sick or have a doctor's appointment or you're out of town, just call the school and tell them. They'll pass it on to me. But no *free* misses this year." He looked at his team for agreement. "We want you on the team for the whole season." He paused. "Okay, great job this morning. We have a whole range of abilities here, don't we? Some of you freshmen and sophomores need to understand that the older girls have been playing longer and really put in some quality time this summer and fall. They improved a lot. You can do the same." Morgan turned to Gloria.

"As you found out this morning, I can get a little vocal in my excitement, and I am excited to be working with you. This is my first year coaching, so I'll make lots of mistakes, so bear with me. Just know that I will always be prepared for practice, that I will always have notes. Also, you can visit me during school in the nurse's office. If you have a question, or a problem, or if you just want to talk basketball or girl stuff, come see me." She stepped back to give Morgan the last word.

"We'll get you lockers next week, but for now, take your jerseys home with you and bring them back Monday. If any of you are having grade problems, take care of them now. I'll be checking grades in a couple of weeks. Remember, one D makes you ineligible for the following week. If you have never played sports before this basketball season, you may not understand, so on Monday, Mr. Vincent, the activities director, will be in to explain the policy. Finally, I want you all to understand this. The twenty-one of us are one team, not two separate teams. Take care of each other. Understand." He looked over this team and then called them to the floor for a hand stack. "Elena, Sofia. What do we say?"

"One, two, three, Miners!"

Several of the girls passed the ladies sitting at the table and thanked them for coming. As Morgan watched, he felt a tug at his shirt. It was Alondra.

"Coach, I won't be able to come every day, so I probably need to quit now." She said this quietly and apologetically, holding out her jersey for him to take.

Morgan put his hand around her shoulders. "No, I understand your situation. Your friends want you to be a part of the team; they have your back. You come when you can, and if you need to leave early, go. Keep me informed. I think your little girl would want her mother to play, to get everything out of high school she can, so she can become the best mother she can. We'll work it out." Morgan handed her back the jersey. "See you on Monday."

At the same time, Gloria was talking with Sofia, who assured her she was physically okay. Sofia told the nurse there were days, however, when she felt depressed, but she would still come to practice if she attended school. Morgan walked slowly over to them and said, "I'm glad you came out. You're going to be a big part of this team." He patted her shoulder when he finished.

Molly asked when Morgan was going to leave, and that she still wanted to shoot some more. He told her that he wanted to go over a few things with Gloria, so she could shoot. Four other girls joined Molly.

"Well," asked Morgan, "what do you think, Coach?"

§

"Ten girls with some basketball talent," Morgan said while his wife fixed dinner. "Well, eight plus Rosa and Alondra. Having Sofia will allow me to try what I've been hoping to do."

"My club ladies had fun. They were impressed with the girls." She tapped his plate with her fork. "Dinner time, dear."

Morgan blinked and smiled. "It was a good day."

§

135

Molly sat in the dark and watched Coach Morgan at his kitchen nook. She wanted so much to sit with them for dinner and discuss the team, but her mother had warned her about taking away his private hours. Molly never felt as if Morgan was bothered by her company; just the opposite. She understood the slow pace of the first practice; it was necessary, but she hoped Coach would divide the team on Monday and start preparing for the first game. Three weeks from today, she thought, twenty-one days. It occurred to her that she didn't know who the opponent was.

Because she shared a bedroom with her brother, she often slept on the couch. As she fluffed her pillow and laid out a blanket, she could still see across the street. Molly thought about her luck as she stretched out, but something Mrs. Summitt had said crossed her mind. "It's not so much Morgan who's providing a lifeline, my dear. It's you."

CHAPTER 15

Practices will be difficult, competitive, and team building. Always!

One hour and forty-five minutes for practice, the first fifteen involved all twenty-one girls on Day Two. Team building. Then Morgan broke the squads up, something he seldom did when he coached boys, but the disparity between the talents of the top players and bottom players was so great that it would do no good for them to be working on the same drills. Gloria had asked for time for her own team and took to the skills development with glee. Pivoting, passing and catching a basketball, layups, set shots. The most basic of abilities that most high school programs develop in feeder programs, but Gloria needed to teach these while teaching her girls the basics of the game itself. Show how things worked in a five-on-five situation, then break it down into one-on-one, two-on-two, and three-on-three situations. The whole-part method. Each night when practice ended, Coach Gloria handed her junior varsity girls one page of terms and diagrams, homework for the next practice. Just as Morgan's ten were his girls, the bottom eleven were her girls. Morgan's girls often referred to him as the OFG, the Old Fart Grampa. Now, Gloria's girls began calling her Mama Gloria. Thirty-years-old and the mother of eleven.

After those first fifteen minutes of group skill work--zig-zag, paired passing, close-outs, and block-outs--Coach Summitt divided the squad and talked with his ten girls. "Well, this is who we go into battle with now." He paused after this sentence and continued to do this after each thought to allow his meaning to be absorbed. "Take ownership of this team, of your part of our success. Own our practices. Own the sweat, the aches, the conditioning. You're going to find that I'm more demanding now than I was during the summer. I won't yell, but I may get a little pointed in my corrections, especially if you make the same mistakes over and over. I'm going to insist on consistent effort, even when you get tired, especially when you get tired. I don't think I need to dwell on this next point because you all seem to get along well, but here, in this gym, in the locker room, on the bus, before and after games, you are family. You are sisters. And families take care of each other. Ownership." He waited. Each girl seemed to like what he had just said. He knew Molly and Bianca and Rosa and Izzy bought in long before now, but the subtle head nods of the others became evident. He began again. "I'm going to teach you to play a style of game no one else in the conference plays, that our town hasn't seen. It won't come easy, but because we have such good team quickness, we need to utilize it. As they say, 'Play to your strengths.' You taught me so much this summer, things this old man needed to learn about girls and what you were capable of doing. Not once was I ever disappointed in any of you. I expect that to continue." His pause was longer this time. What he wanted was for his girls to see his determination and his care. "I've got your back now, too. Any questions?"

He didn't expect any, so he began the first practice with the Oro Hills varsity girls. "Reach down with both hands and feel the floor. Get used to how it feels. It's hard and falling on it can hurt, but I'm going to demand that we *own* the floor. You are no longer *girl* basketball players; you are simply basketball players." Coach Summitt began this practice as he had his last twenty. Capturing loose balls. "Partner up with a ball. Roll it out in front of your partner, and she has to dive on the floor to get it, to secure it. It will hurt but do it anyway. Don't roll over when you get it, because that's a travel. Once your partner gets it, run to her side so she can flip it to you. Again!" After each girl had captured five loose balls, he brought them together. "No broken bones?" he asked with a grin. "There will be so many loose balls over the course of the season. The team that *gets on the floor* will have the advantage. Don't just bend over to pick it up. *Get on the floor!*" On the other end of the gym, the junior varsity practiced pivoting.

Morgan went to the second drill. "Okay, bend over and touch the floor again. Does it feel any different?" He smiled. "Now, we learn to take charges." First, the girls got into a defensive stance and fell back on the floor. "Again." Then, he had them cross their arms across their chest and then fall. They progressed to having a teammate give them a little shove to push them down. Stevie's skinny tailbone made the loudest noise. "You okay, Champ?" She scrunched her face and rubbed her butt, but said she was fine. "Atta girl!" Then to the entire group, "Taking a charge is a momentum booster. It's big, and we have to acknowledge it with great enthusiasm. Bianca will take this next charge by herself, but when she hits the floor, the rest of you will run to her and help her up." She did, they did, and Morgan clapped loudly, saying, "Way to go, Bianca!"

"Okay, layups!"

The driveway time over the summer paid dividends, and all the girls made some right-hand shots. On the left side, most of the girls struggled. "Do it right; get the technique correct first." In the ten rounds, never once did the team make more than four layups. "We'll keep at it every day. It'll come."

The next shooting drill was "Bounce-powers." A quick demonstration and then he sent them to the three baskets on their side of the gym. "Keep the ball high; be quick off your feet; use your right hand; high off the glass." The girls were much more accurate on this shot. Bianca was especially good after a summer of dedicated practice to this shot. Stevie, after missing every left-handed layup, made several of these shots. "Shoot from both sides of the rim." None of this was new to any of the girls; they had all played before, and eight of them had spent considerable time on his driveway over the summer. Morgan knew those hours would pay off as the season progressed. While his squad worked on power layups, he walked to the other end to help Gloria teach layups.

"I've got a handful who can play a little, but the other six are just beginners," said Gloria. "They're eager though. We'll be fine."

The next drill was a four-on-four shell drill, a drill that worked on both passing and defensive footwork, a conceptual drill that began the process of teaching help defense. To the defense Morgan instructed, "Jump to the ball. Put a hand in the passing lane. Help on the back side; get both feet in the paint." To the offense, he said, "Pass away from the defense. Throw it hard. Target hands. Molly, what's the axiom?"

"Every drill's a passing drill, Coach!"

"Good." The girls had never used this drill in their practices, so it was teaching intensive, but they were eager to get it right; there was no resistance. Two girls were always out of this drill, and when Sofia was out and standing next to him, he asked her how she felt. She assured him she was fine. The drill took a little longer than he had planned, but Morgan felt the girls were improving while they did it. The last drill was a full-court dummy drill, no defense, five-on-oh. Molly's group had run this most of the summer and understood positioning. Izzy's shot bounced long into the hands of Bianca, who put it back up for a score. Only Cindy and Penny had a good understanding of the movements in the second group, but everyone finally got to their assigned lanes. Cindy passed ahead to Sofia who shot an air ball. Penny rebounded it and put it back in on the follow. Morgan stopped the play with the girls in place. "Quick shot, but good rebounding position. Sofia, you don't have to make it; you just have to shoot it if you're open. That's your job. We'll miss a lot more than we make, but that's okay. If your teammates know you're going to shoot, they'll be more aggressive to the glass to get the rebound. If you hesitate, they will too, and the defense will gain an advantage. We don't want that."

Morgan took his girls back to their end, giving Gloria back her side of the gym. To end the practice, he had Molly and Cindy passing from the top to the wings to Izzy, Elena, Sofia, Stevie, and Rosa, who all shot the three. Bianca, Penny, and Alondra stationed themselves under the basket to rebound and shoot a follow power shot. The shooters made very few threes, giving the bigs plenty of practice on their most important shot. Passing, footwork, shooting technique. "Details, girls. Be conscious of form. Hands up rebounders. Be quick. Bounce, bounce!"

Morgan ended the practice precisely at five-thirty and sent the girls to the end of the gym where Kane Vincent waited to talk about the eligibility rules. Morgan had them sit and listen, but Molly stood next to her coach, her shoulder bumped up against his forearm. She had enjoyed every minute of practice.

§

By Friday the girls were dragging, but Morgan scheduled a morning practice for Saturday. "Lots of conceptual stuff, no running, just close-in shots, and catered lunch." The girls cheered. "The ladies who were here last Saturday plus a couple of others will be serving, so bring your appetite. No let-down today. Fight through your fatigue." Despite Morgan's directive, the girls did struggle, with the exception of Stevie, Bianca, and Molly. Alondra was especially drained, so Morgan had her sit out of several drills.

Bianca reminded Coach of her responsibilities and her size. "She's really trying, Coach. I'll take her reps, okay."

§

That night, Molly invited several friends to her house for a sleepover. All her friends were basketball players these days, and she, Bianca, and Rosa spent inordinate amounts of time together. The three of them were joined by Sofia, Stevie, Izzy, and Elena.

"Have you guys noticed how, for Coach, Izzy and Elena become one name?" said Stevie. *IzzyandElena.* The group giggled some more.

Elena pretended seriousness. "Yeah, and it should be *Elena* first. I'm older." Izzy threw a pillow at her cousin, hitting Elena on the shoulder.

When the laughing ceased, Molly said, "Coach didn't allow us to get away with any shortcuts or half efforts. If one of us didn't touch a line, he made us all run again. All of us, all the time. So different from last year. It was hard, but I love it."

"Are you guys as tired as me?" asked Rosa. "I don't know if I ever worked so hard in my life."

"I know," said Sofia. "Last year with Coach Abby, we'd run sprints and suicides, but then stand around a lot during drills. OFG has us moving all the time, even when we shoot free throws. We rebound or run, but this is probably just what I needed after my . . ." She paused, not knowing what to call her pregnancy.

Sitting on the floor next to her, Bianca reached over and touched her forearm. "We all know, Sofia, so you can say it. I think it's amazing you've kept up." Sofia nodded and pursed her lips, and Bianca asked, "Do you hurt anywhere?"

Sofia shook her head. "No, just here," and she put her hand over her heart. The girls remained silent for a moment, allowing Sofia to continue, if she wanted. "It's my own fault. First, I get pregnant, and then I don't go to the doctor except the one time. We don't have insurance for that."

"All our moms give us *the talk,* but we don't listen," said Molly. "Stay out of the back seat, they say."

"In this case it was the front seat," said Sofia. She lifted her head and showed a smile. The others laughed a little.

"You know who ought to be here listening to this talk?" asked Izzy. "Penny. She's always out with Benny, and we all know what Benny wants."

The pack groaned.

Molly's mother brought in two bowls of popcorn and sat down. "What are you girls talking about now?" she asked.

"Just basketball, mom. You wouldn't be interested," said Molly.

Bianca still had her hand on Sofia's arm. She knew Sofia's condition could have been her own and was thankful she no longer lived in New Mexico with her mother. She wondered if the other girls were at risk. She knew Rosa wasn't, and she was pretty sure Izzy was smart. Probably Molly too, but Bianca didn't know enough about Stevie and Elena. Both had boyfriends, and high school boyfriends were always digging. Still, she thought, someday she'd like to have a high school boyfriend instead of the men who had always been around her.

§

Just after midnight Morgan got out of bed, put his robe on over his pajamas, and went to the bathroom. Afterwards, he sat at the nook table to jot down notes about the first week of practice. He always had trouble falling asleep again once he was awake in the middle of the night, but before this new coaching gig, he would at least go to bed. He had always been a stat guy, team stats for the most part, and now he was trying to recall how many possessions his old teams used to have per game. Those were up-tempo teams, and he thought they averaged over eighty, or about twenty per quarter. Last year, he counted the number for the girls varsity one game, and they had ten to twelve, or a total of forty-five. Math. If we had seventy-five possessions and made twenty turnovers, that would mean we took fifty-five first shots. Who would be taking those shots? He laughed quietly. *Could Molly take forty of them? Good joke, Coach.* He picked up the pen and slid the legal pad over to himself. Stevie might be able to get eight or ten layups on steals and fast breaks. Izzy will be the first option for the quick three, so maybe eight or ten shots. Elena a handful. Sofia will play at least three positions, so eight. Bianca? If we can learn to throw the ball inside, she could get ten-plus. That would be ideal, and she could get some foul shots. He totaled the number. Even with the other four girls taking four or five shots, that would leave Molly with twenty. Twenty first shots. The league might not expect that the first go-round, and some of those coaches will make adjustments. But, so will I.

On Point

§

"Look," said Stevie. "OFG is sitting in his kitchen." The girls had turned off the lights at midnight, but no one was sleeping.

"What's he doing?" asked Sofia.

"Basketball," answered Molly and Bianca simultaneously.

"We ought to go over and surprise him," said Elena. The girls squealed at her suggestion.

The seven girls put on coats over their pajamas, their boots and stocking caps, quietly snuck out the front door, and ran across the street. Morgan saw them coming and had the front door open with his finger over his lips. For an hour, they talked basketball. Spacing. Help and recover. Live-ball turnovers. Dead-ball turnovers. When to use timeouts. Bench decorum. The girls stayed until one, until Molly's mother came over to take them back.

§

Morgan left at nine on Sunday for Denver to visit Kathy. Andrea went to church and then came home to make a vegetable soup. Morgan would return around dinner. Molly came over just after noon to apologize for last night; she said her mom made her.

"Coach was awake, and we could see him at the table, so we snuck over. I don't think we bothered him at all. The hard part, Mrs. Summitt, was not making too much noise. I hope we didn't wake you up," said Molly.

"It's okay. He enjoyed having you over. When he was teaching, we used to have his AP history class come over on the night before the exam to cram and practice. I think this was good for him." She smiled. "We won't make it a habit, but tell your mother it was fine."

"Where is Coach? Did he go to Denver today?" asked Molly.

"Yes, he got up early and headed down to see our daughter. I'm glad the weather is good."

Molly waited. Then, "Mrs. Summitt, can I ask you something?" Andrea nodded. "It's about your daughter. How come you don't go with Coach to see her? You don't have to tell me if you don't want to."

Andrea took in a deep breath. "Come sit down and have something to drink. Coffee?" Molly shook her head no. "I'll give you the short version, but again, this is between you and me." She poured Molly a glass of milk

143

and herself another cup of coffee, and then slid into the nook on the opposite side from Molly. "Kathy blames me for being in jail. Whenever I go see her, she yells at me, and the visit ends. With Morgan, she stays calm. She began using drugs in high school, and it was very hard on us. She stopped being my little girl and became a stubborn, angry, unrecognizable girl. We got her counseling, but it didn't work. We tried everything, but we couldn't get her to stop. It was difficult for Morgan because all his colleagues knew, as did the students at school. It was hard for her brother too. The police picked her up a couple of times, but because we were an upstanding family in Jefferson County, they gave her breaks. Maybe they were giving Morgan and me the breaks, but eventually, she began stealing to support her habit. She stole some of our things and sold them. That's when I went to the police and had her arrested. It was the hardest thing I ever did." Andrea breathed deeply again and looked directly into Molly's eyes. "Too much information?" Molly gave a slight head shake but remained quiet. Andrea started to speak, but stopped, realizing that Molly was processing her earlier words. She reached across the table and took Molly's hands in hers.

"My mom thinks I butt in in places I shouldn't. I was just curious. I'm sorry if I shouldn't have."

Andrea squeezed Molly's hands. "Don't apologize; I wouldn't have told you if a part of me didn't want to let it out. You've become pretty important to us. I hope in time Kathy will forgive me, but at least she's sober now and safe. There were days when we didn't know where she was, and she wasn't safe."

"You miss her, don't you?" said Molly.

"I miss the little girl, but not the druggie she became. Morgan, I think, has been her rock, and he handles it very well. I think because of the stress on me he retired a little earlier than he would have liked. He doesn't say so, but you and the girls have been absolutely wonderful for his spirits."

"You like us too, don't you?"

Andrea nodded and welled up. "More than you know."

CHAPTER 16

I'm not a big believer in magic, but I do believe in magical.

It was an excellent first week of practice. Over twenty girls came out for the team, and one week later, they were all in. The varsity and junior varsity had determined themselves, and every girl seemed happy. Rosa told Coach Summitt that if he wanted her on the JVs, she would accept that, but he said she was right where she belonged. After the girls had discussed teen sex, especially regarding Penny, Bianca vowed to stop calling her "Big Skinny" and start calling her "Big Beautiful." "I'm still going to push her around to toughen her up, though." Monday of the second week, November 20, brought continued enthusiasm. Practice began at 6:00, the late practice, since the boys went after school. Eleven practices before the first game.

Coach Morgan scrimmaged his squad for the first time on Monday. The varsity went five-on-five against itself and then the junior varsity tried it. Morgan told Gloria he was not going to allow the varsity to beat up on the younger kids until after Christmas, if then. The disparity between the two was simply too great. Both scrimmages were ragged, but it was a necessary step. While the JVs scrimmaged, Morgan debriefed his ten girls about their play. Mostly, he was complimentary, but he was pointed about his pet peeve. "You try to block out every time. No excuses. Maybe you'll miss or she'll out-quick you or the ball will bounce funny, but when the shot goes up, you look for your player." He smiled. There were other concerns that he addressed. "Middle penetration with the dribble is not acceptable. I know it's hard but keep trying. Push her outside and down, and then don't let the ball go back across the mid-line." He spoke directly to Stevie. "I'm giving you a very difficult task, Stevie. You'll always be guarding their best ball-handler, and I want you to give her fits, but inside the three point line, you'll need to adjust slightly. You can do it."

He turned to Izzy. "Sofia blocked your shot early on in the scrimmage, so you stopped shooting. You can't do that. You might have the softest heart and gentlest spirit out here, but when you leave the locker room, you have the spirit of the cheetah. Your job is to shoot that wing three. I didn't say anything about making them; I said shoot them. You shoot; Bianca or Penny or Sofia will do her thing."

"Coach, can I say something?" asked Bianca after raising her hand. Morgan nodded. "This is still a lot of fun."

Morgan pretended disgust. "Then, I guess I'm not doing my job well enough. We'll run extra tonight," but he didn't fool anyone.

§

Monday night, it began to snow. Andrea sat with Morgan as he ate a reheated dinner and told him of her talk with Molly. "She's an insightful girl. Does she ask you about her teammates?"

"She does, mostly about their basketball abilities, about what she should do with them during games. I talked to the girls about our scrimmage at the end of practice, pointing out little things they did, but very specific. Molly wanted to know if my comments to Izzy, who's such a little sweetheart, if my comments to her might hurt her feelings. I don't think they did, but it's nice to see Molly looking out for her teammates. She's done that before."

Andrea nodded her head. "The girls came over here during the summer because of her urging, didn't they?"

"Yes, but I'd like to think I had something to do with that, mostly that I was just relaxed and a teacher. I think not being their coach or even having an idea that I might be, relaxed me. I had no skin in the game, so to speak. Oh, by the way, the girls told me that Stephanie Miles, the really good volleyball player, isn't coming out for the team. I never thought she was; don't know why. Just a hunch."

"Did she give a reason?" asked Andrea.

"Several. Her knee. Tired and wanted a break. That Thulen wasn't the coach, and he should have been. Probably all true. Funny, in all this time, she and I never talked. I haven't thought much about what the team would look like with her in the lineup."

"Will that hurt?" asked Andrea.

"Good athletes are always a good thing, but if she's not into it, it's better she's not a part of this. The girls I have are a close-knit group. That chemistry is remarkable. They are of one heart, even though they don't realize yet where their journey will take them." His head movement affirmed his words. "Besides, we have a point guard, a point defender, and a stallion inside. What else can an old coach ask for?"

§

Kane Vincent called Morgan on Tuesday morning to see if he was available after lunch for a short discussion about his first week. Second lunch ended at 12:45, so Morgan arrived at 1:00. He stopped in at the attendance office and found out that four girls called in because of the weather. Alondra was one of those, but Morgan understood. He then went to the nurse's office, but Gloria was treating a student, so he went to the main office for his meeting with Kane.

"Hey, Coach. Pretty nasty out there," said Kane.

"Not getting any better either. I've got four girls out so far, and I suspect a few more might not make it back for the six o'clock practice. That's why I like the after school block; if they're at school, they make it to practice. What news do you have for me?"

Kane shook his head slightly. "Had a brief meeting with the boss early this morning. Evidently, there's some concern about Bianca's transfer eligibility. It's probably nothing, but Lowell wants me to look into it, just to make sure. I called CACA, but they haven't returned my call."

"Who would be wondering?" asked Morgan. "Who knows or even cares if she's playing basketball?" He paused, looking to Kane for a reason that wasn't obvious. When Kane hesitated, Morgan said, "Is this concern coming from inside our own building, from a staff member? I hope no one here is petty enough to use a student for a gripe against me."

"Lowell didn't say. He just gave me instructions to look into it."

"What's the specific complaint?" asked Morgan.

"The rumor Lowell picked up on was that Bianca isn't living with a legal guardian, and, therefore, none of her records are legal. Maybe she's too old for high school. Do you know who signed off on her physical?"

Morgan ignored the question. "Who cares? You know why she's here."

"Easy, Coach. Let's wait for a response from CACA before we

over-react. It might be nothing." This was why Kane wanted the meeting, to blunt Morgan's initial anger as he rushed to protect Bianca. "How's Gloria doing?"

Morgan understood Kane's tactic, took a deep breath, and answered. "She was a good hire. You picked a good one for me. She does have that edge you warned me about, but I like it. Curious as hell too. Asks me lots of questions; wants to learn, to understand my methods and philosophy. She called me after I had gone to bed last week to question how I wanted something done on defense. Evidently, she had never played a certain cut the way I want it played. Anyway, she came over to the house after ten-thirty, and we discussed it while Andrea slept. She's trying to do it my way, even though she's not totally convinced I'm right. I like that. She knows her JVs are going to get thumped early, but she stays positive with her girls. I like her."

"That's good to hear. The kids seem to like her around school. She stands by her door during passing periods and walks around during lunch to check on the food the students are eating. Reprimands them in a kind manner if their home lunch is crap. Yeah, that's good to hear. Have you scheduled a parent meeting yet?" asked Kane.

"Yes. This Saturday. Doing it on the weekend rather than an evening. Most of my girls' parents work and wouldn't have the energy to go back out again. If I do it on Saturday, I think more mothers would come."

"Just mothers?" kidded Kane.

"I think only four of the varsity girls have a father at home all the time. You know that."

"Do you want a room to hold it in?" asked Kane.

"No, I'll bring them into the gym. Andrea and her book club women will bring refreshments, and then when I'm done, they can stay and watch some of my practice. It's always worked well with the boys, and I have the one o'clock slot on Saturday."

"One last thing, Coach. You seem to be having too much fun with this. Are your goals realistic?" Kane smiled. "This school needs more of that."

§

Fifteen girls attended practice, nine varsity and six JVs, so Coach altered his plans to stress shooting. Perimeter players focused on set-shot threes, post players on powers, and Molly on pull-up jump shots once she had penetrated into the lane. It was a shot Morgan believed she could get at will. From every distance, for each type of shot, Molly was the best on the team. While Izzy, Elena, Stevie, Cindy, Sofia, and Rosa fired three point shots from the wing and corner, as Bianca and Penny went through the power series of post moves, Molly worked on her own, in her own little world. Spin the ball back to herself, triple up, jab step, crossover dribble into the lane, rise up for a jump shot. Again. From the wing, spin the ball back to herself, triple up on either her right or left foot depending on which side of the court she received the pass, and then execute the shot or the move into the shot as precisely as possible. If she felt a problem, she would call Coach Morgan over to watch her, to correct her, and then she would work to improve. Morgan remembered a former all-state player of his who had similar practice diligence. These players were rare birds, soaring in a sky with no ceiling.

After thirty minutes of concentrated shooting, Morgan ran both squads through full court transition drills. "Girls, there can be no hesitation. We are either on the go on offense or challenging our opponent on defense. There is no in-between time. This is who we are this season. Cheetahs!, remember?" Both he and Gloria clapped and yelled compliments to the girls: loud in praise, gentle in correction. From the summer play, Morgan knew the composition of his team, understood the talents and potential of the eight girls who made up the summer roster. His role-players on the perimeter, especially with the addition of Sofia, were becoming 2A varsity players.

Elena's dogged persistence made her a competent defender, and she was not afraid to guard bigger players. While her shooting average was low, her form had improved. She didn't like to be responsible for the ball; she liked the defensive side better. Off the court, Elena had the highest grade-point average among the team and ranked second in the senior class. Her one D at the beginning of the semester had been an aberration. Her cousin Izzy displayed similar skills, but over the summer on Morgan's driveway, Izzy learned to make shots. Early in the summer games, Izzy would look to Morgan for approval when something happened on the court, but at team camp, that trait vanished. Like Elena, Izzy enjoyed defense, but was not as physical as her cousin. Izzy liked being a young lady, wore makeup to practice, and loved wearing the new, more stylish summer jerseys. Izzy reminded Morgan of Audrey Hepburn in *Breakfast at Tiffany's*, minus the cigarette. Izzy would never smoke.

Stevie, because of her hyperactivity, brought an intangible to the defense. Her quickness was unmatched, even beyond Molly's. No team in the conference had anyone like her, and her hands and mind seemed in sync with her body. It was Stevie's ability to frustrate Molly on his drive-way that convinced Morgan to adopt the defensive style of unrelenting aggression that would become the team's trademark. Because Stevie never tired, seldom fouled, and relished getting under opponents' skin, Oro Hills could be in attack mode all the time. However, that body that was so effective on defense was a liability on offense. One of Morgan's few frustrations over the summer was his inability to teach Stevie how to make layups. Fortunately, Bianca made Stevie shoot hundreds of jump-stop power shots, so after a steal, she could race to the basket and make one kind of shot. And of all the perimeter players, Stevie was the worst three point shooter, both in style and effectiveness.

Cindy was to be Molly's substitute, which meant she would not get many minutes during games. Morgan decided she would play the first half of each junior varsity game and then turn over the point guard responsibilities to a freshman. Cindy was Molly's student and took well to the learning. Cindy and Penny were the two sophomores on the varsity and were clearly not as talented as Molly and Bianca, but because of the summer bonding, they were a part of the team.

Sofia was the unknown. Morgan watched her carefully for any signs of physical fatigue or emotional stress. He hadn't noticed anything, but he was vigilant. A senior, Sofia had a year of varsity experience and might end up as a starter in time, but since she could play multiple positions, he envisioned her as his *sixth girl* early on. His compliment comparing her to John Havlicek was completely lost on Sofia. "Who?" Physically mature, athletic, experienced, and tough, Sofia could be counted on, and it appeared to Morgan that she was at peace on the court. Sofia's game fit into Morgan's vision, both offensively and defensively. She could shoot a little, handle the ball securely on the wing, and rebound. Defensively, she liked to bump, liked the contact, and had good instincts to intercept passes. If she were a boy, she would have made a terrific linebacker in football. During Monday's scrimmage, after she intercepted an errant pass, Morgan had instructed her to "find Molly." Sofia stopped, looked at Coach, giggled, and said, "Those words echo in my ears. During school we walk down the halls and Elena is always saying, 'find Molly.'"

Rosa tried. Morgan corrected, but never scolded. The least skilled girl on the team, Rosa was part of the chemistry. Rosa was the *tenth girl*, but it was an important slot. She knew it and Morgan knew it. And Bianca knew it.

At the close of practice, Morgan handed papers to each of the girls about the parent meeting to be held on Saturday. "Make sure someone in your family attends, so Coach Gloria and I can meet them and let them know about the upcoming season. I will answer any questions they have, and they can stick around and watch practice if they'd like. The book club women and my wife will be serving coffee and doughnuts and other treats." Gloria spoke about the importance of practice even when the weather conditions were terrible. Somehow, every girl would get a ride to and from home to attend. "It's not just so you can practice, it's part of what we're trying to teach you as far as making good on a commitment. Whether it's a job or a class or a church group, if you say you'll be there, you will."

"Coach Gloria, we're here because you guys make this fun," said Elena.

Gloria smiled and stepped into the group. "We want you to be here even when it's not fun. Be here because you said you would be, because your teammates are counting on you."

§

Attendance for the second week of practice improved, but someone from the junior varsity was absent each evening. Still, Gloria proceeded without disruption and understood the difficulty of poor kids getting back to school in bad weather. Several of her players lived in trailer courts where the streets were not plowed regularly. Her top five made it each day and no girl missed every practice. By Saturday the roads were clear, and having a midday practice allowed all the girls to be on the court. For whatever reason, the boys coach decided not to practice on Saturday, leaving the gym available for Morgan's girls all day long.

Eleven girls showed up early. The Mountain Matrons arrived at the same time to set up the food table. Snacks had been replaced by a full lunch: deli meats, cheeses, buns, condiments, chips, and potato salad. Kane stopped by at eleven-thirty to address the parents in a meeting where he wasn't reprimanding one of their children, where he could be perceived in a positive light. Since Lowell Exeter always made Kane the *enforcer*, this would be an opportunity for part of the community to see him wearing a different hat. The attending parents were neither early nor late, but arrived near noon as if they had ridden together on the same bus. Morgan, Gloria, and Kane greeted them as they entered the gym and directed them toward the bleachers where they could take off their coats. Food first. Octavia and Lorna enthusiastically ushered them to the tables where the deli spread lay, handing them paper plates and napkins. Mercedes and Andrea stood at the drink table pouring cups of tea or soda or coffee. Orchestrating the entire affair was Queenie with her loud voice. "Y'all don't be shy now. We have plenty," she would say and then make small talk while she pushed the overwhelmingly female group to the food tables.

At least one member came for nineteen of the players on the squad. Morgan had been warned by Kane that attendance at parent meetings was traditionally low, usually about a third of the team number. On this Saturday every varsity player had a family member there or a woman who represented the family, and nine of the twelve junior varsity girls were represented. Three fathers, two grandmothers, two aunts, and sixteen mothers came along with thirteen younger siblings. And one child. Alondra's mother held her granddaughter. Thanks to Lorna and Octavia, whose businesses dealt with predicting food consumption, there was enough food for everyone, although just barely. When all the parents had returned to the bleachers, Coach Summitt introduced himself and Coach Gloria and began the meeting.

"It's nice to see three men here today. It gets a little daunting for this old man when I'm completely surrounded by women. Thank you all for coming, or as Ms. Roberts says, 'y'all.'" Morgan introduced the Matrons and then turned to Kane to allow him to give the administrative line. His words were brief, complimenting the parents for raising such wonderful kids and reminding them to be mindful of their students' grades as the season progressed. Positions were always open on the parent advisory group and booster club, especially for new officers. Kane then went off script to give a brief account of how he chose Morgan to be the coach.

"I know there have been differing stories about my hiring of Coach Summitt. As many of you know, he lives across the street from Molly Rascon, and she and several of her friends began using his driveway as a practice facility last spring. Because of Coach Abby's sabbatical and Coach Thulen's fulltime job responsibilities, *Mr. Summitt,* at the time, put together a summer basketball program. I had assumed Coach Thulen would slide into the head coaching slot for a year, but what with his job and football coaching duties, he was pretty tied up. A couple of the girls, unbeknownst to Morgan, came and talked to me about having him help. I had to twist his arm a little, but he agreed to step in for a season. Being a boys coach in the Denver area for so many years, some of his views have been good for me as we move forward. I didn't know that by hiring him we would get his wife and her friends to assist the program." Kane asked for questions, but received none, so he turned the meeting back to Morgan.

Coach Summitt re-emphasized the eligibility theme, passed out schedules, talked of parental behavior in the stands, "not that any of you might disagree with a referee's call," he said with a smile, and then forewarned the parents about the style of play his team would be employing. "It will look wild and haphazard at times, especially early in the season, but I'd like to take advantage of our players natural athletic abilities and enthusiasm." He elaborated and then asked for questions.

"Coach," asked Elena's mother, "which athletic abilities are you most referring to?"

"Quickness. This team, based on what I observed this summer and this pre-season, has more quickness than our opponents, and I'd like to tie into that to make games difficult for the teams we will play." There were no more questions.

Practice began with station ball-handling drills, moved to layups, zig-zags, and two-on-oh full-court layups. The team then split into varsity-JVs at opposite ends of the court to work on specifics related to their skill level. Morgan worked heavily on four-on-four and three-on-three drills, always completing the drill with immediate transition, setting up the press or breaking the press to the halfcourt line. On both ends of the court, the girls were vocal. On both ends of the court, the two coaches were positively reinforcing the play of the girls. Around two, the action slowed for the girls to participate in their free throw ladder, a competitive drill that allowed them to get water and a brief rest. The girls recorded their makes, ran their penalties, and practice resumed. While Gloria continued to teach her girls the game itself, Morgan spent lots of time on the physical aspect of the game: box-outs, bumping the cutters, and fighting over screens. The varsity returned to pressing/press-breaking, emphasizing ball pressure for the defense and crisp passing for the offense. The focal point of these drills was the one-on-one matchup between Molly and Stevie, which was always physical and intriguing.

"Be as physical as you can without fouling, Stevie," Morgan instructed.

"How much is that?" she asked.

"It will vary each game depending on who's refereeing. Remember the summer games. You'll have to adjust. Start out a bit more cautiously and ramp up the pressure depending on what you can get away with."

Molly's dribbling skills made it difficult for Stevie to steal the ball, but she was brutal on Cindy when she played the point guard spot. Coach called Molly and Stevie over to him while the other eight girls performed the drill. "I want you to appreciate each other. Watching you battle out there is a treat for me, and it makes you both better. Neither of you will face tougher competition this year than what you're getting in practice, so continue to drive each other crazy. Molly, go in for Cindy. Stevie, get Sofia and tell her to move over to Elena's spot."

Next, the varsity went two-on-one against Bianca and the other bigs. Then, three-on-two. So much of the practice focused on odd-number offense, offense after a turnover or in transition. Morgan's halfcourt offense would rely on Molly to break down the opponents' five-person defense. He knew she would be carrying a heavy load, but he had confidence in her abilities and drive. *Please God*, he thought to himself, *don't let her get injured.*

He called over Bianca and Penny to explain spacing in the press. "Triangles. Stay in the middle into the front court, then sprint to the basket. All the other girls must stay wide, but you run straight to the back-side block and get early rebound position. You know what we're going to do when we beat the press." He reminded them that whenever they rebounded near the basket, they were to shoot it. "Don't pass it back out; go right back up. If you want more shots, get more rebounds." Penny was still soft but getting better. *These two next year would be something. Coach Abby will be lucky.* Bianca was Morgan's third piece in the puzzle. 2A basketball didn't require five great players. Oro Hills certainly didn't have five, but it did have a point guard, a defensive menace, and a good-sized center who was rapidly learning her position and what was required of her.

Morgan got Gloria's attention to see if she was ready for her girls to stop. He blew his whistle and called both groups together. "Great practice! Push yourselves in the suicides. We travel to Gunnison in one week." He put the varsity on the line first and blew his whistle. Stevie was always the first to complete the sprints, then Molly out of sheer determination, followed in no particular order by Bianca, Sofia, Elena, Izzy, and Cindy. Rosa and Penny came next, but Alondra carried extra weight and responsibilities. After the first suicide, she was lagging further and further behind. After Molly finished her third sprint, she went back to Alondra and ran with her, offering her encouragement. For the following two suicides, the entire varsity joined Alondra, and Morgan knew he had a team.

CHAPTER 17

Unselfishness is a gift a great player gives to her teammates.

The second half of Monday's practice involved controlled scrimmages for the purpose of preparing the girls of both squads to feel comfortable with procedures. Free throw alignment, inbounds situations, both for offense and defense, timeouts, bench decorum and support. The varsity's summer experience made this exercise a simple refresher course, but the JVs required repeated reminders and, thus, more court time. When the JVs were on the court, Morgan placed his girls in ballhandling drills and the power series. He remembered how confused several of his girls had been during the summer Jeffco League, so he told Gloria to be patient; they would get it.

"Be glad we play on the road for this first game. Tell your team that they'll make these procedural mistakes, but it's okay. By the way do you know you're the *Get back guy?*"

Gloria made a funny face. "What's that?"

"If an altercation occurs on the court, it's your job to keep anyone from the bench from running out onto the court to join the fracas."

Gloria laughed aloud. "Yeah, like any of our girls would. They're so gentle and nice and delicate. Hell, my team doesn't like any of my contact drills. They flinch anytime one of your girls walks past them in a drill or a scrimmage."

Morgan put his hand on Gloria's shoulder. "I don't think we have much to worry about. Molly . . . and maybe Alondra."

The last twenty minutes of practice for the varsity was set aside for inbounds under plays. In all his years as a boys coach, Morgan had used his point guard to throw the ball in, the team's best passer, the player who saw teammates coming off picks, knew when they would break free. For his girls Morgan knew he wanted Molly to receive that inbounds pass; she was the most secure with the ball. She would get the first look, the first opportunity to score or make a basketball play. So, Elena and Sofia would become the inbounders. *Funny*, he thought to himself, *he hadn't made many adjustments because of gender, basketball was basketball. Roll the ball out and get after it. Compete!*

As the girls grouped around the coaches at the conclusion of practice, Gloria nagged about class tardiness and behavior. "It seems like those of you in Mr. Smith's class are taking advantage of his age and hearing. This is a freshman problem and I want it stopped now. If I have to, I'll stand outside his door between passing periods. You certainly don't want that!"

When Gloria finished, Morgan said, "Your behavior around school reflects on the entire team. We're trying to build something special. Get to class on time and behave." He looked at two freshmen in particular to check on their attention. "Now, tomorrow after practice, we'll pass out uniforms. They aren't last year's; they're brand new. I think you'll like them." There was an excited chatter among the team, but the two girls who seemed most quietly delighted were Molly and Izzy. After they stacked hands, Morgan dismissed them. Four more practices before the first test.

§

The varsity scrimmaged halfcourt against themselves for most of Tuesday's practice. Not only did Coach Summitt like his starters, he was able to pit his team against itself in practice to improve. Rosa was still a liability, but not for lack of effort. Alondra had taken to being more physical against Bianca. "She's so pretty, but that don't mean nothin' on the court. She needs to toughen up."

Alondra's statement was true and untrue at the same time. On the court Bianca was conscientious and athletic, trying to be the center Coach envisioned. On offense she moved to the backside to rebound errant shots. She owned the block on the ball side in practice, and when she received a pass, she used the moves Morgan taught her to get a good shot. On defense she was the last line and the team's principle rebounder. Alondra found out, however, that Bianca avoided unnecessary contact during practice, like a matador avoiding the bull. Off the court, in real life, Morgan doubted if there was anyone on the team or in the school who was tougher than Bianca. Despite a childhood of domestic abuse, she stood erect. She understood who in the world could hurt her or Rosa, and it wasn't another basketball player. Since Molly approached her in the cafeteria last spring, since Bianca knocked on Morgan's door asking about basketball lessons, she had been the model of politeness and sportsmanship. That she didn't knock teammates on their butts when they cut through the lane did not reflect her toughness; it indicated a regard for her teammates and an understanding of things beyond a baseline drop step.

As Tuesday's practice unfolded, Morgan was again reminded of his team's strengths and weaknesses. They were quick and had leadership. It was position oriented in that it had guards, forwards, and centers. If Molly and Bianca and Stevie stayed healthy, Oro Hills could win more than it lost, but if one of those three went down, especially Molly, they would struggle to win any game. Second half success might depend on the talent of opposing coaches: could they alter their defenses to contain Molly? Morgan smiled as he watched Molly. Maybe the bigger question was how quickly Molly would grow in her role.

The new away uniforms were a light brown trimmed in gold and tan with *Oro Hills* written across the chest. The shorts were cut at the knees with stripes on the side. As each girl received her uniform, she went into the locker room to change and then returned to the court. Queenie and Mercedes took photos of each girl individually and of the teams collectively. When both squads were wearing their new uniforms, Queenie snapped photos of all twenty-two players, the JVs kneeling in front and the varsity standing in the rear.

§

Morgan continued to work his girls hard on Wednesday and Thursday, not worrying about tiring them out for Saturday. After all, even Saturday's game was but a practice for the league season. He expressed to Gloria his thoughts about having the first game for these girls on the road, far enough away to avoid much of a fan following. Nothing was expected from either the varsity or the junior varsity, not from the principal, the staff, the student body, or the town. Certainly not from the Discovery League. Oro Hills had few believers, just Morgan and Gloria, maybe

Kane because of Morgan's optimism, and the Mountain Matrons who seemed to care little about winning and losing, just about making the girls gain confidence in themselves. To Morgan, a long bus ride over on a Saturday morning, a varsity and junior varsity game, a team meal, and then a long bus trip home with tired girls was all positive. Team building with the opportunity to discuss with his team, and Gloria with hers, the positives of the game. A captive audience. Morgan would have the first opportunity to evaluate the girls' play, before a parent or peer could spoil the fertile soil in which he and Gloria had planted remarkable seeds.

Friday's practice was devoted to walk-throughs and shooting. "You can do this, because we've been over it. Have confidence. Trust your teammates. If we run into a situation that's new, I'll be there to help. Expect some nerves." At every opportunity Morgan spoke with Bianca and Molly, the two girls with the most information to process. He placed special responsibilities on Molly as his point guard. He often told his coaching colleagues that if he didn't have a remarkable point guard, he couldn't coach, and it was common practice for Jeffco coaches to focus their game plans around corralling Coach Summitt's point guard. Over the years he had experienced numerous strategies to counteract those plans, so he felt confident he could help Molly against those tactics. More importantly, he knew of Molly's skills and tenacity. She would be fine.

Gloria continued to talk to her girls after Morgan excused his, so he walked to their huddle and listened. Hiring Gloria had been a stroke of good fortune. She relayed a similar message to her players. They were prepared as much as possible for a first game. They would make mistakes, but all she was asking was that they play hard. She was proud of them. Then, she told them a personal story.

"Like you, I went to a rather small high school with a poor reputation for girls' sports. As a freshman and a sophomore, we still weren't very good, but because of me and a few of my friends, we turned that around. It took a few years, but my senior season we went to the State Tournament. I wouldn't trade all those years for anything, so I want you to think about starting the turn-around for Oro Hills. You guys and the varsity. I'm excited to be your coach. Tomorrow will be a difficult test against a bigger school. Regardless of the outcome, it's our first step, your first step."

§

Kane Vincent called Morgan at his home on Friday night. "I just got off the phone with Lowell."

"Did he call for my number so he could wish the girls good luck?" joked Morgan.

"Hardly. He's worried about what happens if Bianca plays without a parental permission form. Suggested I tell you to hold her out tomorrow until we get better instructions or direction from CACA."

Morgan breathed heavily into the phone. "Is that what you're ordering me to do? Hold her out?"

Kane's head shake was invisible to Morgan. "Actually, I'm calling to tell you good luck tomorrow. If I can, I may drive over. I'm kind of excited to see your girls play, especially that Bianca Steele girl."

§

While the junior varsity struggled in the preliminary game, in the locker room, Morgan spoke softly to his girls, giving them instructions that they already knew by heart. "On defense, keep pressure on the ball. Stevie has the primary responsibility for that, but when your girl receives a pass, get up in her grill. If you're one pass away, get a full body into the passing lane. Make them beat us back door. Block out. On offense, don't be timid with those threes. We're going to be shot aggressive, and we may not make many, but we're going to shoot them anyway. So, anticipate your teammates' shots and run to rebound. Finally, if you get the ball, but don't have a shot, find Molly. Remember, any time she drives, she'll most likely shoot. Run to rebound." He used the piece of chalk he held in his hand to tap the board where these instructions were already written down. "Captains for this first game will be our two seniors, Elena and Sofia. Any questions?"

From the toilet area, the sound of someone throwing up was heard. "It's Rosa, Coach. She'll be all right. She did it a bunch during the summer too," said Bianca.

"How come I didn't know?" he asked.

"Because you never came into the locker rooms or toilets during the summer. She didn't want us to tell you."

"Are you sure she's okay? Do I need to check on her?"

Rosa emerged from behind a bank of lockers with a wad of paper towels. "I'm fine. Really. I'm done now, so we can play." She sat down between Bianca and Izzy, and both girls patted her thighs.

Sofia raised her hand. "Coach, if we start slowly, can we blame it on the long bus ride?" Morgan looked confused. "Just joking. Coach Abby always had an excuse for us."

At that moment, the junior varsity began walking into the locker room. Morgan told his girls to pat them on the back and then head out and warm up. Gloria shook her head and grimaced. "Thirty-five points, but they kept playing hard." At halftime, when Cindy and Penny had played, they were only eleven behind.

"They'll get better, Coach," said Morgan to Gloria.

"Yes, they will, Coach. Yes, they will."

Coach Summit needed no inspirational words to motivate his girls for this first game. They huddled up after warmups and ahead of the tipoff and put their hands together, looking at Morgan before heading out onto the court. He simply smiled and said, "Here we go. This is where we begin." He lifted his girls' hands in unison, and they yelled "Miners!" The first few minutes went well for Oro Hills, and when Gunnison called a timeout just four minutes into the game, Oro Hills led 6-2. Molly scored on a layup and a ten-foot lane jump shot, and Bianca rebounded a missed three by Izzy and powered it back up. Morgan liked the pace of the game. Gunnison started in a player-to-player defense that proved ineffective against Molly's dribble penetration, and against Oro Hills' press, Stevie's, Molly's, and Izzy's ball-hawking flustered them. Gunnison returned to the court in a one-three-one zone which provided the key to stopping Oro Hills' early success. Against the press Gunnison reduced their dribbling and began reversing the ball through the inbounder, nullifying Stevie's effectiveness. At the end of the first quarter, Gunnison led 10-8.

The rest of the game advanced along the same thread. At every position Gunnison was taller than Oro Hills, and every starter was a senior. Their experience and confidence allowed them to adjust more quickly than Morgan's girls could. In the second half, he instructed Molly to dribble to the wings and run the offense from there. That allowed her a little more room to drive baseline or find Bianca on the post. It also pushed Izzy to the corner, opening her up just enough to get her shot away. On defense Morgan pulled his press back until Gunnison tried to run its halfcourt sets. Then his girls attacked like cheetahs, disrupting Gunnison's continuity. Still, Gunnison's zone determined the outcome, and Oro Hills dropped its opener 38-26. Molly had scored sixteen, Bianca seven, and Izzy made one three.

In the locker room after the game, Morgan sat down with his team. "Well," he started, "that was a pretty good team to open the season against. Still, I think we did several things we can build upon. Even though they handled our press, our halfcourt defense was better than I thought it might be this early in the season. Only their size allowed them to score. You battled inside, and for the most part, we blocked out hard. Our ball pressure caused a lot of turnovers. Now, we need to get better in transition when we have an advantage on the fast break. We will. I'm confident of that. On offense, even though they made it tough on us, I didn't feel as though you abandoned what we were trying to do. Having those taller girls on the wings made it hard to get off our threes, didn't it?" Morgan looked at Izzy and Elena and Sofia in particular, and they all nodded their heads. "But, I'm proud of you because you kept looking to shoot. I think all of you got at least two three point shots off. It was a little better in the second half when I slid you to the corner, wasn't it? I know you were rushing a little because of their height, but you'll figure that out. Rosa, you put up a good shot in the fourth quarter."

For Molly and her teammates who were on the team last year, this was an entirely new post-game review. Morgan continued, giving specific examples of play for each girl, always in a positive manner. Coach Thulen and Coach Abby merely said, "Nice game, get dressed." Molly wanted Coach to reconstruct the game all evening, wanted him to talk about the play in the third minute of the second quarter where she dribbled past the point girl on the zone and was able to dish the ball off to Bianca for the basket. Why couldn't they do more of that? "Molly, that was excellent. What Gunnison did after that was assign the middle girl in the zone to stay there and wait for you. She had no other responsibilities than to guard you. She was their best defender and always had help after that. Still, you kept challenging her. Keep doing that." Morgan mentioned each girl by name, saying something positive. Then, he stood.

"We lost. It won't be the last time, but we sure as heck aren't going to lose a lot more. You showed me a lot of fight, but I wasn't surprised because of this summer. Sofia, you being on this team gives us a big boost." To the junior varsity girls who were standing in the back of the locker room listening, Morgan said, "Thank you for your support. Keep working and you'll get your wins too. I have to leave the room while you change. If you have any bumps or owies, tell Coach Gloria. She's a nurse, remember. And hey, I'm very proud of all of you tonight."

On the bus the girls dug into the sack lunches provided by the school, supplemented by snacks brought from home and the oranges and apples provided by the Mountain Matrons. The team didn't know it, but they had been adopted by a book club. After a half-hour of eating and laughter, the girls snuggled into their blankets and pillows and settled in for the remaining two-plus hours. Morgan understood now why Molly had told him that she liked the bus trips. He pulled his legal pad from his briefcase and began to make notes, quietly reviewing the games with Gloria. She, too, jotted notes on a pad.

"Don't shortcut the process, Gloria," advised Morgan. "You can't make up thirty-five points in a week. Stay with teaching skills and basic fundamentals. With Penny and Cindy, you're going to win a lot of first halves. Jenny is coming along nicely as your replacement point guard. Try using her like I use Molly."

"Oh, the humanity . . . !" moaned Gloria softly.

Near the end of the first hour of travel, Bianca slid into the vacant seat next to her coaches. "I can't sleep. Mind if I sit here and listen to you guys talk basketball?" She wrapped a pink blanket around herself, pulled her long legs up underneath her body, and smiled.

"You were a stallion out there today, Bianca," said Morgan.

§

Morgan drove to Denver again on Sunday morning to visit his daughter. He told her about the game and wanted to know about her cooking class. She seemed to think it held promise for a career after her release. She asked if her dad might be willing to help her with some college when she got out, a degree in culinary arts from Metro State. He wiped something from his eye and told her that of course he would.

163

CHAPTER 18

The game is what you play, not who you are.

Heading into the first game, Morgan had instructe d his team on attacking a two-three zone, the traditional, time-tested zone. The one-three-one zone, especially how Gunnison adapted it to control Molly, presented different obstacles. Still, Morgan decided not to de-emphasize the larger goals in an attempt to win the game they had just lost. Odd fronts or even fronts against the zones. Screens against any type of defense. "Remember, Gloria, it's still December and we don't start league until the weekend before Christmas. We have time."

Friday's home game, the second game, would be an entirely different challenge. Vail Valley was in its second year of existence, a private 1A school. Oro Hills lost to them a season earlier in a game decided by a single point, the closest the Miners came to winning last year. It was the only game Vail had won. Elena said they had overlooked them, assuming they would get an easy win. Morgan made the point to his team that every team was a threat, and none could be taken for granted. He asked them to recall tiny Holt from team camp. In his mind he wondered how Oro Hills could take any other team for granted. *Each game is an opportunity.*

Attendance at the four late practices had been perfect, except for Alondra, whose daughter was fighting the flu. Alondra missed two days of classes and all four practices, but Morgan told her that if she could make it to the game, then suit up. She most likely wouldn't play, but he and the girls wanted her on the bench. Some of the JV girls did not know the situation, so Gloria spoke with them about special circumstances, about how fair didn't always mean the same, about supporting teammates all the time, even when you didn't know all the information. It was a good teaching moment, and Morgan appreciated how Gloria handled it.

§

Cindy and Penny provided the junior varsity with a nice cushion by halftime. 16-9. However, the JVs struggled without their leaders and lost 24-22 in overtime. As Morgan had told Gloria, a halftime victory. He allowed his varsity girls to stand in the corner behind the Oro Hills' bench and cheer for their teammates during the overtime. He had completed his pregame instructions, and they wanted to watch the ending of the JV game. Each varsity girl high-fived every junior varsity teammate on her way to the locker room, and then they went onto the court for warmups. It was a sparse crowd, again made up of mostly family members, Mountain Matrons, and Vail parents. Molly's mother was able to attend and sat with several other parents. Morgan convinced Kane and the custodians to put two extra degrees of heat into the gym this season.

Vail's girls resembled Oro Hills in size and class makeup. Neither side gained an advantage there. Where there was a discrepancy was in quickness, and Oro Hills had a decided edge. From the outset it was clear that Stevie, Molly, Izzy, and Sofia would control the pace of the game. Like last week's game, Vail started in player-to-player, but quickly switched to zone when they could not defend Molly. Vail used a two-three set which didn't stop Molly's penetration, allowing her to attack the paint for easy jumpers, dump-offs to Bianca, or kick-outs to Izzy and Sofia. This time it was the opponent who could not adjust. On the defensive end, Stevie provided the first reason for the Vail guards to seek psychiatric counseling at one of the exclusive clinics in their area. Vail committed thirty-seven turnovers and Oro Hills posted its biggest victory margin in school history. Cindy, Penny, Rosa, and Alondra played the entire fourth quarter, with Elena, Izzy, and Sofia alternating at the fifth position. As the teams congratulated each other after the game, Vail's coach could only say, "Wow!" She asked how many move-ins Oro Hills had received.

As Morgan and Gloria headed for the locker room to speak with their team, Kane Vincent shook Morgan's hand and simply said, "Break 'em up." Later that night Morgan phoned the score in to the two Denver newspapers. "Oro Hills 52 Vail Valley 14."

§

Coach Summitt addressed his team's first two games at the beginning of Saturday's practice. "We didn't get low after our loss to Gunnison, now don't get too high on yourselves from Friday. Vail Valley is not a good team. They may not win a game this year, and they're a 1A school. We were able to practice the things we've been emphasizing, but that game is a false barometer. Every team we play from here on in will be better than Vail." He went silent for a moment to check on his girls' response to his statement. When he was satisfied, he continued. "Next up is another team I know nothing about, Pueblo Metro. They're a bigger school that's been struggling the last couple of years. They've started out oh-and-three, but their competition has been all 3 and 4A, so let's not allow their record to fool us. They haven't been blown out in any of their losses. We'll get on the bus at noon on Tuesday, so on Monday, I want each of you to check with your afternoon teachers to remind them of this. They're supposed to get a list of who will be missing class, but they get so busy that sometimes they'll forget."

The twenty-two girls began their station drills, and the two coaches walked to each of the six baskets making small talk with their players. Morgan always liked this part of practice, one of his favorite times, when he had one-on-one time with his players. Today, he worked with Rosa on her ball security. "Get those elbows out. Rip it hard and low when you're closely guarded. You know, I think if you were going to Vail Valley, you might be a starter on their team."

Later, Morgan used six JV girls to defend five varsity girls while Cindy ran the point. His rapidly improving squad suddenly looked weak without Molly running the show. He knew of her value to his team's success, but moments like this reminded him of his team's fragility.

"Cindy, look inside. Get the ball to Bianca." He told Molly to stand on top and coach Cindy while he stood under the basket and worked with Bianca and the bigs. Gloria substituted herself into the post defense position to give Bianca a real challenge. Not having Molly to get her the ball made Bianca work harder, and when she received the pass, making her post moves against Gloria was difficult, but she listened to Morgan's instruction and scored occasionally. Each time, she smiled with satisfaction.

"Nice, Bianca. Again," said Morgan.

On Point

§

Pueblo Metro's record indicated accurately their abilities, and Oro Hills surprised them with a 43-38 win. Metro's coach understood what pre-season games were for and kept her team in man defense the entire game, giving Oro Hills needed practice in its halfcourt offense. As the game proceeded, Molly and Bianca became more efficient. The Metro center lacked Coach Gloria's strength and savvy, and Saturday's practice repetitions reaped immediate benefits. Bianca scored four of her six baskets on post moves after receiving a pass from Molly. Her other four points came on rebound put-backs off missed threes. Oro Hills shot oh-for-thirteen from beyond the arc, but, as Morgan reminded his girls, they rebounded eight misses, Sofia getting four of those. Keep shooting. Anticipate and run to rebound.

§

Three pre-season games. Two wins against a single loss. The statistics kept by the Mountain Matrons provided an accurate look at the efficiency of each girl. They kept statistics for Gloria's team too, but she called them the "inefficiency" of her girls. Conference games loomed, first on Saturday and then on the last Tuesday before Christmas break. After the holidays Tuesdays and Saturdays were game days until the final week of the regular season when the last game was on Friday, February 16. The playoffs began with the league tournament first. Morgan nodded. Pre-season, regular season, playoffs. Trust the process. Don't be fooled by early results, either wins or losses. Play for the conference tournament. The top three finishers went on to the final twenty-four; then sixteen teams advanced, then to the real State Tournament, the Elite Eight in Colorado Springs. *Don't get ahead of yourself, Morgan*, he warned himself.

§

On Wednesday Kane Vincent stood in his office looking out over the front sidewalk to his building. Two hours earlier, just as students were arriving for first hour classes, CACA called to tell him that for the time being, they saw no reason why Bianca Steele could not continue to participate. Unless new information came across their desk, Oro Hills should act in her best interests. Kane called Morgan with the news, starting his day off on a bright note. Lifting clouds and providing opportunities were the reasons Kane moved into administration. Now, he needed to call his girls basketball coach again and ask him to come in on another issue. *Issue! What kind of a word is that?*

Kane didn't stew long. After placing his call, he went to the attendance office for the girl's records and then to the nurse's office for what Gloria had on file. He asked her to come by when Morgan arrived. Back in his office, Kane made a few notes, but mostly thought about Mrs. Marta. She was one of Oro Hills' best teachers, demanding, yes, but kid-centered and a team player. Why was she taking such a rigid line on this? She came into his office after first period frustrated that students were missing too many classes for athletic contests, yesterday being the most recent example. Well, she wasn't going to allow it to weaken her standards, and if a student was absent when there was a test scheduled, then there were consequences. Mrs. Marta would report an F on this week's eligibility report for Sofia, making her ineligible for this weekend's game.

Sofia missed a month of classes because of her miscarriage. She started the fall semester knowing she would most likely have to drop out as her pregnancy progressed, but she had never been a slacker. An A and B student with college potential. At the time Sofia's mother said her daughter's eighteen absences were not just a medical recovery decision, but the emotional depression that wouldn't leave her daughter, mostly guilt and sadness. Sofia's grief from the miscarriage left her numb and fatigued. It was Elena who had come to the house to sit with Sofia and get her back in school, and it was the basketball team that helped her spirit return. Mrs. Marta had been one of Sofia's strongest supporters when she returned. What was this all about this morning?

Kane placed his pen on the desk, raised his hands to his chin as if praying, and stared. After a few moments, his fingers began to gently clap, and his jaw thrust out. He stood, left his office giving instructions to the secretary to have Coach Summitt and Gloria wait in his office if they arrived before he returned, and walked to Mrs. Marta's classroom. He knew his teachers' schedules by heart, and this was her planning period, a time she always used to grade papers or tweak her lessens. She was not a lounge rat like many others, nor did she need a smoke. She had her own coffee pot and would sit at her desk working through the hour. Kane knocked politely on her door and walked in.

"Can I interrupt you for a few minutes?" he asked.

Mrs. Marta took a deep breath and nodded.

Kane sat in the student desk directly in front of her desk. "I think this is the first time since I've been here that you and I have had a sharp disagreement, and I'm uncomfortable with it. You're as good as we've got here at Oro Hills, and I respect you a ton." He paused to let that sink in. "I called Coach Morgan after you left my office. I asked him to come in, so I could tell him in person that Sofia wasn't going to be available to play in the next game. I didn't want him hearing it through the grapevine."

Mrs. Marta nodded. "I respect that. Are you here to make me change my mind?"

Kane shook his head. "I don't expect that will happen, but I would like to understand your reasoning a little better. Kids missing class for activities has always been a hassle, but it's part of our curriculum in one aspect, because we think, in the long run, extra-curricular activities are important. That's why I have a job here, and in all honesty, I believe it." Again, Kane paused. "I guess my question is, why Sofia? I mean, she's not only a conscientious student, but you were the one teacher who took her under your wing during this difficult time for her. You sent assignments home for her during that time." Kane let it stand there, hoping Mrs. Marta would work her way through her decision, so he could understand.

"Sofia missed a lot of school. She needs to be in class every day now to make up her work. Even at best, she's only likely to earn a C. English is an important class for her." She stopped, hoping Kane would interject something. When he didn't, she went on. "I was talking with Coach Holmes yesterday, and she agreed. You know Sofia didn't go out for volleyball this fall, and she was a two-year starter. Now, she's missing class for basketball, and Mr. Summitt isn't even teaching in the building."

Kane chose not to respond directly to Mrs. Marta's statements. There had been an undercurrent of resentment against Morgan Summitt since his hiring, but to directly challenge her position would put Kane on the other side. "To get coaches, we often have to hire non-teachers. All of our assistant football coaches are non-educators, plus there are several others."

"It wasn't fair that you didn't hire Mr. Thulen for this year with Abby away. And then you wouldn't let him be the assistant either."

Kane nodded his head. "One of the reasons I came directly to you is that I trust you. You've always been fair. I'm confident what I say to you stays in this room. I was all set to slide Ed into Abby's position for the year, and when Abby made it official she would be taking a year off, I called Ed to come in so we could sign the contract. That was in May before the year was out. To set the record straight, I asked him four times to come to my office for that very purpose, and each time he either put me off or missed the appointment. Had he come in any one of those times, he would be the coach now." Kane caught himself rising to attack and backed off with a deep breath. "The last time I asked him to come in, he reminded me how busy he was with his two jobs and summer football, but he'd make it in when he could. Darlene, you're about to declare a student ineligible because she missed one class, an appointment. I know neither you nor the rest of the faculty knew of Ed's behavior about signing the contract. It was a simple thing. Come in, sign the contract. He didn't take the time or show the courtesy to do so."

"I didn't know that."

"There's no reason you should have known. It was between Ed and me. He's also the one who said he wouldn't be the JV coach if I hired Morgan. Morgan did not ask for the job, never hinted he wanted it. Three girls came in to talk to me about it. They told me they had talked to Coach Thulen about some summer practice, and he told them he didn't have time. Darlene, it was my intention of hiring Ed all the time, but I realized he wasn't our best option . . . for the kids." He paused.

"He's given a different version, you know."

"I'm sure he has. I'm sorry for that."

"Sofia still missed class," said Mrs. Marta.

"It wasn't unexcused, and there was a list out on Monday. I take responsibility for getting it out late. You should have been given that list on Friday at least." Kane paused again. "That's not Sofia's fault. Darlene, you were the teacher who most stood up for her, who said *we* could get her through. That's why I don't understand this." Kane stopped and waited.

"This one time, Mr. Vincent." It was a formal statement. "I'll have her make up the test tomorrow or sometime, but you have to promise to get those excused lists out earlier. It throws my lesson plans into disarray."

Kane thanked her and rose.

"I know Sofia couldn't play volleyball. She told me last fall how much she was missing it. She used to tell me everything."

Kane nodded. "Pull her aside this afternoon, give her the dickens about missing class, and then hug her and tell her you miss talking with her. I think she'll warm right back up to you. You were the one teacher who was there for her."

§

Morgan and Gloria were going over practice plans when Kane returned.

"Sorry to keep you waiting. Had to clean up a student thing."

Morgan understood. "You called me with good news while I'm still in my pjs, and now you have me down here for bad news?"

Kane poured himself a cup of coffee, sat down behind his desk, and put Sofia's records off to the side. "No. Just wanted to wish you good luck against Tutwiler on Saturday and remind you that Academy Prep beat us by fifty-five last February." He smiled. "Oh, and to get your excused list for that game into me tomorrow. No excuses. I need to get it out to the teachers on Friday or they'll have my hide."

CHAPTER 19

Great point guards don't play on the outside thirds, Molly.
Attack in the middle.

Tutwiler. A miniature version of Academy Prep, located along the Front Range south of Denver, created seven years earlier by over-protective parents, Tutwiler's athletic successes came in tennis, golf, and gymnastics, sports where outside coaching ranked above the school's coaching staff. A feeder system for club sports. Private lessons. Their reputation for team sports was talent without toughness, according to Kane Vincent. Truly talented football and basketball players transferred to one of the numerous 5A schools in the county in search of college scholarships.

Morgan was skeptical as he prepared his game plan. Tutwiler's pre-season record was oh-and-three, but the games were competitive against some larger schools. Oro Hills' two victories, important for his girls' confidence, came against weak opponents, one only marginally more talented than his JV team. Tutwiler put up nearly thirty-five points in each game while surrendering forty. *Ironic*, thought Morgan, *that Oro Hills' opening two games were against the two privileged teams in the conference.* After that, every school was hard scrabble like his own. Academy Prep won the conference a season ago with an unblemished record and was then swept out of the playoffs in the round of sixteen. Tutwiler finished third in both league and districts and lost big in the opening round of the playoffs. They had been oh-and-three in pre-season last year too.

On Friday Morgan had spoken to his girls about goals. "What is a realistic goal when you and your teammates have never won a game in high school?" Now, a month into the season, Oro Hills had two victories in a row. A winning streak. Morgan cautioned that certainly two teams, A-Prep and Benson, would be major obstacles, and the others, with the exception of St. Joseph's, seemed to be on Oro Hills' plane. On the other hand, he doubted any of the other schools participated in the summer like Oro Hills had. Morgan wanted his team to be optimistic, which his girls were, and to begin to see the playoffs as a possibility. He also knew that a poor start might dampen their spirits, make them say, "Here we go again. Same old, same old." Morgan remembered some of his boys teams, where they started and where they ended up. Those teams were either 4A or 5A depending on the student count, but every year he had some talent. It was Izzy who said she wanted to get better, learn to compete, and win a few games, so that next year, when most everyone returned, the team could make the playoffs. Her cousin concurred that she, too, would like to win a few games even if she wouldn't be around the following year. It was Bianca who said next year was not a given, that the team ought to put the playoffs on this year's list of goals, and Morgan heard a larger view than simply basketball. Molly agreed, but went even further.

"The boys congratulate themselves whenever they win a game in districts. That's no goal. To get to the real playoffs, the games after districts, we need to win two district games. We can do that. Bianca is right. Next year will be next year. We can't know, but we can do it this year. I don't care about last year's record; it wasn't us. I think Coach wants us to see beyond our little town and not be afraid. Let's make our goal the State Tournament. Maybe we won't make it, and based on our school's history, we won't, but let's set a goal to be the first."

It was Sofia who spoke first, simply, "I'm in."

Morgan nodded and smiled. "Okay. Okay." He looked to Gloria who grinned broadly.

§

Once upon a time in Oro Hills, way back in Morgan's youth, townspeople and students filled the Elm Street Gym for high school basketball games. It was a different time, fewer diversions. There were no girls games; girls were cheerleaders and on pep squads. Games were always on Friday or Saturday nights, none of these Tuesdays or Saturday afternoons. Opponents came from geographically close towns, and rivalries had developed over decades. The state athletic board didn't devise leagues and send teams to play against schools they had never heard of. You played the next town over. Protect your bus, watch out for a sucker punch. Morgan missed the spirit surrounding those games, missed what they brought to the town, but it had to evolve. Allowing girls to play rather than root from the stands was exactly the right thing to do. To fill a gym in 1995 called for a concentrated plan, but it required a talented, exciting, winning team. As his girls went through their warmups, Morgan looked across the gym to the crowd. It seemed a little larger than last year's, a few more students, but still sparse. One of his goals was to fill the lower bleachers with students later in the season and put a fair number of the old guard in the upper level.

Tutwiler did not follow the script. They battled for every rebound, dived on the floor for each loose ball, trapped the wings with good success, and extended their elbows in the paint. Tutwiler's coach switched defenses frequently to confuse Oro Hills, but Molly adjusted well, and regardless of the defense, she penetrated into the lane most every posses-sion. Tutwiler forgot they were supposed to be prissy, pampered, and protected, and even though Molly got into the paint, she took a physical beating.

Oro Hills trailed 10-8 after the first quarter and 21-16 at half. In the locker room, Morgan instructed his three guards to get even more aggres-sive in the backcourt, fouls were not a problem. He showed Sofia how to anticipate the middle pass against Tutwiler's press break. He told Molly to dribble to the wing, pushing Izzy or Elena or Sofia to the corner or through the court to replace her at the top of the key. He complimented Bianca and Alondra on their physical play, warning them that the second half would only get more physical. As they stood with hands in the circle, he said, "We're in good shape; we'll get a run here soon."

More than the pre-season games, more than any game in the Jeffco Summer League or at team camp, this contest tested the mettle of Morgan's girls. Tough, complex, intense. Two teams trying to impose themselves on the other. Morgan found himself standing in front of the bench for the entire second half, communicating with Molly at every whistle, encouraging his girls to give a little extra, talking with officials on each call. This was basketball! His prophecy for a third quarter run proved inaccurate, and Oro Hills hadn't closed the gap at the end of the period, trailing 33- 27. Heading into the fourth, he told his girls their pressure was taking its toll, that Tutwiler was tired and ready to make mistakes. As they broke the huddle and headed back on the floor, he put his arm around Molly and told her to look for her shot on every possession. Bianca popped Molly on the forehead, smiled, and said, "Do what he says."

Tutwiler wilted in the fourth quarter, just as Coach Summitt predicted. Sofia got three steals in the backcourt, and Molly erupted for six baskets. Oro Hills won 41-37. As the teams congratulated each other, the Tutwiler coach shook Morgan's hand and told him the altitude finally got to her girls.

Morgan allowed her to keep hold of her fantasy. "Yeah, it's tough up here for four quarters. It'll be different when we play at your place." He didn't believe it at all. Tutwiler faded because Oro Hills pressured the entire game. His kids, from across the tracks, were mentally tougher in the fourth quarter.

In the locker room, the girls hugged and yelled, just as a team should do when they win a tough game. Morgan and Gloria congratulated them, went over a few details, and told them they needed a great practice on Monday in preparation for Tuesday's trip to Academy Prep.

§

The eligibility report came out on Monday, and it hit the team hard. Five girls, two from the JVs and three on the varsity received a single D and were ruled out of Tuesday's contest with Academy Prep. None of the twenty-two girls on the team had an F. Penny's D was in social studies, and it was accompanied with an A and five Bs. Stevie earned four As, two Bs, and a single D, in math, a subject which had always given her problems, despite her getting extra help from a tutor before school. Rosa had all Cs and the one D. Kane brought the bad news to Morgan and Gloria before practice, shaking his head in disbelief. Stevie had always been on the honor roll; this came out of the blue. The report blindsided Stevie and brought her to tears, because she had been told on Thursday that she had a high C. What had she done in one day to bring it down so far? Mr. Vincent told her he had gone to her teacher to make sure there had been no error in reporting and was assured it was simply a matter of a low quiz score on Friday. Stevie acknowledged that she had done poorly, maybe should have studied the new material more on Thursday night, and asked Mr. Vincent how many games she would miss. He told her she would be able to make up credit during the first week back in January. He warned her and her teammates that the semester ended on the first Friday in January, and a D for the final report would render them ineligible for six weeks.

As Kane turned to go, Morgan caught up with him. "This is not right. An honor roll student who works hard could be ruled out for an entire season in a course she's actually passing. This is bullshit, Kane."

§

When the team met to leave for its game on Tuesday, Rosa was not there. Morgan asked Bianca where she was, and Bianca said Rosa was going to stay at school and attend classes. As she spoke, Bianca kept her head down.

Morgan lowered his head and looked up to Bianca. "What are you not telling me, Bianca?"

Bianca raised her head. Her lips were pursed tightly. "She thinks you don't care if she doesn't go. You made a big deal about Stevie, but you didn't say anything about her."

Morgan blinked hard, realizing his mistake. A barely audible "shit!" came from his mouth. "Where is she now, Bianca?" he asked. "I'll go get her."

"She went home for lunch and hasn't come back yet."

Morgan thought for a moment. "Come with me." He walked to the coaches' office and called Andrea. "Good, you're still there. Hey, I need you to do me a big favor right now. I want you to go pick up Rosa and bring her to school as fast as you can. Don't leave yet; I need to make sure she's there, but I'll call you right back."

Morgan pushed the button on the phone down to disconnect and then handed the phone to Bianca. "Call her. Tell her to get her pillow and blanket, but that she's going. The bus won't leave until she gets here."

Rosa answered, and Bianca told her what Morgan had just said. Bianca told her that Mrs. Summitt would be right over to pick her up. Morgan took the receiver from Bianca and spoke. "Rosa, it's me, Coach. Hey, I'm sorry. We'll wait for you." He called Andrea back and said Rosa would be waiting for her.

Morgan shook his head. "Old men. We can be so stupid." He walked Bianca back into the gym and then went to Gloria. "Get everyone loaded up. I need to find our A.D. If I'm not back when Rosa gets here, go without me. I've got to get something off my chest, and it may take a while. You've got both teams if I can't get there." He didn't wait for Gloria to respond, just turned and headed up the stairs to Kane's office.

§

Against Academy Prep Morgan moved Sofia into the starting lineup and tried Izzy at Stevie's position in the press. Hard as she tried, Izzy could not perform Stevie's role. With just two subs, Molly played the entire game, as did Sofia, and both were spent in the final minutes. By then the game had been decided, even though Oro Hills played as hard as they had against Tutwiler. A-Prep double-teamed Molly the entire thirty-two minutes. In the visitor's locker room, Morgan honestly told his team they had performed well and he was proud of them, despite the score. There were several positive things to take away, he told them. Izzy hit two threes and Elena one. Bianca and Alondra contained A-Preps bigs until Bianca fouled out early in the fourth. Molly was held to eight points, but she felt she had let the team down. She was the only one who thought that. Academy Prep 48 Oro Hills 27. Morgan gathered his girls and sat on the metal bench with them. He was somber.

"I need to make an apology to you all, but especially to Rosa and Penny." He looked at Rosa and went on. "I let you think that some girls on this team are more important to me than others. Yesterday, I let today's game cloud my judgement, and because Stevie's role in the outcome of our games may be heavier, I screwed up. I popped off to Mr. Vincent about the one-D policy using her as an example, and I think I sent the wrong message to the people I most care about." He paused. "All of you, each and every one of you, no exceptions, are my team. You are my girls, and we take this journey together. Rosa. Penny. I'm sorry."

On the bus ride home, Gloria said to Morgan in a whisper, "That could have been a whole lot worse. Our kids really battled. It may have helped you if Cindy didn't play in the JV game. We weren't going to win anyway."

Morgan chuckled. "Cindy had a good JV game. She got some valuable experience. Playing the whole game was necessary since Penny couldn't. This loss won't be a setback at all. We'll be just fine."

"By the way, who was the old man you were laughing with while we were waiting for the girls?" asked Gloria.

"Jake. An old high school teammate. He was bragging on his grand-daughter, the big girl who played so well, bragging about the facilities and advantages of Academy Prep. He's right, as far as it goes. With the reforms that are needed in education across the board, poor and rural schools will find it harder to compete. They'll become even more invisible and easier to neglect. There's this certain flaw, almost a madness, about our country, this attitude that one group or another is inferior because of wealth or color. The current lie is that public schools are inferior simply because of who the students are. If that's true, then nine out of every ten kids in America are receiving an inferior education. How is that in the *land of opportunity*?"

"It's a rigged system, for sure, and it only seems to be getting worse," said Gloria.

"I laughed to be polite, not because he said anything funny. Sad." Morgan paused. "I'd sure like to play them with a full compliment."

Gloria reached across her body and patted Morgan on the shoulder. "What did you say to Kane before we left, if I might ask?"

"I told him that it wasn't the Stevies and Pennys who were most hurt by the one-D policy, that it was those students who live on the edge with their grades. Poor kids with poor academic skills and little home support. A third of our students will adjust to the policy, the Stevies, but two-thirds will drop away or not even go out for sports, because they know they'll be ruled ineligible at some point and don't want to go through the hassle or disappointment just to get dropped from the team."

"What did he say?"

"It's what he didn't say. He knows what's happening, but he's the junior administrator whose boss has told him the teachers drew up the policy and think it's great. I know he's been gathering data to back up what I say, what he believes, but he's kind of stuck, and he's angry. He told me to get on the bus and go beat Academy Prep. He called them the 'Evil Empire.'"

On Point

§

Oro Hills' last game before the Christmas break took place on Saturday afternoon, December 22, in west Denver. By mutual agreement the game was moved from Friday so as not to disrupt more school at the end of the semester. Slater High had won its first two league games and one of its three pre-season games but had not played either A-Prep or Benson, the two teams by which the rest of the league gauged themselves. Again, Oro Hills would be short-handed without Stevie, Penny, and Rosa. Gloria convinced Morgan to play Cindy entirely on the varsity for this game, which would allow for brief periods of rest for his guards. Having three practices with the reduced lineup provided Morgan the opportunity to alter his press and halfcourt defenses to best suit his players. Still, without Stevie pestering the opponents' guards, the game slowed down. There were fewer possessions each quarter.

From the opening tip, it was clear Slater had received a scouting report on Oro Hills. Two girls covered Molly on each trip down the court. While they couldn't stop her, they did slow her path into the lane, limiting the damage she could inflict. Morgan subbed in Cindy for Elena, in effect having a second point guard, which allowed Izzy and Sofia to get off their threes. Each made one in the first quarter, and Bianca powered in two of their misses. At the end of the first quarter, Oro Hills led 10-9. Slater made its adjustments, switching to a box-and-one on Molly. Molly had more space and took advantage of the Slater guard, scoring three baskets in the second quarter, but no one else scored. At half Oro Hills fell behind 18-16.

The game turned physical in the third quarter, as the Slater guards pushed and grabbed Molly constantly. Morgan couldn't get the refs to call the fouls, so Slater amped up the contact as the game progressed. On successive plays late in the third, Molly was knocked to the ground, only once getting a call. Morgan pointed to the red bruise on Molly's cheek, but the officials ignored him. During the break before the fourth quarter, Morgan gathered his troops.

"We protect our own. Sofia, Bianca, Alondra. Set the hardest picks you can at the top of the key for Molly, then roll to the basket. Molly will find you. On defense bump every cut and clamp down on #22. We're only down eight. Izzy. . ." He stooped so that his eyes were even with hers.

179

"Let it fly!"

A rugby match broke out in the gym, and the tide turned. Oro Hills clawed back to within one with twenty seconds left in the game. Molly fouled the Slater point guard hard to stop the clock; the Slater coach screaming for an intentional foul. Slater missed the front end of the one-and-one, Bianca rebounded, and Oro Hills called time out. Morgan instructed Molly to go hard to the hole when she got the ball, not to wait for the last shot. "Run to Rebound."

When they broke the huddle, Molly found herself surrounded by three Slater players. Izzy inbounded the ball to Sofia, who did her best imitation of Molly, dribbling directly to the basket for a layup. She received a slight bump at the basket and the ball rolled off the rim. Bianca rebounded in the traffic and bounced up with the follow, but it too rolled off. She grabbed it one last time and shot it just as the buzzer went off. This time the ball went in. Morgan looked to the outside official and saw that he was waiving the basket off, that the ball hadn't left her hand before time expired.

It seemed to Morgan and Gloria that both teams showed new-found respect for the other when they exchanged high-fives in the post-game. Combat can do that, and this was the most physical game Oro Hills had ever played. First Tutwiler, thought Morgan, and now Slater. In the locker room, Molly and her teammates had their heads bowed, hiding the tears. Stevie and Rosa patted their backs to console them. Morgan and Gloria sat on the benches with them.

"Hey, hey," he said. "Lift your heads up; you've got nothing to be ashamed of."

Sitting next to Morgan, Bianca sniffled and spoke. "It's my fault, Coach, I didn't get in balance for that last shot. I should have made it."

"You did make your last shot. It just came a half-second too late. You have nothing to apologize for." He put his arm around his big center and pulled her to his shoulder. "All of you, that was a terrific game." He waited before speaking again. He kept his arm around Bianca and turned to Molly. "Molly, remember last summer when you asked me what it felt like to win?"

Molly nodded.

"When you win, it makes losing that much harder."

Sofia had been the only girl not to sit down when they came into the locker room. She had gone back to the showers to cry. Gloria heard her, rose from the bench, and went to console her. Sofia had her jersey pulled up over her head when Gloria found her. Mama Gloria put her arms around Sofia and told her what a great game she had played. Sofia turned into Gloria's hug and continued to cry.

Finally, Sofia said, "I can't stop thinking about my baby."

§

Players recover quicker than coaches after tough losses. The early quiet of the bus ride home eventually turned to laughter. Gloria sat with her team and talked about Christmas and the silly things her girls had done in the game. "We're getting closer."

Morgan went to the back of the bus to chat with his team. Colorado's mandatory nine-day break from contact between players and coaches over the holidays extended from December 24 through January 1. No practices; no coach-player contact. Family time. Morgan had always railed at this week-plus as wasted time. He knew his kids wanted nothing more than to be in the gym together. He had arranged for the Elm Street Gym to be open in the afternoons beginning the day after Christmas for five days, two hours each day. One or more of the Mountain Matrons would supervise, but neither Gloria nor Morgan could be there. In Indiana, in Kentucky, in Georgia, in California, in those states where basketball was taken seriously, there were no *mandatory family breaks*. Morgan went to great lengths to follow his state's guidelines, to follow the rules.

"You don't have to be there. Family comes first. Go as many days as you want; don't go if mom wants you to be with the relatives."

"What will you and your wife do for Christmas?" asked Elena.

"Tomorrow, we'll go to Denver to spend a few days with our kids. Then next week, we're flying to California to see Mrs. Summitt's sister. A short vacation away from the cold." He paused. "Any of you leaving town?"

Not a single girl raised her hand. Ten girls, all of them staying in Oro Hills over the holidays.

Molly laughed. "Coach, we're all poor kids. We don't go on vacations like you. Sometimes we leave town to visit relatives, but we don't call them vacations. We go visit cousins."

§

Kane Vincent worked much of the break, spending several hours each day after Christmas at his desk in the high school.

Queenie Roberts bought Mercedes a new saddle and herself a BMW for Christmas. She drove it into town each day to supervise the Elm Street Gym, always picking up one or more of the Mountain Matrons to keep her company for the two hours. Most of the varsity girls showed up each day, Alondra being the exception, and several of the JVs came regularly. Queenie's voice and laughter could be heard over the bouncing basketballs, squeaking sneakers, and floor talk of the girls. She sat along the sidelines pretending to read her latest novel or shuffling a briefcase full of papers, but really holding court, which, said B.J. on Thursday, was apropos for a lawyer from Birmingham, Alabama, surrounded by poor kids.

"I saw y'all in the Christmas concert last week," Queenie told the girls during a water break. Molly had taken to running a formal practice, including scheduled breaks and conditioning. "Y'all were dressed up so pretty, I hardly recognized you."

Early in the week, Bianca had asked Queenie if she wanted to shoot a few baskets, but Queenie declined. "This jiggly body doesn't belong on a basketball court, honey. Maybe once, but now it's very comfortable on a couch." After a subtle comment by Andrea at a book club meeting in early December, Queenie had asked Morgan about Bianca and Rosa, about their resident status living with an aunt a state away from their mothers. She inquired about these two girls who seemed, as she said, "joined at the hip," since she herself had grown up dirt poor in the home of her grandmother. She and Bianca stood about the same height, but where Bianca was fit and swift, Queenie's body resembled the Pillsbury dough boy. Unlike Mercedes, who professed a desire not to be touched by anyone under the age of thirty, Queenie gave free hugs to all the girls. Queenie and Mercedes never had children of their own and never would, but the Oro Hills Lady Miners moved into their hearts.

§

Molly called Morgan on New Year's morning to see if she could run over. She wanted to come over on Sunday night, the evening he and Andrea had returned, but resisted, believing they might want to rest and settle back in after their trip. Molly was eager to tell them about the practices at the Elm Street Gym, about the remarkable progress Bianca seemed to have made. Morgan told her to bring her appetite when she came because Andrea was cooking a full breakfast.

"Coach, everyone except Alondra showed up every day. She wanted to but couldn't. Lots of company and the baby. We did all the drills you taught us and ran our butts off. Bianca said she never wanted to miss another shot like she did in the last game, and she worked on her post moves all the time. She made Penny work with her too, mostly to play defense against her, but they worked hard."

Morgan and Andrea needed no prompts to get Molly to tell them about the basketball practices. Morgan had hoped open gyms would allow the girls to avoid slippage, but judging from Molly's description, the workouts allowed the girls' development to continue, maybe even given Oro Hills a slight edge in the upcoming games. As Coach Summitt listened, his smile grew. After a few years as a high school boys coach, he had learned that when his players took ownership of their team, success was insured. Not in the sense of winning always, since victory is not a given, but in the sense of educational goals. Oro Hills was Molly's and Bianca's and Sofia's team, and he was just their coach. Another bridge had been crossed.

§

Formal practices started again on January 2. Classes began the following day, so Morgan could hold two practices on Tuesday. Alondra attended both and had lost some conditioning compared to the other girls. Morgan understood. Gloria's junior varsity took a step or two back over the break, but a few of her important pieces hadn't. Two practices on Tuesday, one on Wednesday, Thursday, and Friday, and then the first game of the new year, of 1996. Eureka, the other poor mountain town in the Discovery League whose future had dimmed with the shuttering of local mines. Eureka, with a similar mascot. The Orediggers.

§

The Oro Hills faculty met before school for a quick meeting in preparation for the last week of the first semester. Bookkeeping mostly about when grades were due. Three days of review and finals, a schedule built to promote poor results after the eleven-day break for the students. At least the teachers were aware of the pitfalls and had given their more important tests before Christmas. Most of the teachers used this short week to allow for extra credit and makeup assignments to be turned in. As with all faculty meetings, Kane ran them, planning and delivering the information to be dispensed. The faculty appreciated him because he stuck to the agenda, was brief and succinct, unlike Lowell, who rambled and wasted their time. On this Wednesday Kane added one item to the agenda.

"One last thing," he said, "I am suspending the one-D eligibility policy for the remainder of the year." He held up a folder full of papers. "Our own data, that I've spent the last few months collecting, and all of my Christmas break analyzing, shows how counter-productive it is to achieving its stated goals. On paper, in theory, it makes sense; we want to hold our kids to a very high standard, but we've seen a significant decrease in student participation in extra-curricular activities over the past three years since the policy has been in place. I read over the minutes from the committee that drafted this policy four years ago and discovered that we were supposed to have a review of the policy each year, since it was such a demanding requirement. We haven't done that. I know some of you will have questions, so come see me at your earliest opportunity and we'll talk about it. Maybe I can sign you up for the review committee. In the meantime, we'll follow the CACA guidelines for athletic eligibility."

CHAPTER 20

Hand-me-downs are a fact of life, Coach.

Eureka's rust showed, and Oro Hills seized control of the game early. Stevie's ball pressure, combined with the overplay in the passing lanes by Molly, Elena, and Izzy provided Sofia and Bianca with easy opportunities for steals. Stevie stole the dribble seven times from Eureka's guards in the first half alone. Eureka reminded Morgan of the Oro Hills varsity a year ago, a team without direction or sugar mamas. For the first time in her short career, Molly registered double-digit assists, which she attributed to having teammates who could now make shots. Stevie scored ten points, as did Bianca, and Rosa made her first basket. Oro Hills 49 Eureka 20, evening Oro Hills' record in league to two and two.

That same night, Academy Prep beat Benson 45-41, the closest game A-Prep had played in the Discovery League in its three years of existence.

§

Rosa and Alondra both had a D on their semester report cards, as did two JV girls, but all remained eligible for the rest of the season, as long as their weekly grades were satisfactory. Kane heard some rumblings through the grapevine about his unilateral dismissal of the eligibility policy, but only one teacher came in to talk about it. The boys basketball coach, whose team's numbers had dropped from twenty-seven at the beginning of the season to just sixteen after Christmas, maintained that Oro Hills was the type of town that needed to have such a policy in order to keep the few college-level students challenged. Kane reminded him about the previous season when low numbers forced the boys program to cancel a handful of JV games and about the finagling that occurred to enable one of his better players to participate in the district playoff game.

Still, Kane respected his coach for coming directly to him rather that bitching about it behind his back. Lowell Exeter learned about Kane's action later that morning, dropped in after lunch to tell Kane it was long overdue, and never said another word about the policy.

Kane attended the girls practice on Monday afternoon. He sat in the upper bleachers with a coffee and his notebook. During a water break, Gloria hustled up the stairs two at a time to see if he needed to speak with someone in particular.

"No, just needed a break from the rat race. Long day, lots of feelings to sooth and crises to avert. Your practices are a nice break, sort of a yoga exercise for me before I head home." He asked Gloria to sit for a moment. "How are you holding up? Your kids haven't won a game yet."

Gloria's face lit up. "I've got twelve of the nicest girls who are trying their hardest. Some of them played in junior high just for fun and came out only because Cindy and Penny talked them into it, or because they heard how much fun the older girls had over the summer. But every one of them has bought into this. They're eager little bunnies. It helps that Morgan is so calm and his team is winning some. I can point to them and tell my team the varsity didn't win any games last year but are now successful."

"Morgan is pretty even tempered, that's for sure," said Kane. "On the outside anyway. It's a learned skill, Gloria."

"He makes me laugh. I spend a fair amount of time with him at his house sharing a beer or having dinner. His wife and I get along great. I've adopted some of his traits. I don't cuss around the kids like I did the first few weeks, and I've found myself complimenting my girls more for their trying even when they screw up."

"Maybe I need to spend more time around Morgan. You need to get down there, but when practice is over, I want to talk with the two of you. My turn to bring you some good news."

When Kane realized he was relaxed watching the girls practice, he smiled. He hadn't come to practice for that purpose; he wanted to tell Morgan about the suspension of the one-D eligibility policy. Kane listened to the chatter on the court. "Pick it up girls! Good! Let's try it this way and see if it works better. Again. Again," from Morgan or Gloria. From the players, "I've got the ball; I've got the ball. Help. Follow your shot. My fault; I should have let you know." And the loudest voice of all from Molly Rascon. "Fill your lane; I'll see you. Cut hard! You were open; shoot it, Elena, and please hit the rim. Talk on the screens, Alondra, or you're going to get us killed."

When practice ended, Kane descended to the court. Morgan was checking off drills on his practice plan and making notes in the margin, while Gloria looked over hers. "Did you get everything covered?" asked Kane.

"Never good enough," said Morgan, knowing that Kane would understand. "Never enough time either."

"The one-D policy has been suspended for the remainder of the year. We'll be operating on the state guidelines for now. You can sleep better tonight."

Morgan nodded. "I'll bet you took some grief for this."

"Not as much as I expected. Thank God none of your girls are problem kids around school. You've had the eligibility problems, but no unexcused absences or real classroom behavior issues."

"They better behave, or I'll turn Gloria loose on them." Morgan folded his plan and put it in his pocket. "You know if you keep making these radical moves, you'll be looking for a new job soon, don't you?"

"Well, if I go down, I know you two will keep me company. Might as well go out with our principles intact. It's so easy to forget why we do this when no one expects much from the students." Kane stopped himself. "That's not fair. I just broad-brushed my teachers. Almost all our teachers are busting their butts to get our kids ready for the next level. The teachers aren't the reason for our poor scores. The scores are as good as they are because of the dedication of our teachers."

Morgan put a hand on both Kane's and Gloria's shoulders. "Low expectations have lots of enablers. They all have excuses or gripes. I've been fortunate this season. You two have had my back. We need to convince the school powers that be, that success will help these kids graduate. Little successes like winning a few games will help them achieve big successes." Molly, Bianca, and Rosa emerged from the locker room and sat on the floor to wait for their ride. Morgan tilted his head in their direction. "I was given something special with those kids, with this whole team really. They don't know it, but they're creating a whole new standard for how teams practice and play. I'm an old fart, but I've never experienced a group quite like these girls. We can't let them down."

§

Oro Hills split the two games for the week again, beating Arroyo and losing to Edgewater, staying in the middle of the pack. Molly made free throws down the stretch to keep Arroyo at bay, but the girls went oh-for-seventeen from beyond the arc and lost by a basket to Edgewater. In the locker room after the Saturday loss, Morgan explained the process again to his team. "I'm on board with Molly's goal of making it to the State Tournament, the final eight. Maybe tonight, if we would have scrapped the threes, we could have won. Maybe. No guarantees. But down the stretch, as we play in the district tournament and move on, we're going to need that piece of our game. Teams will clog the middle and double-team Molly or play goofy defenses to take away Bianca's game. If we don't trust the process, we'll be settling for something less. We are not going to be a team that settles."

§

The league order was taking shape after six games. A-Prep was unde-feated, followed by Benson who had lost just the one to Academy. Slater claimed third place for now, and the next four were up for grabs between Oro Hills, Tutwiler, Edgewater, and Arroyo. Eureka defeated St. Joseph's for the eighth spot, while the latter remained winless, taking over the spot occupied by Oro Hills last season and the season before and the season before. Next up for Morgan's crew was an away game with Benson on Tuesday and St. Joe's on Saturday at home.

§

Morgan drove home from Denver on Sunday afternoon thinking about how to attack Benson on Tuesday. He was glad he was heading into the mountains on I-70 rather than down from the ski areas. Traffic was at a standstill in the eastbound lanes, as it usually was during the winter. Morgan's daughter had given him a recipe for Andrea, a sign that maybe she was moving past the anger for her mother. Morgan knew his team needed a signature win, a foundational win. Benson could be that victory. Benson played the basic two-three zone, so Oro Hills would need to make three or four threes, and his defense would need to create twenty-plus turnovers, which Morgan believed could be achieved. Benson's strength was in its size, not its ball-handling abilities. While Bianca would be tested for thirty-two minutes, maybe Stevie, Molly, Sofia, and Izzy could balance that out. As always, Molly's teammates would ride on her shoulders. *So do I*, thought Morgan,

§

When Andrea called her husband to the phone on Monday morning, he had a sinking feeling. Kane asked if Morgan wanted the bad news over the phone or did he want to come in. Morgan told him to just tell him.

"CACA just notified me that Bianca can't play. Your friend Clarence Robinson apologized, but said both Academy Prep and Tutwiler had questioned her eligibility. He said he couldn't give me the specifics of their complaint due to confidentiality rules, but somehow they found out that she's not living with her parents or a legal guardian."

"Oh hell, Kane." Morgan's hand turned white around the phone handle. "The two rich schools in the conference who recruit players outside their boundaries lodge this crap? I wish I knew who gave them their information. I'd kick his ass." Morgan paused. "Sorry, Kane. I know you've been trying to manage this. Bianca doesn't know this yet, does she?"

"No. I figured you would want to tell her and the team."

"I do, yes. Do her a favor and don't tell anyone else about this. You know how bad news leaks out to find the victim. I'll ponder how to tell her and how to hold onto her. We have the late practice, so I'll meet with her right after school. Could you have her and Rosa come to the office just before school lets out? I'll talk to them in your office if I could and then bring them home or over here between then and practice." He went silent for a moment, and Kane waited. "I'll tell the team too at practice."

Kane spoke in a hushed tone belying his words. "More bullshit, Coach, and I don't know how to fight it. This is where we need a strong principal with connections."

"It's not your fault, Kane, so don't beat yourself up. Bianca has been through worse, and her teammates will support her. Andrea and I will too." Morgan hung up the phone, but didn't move. Andrea stepped over to him, laid her head on his shoulder, and wrapped her arms around his waist.

For the rest of the morning, Morgan paced. Around noon he asked Andrea if she could bake cookies for the team. "Maybe have your book club ladies do up something special."

"Very special," she said and then let her husband continue thinking. She called the Matrons without telling them the reason, but saying it was important. On her last call, she handed the phone to Morgan.

§

The most difficult aspect of coaching is not losing, it's making the cuts after tryouts. Kids play all their young lives with their friends to make the high school team, especially the varsity, and when they get to their junior or senior year and are told they aren't good enough to make the team, it's devastating for them. Coaches try to cushion the blow, but it hurts. It's the worst day of the year for most coaches. This day, Morgan knew, could be the worst coaching day of his life. Not the worst day of his life by any means, that was the ordeal with his daughter Kathy. A series of worst days, but today was certainly hard.

Kane met Bianca and Rosa at the office counter and led them to his office where Morgan was waiting. He rose and touched both their shoulders.

"Hey, how were classes today?" he asked.

"Good," answered Rosa, but Bianca hesitated, and Morgan noticed.

"Have a seat," he said, and he sat in the chair he had pulled up in front of them. "This morning we got word that you can't play for a while. The state association is saying that since Rosa's aunt is not your legal guardian, you're ineligible. It's not anything you've done, so don't blame yourself, and I'm going to keep trying to make them understand." He paused, reached out and took both Bianca's hand and Rosa's. Rosa was confused, and it showed in her narrowed eyes, but Bianca maintained a stone face. Morgan felt her grip loosen, while Rosa's tightened.

"Is it just for our next game?" asked Rosa.

Even though Bianca's hand was limp, Morgan refused to let it slide out of his. "We don't know. I spoke this afternoon with two people. The first is an old friend of mine who works for the state association, a good man, and we're trying to find a quick solution. I also spoke with a lawyer to get some advice. That call was more encouraging, but still, for now, frustrating."

"What am I supposed to do?" Bianca finally asked. Her voice showed both despair and sadness, it seemed to Morgan.

"Well," said Morgan, "the first thing I want you to do is trust me. I am not going to let this go, but more importantly. I'm not going to let you go." Tears came to Bianca's eyes and her grip tightened again. The three of them sat in silence for a moment, each processing the unexpected news from a different perspective. The emotions passing through the touch conveyed much more than any words could say.

"You'll fix this, won't you, Coach?" said Rosa.

"I'm going to try, but I can't promise that. I can only promise that I'll do my best, but as I said, the two of you are my kids, and I won't let this hurt any other part of your lives."

In time Morgan explained more details to the girls. Bianca would still practice with the team, travel with the team, sit on the bench, in every way remain a part of the team. He would expect her to continue her excellent work in the classroom. He knew there could be days when she felt like staying home or not suiting up for practice, but he would not allow that.

"Rosa, I want you to tell me if Bianca has a bad day, especially at nights."

"Coach," said Bianca, "this will only make me work harder. I won't let you down."

Morgan let go of the girls' hands and pulled them closer to where their heads touched his. "You never have; why would I expect anything different. You either, Rosa."

He waited until the halls cleared and then drove them back to his house for a snack before practice. He told them he would tell the team near the end of practice, a short practice where he would figure out who would take her spot in the lineup for Tuesday's game.

§

Morgan decided on Sofia, to move her to the back spot on the zone, and to have her guard Benson's all-conference center. He had confidence she would battle. Alondra would sub for her, and when she did, Morgan could move Sofia back to the Rover spot on the press. Penny might fill the gap if more responsibility was placed on her shoulders. After free throws Morgan gathered his girls and explained the situation.

"For now, Bianca has been ruled ineligible because of a gap in her records. We're trying to get it straightened up, but it may take a while. Each of you will need to step up a little more. Alondra, Penny, we'll be depending on you to take her minutes. You can do it."

§

Not surprisingly, Molly visited Morgan after a late dinner. Andrea fixed them hot chocolate and went to the living room to read, to leave them alone to talk about the Bianca Situation.

"She practiced so hard tonight, like I've never seen her before, but she hardly said a word. Is she going to be all right?" Molly's expression mirrored Rosa's from five hours earlier.

Morgan often worried that Molly took ownership of problems greater than her age warranted. Her jobs, the part she played in raising her brother Alex, and for the part she played in raising her mother. She was the team leader, this team's founder, really, who carried its ultimate success on her shoulders. Five-foot-three shoulders. Morgan hesitated to add another piece of straw to her back.

"I think so, in the long run. It's just these next few months I'm concerned about. How much of Bianca's past do you know?" Morgan held the secret to Bianca's background of abuse, the episodes with her mother's boyfriends, the runaways, the escape with Rosa to Oro Hills.

"More than you might think, Coach. We've spent so much time together since we started shooting together on your driveway. The trips to Golden in your van and team camp were like teenage girls' heaven. Ever since then, Bianca and Rosa have slept over several times. Rosa tells me about her. I know her mom is a drug addict and that she's run away a couple of times."

"What's Rosa's aunt like?" Morgan had met her, talked with her only briefly, but had not seen her at a game.

"She's nice. Works hard. She's a house cleaner for a motel out of town, and I think she might do something else too. But nice. She's just too tired to fix supper a lot of times, so Bianca and Rosa make their own. Rosa worried for a while that she would send them back, but she thinks her aunt is okay with them now. They're really good kids, Coach, no problem."

Morgan mused. "Good kids, huh? Sort of like you then?" Molly smiled. "Molly, my hope is someone will see the real problem here and make the right decision immediately, that someone will understand basketball is sort of a lifeline for Bianca. Not an end all, but for now, a lifeline to her future. If she can't play the rest of this season, you and I and the rest of the team will need to always make her feel a part of this team, even when she's not able to wear her jersey. I'm just glad Bianca has Rosa and good friends like you."

"Why can't someone just do that? What's the problem? Geez!"

Morgan decided. "Molly, if this was a problem for a girl at Academy Prep or one of the Douglas County schools where the players' parents have some money and influence, I don't think this would be a problem. Bianca, and to some extent the rest of you, are vulnerable because you don't have those connections. I don't know how information that was supposed to be confidential leaked out, but it did, and someone with no character used it ingenuously, just to gain an advantage in a high school basketball game." Morgan paused as he considered another reason. "Maybe someone has a grudge against me and thinks by prohibiting one of my girls from playing, he's settling a score. I don't know; I can only speculate."

Molly kept her eyes on her coach. "Pretty sad."

"Yeah, little people." He let that thought hang in the air for only a moment. "Still, there are some people who are trying to help. Mr. Vincent has known this all season and has kept a lid on it. He's put himself in a precarious position. That's not information I want you to tell anyone else about; it's just between you and me. He's still trying to work something out. There's a friend of mine at the state association who understands poor kids, was one himself, and he gets it. He's trying. There's a lawyer who's working for free to come up with some strategy to get Bianca reinstated as soon as possible. So, there's lots of good people in her corner."

"What do we do until then?"

"You continue to be her good friend, and I continue to be her coach."

"Can we win our game tomorrow without her?" asked Molly.

"No doubt about it, it will be tougher without her, but we'll get on the bus and show up, like we always do, and battle like crazy." Morgan smiled slightly. "And you, I want you to take more shots tomorrow, especially in the lane, since Bianca won't be there to rebound the back side. Alondra and Penny aren't as talented at catching the ball on the break, so pull up and shoot."

Molly nodded. "So, my assist total will be down?"

§

Starting Sofia limited the effectiveness of the press, so three minutes into the game, Morgan pushed her forward to halfcourt to be the Rover. Penny and Alondra would have to cover the basket against the taller Benson Bobcats. The rotations and substitutions would then be the same as previous contests, except Bianca wouldn't be in the game. Morgan told Bianca and Gloria to sit at the end of the bench closer to the defensive basket and yell out instructions to Bianca's replacements. In their half-court defense, Morgan instructed Alondra to front the low post, but had Penny play topside and only show a hand over the top. "We're going to have to box out like our lives depend on it. Stevie, your girl never goes to rebound so run inside and front-block Penny's girl. Help her out. Molly, check yours just for an instant and then get to the paint to see what you can get."

After falling behind in the early minutes, Oro Hills calmed down and began to execute against the Benson zone. Alondra set high screens against the guards for Molly, who couldn't get around Alondra's big body, allowing Molly to get into the lane for the shots Coach Summitt had asked her to take. At the end of the first quarter, Oro Hills had tied the game. The Mountain Matrons attending the game, Andrea, B.J., Mercedes, and Queenie, stood and clapped as their girls came to the bench. Four women, ten family members, and the twelve junior varsity girls were the only Oro Hills fans in the bleachers.

Benson's coach altered his press break in the second quarter, looking to throw over the top along the sidelines, and by halftime, his team led by four. Morgan believed his four guards could adjust their pressing patterns, but of greater concern was his bigs. Alondra had played more minutes than ever and was tiring. Penny's play surprised her teammates, but she had been knocked down a handful of times and picked up three fouls defending Benson's center.

As the girls sucked on oranges at half, Morgan provided more instruction. "Elena, when you're not in the game, I want you to sit with Coach Gloria and let her tell you how to defend #55. We might need you to do that later in the game. Izzy, you're doing a nice job of drifting away from Molly on her drives. Keep that passing lane open for her, and fire it up when you get it." He made just a few more simple adjustments and then sent his girls back on the floor.

Izzy's three pointer and a steal and layup by Stevie immediately erased Benson's lead. The score leaned forward and back throughout the third quarter. The first whistle of the fourth quarter ended Penny's game. She played like a champion, Morgan said after the game, and her teammates agreed. Alondra ran out of gas and Morgan replaced her with Elena. "Full front down there. Just battle. If you need help, look to Bianca on the bench." Molly's ten-foot jump shot in the lane at the four-minute mark gave Oro Hills its last lead. Stevie picked up her fifth foul on the next possession, necessitating Molly to take the point on the press. Cindy took over Molly's position, but Benson broke it consistently from there on in. Their all-conference center, relieved she was being guarded by a five-foot-six guard, took the game over, and Benson survived by five.

In the locker room, Morgan saw a determination in his team. Penny told Bianca, "We would have won with you in there," but Bianca replied that she wouldn't have played any better than Penny had. Molly led all scorers with twenty-two. The tears of earlier losses were gone, replaced by disappointment and resolve. While Morgan waited outside the locker room door for his team, he spoke briefly with Andrea and her friends.

"Anything?" he asked Queenie.

"Coming along," she replied.

§

Saturday's game with St. Joe's provided the needed win for Oro Hills, who scored a season high fifty-seven points. The junior varsity won its first game, and the varsity league record stood at 4-4 after the first round. After team camp, Morgan had told Andrea he thought Oro Hills could win a half-dozen games during the season. Now, only half the season in, they had reached that total. Two of their wins came against quality opposition, at least for the Discovery League, against Tutwiler and Arroyo. The other four were against very weak opponents, two in league and two in the pre-season. The true tests were now at hand, and Morgan hoped his girls could get five of the final eight in league and draw a weaker team in the first round of the district tournament. *Oh, how his team needs Bianca Steele.*

§

On Monday morning Rosa Leon's aunt began her new job as a house-cleaner at a local motel, Anita Pagel's old motel. Rosa's aunt was also hired for part time weekend work as a server at Lorna McCaffrey's coffee shop. Queenie Roberts filed a motion at the county courthouse to grant tempo-rary custody of Bianca Steele to Ms. Leon, effective immediately, based on the best interests of the child. She presented documents to the court show-ing abuse and neglect, and a statement from child services in Espanola, New Mexico, that Bianca's mother had been deemed unfit several times because of her drug abuse. Queenie included a letter from Bianca's mother saying she would not contest the custody change at this time. Queenie was told the court would act upon the motion within the month, to which Queenie said, "By the end of the week will be fine. I'll come back on Thursday." From the county courthouse, Queenie and Mercedes drove to Denver to meet with a director from CACA informing them of these actions. The underlying message was that a lawsuit could be filed at any time against the state association if they delayed acting when the court gave custody of Bianca to Rosa's aunt.

Kane Vincent gave Lowell Exeter a heads up on Tuesday morning. B.J. Pacheco met with Mr. Exeter at lunch to tell him she was considering an article in her newspaper about his failure to come to the rapid support of one of his students. Lowell called the state association to see if there was something that could be done immediately to allow Bianca to resume her participation in basketball.

§

Bianca did not suit up for Tuesday's game against Tutwiler, but Molly, Stevie, and Sofia led the visitors to a victory anyway. Oro Hills came out hot, with Molly and Izzy each hitting a three point shot in the first few possessions, and Stevie making two steals which turned into layups for Molly. The quick 10-0 lead seemed to deflate Tutwiler, and the rematch did not resemble the earlier game. Tutwiler made a small run at the beginning of the fourth quarter, but baskets by Molly and Sofia ended the threat. Oro Hills 41 Tutwiler 33. Next up, Academy Prep at home on Saturday.

§

Mercedes called Morgan on Friday afternoon from Idaho Springs, the site of the county courthouse. The court had not ordered the custody change as of yet, but Queenie was still obnoxiously battling the bureaucracy. "Persistent nudging," as she called it. If the order came down today, they would let Morgan know before practice.

The call didn't come, so Morgan prepared his girls for their fourth game without Bianca. They had won two of the three, but St. Joe's and Tutwiler were not Benson and A-Prep. Penny's growth surprised everyone, especially on the defensive side of the ball, but her offensive production fell short by about eight points per game from Bianca's. Gloria convinced Morgan to keep Cindy all to himself for the A-Prep game. "Molly needs a short blow occasionally, and my Jenny needs to start. We'll get clobbered anyway, so put your best team on the court. You never know."

As he had since her suspension, Morgan gave Bianca quality practice time. She ran with the starting five at times, turned her jersey inside out and played defense against Penny and Alondra when they were with Molly, and diligently worked on her post moves during the drills. Bianca climbed the free throw ladder steadily, and now she was battling Molly and Izzy for the top spot. Excluding Molly, Bianca shot more game free throws than the rest of the girls combined. She had grasped Morgan's directive to take her power shots into her opponent's chest to draw the foul. On this Friday, however, both Morgan and Molly sensed a disappointment in Bianca's demeanor. Even though Morgan warned her that her return could not be predicted, Bianca wanted desperately to compete against Academy Prep. Half-way through practice, as the girls worked together on game shots at game speed, Morgan took Bianca aside.

"Did I ever tell you how much I respect you?" he asked.

Bianca nodded. "I know, even when you don't say anything."

"Tough day, huh?"

"I just wanted tomorrow to be the day. We can beat those guys"

Before he could say anything else, Queenie entered the gym and marched directly up to Coach Summitt. Kane Vincent stood at the doorway.

"Coach, you want to blow your whistle and gather up all your little darlins? I have an announcement." Queenie did not make eye contact with Bianca. When the girls were gathered, Queenie opened a manila folder, raised her reading glass from the chain around her neck, scanned the document, nodded, took off her reading glasses, and said, "What it says is that y'all have your teammate back."

Pandemonium broke out. The girls hugged Bianca and clapped for her. There were no tears in Bianca's eyes, just a huge smile on her face. Rosa began to cry, and Molly's smile may have exceeded Bianca's. Queenie leaned into Morgan's chest to take the whistle. She blew it, and quiet returned.

"Okay, now y'all know the news, so let's quit wasting valuable practice time and get back to your shooting drill. This time, though, how about making a few more." The girls laughed but dispersed to their respective baskets. Bianca remained and now tears formed. She moved to Queenie and hugged her. Morgan moved away to a side basket to pretend he was correcting Stevie's shooting technique. The last hour of practice flew by, but at a level of efficiency and energy never before achieved in the Oro Hills gymnasium.

§

As for every game he ever coached, Morgan wore a tie. He always came to the gym with a sports jacket too, but he didn't always have it on during the games. This Saturday afternoon he left it in the locker room. He stood in front of his bench watching his girls warm up, looked over the people in attendance and decided there were almost enough to be called a crowd, turned to find his wife like he always did, and noticed his old high school teammate too. Four weeks in a row, Oro Hills had split the games, a win and a loss. A victory against Academy Prep would break that habit, push them to a six and four record, end Academy Prep's claim as to have never lost a game to a Discovery League team, and be that foundational win.

Morgan knew his team was still a heavy underdog, but he also understood how far his girls had traveled. As he scanned the crowd, a peculiar thought entered his head: he wondered if the person who leaked Bianca's records was in the gym. He might never know, but he did wonder. The buzzer sounded, ending that thought, and bringing him back to the present, back to the faces of ten girls who believed.

After the national anthem, the Voice of the Miners, a junior high Spanish teacher, introduced the starting fives. Elena, Izzy, Stevie, Molly, and Bianca Steele. The girls were joined by their teammates at center court for their stack before returning to the bench for Coach Summitt's last words. "Take a deep breath and pull back your emotions just a little. Remember the keys that we talked about. Pick up in the back court, but just contain early. Let's see how they choose to handle our pressure. No fouls back there, Stevie. Elena, you've got a tough cover; don't help much. Bianca, half-front and try to deny the pass into the post. Izzy, you're going to have a good shooting game. Let it fly early." He looked over his team and sent them out on the court. As always, when the team broke the huddle, he put his arm around Molly's shoulders and said, "This is your team, take care of it."

And as always Molly responded by tapping Morgan's belly and nodding. No words, just the tap and the nod.

A-Prep won the tip, but turned it over when Bianca tipped the entry pass away allowing Molly to get the steal. Racing up court, she veered right, passed ahead to Izzy, who fired up the quick three. It was long, but Bianca outran the A-Prep center to the backside block, secured the rebound, and powered it up to score. "Game on," said Gloria to Morgan on the bench.

Despite A-Prep's best efforts, its guards could not deny Molly the ball or prevent her from getting Oro Hills into its offense. Still, there was a reason A-Prep was undefeated and ranked. Near the end of the first quarter, with Bianca on the bench for a blow, an Academy sub ran over Molly, who stayed on the floor for a moment. Morgan prevented Nurse Gloria from running out to check on her, giving Molly a moment to collect herself and stay in the game. She stood and motioned to Morgan that she was okay. Besides, it was a charge and Oro Hills gained possession of the ball. Morgan then called time, mostly to give his charges a little breather.

Morgan crouched and smiled at Molly. "Nice job, kid. Remember what I told you; point guards can't get hurt." It was a standing joke between Morgan and his point guard.

"I know, and I can't get in foul trouble either."

"All right, if they're still in that zone when we come out, I want you to hold the ball near the halfcourt line for the rest of the quarter. Don't attack until we get to ten seconds left, then run *Lakewood*. Let's see if we can end the quarter with the lead." He looked to his team for understanding. "Sofia, find the gap and get your feet set. If Molly gets you the ball, don't hesitate."

The girls stood and Morgan leaned into Molly. "If they deny Sofia, you're on your own."

Academy Prep allowed Oro Hills to hold the ball. At the ten second mark, Molly dribbled quickly to the left elbow, drawing the wing guard to help on coverage. Stevie set a down-screen and Sofia drifted up, received the pass from Molly, and drained the three. A-Prep inbounded the ball with a long pass in the direction of the girl who had knocked Molly down two minutes earlier. The pass was contested by Alondra, who collided with the Academy girl, sending her into the bottom of the bleachers. A non-shooting foul was called on Alondra, ending the first quarter with Oro Hills leading 12-10. When she returned to the bench, Alondra tapped Molly on the head. "We're even now."

Academy Prep regained the lead at half, extended it to seven after three quarters, and won by five, 39-34. To his girls after the game, Coach Summitt explained what a *foundational game* meant. He didn't say foundational *win,* he understood this had been a stepping-stone game, and he wanted his girls to know what he knew, that Oro Hills had entered upon a new plane. They wouldn't be taken for granted ever again.

§

On the return from Denver on Sunday afternoon, Morgan mused to a relaxed Andrea about his year. "I think you understood more than me about my missing coaching. Teaching too, but the coaching at this point in my life. It's funny. I'm having breakfast and a special young lady starts shooting baskets across the street. You sent me over, remember? I told her I could help, and she told me she couldn't afford to pay me. Pretty typical of her, now that I look back on it. I was just going to make a few suggestions. Then I go buy a backboard and put it up on our driveway. It never occurred to me I would be coaching again. Even when the other girls started coming over, it was just something I could help with. Molly asked about summer programs, and I knew something about that, so I helped. Never raised my voice like I did when I coached, never made them run, never said they had to attend." He paused to turn off the interstate.

"You're a little more into it now," said Andrea.

"You've noticed. When Kane asked me to do this, I wondered how I would react. I thought I'd fall back into the old Morgan style, but I haven't. I don't yell, but then I've never had to with this group. Molly sort of keeps everyone focused, but Bianca does too."

Andrea smiled warmly. "Bianca. What a wonderful, wonderful kid. She and Rosa are just so, I don't know, humble, but strong. They love you, you know."

Morgan made an uncomfortable grin. He knew they did, but he wished they understood that his actions were the visible acts that helped them, and that the work of Andrea and her book club women enabled him to work his magic. *Magic*, he thought. "This whole team, from Molly and Bianca down through the whole lineup, just fell into my lap, and it's strange. It's the perfect mix for my style."

"They remind me of your '88 team, all heart."

"I haven't compared this team to any of my old teams, but I guess in some ways it does. That team started out with a string of losses and ended up in the State Tournament," said Morgan.

Andrea remembered because there had been a small movement of disgruntled fans to fire her husband. "*Oh-and-eight to final eight.* That was the newspaper headline, if I recall. What I was referring to, however, was the type of kids on that team. Nice kids, every one of them. They came over to the house a lot too."

"You're leaving out the part where we got drilled in the first round of State." He laughed. "But you're right; they over-achieved just to get there." He paused for a moment. "I'm not sure this bunch of girls is overachieving anymore; they're pretty good and so balanced."

"What do you mean by 'balanced?'" asked Andrea.

"I have a quality player at each position and a sub for each one of them. Sure, if Molly wasn't in the lineup, the rest of them might look like they've never played before, but that's the beauty of the whole thing. On last year's team, Molly wouldn't have been allowed to be the focal point; those girls wouldn't have bought in, but these girls couldn't care less about egos. They're just friends enjoying the moment."

Andrea reached over with her left hand and placed it on Morgan's forearm. "Not sure I agree with you on that, at least that this is just for the moment. I'm not sure you believe it either. This is why you've always coached, for the lessons beyond the game."

§

While the Summitts were in Denver, Molly and Stevie practiced on the driveway. Molly saw Stevie at church and asked her to meet her at Coach's house to work on something, a tip she had read about in her basketball book.

"You're so good at stealing the ball off the dribble, Stevie; what are you looking for?" asked Molly.

Stevie slapped the ball out of Molly's hands. "I don't know exactly. Just like that," she said referring to slapping the ball. "If my girl isn't paying attention, I guess."

Molly understood Stevie's quickness was the key, but there had to be more. "When you're guarding me at practice, what are you looking for? You're the hardest person for me to get around."

It was clear that Stevie hadn't over-analyzed how; she simply reacted, but Molly wanted more. Stevie handed Molly the ball and told her to start dribbling. They had practiced this drill nearly every day at practice in the center circle; Molly dribbling and Stevie trying to take it away.

"Your cross-over is really good, especially when you're squared up on me." For the first time, Stevie was viewing her play from the outside. "It's when your body is turned like you're protecting the dribble that I kind of think I can steal it. Do that for me."

Molly dribbled with a low crouch, dribbling with her left hand, her right leg nearer to Stevie and her right arm at a ninety-degree angle, in a protective armbar. From this position Molly's head was up surveying the defense, identifying weaknesses, directing her teammates in their movements.

Stevie nodded. "When you're like this, you either spin dribble or have to drop-step to change direction, and I think that's when I try to steal it. I'm not sure."

Molly had Stevie defend her while she was in this position. Molly couldn't remember ever losing the ball during a game from this position, but it didn't matter. She understood her vulnerability to a quick defender from this position; Stevie had identified a weakness.

"Crowd me," she instructed Stevie. "Closer." As often as not, Stevie disrupted Molly's movements, making her lose the dribble or at least forcing her to pick it up. It didn't matter whether or not the ball was in her right hand or left; Stevie had an edge.

"When you're on the move, Molly, I can never get it, because you're always squared up and can change directions easily. You're moving forward. It's when we're in the halfcourt offense and you're standing still, that's when I have a chance. Also, when you're on the wing where Coach wants you to start the offense a lot."

The drill stopped while Molly internalized the information. Morgan kidded her about these moments, had used a phrase to Gloria in front of the entire team as a way to tease her point guard, but also to admire her determination to improve. Bianca had picked it up and began using it. "Molly's having an epiphany moment" she would yell, and the team would giggle.

"Teach me to do that," said Molly.

§

Slater. A home game with a slightly larger crowd; a few more students, a few more townspeople. Oro Hills lost to Slater in the last game before Christmas when Bianca's put-back came just after the buzzer sounded. Slater held the third spot in the standings, the spot Morgan hoped to wrestle away from them for district seeding purposes, the spot away from Academy Prep in the second round. Slater's coach was a wily pro who understood that beating Oro Hills meant containing Molly Rascon and leaning on Bianca Steele, keeping her off the offensive boards. Morgan expected more goofy defenses from Slater to achieve those ends, and he hoped he had prepared his girls for these odd sets.

"Remember," he told them in the locker room before the game, "explode in transition and get a shot before they can set up. The more the game is at our pace, the better our chances."

Slater employed a diamond-and-one at times, a triangle-and-two at others. One defense on the make, another on the miss. Their transition to defense forced Oro Hills to execute in the halfcourt, for Molly to create shots for her teammates in a new environment. A game of fits and starts, but Morgan could see his point guard lifting her game, seeing the changes, finding ways to get Izzy open on the wing or Bianca free for a bunny. Finding ways to free herself from the constant pressure being applied by Slater's guards.

At the end of regulation in a game played more at Slater's pace, the score was tied at 32. The overtime turned toward Oro Hills' style, a free-flowing affair. To Morgan's consternation, however, the officiating tightened, and two quick whistles put Stevie on the bench, joining Sofia. It seemed to Morgan that roughness was allowed near the basket with the bigs, but not tolerated on the perimeter, much to Oro Hills' disadvantage. Still, the game came down to the last possession, with Slater leading by a point after a wild hook shot by their center. Molly received the inbounds pass from Elena, went between her legs with the dribble to get past the two Slater guards, and raced down the sideline, only to be knocked out-of-bounds by a Slater forward in front of the scorer's table. No foul. After a few moments of discussion, the referees awarded the ball to Oro Hills for the last shot, an eerie replay of the pre-Christmas game.

Morgan nodded confidently. "We've been here before. Last game, they triple-teamed Molly on the inbounds, so let's try this. Molly, you throw it in. We should be able to free up Bianca on the screen. Get it to her." On his clipboard, he diagrammed a staggered screen to free up Molly to receive the return pass from Bianca. "Get it and go, Molly. The rest of you, run to rebound. Izzy, drift to the corner for your shot; it doesn't need to be a three. If Molly gets mugged in the lane, she'll find you. You won't have time to make a move, so catch it and shoot. Get your feet set early."

Oro Hills broke the huddle; Coach Summitt putting his arm around Molly, and Molly tapping his belly. The referee handed the ball to her. Bianca broke free near the dividing line; Molly threw her the ball and broke toward the basket, receiving two screens as she ran. She cut back to Bianca and got the ball. Without hesitation, she dribbled hard toward the free throw line where three Slater defenders met her, just as Coach Summitt had foretold. Molly's pass to Izzy hit her in the hands for the final shot.

Izzy's sixteen-foot shot went eleven feet and was off-line by another three. B.J.'s newspaper photo the next day would show the Slater defender's arm collapsed across both of Izzy's arms, but no foul had been called. The Slater defender knew she had committed the foul; it showed on her face. The young official standing on the baseline next to Izzy had raised her fist signifying a foul. Two shots. But the older official came running in to signal the game was over and no foul was to be assessed, over-ruling his junior partner. Before scurrying out of the gym, he had turned to Morgan and said, "It wasn't intentional, Coach, and the shot was already off. The contact didn't affect it."

Morgan stood in front of his team in the locker room, some with their heads down, a few with their eyes on him waiting for an explanation they could understand. "Hey, hey, eyes up," he began. "That was clearly a foul; you know it and I know it. Having said that, we can't change it. Referees are fond of saying that they don't want to be the ones to decide the outcome of a game on one call. That's not fair. I should say, some referees say that. It's a copout. By not making the call, they took our chance away from us. Izzy should have been awarded two shots to determine the game or to send it to a second overtime." Morgan paused, rubbed his chin, and continued. "But now we need to move on. As in all things, we can't change what's behind us, but we can forge the path in front of us. That's what we're going to do. The next three games will most likely decide whether we finish fourth, fifth, or sixth in the standings, and that will play a big part in determining the success of our post-season." Again he paused, realizing his past few remarks were most likely not being processed by his girls at this moment. They needed to hear something else. He took a step forward and sat on the bench between Molly and Stevie. "You played your guts out again, and I was so proud of you. Every game, you guys grow and my pride swells. This old man, your OFG, can't believe how lucky I am to be hanging around such a terrific bunch of girls. So," and he dragged out the word, "this is what I'm going to do, this is what we're going to do. We're going to come in tomorrow and practice with a purpose, and again on Thursday and Friday. Then we're going to get on the bus on Saturday and go beat Eureka and then come back next week and win two more. Our regular season has just two more weeks, but I figure we ought to set our sights on dragging all this fun out for another two or three after that. So, we got a raw deal tonight and it hurts, but we can still determine our own path. These things tend to even themselves out; basketball's funny like that. In addition to being so gol-darned fun, it teaches you things about yourself. This is one of them. We can take a hit and bounce back stronger, and that's just what we're going to do."

It was a promise Morgan was making to his team, for his team. They all stood and stacked hands. "Miners!" Coach Summitt left the locker room to Gloria and the girls, went out to the gym to receive his kiss from his wife, and to speak glowingly to anyone who would listen about the effort and determination of his team.

CHAPTER 21

The enemy of our girls isn't a person; it's low expectations. It robs them of their uniqueness and potential greatness.

On Saturday Oro Hills traveled to Eureka, the other mountain mining town in the conference, and demolished them. Molly finished the game with no turnovers, her first such game ever, and the team committed just nine total turnovers. "Every drill's a passing drill," said Molly to her team after the game, to which Coach Gloria added, "and a catching drill." Oro Hills won 70-18. Morgan called off the press after the first quarter; neither Molly nor Bianca played in the fourth quarter; Rosa, Alondra, and Cindy all scored field goals, the first time that had happened; and Big Beautiful tallied nine points. *The Bench*, minus Sofia, had outscored Eureka.

Queenie, Mercedes, Andrea, and B.J. had gathered up Rosa's aunt, Bianca's new guardian, and driven her to her first game. She was quiet at first, but Queenie allowed nobody to be shy long, and by the time they positioned themselves in the bleachers behind the Oro Hills team to keep statistics, Tia Maria laughed openly and cheered loudly for her two girls and the rest of the team.

Morgan remained subdued both during and after the game. His team performed at a level he could not have imagined three months earlier, but his thoughts centered on the opposition, a team that seemed to have filled the void left when Oro Hills climbed out of those shuttered mines. As the teams congratulated each other after the game, Morgan saw an acceptance of low expectations on the faces of Eureka's players and coach, the same expression he saw on Oro Hills' varsity last year. He also didn't see a Molly Rascon anywhere on Eureka's squad.

For the sixth straight week of the conference season, Oro Hills had split its two games, a win and a loss, evening their league record at 6 and

6. Middle of the pack along with its next two opponents, Edgewater and Arroyo. Most likely, these teams would secure the fourth, fifth, and sixths seeds going into the conference tournament, with the fourth seed getting the home-court advantage against the fifth-place team, while the sixth seed traveled to Slater. Edgewater held the advantage with first-round wins over both Oro Hills and Arroyo, and they were hosting Oro Hills on Tuesday.

§

In the first meeting, Oro Hills didn't make a single three-point shot and lost by a point. This time, however, Molly hit two from beyond the arc, Izzy two, and Sofia one, all in the second half, and Oro Hills surged past Edgewater 44-38. It had been a game of starters. Except for Sofia's five points, no bench player from either team scored or played significant minutes. For at least the next four days, Oro Hills held the fourth position in the standings.

Arroyo was the hard-luck team in the conference, losing a handful of games by a single possession without winning any close games. "A better team than their record," Coach Summitt cautioned his girls. Oro Hills played before its largest audience on Saturday and continued with its hot shooting and reduced turnovers. Molly's mother sat with Rosa's aunt and a dozen other family members, their behavior so different than a year earlier. The Miners' pressure defense and rebounding advantage, led by Bianca, Sofia, and Penny prevented Arroyo from establishing any type of rhythm, and Molly's twenty-two points led Oro Hills to a comfortable 53-36 victory. For the first week since the pre-season, Oro Hills went two-and-oh, bringing its record to 8 and 6.

§

For several weeks, Morgan and Gloria had been working with Kane to encourage attendance. Increased newspaper coverage, including photos, seemed to have informed the townsfolk of the girls' success. With Morgan's prodding, Kane set Tuesday's game with Benson as "junior high night," with both the seventh and eighth grade girls teams playing a six-minute game on the high school gym floor beginning at four. Andrea and the Mountain Matrons purchased tee-shirts for the younger players with *Future Lady Miners* screened across the front of the shirt, and *No Limits* across the back. Gloria's idea. The concession stand, which had only operated for the boys games, would offer every snack for half-price. The morning announcements on both Monday and Tuesday encouraged student attendance at the game. Finally, Kane pressured the band and drumline, along with the cheerleaders, to perform for this game.

On their own Lorna McCaffrey put up a banner in her coffee shop, and Octavia Wick reduced the price of beer to patrons at her bar who promised to attend the game. Mitzi Risso gave no homework assignment for Tuesday night and asked her colleagues to think about doing the same thing. Kane sent a memo out to the faculty that there would be a special section roped off behind the team's bench especially for them with free popcorn.

The second-place Benson Bobcats arrived to a nearly full gymnasium to face an opponent whose center would be allowed to play in this game. Benson's only losses were to Academy Prep, both in close games. Their margins of victory against the rest of the league had expanded in the second-round of league play, and they came confident and ready. For the first time since its creation, the Discovery League had two legitimate teams capable of winning more than a single game in the post-season. Benson did not intend to be blind-sided tonight, not by an upstart with a history of ineptitude. Benson had scouted Oro Hills and knew its tendencies, knew its center returned, and knew Molly Rascon was among the best in the league. Benson's coach did not intend to allow his team to take a step back.

Bianca's presence made a difference. Slight adjustments by Coach Summitt allowed Molly to get inside Benson's two-three zone. There, she was able to score, set up Bianca for her power layups, or kick the ball out to Izzy, Elena, and Sofia. On defense Bianca's size and strength negated Benson's previous advantage which it had exploited against Penny and Alondra a month earlier. Stevie stripped Benson's point guard of her dribble early, making her nervous and unsteady for the remainder of the game. Through it all, however, the Benson coach rallied her girls and made adjustments to keep her team in the lead, and Oro Hills trailed throughout. In the last half-minute of play and down three, Molly stole a weak Benson pass and drove the length of the court for a layup. Immediately thereafter, Stevie tipped the dribble away from Benson's guard and Elena recovered it. Morgan used one of his remaining two timeouts to advance the ball to the sideline in front of his bench. With the second timeout, he set up the special play he had taught the girls since their loss when Izzy had been mugged trying to get a last-second shot away.

Sofia would be the inbounder, and her soccer skill of a two-handed over-head pass was the key. She would need to throw a precision pass from in front of the Oro Hills bench to the far corner where Molly would have to locate the ball in flight, catch it, and pivot back to the basket for an uncontested jumper. Along her path, she would receive screens from Elena at the top of the key and Bianca at the far-side block.

With clipboard diagrams Morgan reminded each girl of her details, details that had been practiced at every practice for just this moment. "Sofia, make a good fake to the corner to move your defender's hands. Molly, fake up like you're going to get the pass high, then back cut hard. Elena, set your screen and don't move. Don't allow the ref to call you for a moving screen. Izzy, remember, if they grab Molly and don't allow her to back cut, you'll get the pass. Shoot it; we'll have no time for a second pass. Bianca, nobody gets through your screen." He looked at her and smiled, knowing no Benson player would get close to Molly once she cut through the lane. As they rose from the bench, Morgan felt the gentle tap from Molly on his belly. Three hundred fans rose in unison with their team.

The old referee, already exhausted from the pace of the game, handed the ball to Sofia. She slapped it hard, and four Oro Hills players moved together, as of one body. Sofia ball-faked to the near corner, then straightened herself and threw a strike to the far corner. Molly had no defender within eight feet of her. She caught the pass, pivoted on her left foot, and drained an eighteen-foot jumper. Oro Hills 41, Benson 40, and the Lady Miners had their fourth straight win and a lock on the fourth seed of the conference tournament if they took care of business against the last place team on Saturday.

After walking through the post-game congratulatory line, Morgan instructed his team to stay on the court in their sweaty uniforms and mingle with the crowd, to soak in the smells and feelings of this after-noon. He received Andrea's hug and several from his sugar mamas before sneaking into the locker room to be by himself. This day, this victory, belonged to the girls. If the shot had not gone in, he would not have cared for himself; he knew the margin of victory is always razor-thin, and as the saying goes, *it cuts both ways*. But he was grateful for Molly and Bianca and Sofia and Elena and Izzy and Stevie and Alondra and Cindy and Penny and Rosa. Grateful was too mild. He loosened his tie and then took it entirely off from around his neck. A wide tie with orange basketballs on a blue background, one of more than a dozen Andrea had purchased for him over the years. An old tie, but one of his good-luck ties. *Needed it tonight*, he thought. He folded it carefully, tucked it into his coat pocket, and then sat on the locker room bench. A part of him wished this could be the last game of the season, because he knew that nearly every team loses its last game every year except in the consolation games at State and that brings tears. End it tonight on a shot that brought smiles and shrieks to his girls, with Molly being hoisted in the air by Sofia and Bianca, with the school band striking up the Oro Hills' fight song. With Rosa hugging him, her face buried in his chest, one that felt like the ones his daughter used to give him when she was in junior high. Morgan wiped away a tear and thought of the scene from his favorite movie, *Chariots of Fire*, when an old coach, denied entry into the Paris Olympic Stadium, hears the English national anthem and knows his runner has won the gold medal, knows that he has given his sprinter those extra two steps needed to win the 100-meter dash.

Morgan sensed he was not alone in the room.

"Wondered where you were hiding."

Morgan cleared his throat and smiled warmly. "This is their time. I needed to step away and compose myself."

"Nice play. You probably knew Molly was going to make that shot though, didn't you?"

"I was more concerned about Sofia's pass," said Morgan. "That's the key component. And Bianca's screen. Nobody sees those things, just the shot."

"I suppose you're going to ask me for a raise now, especially since I spent your salary for this year on warmups. They're supposed to be delivered tomorrow."

"Just in time for the playoffs."

Kane pushed himself off the wall. "I'll unlock the door and let the girls in for your post-game talk. This school needed this. Mind if I remain in the background and listen?"

Morgan stood up with all the grace of a sixty-five-year-old man lifting himself off the couch after watching a long movie. He stepped to his athletic director and shook his hand. "Couldn't have done any of this without you, you know."

Kane nodded. "Let's keep that between you and me. You can buy me a couple of beers and we'll drink them out by the river this summer. You can thank me then." The two men looked each other square in the eye and nodded, and then Kane turned to unlock the locker room door.

Twenty-two girls pushed into the locker room, still laughing and touching, still exuberant about the victory. *No*, thought Coach Summitt, *maybe this shouldn't be the last game of the season.*

St. Joe's had not won a game, but Morgan used last year's final JV game to drive home his warning. Without a win, Oro Hills had pushed Academy Prep's junior varsity to the last few minutes of play. Molly and her teammates headed the warning and won easily, 66-23. Again, Cindy, Penny, Rosa, Alondra, and Jenny from the junior varsity played much of the second and fourth quarters. The Oro Hills JVs earned their fourth win, ending their season with a victory. A satisfying bus ride home. Molly's hopes of becoming Oro Hills' winningest team ever were achieved. 10-6 in league, 12-7 overall as they headed into the league tournament. The girls had looked sharp in the new gold warmups and brown shooting shirts. They would be the fourth seed and host number five Edgewater on Tuesday. If they won, they would travel to Academy Prep for games on Friday and Saturday, the Friday opponent being A-Prep.

If they won on Tuesday against Edgewater.

CHAPTER 22

When you meet your goals, you'd better be
ready to make new ones, to reach higher.

M olly watched film with Coach on Sunday evening after dinner, something she relished doing. Film study helped Morgan, always had. His friends back in Lakewood teased him about the amount of film he watched, told him that drinking beer and meditation was just as valuable as taking stats or knowing which out-of-bounds play the opponent ran in the third quarter. The rest of the team seldom watched, and Morgan didn't think his players needed to watch; they saw the wrong things. There was a reason it was called film *study*. Tonight, the two partners analyzed Edgewater. She wanted to study the second Academy Prep game too, but Morgan nixed that. "If we don't beat Edgewater, there will be no A-Prep game." He doubted if his team had seriously considered that fact, that the season could come to a sudden end on Tuesday.

"Did you ever have a team that got upset in the early rounds?" asked Molly.

"One in particular. Colorado didn't seed teams until the late Eighties, if my memory serves me accurately. Tournaments were organized at the beginning of the year; the league champions advanced, but who they played was set up before the season began, not by seeding. No second or third place teams were invited to the big dance." Morgan paused the tape. "We were ranked as high as third in one paper, but we came up against the number one team in the quarterfinals. Would have been a great final. I had a terrific bunch of kids, very deserving to advance. Played a heckuva game but lost by a basket at the end. It hurt. Later found out that the other team's coach probably used an ineligible player, but whatever, we got bounced. 4A doesn't play consolation, so our season ended. Tough one."

"How did they respond?" asked Molly.

Morgan thought about brushing off Molly's question, but he had been honest to this point in answering her questions. "They took it hard in the locker room, of course, but when we arrived back home, most of them went out and got drunk. Disappointed me."

"We would never do that," said Molly. "None of us ever want to disappoint you."

"No fear of that." They smiled at each other and Morgan restarted the tape. "See how they over-commit to the double-team on you? The helper comes up too wide. Just push the ball past them and jump through . . . like you did here. See? Good."

"Do you think they'll cover out on the wings since we hit our threes against them the last time?" asked Molly.

"I hope so. It'll open up the middle for you."

§

The crowd wasn't as large as for the Benson game because there were no special promotions, but the student body filled the lower bleachers. Molly's mother, Alex, and most of the team's families sat together. Kane roped off a faculty section behind the team again, once more providing popcorn. He noted that both the football and volleyball coaches were seated with their colleagues. Mrs. Marta wore a gold sweatshirt. The band did not play except for the anthem, but the drumline kept the noise level at unacceptable decibels. In their pregame greeting, the Edgewater coach complimented Morgan on his team's success and on the sportsmanship of his team.

"I walked into a gold mine. I think it's them who improved my behavior," said Morgan.

Just before warmups ended, Stevie ran over to Coach Summitt with a disgruntled expression. "Look who's refing. Those are the ones who fouled me out last time."

Morgan knew, but patted Stevie on the back. "It'll be fine. You're just going to have to do your terrorizing by being that much quicker. Edgewater's guards already are afraid of you. I expect them to not want to try and dribble when you're guarding them. Let's see how they adjust; maybe we can cause turnovers by getting in the passing lanes. Don't pick up a quick foul, and we'll go from there."

Edgewater's plan of attack was to throw over the top of Oro Hills' press, but it was a plan they hadn't used during the course of the season. Time after time their passes sailed out of bounds or into the hands of Bianca, who recognized that Edgewater's guards threw quickly, looking mostly for a particular forward who wasn't as athletic as Bianca. By halftime Oro Hills had a nine-point lead and Edgewater was frazzled. Stevie had no fouls, and most of Oro Hills' offense was coming via the turnover or the fast break.

"This isn't over by any means," warned Coach Summitt. "Let's turn up the pressure on their guards, Stevie. My guess is they'll try dribbling past you in this half since their passes aren't working. Molly and Izzy, deny. Elena and Sofia. Look alive in the middle. Full front #33."

Bianca raised her hand. "Coach, I can outrun their girls on the break. Tell everyone to shoot quick, and I'll get the rebound."

Morgan nodded. "Got that, girls?" He smiled, brought the girls' hands into the stack, and said, "Let's be cheetahs this second half. Go for the jugular right away."

Edgewater collapsed in the third quarter, not scoring a single point, while Oro Hills tallied eighteen and led by twenty-seven at the close of the period. Morgan breathed a huge sigh of relief. The season wasn't going to end tonight. He put his team into a delay game for the first half of the fourth quarter, mostly having Molly dribble away from the defenders. Edgewater came out of their zone eventually, but at the four-minute mark, Morgan substituted Cindy, Penny, Rosa, and the two freshmen junior varsity players to finish off the game.

In the locker room after the game, a sense of accomplishment hung in the air, slightly different from the jubilation of the Benson victory. "Tough one Friday, girls," said Morgan with a smile. "I don't need to tell you who we'll be playing. We'll meet at my house in twenty minutes for a little dinner, and then everyone is to head straight home and get some sleep. I'll expect each of you to be on time for your first class tomorrow morning." He turned to Gloria. "Anything, Coach?"

"Just want to say how proud of you we are. The whole school is. The women have refilled your water bottles, so hydrate tonight. I want every one of those bottles empty by the time you get to Coach Summitt's house."

They team stacked hands and, instead of "Miners," yelled "Cheetahs," and cheered briefly. Morgan left the locker room to find Andrea and Kane. After dinner he would send the girls home and break out the Academy Prep game film. Molly would walk across the street to pretend she was going to sleep, but when all the other girls were gone, she would return and watch the tape with her coach.

"These girls have never been here before," said Andrea to her husband as they lay in bed.

"Never won a league playoff game."

Laying on his back, Morgan reached over and took Andrea's hand. "Nope, but then again, they've never done any number of things before."

"What do you think about Friday's chances?"

"I kind of wish our last game hadn't been so close. We won't surprise them, that's for sure. They're ranked number four in the state, undefeated, confident, and playing on their home floor. It'll be difficult." Morgan squeezed Andrea's hand. "But we'll show up."

"You didn't mention the long bus ride," teased Andrea.

"Yeah, but on the bright side, our new warmups and shooting shirts are as pretty as theirs."

§

Two blocks away Bianca Steele, just as she did after every game, took out her spiral notebook and wrote down an evaluation of her play. She included her stats, fourteen points and thirteen rebounds, but only as a point for improvement. She noted each shot, make or miss, and why. She listed the number of points for the girls she was defending and if she could have done something better to stop them. She knew during and after each game those statistics, as if she was sitting with the Mountain Matrons charting the game. Every play, every possession, every sequence etched on her brain to be recalled later that night. She noted Rosa's stats; three points on her very first three ever late in the game. The starters on the bench had jumped up and cheered. When she finished with the personal information, she wrote in perfect cursive: *Acero*. Then, she replaced the notebook in her dresser, bid goodnight to Tia Maria, and said her prayers.

§

At practice on Wednesday, Morgan took his girls upstairs to a classroom to explain the District Tournament, the first round as it had already unfolded and the semis and finals. On the green chalkboard, he diagramed the bracket. "I think you probably knew, but the first round was an elimination game. If we had lost, our season would be over. I didn't say anything about it, because I didn't want to put any extra pressure on you. Needless to say, we didn't." A few of the girls cheered. "There were no upsets last night; all the higher seeds won on their own home floor. Now, the tournament moves to Academy Prep's gym because they're the league champion, and the champion hosts the semis and finals. On Friday Benson plays Tutwiler at five, and we play A-Prep at seven. It will be a loud environment and almost none of them will be cheering for us. The three other schools are lots closer and will bring fans, so be ready for that. We've been underdogs all year anyway."

Penny raised her hand. "If we lose, are we out?"

Morgan smiled. "No, we aren't. Let me run through this. Three of the four teams left will advance to the round of twenty-four which begins next week. For us to be included, we need to win one of this weekend's games. There are several scenarios. One, beat Academy and whoever wins this game." He pointed to the other semifinal contest on the board. "Two, beat Academy and lose the championship game. Then we would be the number two seed next week. And three, lose to Academy but then win the third-place game. That would get us to next week also. In the unlikely circumstance we lose both, then our season will be over on Saturday." He noticed a few of his girls were still a little unsure of the playoff picture. "Three of the four teams left from our conference will continue to play next week. Twenty-four teams in 2A will be left. I intend for us to be one of them. The way we're playing now, I think we have a real good chance."

Izzy raised her hand. "When would we play then?"

"Remember, I said twenty-four teams advance to next week. All the teams play against teams from other conferences. Depending on where we finish in our tournament this weekend, we will play on Friday or Saturday or both. Starting next week, winners move on, losers are out."

"So, don't lose," said Molly. "Win this week and next, and we go to State."

Morgan allowed Molly's remark to set in. Then, "At the beginning of the season, nobody expected Oro Hills to be here, to be one of our league's final four. Certainly, Academy Prep was picked to be the champion since they've never lost in this league in the previous years. Benson was a good bet for second, and Tutwiler is no surprise. But we are, and we'll show up with our twenty supporters and battle." *Battle* was a descriptor Morgan always liked to use. "I like our chances, and I don't mean just to win one game, but to win it all. Yep, we're the underdogs, but you have improved so much, more than any other team I've ever coached, and have a chance. Like my wife likes to tell me, if you have a chance, you've got everything."

§

Academy Prep's gym held thirteen-hundred people, and every seat was taken. Morgan shook his head; *2A school, my ass*, he thought. Benson and Tutwiler brought solid contingents, but the majority were wearing powder blue colors. As the Oro Hills girls stood with their coach waiting to be escorted to a P.E. locker room, they seemed a bit awestruck by the setting, and Morgan knew arriving early had been a good thing.

In the locker room, Morgan sat with his girls, hoping to settle them down. "Well, this is going to be fun. Molly, you're just going to have to do this on your own, since none of you on the court will be able to hear me." He looked first at Molly and then to the rest of the girls. "Just kidding."

"Just like *Hoosiers*, huh, Coach?' said Molly.

"Except for the fact that the Indiana championship game was probably played in front of fifteen-thousand fans, no difference." He paused. "Leave your stuff in here. Gloria has the key. We'll make sure everything is secure. We'll go out and find seats together and watch Benson and Tutwiler for the first quarter. Then, we'll come back in here and dress so we can shoot at halftime. He looked to Rosa. "Make sure you find time for your ritual." He smiled broadly at her and the team giggled. "You're pretty special, you know. Okay, let's go out and watch a little basketball."

Tutwiler and Benson both played zones and the score stayed low with a minimal number of possessions. When Oro Hills took the floor at halftime, the first game score was 13-12 in favor of Benson. Molly commented to Bianca that both teams must be saving their energy for Saturday's games with Academy Prep and Oro Hills. While the Miners and Antelopes shot, Morgan stood near the corner of the end line and considered his pre-game words. He wouldn't need to hype the game for his girls, just review the game plan. Morgan noticed Kane and three teachers sitting above the Tutwiler bench, the visitor's bench where Oro Hills would sit. Andrea and the book club hadn't arrived yet, and the eight junior varsity girls who traveled with the team were gathered in the balcony waiting for seats to open up after the first contest. He knew the referees for his game and felt comfortable they would not affect the flow of the game, wouldn't call ticky-tack fouls. Stevie and Bianca could play to their strengths. Morgan watched his girls shoot mostly in silence, while the A-Prep team clapped, danced, and sang. Loose as geese. *Why shouldn't they be?* he thought.

Back in the locker room after halftime, Oro Hills sat on the benches, stretched, or walked around nervously. They read Coach Summitt's keys on the whiteboard and sipped water, while Coach Gloria spoke to each girl. Coach Summitt watched Benson begin to put distance between themselves and Tutwiler, just as he predicted they would. There were Academy and Benson in the Discovery League, and everybody else. If indeed, as expected, the championship game pitted those two teams, it would be a barnburner. Two good teams that were just a cut below the best 2A teams in the state. They were closing the gap; maybe a Discovery League team could win a game at the real State Tournament.

When the horn sounded ending the third quarter, Benson led by seven. Not an insurmountable lead by any means, but Benson was in control. Morgan turned and went to join his girls for the biggest game in the history of Oro Hills girls basketball. He gathered his team and reviewed his keys, focusing on the press at the game's outset.

"Remember what we practiced. We'll be in a zone press. It will look like our usual man press, but we trap hard when A-Prep crosses the timeline. Hit 'em hard there with high hands; make that first trap tight. Elena, most likely Academy will go down the right side of the court, which means first pass out of the trap will come toward you. Bianca, cheat towards the ball side and dare them to throw cross-court. Be aggressive and get the steal.

Close down the passing lanes."

§

Molly heard the crowd, but it didn't frighten her. It amped up her desire to play; she wanted to be the focal point of the Academy Prep jeers. In the layup line, she went hard and then sprinted to halfcourt to toe the timeline. Once, she reached across and swatted the younger Academy Prep sister on the fanny as a sign of sportsmanship or gamesmanship, depending on the point of view. The older sister was a second-team all-stater last year, and the two of them were the strength of the team. Both were Bianca's height, although neither was as strong. They controlled the paint every game, seldom roaming farther out than ten feet from the basket. Athletic, determined, and, as Molly described them, *privileged*. Neither girl had lost a league or district tournament basketball game in high school.

The Antelopes' crowd stood in unison in anticipation for the tip-off and would remain standing until their team scored its first basket. Coach Summitt turned toward the task at hand, turned to his girls with last words, *Don't wait!*, stacked hands, and sent his girls out to do battle. He hugged Molly around her shoulders, and she tapped his belly. As he turned back from the bench, Bianca stood directly in front of him.

"I'm not coming out tonight." It was not said in defiance, but as a promise. Morgan beamed.

Academy Prep controlled the tip, but Stevie stole the ball before A-Prep reached halfcourt, creating a two-on-one situation with Molly. One quick pass and Molly had a layup. The faux girl press confused A-Prep, and they passed ahead into the waiting Oro Hills trap. "High and tight," Morgan had instructed. "Don't wait!" The Academy guard panicked slightly, and Elena intercepted the pass thrown into the heart of Oro Hills' press. A three-on-two situation this time led to another Molly Rascon basket. Academy's inbounds pass flew into their bench with their coach catching the ball. He slammed it down and called time-out. Their crowd was still standing.

Morgan leaned in close to his girls. "We'll run *Carolina* on this possession to Izzy's side. Let it fly, Izzy. Stevie, front block #50 in the middle to free up Bianca. After we score, we change to our regular forty-press. They won't expect it."

Izzy's three skipped long off the rim into the waiting hands of Bianca who powered it back up and in and was fouled. Her free throw made it 7-0 and the tone had been set. The lead forced A-Prep to play catch-up, which they were unaccustomed to doing. The pace allowed Molly more space to attack fullcourt, more opportunities for her teammates to run, and Oro Hills could run.

The Academy Prep crowd finally sat after two minutes. At the end of the first quarter, their team trailed 17-12. Their guards hadn't figured out what Oro Hills was doing defensively, as Gloria kept saying to Morgan on the bench. "Their coach has to tell them each trip down!" The second quarter was more of the same, up-tempo favoring the underdogs, and when the teams went to their locker rooms, Oro Hills still led 33-29. Molly and Stevie had played all sixteen minutes. Bianca took a forearm across the bridge of her nose mid-way through the second period and came out for two minutes, but Penny stood up toe-to-toe with the *sisters*. Sofia had more minutes than Elena, but the trio of Izzy, Elena, and Sofia battled A-Prep's talented forwards to a stand-off.

Coach Summitt's first words were not about strategy. "At various times in your life, you'll be given opportunities to perform at the highest levels with great passion. If that time comes when you're with friends or family, it's all the better. At those times seize the opportunity with courage. This basketball game tonight provides us with an opportunity. Clear your mind of every thought about *what if* and focus on *right now*." Standing behind the team, Gloria rubbed her bare forearms.

"Now, in their locker room, their coach is telling them to calm down, that they're okay, and maybe the sisters hear him, but their guards are not all in. They've been wounded." He allowed for his words to be processed. "We've been working on our run-and-jump press for a month. No traps now, everyone moves into passing lanes or rotates hard. We'll be vulnerable for an instant, but I don't think their guards will react fast enough to be consistently effective. We'll get more than we lose, so stay in your cheetah mode." He looked to Gloria. "Anything?"

Morgan's assistant coach smiled and said softly but intensely, "Be shot aggressive and run to rebound. This game will come down to the wire, but you've been given a chance. That's all Coach ever wanted for you."

She paused. "A chance."

"All right, everyone up and in."

§

The second half was more of the same, the league champion caught in the claws of young cheetahs led by two sixteen-year-olds who had never had such an opportunity in their lives. Molly was certainly the most talented player on the court, but at every other position, the champion held the ability and experience edge. Morgan stood at courtside and wondered if his girls could hold up on heart and grit. Late in the third, A-Prep took the lead, but Bianca wrestled a rebound from the older sister to score at the buzzer giving Oro Hills a one-point lead heading into the fourth, 50-49.

"Keep this game ugly!" screamed Molly as her girls gathered at the bench. "Don't let them be pretty!"

Morgan was calmer. "Having fun down there, Bianca?" he asked. He knew the answer. "No one's in foul trouble, so stay tight. How's your lip, Sofia?" Sofia shrugged it off. "Okay, fake the jump on the trap now, and stay with your girl. Their guards are frazzled. On offense, Molly's going to attack the basket on each possession, so Stevie and Izzy, get back." Morgan complimented Penny for her two minutes and sent the team back to the floor.

The home crowd stood constantly in the fourth, their cheering displaying a nervous tone rather than the confident, celebratory noise of the past seasons. Still, experience, talent, and a deep bench gave A-Prep the advantage, and Morgan knew it. He understood that will and determination have limits against a team that also possessed those traits and was well-coached. Morgan would select the precise moments to use all his time-outs to give his girls a breather, saving just one for that last possession, if needed.

When Oro Hills had boarded the bus after the pep rally, Kane Vincent asked Coach Summitt what he hoped the score would be to give his team a chance. Morgan said he thought the higher the score, the better. If it got into the fifties, Oro Hills would have a chance. At the two-minute mark, when Morgan called his third time-out, the score was tied at 60. "Okay, the sisters are playing behind Bianca to keep her off the glass, so our first look on this possession is inside. If you can read her numbers, throw it inside. Sofia, flash to the near elbow and see if you can drag your girl with you. Bianca, that should allow you to drop-step baseline. Go up strong."

"Is there any other way, Coach?" said Bianca with a grin.

"Stay in our tight forty-press. Deny your girl, Stevie. See if we can keep her from bringing the ball up court. If your girl has it, Molly, and we have the lead, take a chance on the steal."

They broke the huddle and Molly tapped Morgan's belly. Rosa stood next to him and put her arm through his. Molly received the pass in the backcourt and dribbled forward, in no hurry to force a play. She did not look to give it up, motioning to Izzy to clear her wing and replace Molly at the top. Stevie held to her opposite wing position, while Bianca and Sofia set low on the blocks. Sofia turned to screen the Academy girl in the middle of their two-three zone, and Bianca came under and set up on the near block closest to Molly. When Sofia flashed high, Molly threw Bianca a bounce pass. She moved forward slightly to receive it, located the older sister, and drop-stepped to the basket. Her shot found the bottom of the net and the younger Antelope sister fouled her. Bianca's free throw gave Oro Hills a three point lead. Stevie denied her girl the ball forcing A-Prep to go to their off-guard, just as Morgan had hoped. Molly remembered the tactic Stevie had shown her. With every Oro Hills defender denying her girl, the Academy guard was alone against Molly. Molly faked one way and stepped forward quickly to steal the ball, breaking free for the layup and giving Oro Hills a five-point lead with less than a minute to go.

Academy Prep took one last three that careened off into Bianca's hands. She passed to Molly who dribbled away from the Antelopes until they committed a desperation foul with just twelve seconds left. Molly made both free throws, and Oro Hills had the win, 67-60. The Evil Empire had fallen, had lost its first Discovery League game ever, and Oro Hills would play Benson for the league's top seed, for the District Championship. A-Prep's fans stood in stunned silence as they watched their team walk through the post-game congratulatory line. With tears in their eyes, the Academy girls tapped the hands of Oro Hills' girls, but said little, not out of disrespect, but in disbelief. A year earlier they won by over fifty points. What had transpired over the past year?

Morgan knew. His team had flat out out-worked the league champion, not just on this night, but over the course of the year. The Mountain Matrons stripped away the veneer of poverty; Kane and Queenie allowed for all the girls to participate; Morgan and Gloria created a framework built on their girls' particular physical skills; Molly Rascon saw an opportunity and seized it. She and her teammates wrestled away something that was precious from the team that had previously clutched it. When the final buzzer had sounded, the Cheetahs walked through the sportsmanship line and then sprinted into the locker room. Molly knew that every bead of sweat over the past eleven months had been worth it.

When Morgan finally calmed his players, after his words of praise and pride, he told them of the U.S. hockey team that upset the Soviet Union in the 1980 Olympics. "They were a bigger underdog than we were, maybe the biggest of all time. That game is called the 'Miracle on Ice,' but what we seldom remember is the game was in the semifinals of the tournament, not for the gold medal. The U.S. team still had to win one more game to get the gold," said Morgan.

"Did they win?" asked Izzy?

"It was a tough game, but yes, yes, they did."

"Someone ought to make a movie about it," said Rosa.

§

On Saturday, the disappointed Academy Prep fans cleared the gym after they received their third-place trophy, leaving the championship game to be played before a crowd of maybe five hundred, mostly Benson Bobcat supporters. Fatigue created a sloppier game for both Oro Hills and Benson. Morgan went to his bench often, including Alondra and Cindy, to spell his tired starters. Penny played well in her six minutes, and the game was decided by the three point shooting of Izzy, who hit five threes against the Benson zone that focused on stopping Molly. Izzy's instincts and footwork, coupled with her confidence, provided Morgan with the weapon he'd counted on at the start of the season, although he never dreamed she would make five threes in a single game. Moreover, two of the threes she missed were rebounded by Bianca who powered them back in. Eight shots for nineteen points, almost half of the points in the championship game on just eight possessions. Benson concentrated on Molly, but was only partially successful, and leaving Izzy unguarded on the wing cost them the game. By winning the District Championship, Oro Hills received one of the 2A classification's prized number one seeds in the round of twenty-four, meaning they would receive a first-round bye into the round of sixteen and host a game on the next Saturday. One win to the State Tournament, to the Final Eight in Colorado Springs.

CHAPTER 23

He told me never to be scared of a basketball game.
After that, I never was.

On Sunday Morgan and Andrea drove to Denver to tell their daughter about the game. In the early afternoon, he met with the other Discovery League coaches at Edgewater High School for the conference meeting.

On Monday Kane displayed the championship trophy in the commons area for the student body to see, and Gloria initiated an impromptu pep rally during lunch for the girls. Elena received her letter of acceptance from Western State College and was called to the office to be given a certificate confirming she would be receiving a tuition scholarship.

When the girls went to the gym for Monday's practice, Gloria told them not to dress out, to just wait on the bleachers until Coach Summitt arrived. They would not hold a physical practice but would receive information about their upcoming opponent. Kane came in with their trophy and bottles of soda. He told them how proud he was of their accomplishments, how they had earned it, and wished them good luck on Saturday. Morgan had called him earlier with information about the possible opponents, but Kane kept mum on that.

"I'll get it engraved with all your names, and it will go on permanent display in the trophy case in the hall opposite the main office where every visitor will see it. You've made Oro Hills history, the first girls basketball team in the school's history to win a trophy."

Morgan arrived shortly thereafter. "One more day of rest before we get at it again tomorrow. This is what I learned today. We will play on Saturday, or should I say, we will host on Saturday." He smiled and the girls cheered. "We were given the number sixth-seed for the tournament, which I expected since we were only fourth in our league, and the state considers our victory an upset. I also think they wanted to give Academy Prep the highest non-champion seed and didn't want them to play against us again until the State Tournament."

Molly interrupted. "Didn't want us to kick their butts again." Her teammates clapped.

"Anyway, we will play the winner of tomorrow's game between Manitou Springs and Rangely. They have records similar to ours and Rangely is hosting. I think both came in second in their leagues. Either one will be a tough game, so our practices have to be sharp. I know you'll want to rest on your laurels and take it easy, . . ."

His girls booed at his kidding.

"Last thing. I was at the conference meeting on Sunday, and all the league coaches told me to tell you good luck and congratulations."

"Even Academy Prep, Coach?" asked Molly.

Morgan nodded. "Yep, even him. He said they'd meet us in two weeks when we play for the State Championship. Said something about having a score to settle."

Mr. Vincent stepped forward with his hand up, asking for a few words. "I've received calls from several former Miners congratulating you." He waved his arm to the hallway behind the bleachers. Seventeen Oro Hills coaches and teachers entered, including Coach Thulen and Coach Holmes. They were all clapping.

Coach Holmes spoke for the group. "We are so proud of you. You've shown us what hard work can accomplish. Now, all of us have a higher bar to coach to. Thank you." She stepped back, took a card from Mrs. Risso, and handed it to Morgan. "This is signed by all the faculty. We wish you good luck."

§

On Tuesday night Rangely, the second-place finisher in both the Western Slope regular season and tournament, beat Manitou Springs. They would travel to Oro Hills in the round-of-16, the winner advancing to the State Tournament the following week. Rangely's overall record was better than Oro Hills', and they played in a tougher conference. Through phone calls and newspaper accounts, Morgan was able to piece together a

Roger Johnson

basic scouting report. Tough, methodical, disciplined ranch kids. Mostly a zone team that wanted the score in the twenties and thirties. Oro Hills would have its hands full. He wondered if they had a scouting report on his team.

Coach Summitt challenged his girls on Wednesday's and Thursday's practices, going five-on-five both days. He had Gloria play the post against Bianca, all the time teaching as she was bumping Bianca. Bianca liked when Coach Gloria played, and the two had formed a close relationship. Morgan knew every positive relationship Bianca formed with an adult was a valuable one. Her history with adults' trust had made her suspicious.

§

Molly renamed their full-court press "Cheetah," but Oro Hills had added the wrinkles to it. In every victory this season, the press provided an advantage, regardless of how the opponents prepared. Morgan began the summer with a full-court press that he called "Forty," using the terminology of North Carolina coach Dean Smith, one of his heroes for how he used basketball to grow the character of his players and to fight racial discrimination. But his girls' quickness and maturation allowed Morgan to expand the defensive arsenal. Because of summer play, because of the time the girls spent on his driveway, he envisioned their offensive development, but he did not predict how crazy-good the defense would become. Gloria's term. Morgan laughed at his good fortune over the past year. Kane's support, Gloria's enthusiasm and curiosity, her different set of eyes, these wonderful girls, and the Mountain Matrons.

§

Morgan knew Friday could be his last practice with this special group, that a loss to Rangely would end his magical season, but he tried to push that image out of his mind and focus on finding one last thing to improve. Maybe Stevie's blockout technique, Sofia's three point shot, Bianca's baby-hook, or maybe how Molly attacked a goofy zone. Friday's practice was to go over details, shoot lots of game shots, and to establish their confidence, all things they did every day. Maybe it was to fortify his own confidence. Morgan understood Rangely could be the toughest opponent of the season, better maybe than Academy Prep and Benson. He didn't know

228

for sure. But if his girls could win this one, every opponent at State would be better than any previous one.

The Rangely Panthers versus the Oro Hills Miners. "Both schools seem to be misnamed," said Gloria. "Should be the Elephants versus the Cheetahs." She and the team sat on the locker room bench while Morgan wrote a few more notes on the board. He underlined his last key, set the chalk on the ledge, and turned to his team. "Do you know how to eat an elephant?" No one answered. "One bite at a time," he said. The girls smiled. "And that's how we'll win this game; one possession at a time. When they have the ball, you will scratch and claw, you will put pressure on the ballhandler and deny the passing lanes. When they shoot, you will put your butt on their thighs. When we have the ball, Molly will attack the lane, and the rest of you will look for your opening. When the shot goes up, you will beat your girl to the rebound. We will continue to play the game like we have over the last month. Trust yourself. Trust your teammates." He stopped. He set his jaw. "It will take a few minutes to establish ourselves, but don't worry. Just keep pushing and we'll get control." He looked over his squad and nodded. "Last home game. Own the floor! Own this court! Let's go get 'em!"

Rangely's deliberate style made it difficult early, and they led after a quarter, 7-6. Morgan saw no panic in his girls. Stevie's pressure forced an early second quarter turnover and Oro Hills gained the momentum for a few minutes, enough time to seize the lead at halftime, 19-13. Because of the slow pace, none of the Oro Hills girls had more than one foul. Rangely's plan was to stay in a tight zone, prevent Molly from penetrating the lane, and keep Bianca off the boards. Rangely's bigs were only five-nine and five-eight, and Bianca was wearing them out. Both had three fouls. Still, Morgan cautioned his girls. "Get out on their threes; both wings can shoot. Don't let them have an Izzy-type game. Stevie, in the halfcourt, just contain #11. If she gets careless, then strike, but in the halfcourt, contain with good pressure."

The third quarter was played out like the first quarter, with Rangley winning by a point, trailing 27-22. But Oro Hills' guards had planted the anxiety seed in the minds of Rangely's guards, a seed that germinated on the first possession of the final quarter. Stevie stole the dribble, passed to Izzy, who fed Molly for a layup. On the ensuing possession, Sofia intercepted a cross-court pass. Her pass to Stevie led to an easy score, and the lead was nine. It never got closer. When it reached thirteen, Morgan ordered a delay, and Molly protected the ball. Rather than foul, Rangely acquiesced, never coming out of their zone. Oro Hills would be playing three more games as one of the final eight 2A teams at the State Tournament. No Oro Hills girls basketball team had won any tournament game, and now, Molly's team had its second trophy, sixteen wins, and an invitation to the Big Dance. As Morgan told his team after their celebration, while Elena cradled the trophy and the girls locked arms, "A little talent goes a little way, and a lot of talent, coupled with hard work and trust, can go a long way."

§

In her notebook entry, Bianca evaluated her play, as always, and on a separate line wrote, *Bianca Acero, center, Oro Hills High School, Regional Champions.*

CHAPTER 24

Do your best and that will be good enough.

M organ had been wrong. Rangely was not as talented as Academy Prep or Benson or Slater, at least his girls didn't think so, and Oro Hills showed how far they had traveled. The team had received a fortunate draw. Academy Prep hadn't been so lucky and was beaten by one of the Eastern Plains' powerhouses, Simla, the top seed for the tournament. Benson was eliminated by a Denver private school. Winning the Discovery League tournament had given Oro Hills the opportunity to play a weaker team, and now it was going to State. As Morgan sat with Molly, Bianca, and Rosa at his kitchen nook on Sunday evening looking at the brackets, something basketball geeks did at this time of the season, he could only wonder if his girls knew what they were up against for their next three games. Oro Hills' first opponent would be Fowler, a traditional participant in the tournament, the '93 champion. Next up would be either Ellicott or Sanford. Ellicott was the two-time defending State Champion but had been beaten out in their own conference by Simla. Sanford had just a single loss all season, but drew Ellicott because Ellicott had to advance as a number-two seed out of their conference. Oro Hills was in the same bracket with Sanford, Fowler, and Ellicott. The three of them had fewer combined losses for the season than Oro Hills had. Realistically, Oro Hills might be looking at winning its only game in the seventh-eighth place game next Saturday morning, and even that would be an upset.

"Well," said Morgan to Molly, "you got what you wanted, to go to State. We achieved our goal."

"New goals," said Molly. "What do you think is possible?"

Morgan laughed aloud. "At the end of last season, back when I was the only one in the stands watching you play junior varsity, I thought you should have won four or five games at that level. I thought with a different style of play, you guys could win three or four *varsity* games this season. Then we played over the summer and you two," Morgan nodded to Bianca and Rosa, "came on board, and I thought maybe a few more in the Discovery League, maybe a half-dozen. Ten, tops. So, what's possible? With you guys, I guess darn near anything."

Rosa smiled. "Yeah, I made the difference."

When they stopped giggling, Bianca asked Molly's question again. "What's possible, Coach?"

"Basketball's a fair game. Each team starts out with the presumption of equal possessions, and what you do with those possessions determines the outcome. Take good shots, make your fair share. Limit their good shots. A team can add to its possessions by getting offensive rebounds, second chances. We can limit their possessions, in effect, by causing turnovers. Of course, other things affect this. Are we tall enough to get those rebounds? Are we quick enough to get turnovers? I think we are; it's how we play, our style. Still, the other team will have its particular physical advantages, plus our first two opponents, at least, have experience and tradition in their favor. We'll need to overcome that."

"But we can do that?" asked Bianca, looking for assurances.

"Yep, we have a chance."

§

"Two nights at Motel 6 off I-25. Only a couple of miles to the gym from there. Will that work?" asked Kane.

Morgan nodded. "Yeah, just get assurances from the motel that we can get a late check-out on Saturday if we play in the afternoon or evening."

"Longshot, huh?"

"The longest. Realistically, we can compete with Yuma and Paonia. Most likely after two losses. Our first two opponents are beasts."

"What do you know about Fowler?"

"Not much. Up-tempo like us, good guards, an all-state senior center. They dominated a pretty good league and beat some 3A teams early. Their seniors have been to four straight state tournaments."

"'93 champs, huh?" said Kane. "Do you want me to call them and tell them we surrender?"

"Nah, we'll show up regardless."

§

Morgan held Monday's practice from four to five-thirty. He wanted his girls to be able to hang around the halls after school to receive the accolades from their friends. Many of the Oro Hills students didn't know about the victory or what winning Saturday's game meant. State tournaments were not part of their experiences, but as word filtered out, students would congratulate the team.

Practice ran like those normal practices during the latter part of the season. A little shorter, but just as intense. Morgan spent additional time on rebounding, concentrating on box-outs. He had Molly review the special situation plays and the out-of-bounds sets. "Execution, girls. We need to be precise. Our beauty isn't going to impress Fowler."

Practice ended precisely at five-thirty, at least the floor work. Morgan sat them down in the bleachers, passed out detailed itineraries, and talked about the experience. The Mountain Matrons arrived with pizza and sodas, Gloria talked of her Wyoming State experience, and Morgan closed with stories of his boys teams that played in the tournament. He understood this team could lose all three games, but he wanted them to know this coming week was about much more than the final score. For him, since the days when he played at the Elm Street Gym as a fifth-grader during World War II, basketball had been his sanctuary, and this year, especially for Molly and Rosa and Alondra and Sofia and Bianca, it was theirs.

§

Wednesday's practice was the last one of the season. Because Oro Hills was playing in the State Tournament, Morgan could use it to encapsulate the year. After an hour of shooting and reviews, he sat them down one last time. "I know I've talked a lot about the experience, but tonight I want to talk about something else. Tonight, I want to talk about the here and now." He let that sit for a moment. "You are one of eight, one of the last eight teams to still be playing basketball. About sixty other 2A teams are running track or playing soccer or chasing boys fulltime." The girls laughed. "We lost our first game of the season. Since then, you've been moving along the curve to excellence, and now, you have a chance to take another step. The here, the now, is about . . . winning."

§

At the pep rally on Thursday morning, Elena and Sofia, the two seniors, spoke. Morgan was proud of their words. They spoke of *family* and thanked the student body and faculty for their support. They promised to make them proud. Since the team would be spending two nights in a motel, the junior varsity could not accompany the varsity on the bus. Just twelve girls and two coaches. Five of the Mountain Matrons were driving down and staying in the same motel.

Molly took it all in, each practice, each post-practice talk, every suggestion by her coach, but she wanted the pep rally to be over quickly, so she and her teammates could get on the bus and get to Colorado Springs. At home she had been irritable with her mother and brother. Her mother explained why she would be unable to attend, that work came first, and that hurt Molly. She wondered if her dad would attend, but she wasn't going to call him. He probably didn't even know Oro Hills was playing. He'd never followed her basketball career before. Morgan noticed and was concerned, but when the bus left the school parking lot, he noticed the change. She left those concerns behind. Bianca was Molly's best friend, and Molly was Bianca's second-best friend behind Rosa. The three of them sat together in adjacent seats, snuggled into their blankets, and reminisced about the season, along with the rest of the team. Nervous talk.

"Hey, Coach, what's Fowler's nickname?" yelled Molly from the back of the bus.

"Grizzlies," answered Morgan. "Just like Adams State College."

"So, Cheetahs versus Grizzlies. Good sign," yelled Molly.

§

The bus stopped in south Denver just after one o'clock, so the girls could have a pre-game meal. Morgan and Kane planned every detail, and if by chance something had been left out, Andrea and the book club women covered it. Tournament experience was valuable not only for

234

the players, but also for the coaches. Arriving in Colorado Springs, they went straight to the motel where Morgan would have them dress for the game, and he would apprise them of the rituals of a State Tournament game. Gloria realized how often he used the term *state* as he spoke to his team. *State* this and *State Tournament* that. Reverently. He plugged them into this environment, letting them know they belonged. He told Gloria the team had its rock, Molly Rascon, but that every other girl might get caught up in the hoopla, and it could affect her play. When Gloria had asked why not Molly, he told her about the nightly talks the two of them had at the breakfast nook talking basketball, talking life. *Molly has a filter,* Morgan told Gloria, *and a focus.*

The girls dressed in their rooms and then gathered in Gloria's room for a final inspection. Little things: the ribbons used to tie their ponytails, or the double-knot Morgan insisted they used to secure their shoes, details. When they walked out onto the college arena floor, a larger floor than a high school gym floor, there would be the noise and the lights and the professional sound system creating distractions, but within his control, Coach Summitt would limit those distractions. Gloria inspected each girl, straightening her shooting shirt or checking Izzy's makeup. Reassurance. When Mama Gloria was satisfied, she called in Coach Summitt.

"I tried to get the Hilton Hotel downtown, but it was pre-booked by Academy Prep," he said. "Oh, they aren't here, are they?" The girls laughed. He looked to Rosa. "You okay?"

"So far. Coach Gloria said she'd have the key to the bathroom at the arena in case I needed to throw-up there."

His smile registered his love for her and her teammates. "Okay," he began, "since we're here, we might as well do some damage. All year long I've spoken about *going into battle.* We have been just us, for the most part, our little band of sisters. No difference tonight. We'll have a few extra supporters in the stands, but they'll be swallowed up by the fans from the other towns, teams whose traditions have taught them how to prepare for the State Tournament. Tonight, on this first trip to the Big Dance, you'll have to rely on my experience." He looked over his team. Gloria thought at that moment he was putting a wool comforter around his team. *I've been here.* She understood what he was doing, asking them to trust him to handle their insecurities, to enable them to just play the game. "Our officials tonight are from the Northern Colorado area, so they won't know you or the Fowler team. No advantage or disadvantage there. We'll only have twelve minutes to warm-up, so go right to the first layup drill. Get lots of looks from your particular shot area, check the backdrop. Wings, that will be especially important for you. Shoot some threes. We'll be seated towards the end of the court rather than close to the scorer's table, so communication will have to be altered just a little. Look to Molly for instructions; she and I have worked this out. There will be no anthem, so when the buzzer sounds to end warmups, just run to the bench. The player introductions will be short. Line up like we normally do; just know that the pre-game routine is shorter. Since we're the visitors on the scoreboard, we'll be announced first."

Morgan went over the game plan for the first time, but it was basically *Play like we play. Take the game to them.* Gloria approved; no radical changes. *We're good enough just as we are.* Morgan covered a few items specific to each girl, reminding them of assignments that might be forgotten due to nerves, but mostly reassuring each girl by name to calm her.

"Bianca, I like how your baby hook is coming along, but don't forget to take those put-backs right into their big girl's chest. She'll be off balance on those. Let's see if we can get her a couple of early fouls." Morgan looked to Gloria as he always did. "Anything, Coach?"

Gloria shook her head. "I think you covered everything, Coach. I'm just excited to play this first game at State." She looked over the girls. "You can do this. Believe in yourself."

Morgan looked to Molly. "Anything you'd like to add?"

Molly nodded. "I set our goals too low. Just *get to State?* We're here. Let's win this first one and see what's next. Stevie, lead the way."

§

When the team arrived at the arena, it dawned on Gloria that none of the Oro Hills girls owned a letter jacket. Students from the other schools, athletes from all sports, both male and female, walked around the arena wearing colorful jackets with leather sleeves and a letter on the front left side decorated with balls and stripes. Most of these jackets had the students' first names written in cursive on the back. Gloria remembered hers from Wyoming. It had been expensive, but it was a symbol of achievement in small towns where high school sports were valued, as were high school athletes. Her parents bought it for her, saying she would have to work to pay them back, but never sticking to that deal. They were proud of her. Gloria added another bullet to her mental list of things needed to be done in Oro Hills to change the losing culture. She smiled to herself that the first bullet could be checked off. *Have a winning team.*

§

As a recent state champion and being only an hour-and-fifteen minutes to the southeast, Fowler brought the whole town. That and their boys team had also qualified and were scheduled for the six-thirty game. An entire corner of the arena dressed in purple and gold. On the opposite corner sat maybe seventy Oro Hills supporters, a few wearing brown or gold. The Fowler supporters may have bolstered their team, but it did not seem to bother Oro Hills. It was the norm. Games had begun at nine that morning, alternating boys, then girls, then boys. This would go on for three days non-stop, with teams advancing into the championship round with a win or to the consolation bracket if they lost.

After arriving at the arena, Morgan took his team to their locker room for a few last words, to allow them to use the toilet, to let Rosa throw-up, and to experience another part of *State*. The four o'clock boys game would end on time, since it wasn't close. A CACA official knocked on the door, stuck her head in the locker room, and signaled three minutes before Oro Hills could take the floor.

"Everybody up, hands in." Morgan put his right hand in first, palm up. When his team had their hands in, he put his left hand on the top and did something he never had with this team. He closed his eyes and thanked God for the privilege he had been given to coach this team. "Okay, when the referee tosses the ball in the air, get after it like you always do. You have improved every game out this season; no reason to think we won't be a little better tonight. Expect the best opponent you've ever seen, but trust me when I tell you that you deserve to be here. You've earned it. Do not be afraid. Do not doubt yourself. Do what you do best. No hesitation." His jaw was set, and he liked what he saw in his girls' eyes. A six-foot-two, sixty-six-year-old gentle man standing among twelve teenagers in a place they'd never been before, never imagined being. "Sofia, Elena, send us out."

"One, two, three, Cheetahs!"

§

As his team arranged themselves around the center jump circle, Morgan heard the Fowler radio announcer broadcasting from the table next to the Oro Hills' bench. "Fowler's opponent is a surprise to the tournament, its first trip to the State Tournament ever. Many observers believe Oro Hills, with their seven losses and finishing fourth in a weak league, should be seeded number eight in the tournament, but since two top seeds in other district tournaments went down, Oro Hills, by virtue of their victory in their District Tournament, is seeded sixth. I think our girls may have been given a gift tonight. Still, we've seen upsets before, so we can't get over-confident." Small town radio announcers seldom learn that kind of information on their own. Most likely, it came from Fowler's coach. *Well, coach, let's let this game play out, just for kicks.* A younger Morgan Summitt might have said something to the announcer, but OFG Morgan just smiled. On paper, the announcer was probably correct, but this team had never played on paper, had never followed the script. The near official turned to the scorer's table to say something, delaying the start of the game. Molly jogged over to her coach.

She popped him on the belly. "Forgot that." She turned and joined Stevie in a safety situation.

Fowler's experience allowed them to grab an early lead and maintain it through the first quarter, but Morgan liked what he saw from his team. After one, Fowler lead 15-8, but Oro Hills had not turned the ball over once. Fowler's six-two center led a balanced Fowler attack with six points. Molly and Bianca each had four, but Izzy and Elena had some good looks from beyond the arc. Stevie missed her two layups after steals, shots Morgan felt she had been fouled on.

In the huddle, Morgan addressed his point guard first. "They want you to give it up in the halfcourt, that's why Izzy and Elena are always open on the wings. Let's try this. Dribble to the wings. Izzy, cut through and go to the top. Sofia, come all the way across and screen for Molly. Molly, keep your dribble alive and attack the paint. Bianca, be ready if the big girl drops off on Molly. Izzy, if Molly kicks it out, let it fly. Stevie, nice job of getting back until you're replaced."

Coach Summitt's adjustments made a difference on the offensive end. Molly scored three quick baskets on twelve-foot jumpers, closing the score to 15-14. Fowler called time out. When play resumed, Molly found herself being double-teamed even when she didn't have the ball. Morgan heard the Fowler announcer say, "Coach Barnes is not going to allow the state's leading scorer to operate freely. He's decided to force someone else on the Oro Hills team to step up. Gotta say, though, this little Molly Rascon is as good as we've seen all season." *Damn right, she is,* thought Morgan.

Fowler's new strategy made it difficult for Oro Hills to score, and the Grizzlies poise against Oro Hills' press allowed them to right the ship and build their lead to ten just before half. With fewer than twenty-seconds left in the quarter, Molly launched a three from four feet behind the arc that found the bottom of the net. Fowler, trying to get one last shot, hurried and got careless. Sofia intercepted a sideline pass, kicked it out to Molly who found Stevie alone at the basket. Her jump-stop layup just before the buzzer closed the margin to five, 31-26.

The five-point blitz renewed Oro Hills' confidence. In the locker room, Morgan had to tell his girls to sit, to take a deep breath, and to listen. "What just happened at the end of the half?" It was a rhetorical question. "We played just beyond our comfort level, maybe because you got a little desperate, but it doesn't matter why. Step off the ledge, ladies. Trust." It occurred to Bianca that her coach had never used the term *ladies* before, at least that she could recall. Always before it was *girls.* She heard her name. "Bianca, Fowler is not going to allow you to post up. The big girl and #45 have been told not to allow you to catch the ball on the block. So, don't. Drift under the basket for a two-second count and then, step out. This second half, I want you to get every missed shot and then power it back up. You're going to be the difference. I know you can do that."

Penny interrupted Morgan. She addressed Bianca who was sitting next to her. "*Big Skinny* isn't sitting on our bench. It ain't me. It's Fowler's center. Rip her up like you do to me every practice. See her and then imagine it's me." Penny patted Bianca's thigh.

Morgan nodded. "On our press we haven't had much success yet but keep at it. I have a feeling that last turnover might cause them to start thinking too much. Stevie, do you have a half-step more quickness in you?"

There wasn't more to say, no inspirational words. He told his team to just be his team and sent them back on the court. He put his arm around Molly and told her not to wait. "You've waited long enough for this."

Fowler's coach most likely told his team not to panic, that Oro Hills got lucky in the last few seconds. "That shot was way out of her range and then we got careless. Stay with what we're doing and don't turn it over. We'll be fine. Keep their big girl bottled up. She didn't score in the second quarter."

Morgan never heard the Fowler radio announcer again. The crowd became louder with each possession, and Coach Summitt's attention was completely on his team. He stood the entire second half, as close to the play as he could get. He shouted instructions to Molly occasionally, but more to Sofia, Elena, and Izzy. He encouraged Stevie to attack every single defensive possession. He turned his head to his bench players to congratulate them on his team's good plays. The pace of the game continued to be in Oro Hills' favor, but Fowler countered and used their size and experience to maintain their five to eight-point lead. Oro Hills scored sixteen points, six by Molly, two by Elena, and eight by Bianca. Still, the Cheetahs trailed by six going into the last quarter, 48-42.

"If we run that baseline screen for you to get your shot from the corner, Izzy, do you think you can knock one down?" Morgan tapped his fist on Izzy's knee. She nodded. "Okay, Molly, let's run it to the left side. Then, we change from our forty-press to our run-and-jump."

Izzy's three closed the deficit to three. Fowler's off-guard traveled when Sofia darted up to her unexpectedly, and Bianca rebounded Molly's missed jump shot and scored. Down one. For the next seven minutes, Fowler called on every ounce of experience to maintain their lead, as Oro Hills ran and bumped and poked and dived. Composure versus chaos. On every trip up the court, Sofia or Bianca set a high screen for Molly and rolled to the basket. On every fourth quarter possession except three, Oro Hills shot within fifteen seconds of crossing the time line. A lesser team would have folded, but Fowler found ways to limit the game's possessions by extending their time with the ball. Fowler's coach used his timeouts to stop Oro Hills' runs, and his two senior guards used their size to over-power Stevie and Izzy, to keep the Grizzlies in the lead.

Despite scoring twenty-four points in the quarter, Oro Hills still trailed in the last minute by two points. Stevie had fouled out at the two-minute mark, and Izzy followed with forty-seconds left in the game and Fowler running a delay. Morgan had a few seconds to ponder his substitute. Penny. Alondra. Cindy. Rosa. He turned to Gloria. "We need quickness." He turned back to his bench. "Jenny, check in." His instructions to the former JV point guard were simple. "Face guard #24. Don't let her catch the ball. Slide over every screen. Get a deflection or a foul. Don't let her catch it!"

Jenny mimicked Stevie and denied #24. Fowler passed to Sofia's girl who clearly did not want the ball. Her weak pass nearly went out of bounds under their basket, but Fowler's Big Skinny recovered it. Bianca intentionally fouled her, as Morgan had directed. One-and-one with eighteen-seconds left. Every command ever uttered by a coach when the opposing team was shooting a free throw at the end of the game and the trailing team needing the rebound to win came from the Oro Hills bench. Plus, one reminder. "Bianca, find Molly and sprint the court."

Big Skinny's free throw rimmed off, and Bianca corralled it. She passed to Molly and both headed up court. Just over halfcourt, Molly split the double-team and drove to the lane. She veered right to improve her angle, and when the Fowler defender stepped up to stop the layup, Molly laid a soft bounce pass to Bianca for the power layup. Setting her feet, she took the ball straight up into Big Skinny's chest. The shot was good, and the referee called a foul with just two seconds remaining in the game. One free throw. Fowler was out of time-outs. Morgan knew Molly would know not to foul, so he motioned her to get on the lane and encourage Bianca. He called Jenny, Sofia, and Elena over and told them not to foul, but to steal any truly bad pass.

Fowler's fans yelled louder than seven-hundred farmers should have been able to, but it didn't matter. Molly stood in front of her teammate and told her to shoot the ball and stand perfectly still. She was not to run to rebound or move after she made it to play defense. "You have one task! Make this and stand still! I'll do the rest."

Bianca's free throw swished, and Molly deflected Fowler's quick inbounds pass. The buzzer sounded, and Oro Hills was moving on, going right on the bracket.

§

Basketball locker rooms after a State victory are about the best place in the world. After the jumping and screaming, after the hugs, Morgan sat on the bench with his team. They quieted down and waited as he regained his composure. He breathed out heavily and shook his head.

"That was something!" He kept shaking his head. Gloria walked up behind him, wrapped her arms around his neck so that her cheek touched his, and then kissed him on that cheek.

"You guys finally did it," she said. "You rendered Coach speechless." The girls clapped and cheered. She kept her hands on Morgan's shoulders and asked Bianca, "Why were you ready to catch that last pass? I would have expected you to be looking to rebound."

"Because their center stepped up to defend Molly. Coach always tells us, 'Don't help up, help across.' When I saw her do that, I knew Molly would pass it."

§

Morgan sent his team back to the motel to shower, change, and eat dinner at a family restaurant nearby. Gloria went with them, and they were joined at the restaurant by the Mountain Matrons, minus Andrea. She and Morgan remained in the arena to scout the Ellicott-Sanford game at eight, the winner to be Oro Hills' semi-final opponent. Ellicott came in as the two-time defending State Champion, even though they were beaten by Simla in their district playoff game. Most coaches expected those two teams to meet one more time on Saturday, although Sanford was a terrific team too. Kane Vincent accompanied the team to dinner, the only male this time. "You get to fill my role," Morgan had told him. Morgan's instructions to Gloria were to get them fed and get them to bed. He and Andrea would eat junk food at the arena and return around ten-thirty.

Oro Hills' victory was the major upset of the first round. Sanford's victory over Ellicott, while mildly surprising, was explainable, but now a new 2A champion would be crowned on Saturday. Fowler, the '93 champ, and Ellicott, the '94 and '95 champ, were sent to the consolation side of the bracket. Oro Hills would play Sanford on Friday night, the last step before the championship game. The loser would play on Saturday afternoon in the third-place game. The number one ranked team in 2A girls Simla would play Denver Catholic on the top half of the bracket. Simla, Sanford, Denver Catholic, along with Ellicott and Fowler were the traditional powerhouses of 2A basketball. *How,* wondered Morgan, *did Oro Hills sneak into the group?*

Morgan and Andrea returned to the hotel to find Kane and Gloria in the downstairs lobby, waiting for the head coach to appear. Gloria told Coach the girls were all in their rooms, probably not asleep, but quiet. Dinner had been wonderfully satisfying, with the book club women fawning over the team. Mercedes and Queenie had chipped in so the girls could order whatever they wanted for dinner rather than being restricted to the amount Kane had budgeted. Andrea excused herself to allow her husband to review the scouting report with Gloria and Kane.

"Will we need to make any significant adjustments?" asked Gloria.

"No. Too late for that. Sanford's in many ways like us. They want to play fast, and they have great quickness. Every position is quick. They may just play us straight up, *mano-a-mano*," said Morgan. "That would be a first in a long while."

"What's the Spanish for girl-to-girl?" asked Kane with a chuckle.

"*Nina-a-nina*, I think," said Gloria.

Morgan leaned back on the motel couch. "They're deeper than we are. They played ten girls a lot. Molly played all thirty-two minutes tonight, and we mostly played with six kids. That could be a factor tomorrow."

"I have to tell you," said Gloria, "Bianca and Sofia mentioned that they were tired, and they looked a little like it. Elena too."

Kane smiled. "Tell them to suck it up. Wrestlers don't get subs at the State Tournament."

Morgan looked at Gloria. "As you get more involved in this coaching thing, you'll understand how difficult it is to make intelligent conversation with wrestling coaches. I get wrestling, but no wrestling coach ever gets basketball." He paused. "We kid, but wrestlers are a special breed, especially at the state level. I admire them more than I let on, and wrestling coaches are cut from that same special cloth."

"We need beers, but probably not tonight," said Kane. "What I do know is that this ex-wrestling coach hired a pretty good coaching duo for these girls."

Morgan nodded. "Gloria, there's an old basketball adage, probably from John Wooden, but maybe not. Anyway, if you have your choice between good coaching and good players, always choose good players. I'm pretty sure it's true in this situation."

"Those girls are making us look pretty darn good," said Gloria. "I told them to sleep in, at least until nine. We'd have breakfast then. What's the agenda after that?"

"I want them to put on their warmup jackets, and then we'll all go to the arena to let them soak up the atmosphere. Make them sit mostly, maybe have them walk a bit during halftime of the Ellicott-Fowler game. I want them to see that game," said Morgan. "I want them to see the company they're in. After that game we'll bring them back for a light lunch and nap. Then, you get them dressed and we'll go back and let them surprise me again."

"How good is Sanford?" asked Kane.

Morgan tilted his head and hmphed. "Do you know how good we played tonight? Well, we'll have to play better tomorrow to have a chance."

§

When Gloria tucked in the girls, she told them she would be downstairs in the lobby with Mr. Vincent waiting for Coach Summitt. Molly told her she'd make sure her teammates were in their rooms and quiet, but what Molly was doing was giving herself backdoor permission to go into each teammates' room to go over tomorrow's assignments. Mostly, she wanted to check in with Elena and Izzy in their room, to fawn over their defensive play so they wouldn't focus on how poorly they had shot, to move them forward. Both of them had made comments at their late dinner about how little they had contributed to the win. Molly reminded Izzy that her three late in the game set up the win. From there Molly visited Penny and Cindy, the two sophomores. Cindy hadn't played; she was good with that, but Molly told her she might against Sanford because "I might need a little rest, so be ready." Penny, though, had played a few minutes when Bianca got popped in the nose and she had done well. Molly encouraged her to be ready for more minutes as the tournament moved forward. Next, Molly went to Alondra's and Sofia's room. Alondra, too, didn't play, but like Cindy, understood and would be ready if Coach called on her. Molly's visit was aimed at Sofia. Molly believed that without Sofia joining the team, they would never have made it out of districts, that her toughness and ability to play three positions allowed Coach to adopt the fast-paced style that had made them so successful.

"You were so good tonight, Sofia, I just wanted to kiss you!" said Molly. Molly was in her pjs, warmup jacket and bunny slippers. "I know that #23 will be seeing you in her nightmares tonight."

Sofia laughed. "You scored a thousand points and tell me I was so good? That's nice of you, but I just knock people down." Sofia looked over to her roommate. "Alondra taught me that, and if I ever back down, she lets me know from the bench."

Molly's last stop was to visit Bianca and Rosa. Both were in bed, trying to sleep. Molly's knock startled them. Bianca got up, looked through the peephole, and opened the door. "You're supposed to be in bed,"

"It's okay. Coach Gloria gave me permission to make sure everyone was in bed and doing okay." Molly walked past Bianca. "We need to talk."

Bianca laughed. Typical Molly, but the jacket and bunny shoes made her look comical. "Are you going to put the outcome of our next game on my shoulders again?"

"Nope," answered Molly. "You and I have done our share. It's time for Rosie to step up." Molly looked at Rosa.

Rosa didn't respond but smiled. Bianca climbed back into bed and pulled the covers up to her chin as she leaned against the headboard. "Are you as tired as I am?'

"It's temporary, Betty-Bee," answered Molly.

"Where did you hear that name? Only Rosa's aunt calls me that."

"That's where I must have heard it then. Anyway, I just want to tell you what a great shot that was at the end of the game. And the free throw. Nothing but net. That took guts," said Molly. "I think in tomorrow's game, we need to win more comfortably so we don't give everybody a heart attack."

"Good plan," said Betty-Bee.

When Molly returned to her own room, Stevie was dancing to her headphones. Molly extended her arms as if to say, *Don't you ever get tired?* Stevie removed her headphones and put them on the dresser.

"Everybody's in. We win again and see what happens on Saturday night. Might be fun," said Molly.

"How are the cousins?" asked Stevie.

"Tired, like the rest of us, but we won't let that stop us. I think by the time the game rolls around, we'll all be rested up. I told them what Coach always tells them. 'Keep shooting.'"

"I talked with my mom. She said she's trying to get some more parents to come down on Saturday. It would be great if your mom could come. And Rosa's aunt and Sofia's mom."

Molly scrunched her nose. "Yeah, but don't count on it. Saturday is my mom's day to work two jobs. Rosa's aunt won't. Maybe Sofia's will. Alondra's can't."

A knock on the door made them giggle and hurry to turn off the lights.

"It's me," said Gloria. "Get to bed. No more talking."

Molly slipped off her bunny shoes but wore her warmup jacket to bed.

CHAPTER 25

One heartbeat, ladies!

Friday, March 8, 1996, 5:00 p.m., Colorado Springs, 2A State Semifinals. Thirty minutes to tip-off. Coach Morgan Summitt sat reviewing his notes while Coach Gloria examined each girl's uniform and hair. Twelve girls wandered the spacious locker room, a carpeted, college locker room for other games, one of four such locker rooms generally reserved for those college teams that played a dozen or so games in the arena each year. This one was the men's locker room. Last evening's locker room was smaller; nice, but more spartan. Ten times nicer than the one back home, but nothing like this one. As Gloria said, "Befitting a champion."

After last night's victory, Morgan's emotions had overtaken him. Tonight, he was calm and focused. His team had grown far beyond his expectations. Far beyond his hope of winning eight or ten games. Molly, Bianca, and Stevie. The triumvirate upon whose vectors Izzy and Sofia and Elena and the others had attached themselves. Molly. The bright star every opposing coach built a game plan around. The best ballhandler in the playoffs, maybe in the state across classifications. The second leading scorer in 2A. Stevie. Invisible in newspaper statistics, unless they listed steals or defensive disrupter. No team had been able to smoothly run its offense against Oro Hills for four quarters. Not one. Bianca. She dominated that eight-foot semi-circle extending out from the rim. Academy Prep's sisters, two talented, experienced, well-coached players lost the battle inside to the quiet, focused, team-first stallion--as did every center she played against when she returned from her *forced exile*. A-Prep and Tutwiler, and some unknown fink, tried to prevent her from playing, but they only stoked the already intense internal fire.

Morgan had three reasons to be calm and confident.

"All right," he said. "Take a seat. Let's go over this one more time." His girls sat in cushioned chairs rather than on a wooden bench. "Sanford's personnel are a lot like us. Quick on the perimeter, tough inside. They take care of the ball on their offensive end, and they try to prevent second shots on the defensive end. They don't want a chaotic game. And therein lies our game plan." Morgan detailed what the girls already knew, gave a scouting report based on one game, talked about matchups, and then called them up for the stack. "Do you know what stairs are for?" He waited. "Stairs take you higher. Made up of steps. So far, we've climbed twenty-four steps. Seventeen wins and seven losses. Sanford is step number twenty-five." He went silent, just looking over his girls. When he knew they understood, he said, "Elena, Sofia."

"One, two, three, Cheetahs!"

All season long Morgan's task had been to get his team to play to the style most suited to their physical abilities and skills. To his way of thinking, all of Oro Hills' losses resulted from his girls not fully implementing this style, not because they were resistant, but because it was a learned team skill and it took time. As the season unfolded, as each girl began to become a piece of the whole, the team became stronger and more efficient. Trust the process, and the process had brought them to the State Semifinals. Big wins over the past month, Benson, Academy Prep, Benson again, Rangely, and Fowler, resulted from twelve girls becoming of one mind, becoming that most elusive of goals, a team. Certainly, it began with Molly Rascon, the first grain of sand in the shell that developed into the pearl. Would it have developed had she moved into another house on another block in Oro Hills, on a block out of sight from the eyes of an old coach, eyes that had seen extraordinary talent and desire before and recognized it again in the body of that five-foot-three-inch dynamo? Would Oro Hills have won just four or five games and been bounced in the first round of the District Tournament? Unanswerable questions, except to the Basketball Gods who sit in on every practice and every game and determine who is deserving.

Gloria Fawkes wondered what style she would have come up with if Kane Vincent had hired her to be the head coach. *Not this*, because her limited experience to that point didn't allow her the vision to create such a team out of these pieces. But working with Morgan over the past six months was a continuing epiphany. She asked him once if all his boys teams had played fast, almost recklessly. They hadn't. He liked the up-tempo game for a variety of reasons, but never did he push a team over the edge, because he said he never had the courage. Retiring, stepping away for three years, allowed him to evaluate his work. Molly, Stevie, Izzy, Bianca, and the others gave him another opportunity to give what the Game of Basketball always asked for. Players! Players released to run and jump and shoot without looking over their shoulders for approval. Players who had been cut loose to simply run and jump and shoot without restraints.

Sanford had better offensive players at three positions and a clear advantage with depth. Bianca provided Oro Hills with an edge at the center spot, and Molly was the best player on the court. Had the game been played between Sanford's starters and Oro Hills' starters with no regard to fatigue and only those ten girls, Morgan believed his team could compete, but games are always played in context. It was the second game against a quality opponent played twenty-four hours after his top six had played 154 of the game's 160 minutes. As the first quarter unfolded, it seemed to Morgan that the Sanford coach received the same memo he had. *Just line up and play the game.* Sanford's slight concession was to play off Stevie in the halfcourt and lean toward Molly. Morgan's counter was to have Stevie "steal rebounds" since no one was blocking her off. Chess. Spasky versus Fisher.

Sanford's Flex offense resulted in freeing its forwards for a couple of baskets in the first quarter. Oro Hills relied on dribble penetration by Molly and pressure defense to cause turnovers. Before either team substituted, Oro Hills led 10-6, but Sanford's second wave was barely distinguishable from its first team. Morgan saw the first bit of fatigue in his top six and went to his bench, to Penny and Cindy and Alondra, hoping to "hold the fort," as he said to Gloria. They didn't, and when the quarter ended, only a rebound follow by Sofia kept the score tied, 14-14.

With four starters back in the game with Sofia, Oro Hills surged again in the second quarter, grabbing its largest lead of the half, six points at 22-16. With four minutes left before halftime, Morgan gave Molly her first break in two games. She hadn't sprinted the court behind Stevie after a steal and then followed that possession with a poor decision in traffic, leading Morgan to realize his point guard needed a quick blow. During her two-minute rest, Sanford rallied to tie the game at 22. Baskets by Bianca and Izzy and a three by Molly pushed Oro Hills back into the lead at half, 29-26, but Morgan knew Sanford's depth would play a key role in the second half, or rather Oro Hills' lack of depth. *Oh, for a feeder system!*

Back in the luxury of the locker room, Morgan's cheetahs fell into the cushioned chairs. Rosa and Jenny handed out orange slices while Morgan and Gloria conversed just outside the door.

"They're wearing us down, minute-by-minute," said Morgan.

"They're using our pace against us, maximizing the number of possessions, it seems," responded Gloria. "Do we need to slow it down?"

"No, that's not who we are. You and I need to keep a sharp eye out for little signs of fatigue and give the girls quick breaks, but avoid having too many subs in at the same time. They're chopping at Bianca's legs every possession. She won't complain, but it's taking its toll. What do you think? Penny or Alondra?" asked Morgan.

"If their first-team center is in, go with Alondra and tell her to push and shove. If they're second-team center is in, Penny can do it. I'll talk to them on the bench."

"Good idea. We can rotate Izzy, Sofia, and Elena. We're okay there. But Cindy and Jenny need to give us good minutes. Sanford just attacked Cindy when she was in. Any suggestions?" asked Morgan.

Gloria grimaced and shook her head.

"Let's go talk to the girls."

Inside, Morgan stood before his soldiers and rubbed his hands together before wringing them out. "That was enjoyable to watch. Two excellent teams going at it." He pointed out a few specifics about guarding the Sanford forwards, demonstrated how Sanford's point guard turned her body away from her team to protect the ball from Stevie, which could give Molly and Izzy a chance to double-team her, and then complimented his entire team on its stamina. "Sixteen more minutes. As tough and gritty as that first half was, I expect both teams to ramp it up another notch. Expect it, relish it. Molly, Stevie, Bianca." Morgan made eye contact with each girl. "Monitor yourself. If you need a quick blow, signal me. Trust your teammates to carry the load for a few possessions." He lowered his chin slightly, looking out the top of his eyes. "Like several of our last games, I suspect this one will come right down to the wire."

The girls stood on their coach's direction, stacked their hands on his, and waited. A CACA official knocked politely, stuck her head in the door, and said three minutes remained before the third quarter began. It was Molly who finally spoke.

"What do you think, Coach? Should we go out there and finish what we started?"

Morgan nodded. "I couldn't have put it better myself. Finish this!"

Morgan and Gloria trailed their team onto the arena floor. Morgan leaned into his assistant and said, "I wonder what the Sanford coach said to his team."

"Probably something similar to what you just said. 'You're playing a damn good team out there; go out and compete.'"

The ebb-and-flow of the second half resembled the first half. Oro Hills would stretch the lead to a half-dozen, and Sanford would battle back, sometimes taking a one or two-point lead. A few minutes into the fourth quarter, two Sanford girls sandwiched Molly, sending her to the floor. Both ran over and helped her up. Elena locked in on her girl, #33, keeping her scoreless after the intermission. Morgan would tell the team later that it was Elena's best game. As Sanford focused more attention on Molly, Morgan instructed Stevie to handle the ball more frequently in the halfcourt, since it was her defender who was double-teaming Molly. Her passes were shaky, but she was able to enter them into the post to Bianca often enough to force Sanford to guard her, returning some freedom back to Molly. Morgan used two of his timeouts to rest his starters in the fourth quarter when Sanford's depth seemed to be getting the best of Oro Hills. The most delicate flower in Morgan's bouquet, Izzy, was spent, but the other starters were holding up. He had used both Penny and Alondra to spell Bianca, just as Gloria had suggested, and each performed well. Cindy and Jenny, never in the game together, provided Molly and Stevie with just enough time for the sprint to the finish. When Morgan was standing in front of her, Rosa shook her head adamantly. Morgan leaned over and gave her a hug. As the scoreboard counted down, Morgan sent Molly, Stevie, Bianca, and his two seniors, Elena and Sofia back onto the court to finish the game. Sanford returned its starters too. The final two minutes of this semifinal contest were played with each teams' best lineups, and no player was in foul trouble.

Both teams executed to perfection, making crisp passes and taking good shots while being defended closely. Neither team committed a turnover and no girl missed her blockout assignment. The game came down to which team had the ball for the last possession, and that team won the game on a contested fifteen-foot jump-hook, 55-53. For a few moments, the victors jumped and screamed in jubilation, as expected, while the vanquished walked to their bench and consoled one another, their coaches hugging each girl and offering words of comfort and praise. A single basket at the end of the game in a city far away from the girls' homes. Seeing their opponent waiting in line to congratulate them, the victors stopped their celebration, gathered around their coach, and applauded. Then, the two teams walked the sportsmanship line, exchanging compliments as they touched hands, and a few hugged.

The Basketball Gods were pleased.

§

Coach Summitt stood in front of his silent girls, silent except for the sniffles. To him, the luxury locker room was too impersonal, as each girl sat in a separate cushioned chair. He wished for the Oro Hills locker room with its cramped quarters and wooden benches where his girls would be forced to rub shoulders or stand behind one another. Most of his girls had their heads down, hiding their tears and fighting fatigue. Rosa's eyes were up, locked onto Morgan. Next to her, Bianca stared vacantly straight ahead, tears streaming down her cheeks. Molly sat on the carpeted floor behind the chairs, her knees pulled up into her chest, and her chin down on those knees. Morgan took a heavy breath and cleared his voice.

"Hey, hey," he said softly. The girls lifted their heads to the sound of his voice. "We're a little too distant like this, so take hold of the hand of the girl next to you. Molly, come up here with me." He took a couple of steps towards his point guard. She stood and walked into his hug, and he whispered into her ear how proud of her he was. Still holding onto Molly, he began.

"In all my years of coaching and teaching, I have never been more proud of one of my teams." He allowed that to register and squeezed Molly tighter. "The game of basketball demands that one team wins and one loses, but in every other way, neither team lost out there tonight. You played to a draw; both teams were winners out there, but they get to celebrate and play in the championship game, and we don't. But it doesn't change a thing in my mind." With his free hand, Morgan wiped a tear from his eye. "My goodness, last year Oro Hills didn't win a single game on either level, and tonight, you played the possible state champ straight up. If they don't win it all, it will be because you took something out of them. That was, without a doubt, the purest basketball game I was ever a part of." He smiled slightly and sniffled again. "I know you're pretty deflated at this moment, but we need to accept this and get ready for tomorrow. We play at four-thirty for third place. Third place! Think about that for just a moment." He noticed a slight change in the demeanor of some of his girls. "Let's clean up here and go back to the motel and shower. Then we'll get something to eat and get our mojo back."

Bianca raised her hand. "Are you going to stay here and scout or are you going to eat dinner with us?"

Morgan knew what Bianca wanted. He had already decided. "I'm having dinner with my team tonight."

§

It was important to Morgan that the girls sat with each other on bus trips and at the various dinners they had had over the course of the season, but tonight, the team was interspersed with the coaches and the Mountain Matrons. He wanted to pull the girls out of their funk and having them sit together wouldn't allow that. Better that Queenie and BJ or Mercedes be at the table to ask questions and tell stories, to make them laugh. Morgan intentionally did not sit with Molly or Bianca, although a part of him wanted to. Instead, he and Andrea sat with his two seniors, Sofia and Elena.

"I understand you've got yourself back on schedule to graduate," said Andrea. "That's really good. Will you be off to college in the fall?"

"I just sent out my applications," answered Sofia. "I hope to be accepted by Western State, and then I can be with Elena. We could room together. If not, I'll go wherever I'm accepted."

"Have you thought about a major?" asked Andrea.

"Finance or business." She smiled at Morgan. "I want to get rich."

"What about you Elena?" asked Andrea.

"Undecided. Coach, do you think Sofia and I could make the basket-ball team?"

Morgan knew this was something neither one would have considered six months earlier. "I don't know, but you won't if you don't try out. My guess is the first year you wouldn't see any time, but if you continue to improve like you did this year, then I think in time you could." He looked to Sofia. "You're interested too?"

Sofia nodded her head. "I know it would be a longshot, but you've taught us that longshots are achievable. Just look at us. A bunch of poor kids from a small town, and here we are." She smiled sentimentally, started to tear up, stood and went to her coach and hugged him.

Queenie noticed, stood, and held up her iced tea glass. "I propose a toast." She waited until everyone held up a glass. "To Sofia and Elena, our two seniors, who stuck it out through the thin to get to the thick. Good luck and God bless." Queenie remained standing while the team saluted its seniors, and then told a story. "Y'all see me as a stereotypical, Southern black woman, what with my accent and carefree attitude, but you'd be wrong. There's nothing typical about me or anyone. I was a happy kid in Alabama, but I was poor like you. Probably poorer than most of you. But I wanted to be more than where my upbringing was taking me, so I went to college and eventually became a lawyer. An angry lawyer. When you see me, you see color, but I feel poverty. I got lucky with a few of my high school teachers who saw something in me when I didn't see it myself. Poor girls like us don't have a big margin for error; we've got to scrape and claw."

"Get to the point," yelled Mercedes from across the room. Andrea and B.J. laughed.

"Okay, okay. My roommate has heard all my stories. The point is, you girls are unique and have accomplished something special. As your *Sugar Mamas*, we are tickled pink and so very proud of you. Don't let it end after tomorrow. Keep scratching and clawing. You've got what it takes."

Food helped, and when the girls returned to their rooms to rest, Morgan felt more comfortable about tomorrow. They would be tired, but they would not be held back by the semifinal loss. They were naïve enough to think that a third-place game was important, unlike those big schools and their coaches who only saw the Big Gold Ball as the symbol of success. Those teams must have failed to eat dinner together after a hard loss.

CHAPTER 26

It's always about the game in front of you.

Because of district tournaments and Morgan's previous trips to the State Tournament, eight in his twenty years or so, Andrea knew he would be restless. Stay up late, toss and turn when he finally went to bed, up early. Three times his teams had played for the championship, coming up short in each game. For all those trips, he brought his teams home each night to sleep in their own beds, to focus on the game ahead of them, but for this team, when he qualified for the final weekend, he was adamant that they stay in Colorado Springs. There were obvious differences. 4A was a one-and-done, no consolation bracket. 2A teams played three days regardless. Lakewood was only a dozen miles from the tournament, while Oro Hills was a couple of hours from the 2A tournament, so busing back and forth made no sense, but it was more than that. Andrea knew. He wanted to give these girls an experience to remember, a memory to last a lifetime, and a vision to draw upon when the next opportunity for success presented itself.

He returned from the bathroom and climbed back into bed. "I didn't mean to wake you," he said.

"Nervous?"

"Just thinking. And I'm an old man who can't hold it through the night." He leaned over and kissed Andrea on her cheek. "Do you think the girls are sleeping?"

"It's two o'clock; I would hope so." They lay still for a moment, each thinking about the girls. "It would have been interesting to be able to remove the ceilings from this place and been able to peer into each room, to see how each pair reacted to this," said Andrea.

"It would indeed," said Morgan, and Andrea felt his head nodding on the pillow.

On Point

§

Cindy and Penny, the two sophomores, had talked about how to get more members of their class out for basketball next season, and about what the team might be like in two years, when they were the seniors. Both fell asleep by ten-thirty.

Jenny and Danii, the two junior varsity players, both freshmen, watched TV and talked of things fourteen-year-old girls normally do, happy to be included on this adventure. Jenny had gotten some minutes during the playoffs, but Danii had not. Playing behind Bianca and Penny, she vowed to work hard to get into a few varsity games next season.

Izzy was asleep by nine-thirty, the earliest of all the girls. She wanted to be ready for tomorrow. When she climbed under the sheets, her cousin Elena went across the hall to spend the time before lights-out with Sofia and Alondra. Elena was in a race to be number one in the graduating class; Sofia had been in that race, albeit maybe for the number four or five spot before her pregnancy but was focused on college now. Alondra had a one-year-old baby and a year of high school remaining. And yet, in Oro Hills they understood each other and held no judgments. Good friends brought closer with basketball, especially this season.

Rosa and Bianca spent the hour before lights out with Stevie and Molly and then were in bed at ten, as Coach Gloria had directed. Bianca wrote in her notebook and then they talked quietly for several minutes until they both fell asleep. Unlike the others, Rosa and Bianca had been roommates for nearly three years, one year in Oro Hills and two in New Mexico. On more than one occasion, Bianca had told Rosa they were the luckiest girls in the world to have ended up in Oro Hills playing for Coach Summitt.

After Bianca and Rosa left, Stevie and Molly stayed awake, trying to fall asleep and be rested for tomorrow's game, but neither could. They tried to be quiet, but their giggles were probably heard by Gloria in the next room. When they were laughed out, they recounted the year, game by game through Molly's vivid memory. Stevie remembered games, but not specific plays within those games, and was surprised at the details Molly could recall. Both thought beating Academy Prep was the best thing, but then Molly began talking about the loss to Sanford and started to cry. She hadn't cried after the game, just buried her head in her arms while she sat on the locker room floor and shook. Now she was letting it out.

"I made three turnovers. We could have won!"

"Molly, you scored twenty-seven points!"

"It wasn't enough."

§

Morgan's thirteenth girl didn't have a roommate this weekend. On this Friday night, after spending time with the girls and then with the adults, Gloria retired to her room. She understood that she lived in the middle, certainly not one of the high school girls, but not quite one of the Matrons either, despite their best intentions to include her. Her age put her in that middle, fifteen years older or younger. The girls on the team were paired up, as were the adults. They all had partners. Before she agreed to help Morgan coach for this season, she had decided this would be her last year in Oro Hills. She would return to the Front Range and quit living by herself. She would go where there were *prospects*. Now, she had second thoughts. She didn't want to continue to be single, living alone, but, damn, this season had been fun and important. She was making a difference. Her JVs won just four games, but she was certain that if she coached them next season, they could win ten or twelve. More importantly, she wanted to help build a program for the high school, to have enough girls for a C team. She laughed to herself. *Maybe Thulen could coach it.* Not such a far-fetched idea; the girls liked him, and he liked them. She and Morgan had never gotten those coaching shirts, forgotten all about them. *Coach Gloria.* Was this her future?

§

Brian Summitt met his parents for breakfast and Morgan introduced him to the team. He sat next to Gloria at the table, meeting her for the first time. The Mountain Matrons were at full strength, as Andrea noted; even Anita Pagel had joined them from Salida, a shorter drive to Colorado Springs than Oro Hills. Octavia Wick, the lone Oro Hills' alum, said that what Oro Hills lacked in quantity for the game, they would make up in quality. She promised that her club would be the loudest women in the arena. Morgan spoke with Kane on the phone earlier and been promised

258

that most of his request would be coming. As the girls began to finish breakfast, Coach Summitt rose to say a few words, to give them their schedule.

"As we've done for the two previous games, we'll dress here and then head over to the arena. Our game is at twelve-thirty and our opponent is Denver Catholic. They got thumped pretty good last night by Simla in the late game. Coach Gloria wants me to remind you to keep drinking water right up to game time." He smiled. "We'll leave here at ten-thirty, so we can get a little shooting in during halftime of the game before us. After the game, we'll get our trophy and come back here to shower and pack up."

Molly asked, "We get a trophy for third place?"

Morgan nodded. "Both the third and fourth place teams get one. Actually, I think it's a plaque, but it's your reward for being successful on this stage."

"Third place, Coach," said Molly.

"That's the goal. After that and after we get cleaned up, make sure your rooms are clean. We'll stop at that food court on the way out of town for a burger to take home on the bus." Rosa raised her hand, but Morgan answered her question without her asking. "Get what you want; we're still paying for everything." He looked down at his notes. "As for the game, as Molly already said, we want to win. For several reasons. Getting to State has been a great accomplishment, but when we arrived, we weren't satisfied. Winning two of three is possible. Third in the state. It's also Elena's and Sofia's last game, and we want to send them off with a victory." He waited for a moment while the girls promised the two seniors that they would go out winners. "Mr. Vincent called me this morning. He's been working on a pep bus for today and has had a little bit of success getting some of your fellow students to come down, but the bus will also be carrying a handful of your parents and families to see you play." Andrea reached over to her husband and took his hand as the girls, whose families had not been able to attend, began to comprehend what their coach had just given them. "Finally, this game in front of us, I think it is the most important game of the season. In a season of important games, it comes down to this. We play basketball to win games, and you've done that seventeen times. Ten times in a row before last night. We certainly don't want to end the season on a two-game losing streak, but that's really beside the point. Playing this game of basketball teaches us to give our best at whatever it is we've committed to at the moment. I think we first saw that this summer at team camp when we played Holt, that tiny school, and they battled us tooth and nail. Remember them? They respected the game. Last night, we saw that again. You and Sanford played the game of the tournament, and both teams respected the game and each other. I wish . . . for you . . . that we would have won, but for me, I'm at peace with the outcome. You did your best, gave it your all, just as you have all season long. For today's game, I will expect no less. You can be tired tomorrow." The girls laughed slightly. "The Oro Hills girls basketball team is playing on the last day of the season, and I know you will battle from the opening tipoff to the final buzzer."

§

Denver Catholic did not shoot at halftime of the leadup game, and the daytime crowd in the arena was sparse. When the two boys teams pushed Oro Hills off the court, they noticed the busload of fans who were just entering the stands. Morgan instructed his girls to go say hi to their families and fellow classmates, sit with them for a few minutes, and then meet him back in the locker room. Gloria would round them up at the four-minute mark of the third quarter. While his team went into the stands, Morgan and Gloria sat together to talk strategy.

"What do you make of Denver not shooting?" asked Gloria.

"I wouldn't read too much into that. Maybe their coach wants to save their legs. If anything, they might come out just a little flat, but we can't count on that. We just need to monitor our kids."

"I was thinking about that. One of the things my girls can do is play zone. You had the JVs play so much of it to get the varsity used to attacking one. Cindy, Jenny, and Penny especially. Add two of yours into the mix and we could give your starters some needed minutes of rest."

Morgan liked the idea. "Good. Talk to those three about playing both a two-three and a one-three-one. It could be effective. I'm starting Sofia today. I told Izzy and she's not disappointed at all."

"Izzy's quite a kid. The most unselfish one of all, I think," said Gloria. "She'd make a wonderful coach someday."

On Point

"They're all unselfish. Amazing group we have."

§

In the locker room, Morgan went over the keys. "D.C.'s colors are blue and white, just like Academy Prep's. When you look at them during the game, I want you to see Academy Prep." He wanted his girls to have a focus to hold on to. "It's the third game in three days, so even when your mind and heart tell you that you can play as hard, your legs may be saying, 'Oh no, you can't,' so Coach and I will monitor you and give you a rest when we think you need one. As always, being substituted for is never in response to a mistake. Mistakes are a part of the game. Be courageous, as you have been all season." Morgan pointed to his keys on the chalkboard. "Fouls. Again, fatigue may cause you to reach instead of moving your feet. Stay out of foul trouble. Molly."

"I know," she smiled, "point guards never get in foul trouble."

"That's my girl." He moved to the second key. "Be shot aggressive and run to rebound. Bianca, they've got some size, but I think you can handle them." He took a step towards his center and gave her a gentle high-five. His third key, the number three on the board, had not been written down. He bent over and wrote on the board *You belong here. You have earned this game.* "Luck did not bring you to this game. True success is earned." He looked on his girls with pride, and they knew. "Elena, Sofia."

"One, two, three, Cheetahs!"

§

Like the beginning of so many games Oro Hills played, Bianca won the tip and Molly scored, either on a layup or a lane-jumper. On this Saturday it was a driving, left-handed layup, and it was followed by Stevie stealing the dribble from an unprepared Denver Catholic guard. Her jump-stop layup gave Oro Hills a four-point lead just twenty seconds into the game. A timeout could not rally the Crusaders, because the Cheetahs had already knocked them down and clutched their throats. At the end of the first quarter, Oro Hills led 19-6, and Morgan had played nine kids. Bianca had taken down every defensive rebound. Rosa sat down beside him when he motioned for her to sub in, but declined, saying she might be ready later in the game. Morgan was okay with that.

The Cheetahs knew only one way to play basketball. Their pressure choked the life out of their prey, and Oro Hills went into the locker room at halftime leading 37-14. Morgan and Gloria warned their girls not to get complacent, not to get over-confident, not to let up, but they knew. Denver Catholic played even for the first four minutes of the third quarter, but then Molly and Stevie struck again. Three quick steals later, Oro Hills had its largest lead. Morgan called timeout and pulled off the press, at least in the full court. For the last three minutes of the game, Elena and Sofia, the seniors, were surrounded by Alondra, Rosa, and Danii.

Morgan instructed Elena and Sofia to accept the third-place plaque, but they pushed Molly to the front to receive it. Morgan and Gloria stood in the background as the girls in unison held the trophy aloft and danced. B.J. Pacheco made her way to the arena floor and snapped a couple of dozen photographs for the Oro Hills newspaper. Only because more games were to be played, championship games, did the Cheetahs leave the court. Morgan wished he could stop time and hold this moment forever.

§

He didn't notice any of his girls sleeping on this last bus ride home. The bus driver had told them that if they didn't stand during the ride, they could be as noisy as they wanted. "Just this one time though!" The girls held the trophy, passing it between them periodically, although Gloria noticed that Molly held it frequently. There were lip prints on the brass plate.

"Girls bus rides are different from my boys trips," said Morgan. "Both are bonding experiences, but there's just a different feel to them. Can't quite explain it."

"Are you sure it's just boys versus girls? Maybe it's upper middle class versus poor kids." Gloria raised her eyebrows. "Remember that survey at the beginning of the season where you asked the girls what the most fun thing about playing was, and several of them responded 'bus trips'? I wonder if they would say that now."

"Look at them. It would be somewhere on the list."

"I guess we didn't have to worry about fatigue in this last game, huh," said Gloria. "Dang, I was all set to use my zone."

"Maybe next year," said Morgan.

"What about next year?" asked Gloria. She turned away from the team, slid over in her seat, and motioned for Morgan to join her from across the aisle. Privacy.

Morgan knew what his assistant was asking but parried for a moment. "They should be back here again."

"No. What about you? What about us?"

"Kane and I have talked. We talked again after the game for a moment. He's been in touch with Abby and she's coming back, but she wants to be transferred into a counseling position. She's also been following the team, as I would expect. She knows what's happened. Does it surprise you that she's returning to Oro Hills?" asked Morgan.

"A little, but who would pass up the opportunity to coach this team?" It was a rhetorical question.

"It's our job. He's not going to give it back to Abby. This is what I proposed to him. Remember, I'm the OFG. I told him I'd coach again next season and you would be my assistant for just one more year. Then, I'll retire again and step away, but he had to promise me that you would get the head job when I left. If Abby still wants to coach, she'd have to be your assistant. This way, I get those six juniors for their senior season, and then you'd have yours after that."

Gloria asked, "You don't want to continue coaching? You're so good at it."

Morgan laughed. "I do some things well, but let me refresh your memory about a few things. First, we didn't have a single player miss a game because of an injury. No sprained ankles or dislocated fingers. Nothing. How often does that happen in a season? Second, Kane set the one-D policy aside. Third, by playing in the Pity League, we were able to develop slowly without getting our heads bashed in early. We were able to gain some confidence. Fourth, Kane Vincent had our backs from day one. He's a remarkable A.D. Fifth, Molly Rascon. Sixth, Bianca Steele. Seventh, Stevie Lizardo. Eighth, the Mountain Matrons. And for me, ninth, Gloria Fawkes. You have been the perfect assistant for these girls." Gloria started to disavow the compliment, but Morgan cut her off. "And tenth, I inherited a group of girls who genuinely liked one another and worked their butts off."

"Still," said Gloria.

"I haven't developed a program. All I've done is mold the clay. I get to do it one more season and take all the credit. You'll be developing the program, creating a feeder system. It will be you who determines the legacy for basketball at Oro Hills High School over the long run, not me. I'm just going to sit in the bleachers and criticize your substitutions, talk behind your back at the bar."

"Have you told them yet?" asked Gloria tilting her head to the girls.

"Just the one. I don't keep secrets from her. The other one probably knows because she's so intuitive. They haven't said anything."

"Now might be a good time."

§

On Sunday morning, despite the snow, Morgan and Andrea drove to Denver to see their daughter to tell her about the State Tournament.

§

The following Saturday, the Mountain Matrons decided to establish a scholarship fund for Oro Hills girls who played basketball.

§

Stevie Lizardo made honorable mention All-State, a remarkable achievement for a player who averaged fewer than five points per game. Bianca Steele made second-team All-State, and Molly Rascon was named first-team All-State.

§

Izzy, Elena, Cindy, Sofia, Jenny, and Danii went out for spring soccer. Stevie and Penny ran track, while Alondra went back to being a full-time mother. And on the Monday after finishing third at the State Tournament, Molly Rascon, Bianca Acero, and Rosa Leon began the '96-'97 basketball season on Coach Summitt's driveway.

The End
(of their Junior year)

CPSIA information can be obtained
at www.ICGtesting.com
Printed in the USA
LVHW081530010221
678020LV00040B/377

9 781736 436806